The One Gold Slave
Atlaind: Book 1

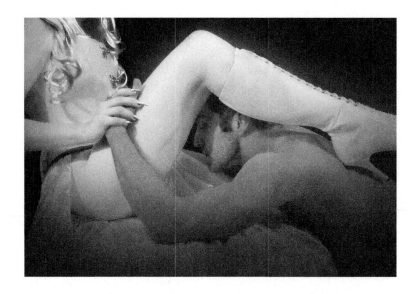

From Author and Photographer
Christian Kennedy

Copyright © 2016 by Christian Kennedy

DISCLAIMER:
This book is a work of fiction. Names, characters, places and incidents are a product of the author's imagination or are used fictitiously. Any resemblance to actual people, living or dead, or to businesses, companies, events, institutions or locales is completely coincidental.

This book is for ADULT AUDIENCES ONLY 18+. It contains substantial sexually explicit scenes with multiple partners, multiple sexual orientations, rough/violent sex and graphic language which may be considered offensive by some readers. All sexually active characters are 18 years of age or older.

Published by Waitingstar Publishing
Edited by Eryn Mills of Tahosa Editing Services
The One Gold Slave
Tales of Atlaind: Book 1 / Christian Kennedy
First Edition - October 11th, 2016
Second Edition - January 18th, 2019
Printed in the United States of America
ISBN-13: 978-0692790014 (Custom Universal)
ISBN-10: 0692790012

Special Thanks:

To You,
who is reading my book.
I sincerely hope you enjoy my work.

To my Husband,
who sets my passions on fire and inspires my writing.

To Tiffany,
who always encourages me to follow my creativity.

To my Parents and Family,
who love and support me
      …and who I really hope don't ever read this book.
      … 'Cause that could get awkward.

Additional Thanks:

To Matthew, Matt, Gilly, Greg, Josh, Amy, Jace and Evan.

Thank you so much for all your insights, feedback, and talent. You are all rockstars.

A Note from the Author:

Dearest Reader,

I greatly appreciate you taking the time to read my book. I have put my heart and passion into these characters and the world of Atlaind. I sincerely hope you enjoy reading the series, as well as viewing my photography.
Pretty, pretty please with whipped cream and a fucking cherry on top, take a moment to write a review of my book or photos at the website where you purchased them. (Amazon, Etsy, etc.) Ratings and reviews are the lifeblood of independent artists getting our work to more people like you. Self-published authors aren't generally promoted unless they have a great number of favorable reviews. So, if you like my work, please help me share it with others.

Sincerely,

Christian Kennedy

The One Gold Slave

Atlaind: Book 1

"It was the most glorious of days. The day I was first owned. I trembled upon the auction block in fear that I would not be chosen. Many bids were placed. My heart raced as I waited to see the face of the Master or Mistress I would belong to. But it was even more wondrous than I could have imagined. When *he* arrived and placed the final bid, he was so beautiful. Looking upon him was like staring into the sun. I thanked the Goddess for her generosity. That night I was fitted with a collar of my very own. I was presented before the entire estate in the grand hall. I was then blessed with the taste of his leather across my skin until I could not tell the difference between my sweat, my blood or my tears of joy. It was then that I knew what it was to belong to a Master. This was heaven."

Landryl, *The Scrolls of the Goddess*

CHAPTER 1: AUCTION

I have an above average cock.

This is a valuable trait for a pleasure slave. More importantly than its size is that I've been trained in how to use it. Not just my cock, but my entire body. I'm quite good at giving pleasure with my hands, mouth, tongue, teeth and even my feet. I am reasonably attractive, I suppose. I'm not exactly muscle-bound, and not really considered a pretty boy, but maybe rough-scruff handsome. My eyes are an intense shade of emerald green that I've been told on several occasions are very beautiful. I do, unfortunately, have a long scar that runs across my chest just under my breastbone that I incurred during the combat trials of my skill placement. It was given to me most graciously by a fellow slave named Zulyin. Surely though, a scar adds character to my body. Some people find scars attractive, I've been told.

These are all things that whirled through my head while I lay staring at the ceiling in the pleasure slave quarters on my last night in the training house. Why the fuck had I never been purchased? What was I doing wrong?

You'd think that by now someone would have had a use for me. I may not be the most handsome. Or the most muscular. Or the most charming. Or the most…anything, really.

In fact, it's probably because of my excessive averageness that makes me so forgettable. All my skills aside, in appearance, I am extraordinarily ordinary. I'm not the best at anything, which doesn't make me stand out. I'm also not the worst at anything, *which again*, doesn't make me stand out. As far as shortcomings go, this must be the weirdest problem to have.

This is why, at the age of thirty, all slaves who have not been purchased go on auction. This is not where I imagined I would end up. I kept myself awake for hours that last night wringing my brain with the why's of my life and how it had come to this moment. I tried to fight my fear of the real possibility that I might die soon. If I wasn't bought at the auction, I would be sent to the Cheritoth, and I did not fancy my chances of living long in the fighting tournaments.

First light brought with it little chirping birds and their songs on the crisp dawn air. I slept in a pile with my closest bedfellows, three males and four females. Our quarters were shared with around forty other pleasure slaves. Older pleasure slaves at the training house were all bedded in one large room filled with pillows and blankets. This made any notion of personal space or privacy impossible.

The floors were covered with soft lush carpets and pillows that made it comfortable, but far from luxurious. Each of us had a blanket that was our own, but most of us slept wrapped around each other, sharing blankets and body heat.

That morning, however, I did not feel warm when I woke up. My backside was chilled as I lay on the outer circle of the small pile of sleepers. All the slaves I'd fallen asleep with were from my training class. Older, like me. Two of them, Trylith and Basz, were to be sold at the auction that day as well.

Trylith was dark skinned with bright amber eyes. I've never understood why she hadn't been purchased as I could never locate any flaw to her. She was lovely, with the firm curvaceous body of a dancer and a warm, inviting personality. The fact that she was still at the training house with us was just absurd.

The other slave girl, Basz, was also beautiful with crystalline blue eyes. Her blonde hair just barely touched her creamy bitable shoulders. Her skin was smooth, pale and sprinkled with adorable freckles. Sadly for Basz, all her allure ended the moment she walked. Or danced. Or moved, really. Her walk reminded me of the little birds on the beach searching for bugs in the sand. In her youth, the training Master had judged that she would grow up to be a beauty. She had. She was tall, which came off poised and elegant while she stood still but turned gangly and clumsy the moment she began to move. She was the most ungraceful creature I had ever witnessed. She possessed no rhythm or balance, which are terrible things to be lacking for a pleasure slave since much of our job required keeping or setting pace with a lover.

Poor sweet Basz...

Basz had been the first girl to share herself with me prior to my lessons with the training Mistress. We had been young and adventurous with each others' bodies. She was not the best I'd ever had at this point, but she would always be my first. In my opinion, her enthusiasm made up for much of her lack of skill. My heart always warmed at the thought of the awkward duckling of a girl who took my virginity.

I got up with the first signs of the sunrise and watched the light in the windows go from dark blue to the pink purple of morning hues. Carefully, I moved each of my arms out of the entanglement of limbs so as not to wake anyone. Making sure not to step on the others as I went, I crept on tiptoes to the doorway. Cold stabbed into the bottoms of my feet as I met the rough cut stone floor beyond our sleeping rugs.

The training house was built of granite and black iron, with dark walnut wood beams and solid heavy doors. In the long main hallway that had to be traveled to get to any wing of the training house, there were prayer tablets set into the wall, carved in sandstone and inlaid with gold. Each had been decorated with delicate carvings revolving around the symbol of the figure eight, the eternal sign of the Goddess.

On each tablet was one of the eight codes found in the scrolls of the Goddess. I knew them well, as did all training slaves. The end of each day was spent saying our prayers, which was to recite the eight codes in unison. I couldn't help myself mumbling each code as I passed them in the hall.

The First Code: "My life for my Master."
The Second Code: "Submission is peace."
The Third Code: "Love is my duty."
The Fourth Code: "Pain is the lesson."
The Fifth Code: "Channeling forbidden."
The Sixth Code: "Unworthy but never unwilling."
The Seventh Code: "Forgiveness is earned."
The Eighth Code: "Every breath is a gift."

To either side of each tablet were wooden handles. They were worn and smooth after years of being gripped by training slaves. Whenever it was deemed that a slave had broken one of the eight codes, they would kneel before the stone tablet, grip the wood handles and receive their punishment, all the while reciting the code until they could learn to behave. Many times the punishment was flogging. Other times, the Masters and Mistresses of the training house would get more creative.

I made my way to the bath chamber at the end of the corridor. White marble bathing tubs were set into the floors in a row against the wall. To the right of the doorway, a wall of shelves held small jars containing scented bath salts and soaps. Directly across from the door was a line of sinks that held makeup, jewelry and various mouth cleansers. And every wall was covered in floor-to-ceiling mirrors for maximum visibility so one could appear their best for potential buyers.

I went to the nearest tub, lowered the plug into the drain and then moved the pump handle up and down to start filling the tub. The water pumps at the training house were old-fashioned. I'd seen ones in royal estates that were just a turning valve. Open it and water poured in until you closed it. Much nicer. After several seconds of pumping, warm water began to fill the tub. Once it was full, I went to the counter across from the tubs to grab some bath salts. I wanted something a Mistress would respond to.

One of my higher skills is mixing fragrances. Aromatherapy is taught to pleasure slaves extensively. Laugh if you want, but scents speak to us on a primitive level. And I wanted to speak on every level I could. I decided on a mix of bergamont, sandalwood and red rose.

Choose me, is what I wanted to say. *Please, choose me.*

The steaming water pulled a sigh from me as I sank into it. On the ledge of slate tile between the tub and the mirrors were grooming supplies. I still had hours before the auction but I wanted to take my time so I would look my best. I washed my hair first. My hair is dark brown, very fine and cut short. I've been told it feels like rabbit fur when you run your hands through it. Women seemed to like to play with my hair a lot. My facial hair, however, was not so soft. I lathered my face with honey soap and let it sit for a moment. It made the skin more elastic and less likely to leave little cuts. I plucked a straight razor from the sterilizing jar and flipped it open. Running my thumb lightly across the blade, I smiled at its edge.

An unspeakable dark thought crept into my brain as I stared back at myself in the blade. My smile melted in the sharp reflection. Maybe it would be better to end the day before it started. Or, perhaps I would just take the blade with me in case things went poorly.

The dishonor of the thought staggered me so much that I cursed as I dismissed it from my mind. Someone would buy me today! I didn't care if I had to sweet talk a King into wanting me. Men aren't my first choice, but I'm not opposed to the concept, either. I was determined that I was finally going to be bought today.

Shaving with care, I ran the blade over the scruff I'd built up. I wanted to get the cleanest, closest shave possible to make me look good. Once finished, I ran my hands over my clean shaven face and neck to inspect my work. It was a good close shave with no cuts. I smiled at myself in the mirror, then leaned back in the bath.

I used the bar of soap from the edge of the bath and rubbed it between my hands, causing a foaming lather, first on my arms, then my chest. My fingers played with the scar on my chest again with practiced habit, before scrubbing down my abdomen. The act quickly became more about enjoying the sensation than actually getting clean. I gave myself the excuse that I would be less likely to have an erection while on display if I took care of it now. This was a lie I was fond of telling myself frequently. On occasion, it took no more than a gentle breeze and the curve of a woman walking by to set my loins on alert. Getting hard has never a problem of mine.

I rested the soap on the ledge and brought my lathered hands back to my stiffening cock. At this point in my life, there was little ceremony to this action. It was more about function than prolonged enjoyment. I have gotten more pleasure without release while servicing a woman than I ever have while making myself cum. For lack of a better word, I found self-pleasure boring. It was not my first choice, ever, unless when done for exhibitionism. If someone watched me or made me perform for them, that could be very enjoyable. Alone, thrusting into my own hand has always seemed like a cheap imitation of the real thing. Another drawback of my skill set. When sex was something you're trained in rigorously, it could get tedious quickly. It turned what should have been one of the most exhilarating sensations into passive routine. I imagine interior slaves or grounds slaves had to spend more time exploring themselves. Perhaps it extended the enjoyment of discovery.

Masturbation is one of the first things taught to us upon becoming a pleasure slave. The idea was that if you could pleasure yourself efficiently, you knew what felt good to another. We had contests, in fact, to see who could make themselves cum the fastest or hold out the longest. The girls always tried to cheat because they thought the teacher couldn't tell. I got what was probably an inappropriate amount of pleasure at the instructor's lessons about female pleasure slaves not faking orgasms. It was a particular sore spot with him, and a point he made sure to drive home with them, deeply.

Nothing arouses me more than hearing, or better yet, feeling a woman climax. My hand moved faster. I squeezed harder as I thought about the girls in my class having orgasms with me for the first time, their short, high-pitched gasps as I held their hips still and thrust into them. The surprise in their faces as pleasure overtook their bodies. At a certain point, their eyes would shut tight as their muscles clenched around me, with the throbbing that pulsed through their body that couldn't be faked.

I came quietly. My rapid breathing and the sound of lightly splashing water echoed around the room. Finished, I sighed wearily and cleaned my hands off in the bath, then removed the plug from the drain and grabbed a towel to dry myself. I still felt a little light headed from my orgasm, but also clean and refreshed. I stepped out of the tub and went to the sinks. I thoroughly brushed my teeth and swished a minty alcoholic cleanser around my mouth until my eyes watered and I spit it out. Lastly, I applied some clear moisturizer to make sure my lips looked more kissable.

I evaluated myself in the mirror, flexing my muscles in a way that would be embarrassing if anyone had walked in. Satisfied with my grooming, I headed toward the garment room.

None of the training slaves own their own garments, and pleasure slaves train mostly in the nude anyway. But on special occasions, like auction days, we are permitted to wear clothes from the garment room. It's a room across from the bathrooms filled with all kinds of fine clothing that are donated by the monarchs if they are anything less than perfect. I'd had my eye on a specific pair of pants that I knew would catch a Queen's eye for sure.

I had to dodge to the side on my way out of the bath chamber, as I narrowly missed being run over by Trylith and Basz. Both were still pleasantly naked and chasing each other. The women laughed as they ran down the hall past me. I smiled and felt a twitch in my groin at the tandem bouncing breasts of my two lovely slave sisters. The graceful stride of Trylith only emphasized

Basz's flailing bound down the hall. I scoffed and shook my head, smiling at them.

"Morning, Brother!" they both chimed.

"You'll wake the entire house," I whispered.

"Oh? What are they going to do? It's our last day!" Basz giggled and slapped my bare ass as she passed me.

"Don't remind me," I mumbled with a sigh. I turned away to head to the garment room across the hall.

I knew exactly what I wanted to wear and part of my waking early was to make sure I got it before anyone else. Finding what I was looking for, I got dressed. This was it. The last thing I would wear as a training slave, one way or another.

The auction block consisted of a raised white marble stage set in the front courtyard of the training house with stairs leading up on all four sides. Black iron torches illuminated an onyx pillar that extended out of the center of the stage. My heart stopped while I watched the rows of polished stone benches out front as they were filled with Kings and Queens from across the land. Each of the monarchs glittered with finery and jewels along detailed leathers or satin. They were all so beautiful, and yet, frightening as well. A few had clawed hands, horns or fangs. Their vibrantly colored hair and wild eyes gave them a beastly quality amidst their perfection.

Master Azur, the King of the training house, walked onto the stage wearing blue leather pants and a matching tunic studded with rubies. At his hip hung a well worn black leather flogger, its silver tipped tresses swung lightly against his leg. His short, spiked hair was a shade of deep blood red. His black soulless eyes no longer contained any whites. They shined like pools of slick oil as he smiled with perfect white pointed teeth at the crowd. I had heard a rumor that he channeled some kind of demon. It seemed to make sense but I would never have asked. I was nervous I'd get more of an answer than I was looking for.

He bowed to his fellow monarchs at the edge of the stage and a polite clap drifted out from the crowd.

"My lords and ladies of the realm!" his powerful voice boomed. "You know me! I do not sell substandard merchandise. A slave with a twinkle of disloyalty would be unmade from my training house without a second thought. You know it to be true!"

Master Azur then spoke of the traditions and honor of the training house. How they were committed to providing the land with the best quality slaves, that the slaves on the auction were no less well trained or valuable than the full price market, which sounded absolutely terrible. I really wished he hadn't made that point as I was sure none of the monarchs believed it. If we were really as good as the other slaves at market I suspect there would be no need for a last chance auction. His statement seemed both untrue and a dishonor on us. The crowd seemed entertained, however. I'm sure they'd heard this pitch before and were still interested in buying some low-cost slaves. I looked around at the faces of the crowd. Plenty of Queens had shown up for the auction. I just had to impress one of them.

Trylith was called to the stage first. She wore a sheer glittering gown of lime green with a plunging neckline and a high leg slit revealing her perfect chocolate skin. A cool breeze fluttered the light fabric of her dress and made sure to display the pert loveliness of her breasts.

"Trylith, a pleasure slave of passion and beauty! Unquenchable in her desires to please," Master Azur said. Before he'd even finished telling them about her skills, a few monarchs started calling out offers to purchase her. That made me feel a little better. At least they came with the intention to buy.

Next to me, Basz stepped forward, biting her lip and tapping her foot anxiously. Her long arms wrapped around her slim waist as she attempted to comfort herself. I pushed my own fears to the back of my throat and bolted a sly smile to my face.

"It's a shame I didn't get to take you one last time this morning. Now you'll be all for the pleasure of your Master." I said, rubbing my hands on her shoulders.

"Yeah..."She said, trying to force a smile.

"Hey," I said, unwrapping her arms from around herself. "You are a gorgeous fucking woman, do you hear me?"

"But...the Cheritoth, Zsash. What if I—?"

I stopped her lips with a soft brief kiss. Basz grabbed me around the waist and hugged me tightly.

"You will not end up there," I whispered into her ear. "You will get up on that stage and stick out those sexy little tits of yours and kill them with that beautiful smile. You understand me?"

She nodded.

"You can do this! All you have to do is convince one of them, just one, that they need to have you on their estate."

"Zsash—" Basz said with wide eyes that I didn't notice at first.

"Just keep breathing and make sure they see how you—"

"Zsash!" Basz said again in a quick, hushed tone, and gave my shoulder a little push toward the stage.

"Huh?" I mumbled. I realized how quiet it had become around me. I looked back and fourth, confused. Until I heard Master Azur call my name for what I hoped was only the second time. I half stumbled through the curtains and up the white stairs of the stage.

I don't know how successful I was at hiding my look of panic, but I tried. I walked with as much confidence as I could muster, trying desperately not to trip and fall on my face. I had chosen my wardrobe carefully that morning to gain maximum attention. Anything to stand out. I wore a pair of sleek silver pants that hung loosely on my hips to show as much of my abs and chest as possible. I liked them because they hung low enough to see the dimples in my lower back and the muscles that led to my groin. I stood with my back straight to project confidence but lowered my head slightly to demonstrate humility. Over the fear pounding through my brain I heard Master Azur listing my skills to the audience.

"A pleasure slave excelling in massage and aromatherapy! This one has a feisty nature and fiery tongue you'll enjoy again and again. He is still young enough to ride, fuck or lick you into paradise. This body could be yours to do with as you choose for as long as you desire. What do I hear now for this slave? " After making a few turns, I stopped in the center of the stage.

Ta da... I thought. I was shocked at the response.

Nothing. No sound. No bids. The royalty before the stage all chatted among themselves, waiting to see what was next. Clearly, I was nothing they felt was worth their time, let alone any money. I suppressed a heaving sob in my chest.

All of it. My life was nothing. I was nothing.

My eyes darted frantically across the crowd, then to Master Azur, who seemed to weigh how long was appropriate to wait before ordering me away. I would be unmade! Stripped of my skill title and sent to the Cheritoth. I breathed a prayer to the Goddess.

I am your humble child, my lady. Please do not let this be my end. Forgive my arrogance in believing myself to have any importance. All I wish is to serve those higher than me in any capacity. Please, let one choose me.

Please choose me. Please...please...

"Choose me!" A voice rang out through the auction with a forceful will. It was so foreign in tone that, for a moment, I didn't recognize it as my own. It sounded bold. Fierce, even.

A thick silence cut through the crowd as all heads turned to me on the auction stage. I then did something I had never done before in my life. I looked up. And not just up, but into the eyes of the royalty. Like an equal.

They all seemed shocked. Surprise and outrage flashed across the faces of Kings and Queens alike. A few even stood with their mouths slightly gaping, brought to a standstill by none other than myself. The insane impulse to demand the attention of the entire royal court was a death wish for sure. But I had gotten what I wanted. They were all looking at me.

A moment later, a roar of disapproval thundered from the crowd and I immediately regretted the last several seconds of my life. I quickly looked back down at the floor. The short streak of power that had run through me, filling me with self-confidence, turned to vapor. The shouts from the monarchy brought me to the realization that I wasn't going to be unmade. I wasn't going to die in the Cheritoth ring.

I was going to die right then and there.

I would be lashed to death or tied to horses and ripped apart. The only thing I had always been so proud of, my loyalty, was also nothing. No wonder the Goddess had abandoned me. Deep down, I was an arrogant, proud slave. Not worth saving.

"Zsash!" Master Azur snapped in disbelief. The knuckles of his hand crashed into my jaw in a vicious backhand that was both sobering and familiar. I knelt down and rested my hands on my knees in the standard form for receiving punishment.

"I—I'm sorry. I didn't…please forgive me, Master." I begged.

"Quiet!" he snapped and unhooked the silver-tipped flogger from his belt, the kind that would draw blood with every blow. Ten lashes were the standard punishment for speaking without permission. Somehow I figured I had earned myself more than that. All punishments were immediate and uncompromising.

Master Azur cursed under his breath as he circled around behind me, shaking his head. "All you had to do was shut the fuck up for a few minutes! But you couldn't even do that. Such a disappointment. Another one to the Cheritoth."

Enraged shouts from the crowd shifted into excited noises of an entertained mob. Master Azur addressed them before commencing with my punishment.

"Let it never be said that I held a boring auction!"

Laughter erupted from the Kings and Queens. I felt my stomach turn as the flogger rose up.

The first lash landed on my right shoulder with swift, hot pain. Then another across my low back. The pain was not nearly as hard to bear as the shame of knowing that I was a complete failure. The metal ends of the flogger left shallow splayed cuts in my skin and bruised the muscles of my back. I fought to control a grimace as the metal tipped tails wrapped around my ribs on the next strike. The crowd seemed excited at my punishment. Each lash elicited a shout of approval. I kept my eyes down, watching small flecks of blood hit the thighs of my prized silver pants. The crimson dots sprinkled all the way to the marble stone floor in front of me. I was faintly aware through the pain of the hot trickle of blood slowly dripping down my back. I gritted my teeth and stared at the floor, trying to block out everything.

Then, something landed in front of me on the stage. It made a clear, sharp, tinkling clatter as it skipped over the marble, danced circularly for a moment, then came to rest before my eyes. Master Azur stopped and the crowd fell silent. My eyes fixed on the object in front of me.

One gold coin.

I stared at it. The small, round metal disc was just inches from me. I could see the figure eight symbol of the Goddess stamped into the metal. I'd never seen a gold coin, certainly not up so close.

Hushed voices whispered among the monarchy while many of them shifted in their seats. I froze. I remained still so as not to do anything that might ruin this moment. If I could have willed my blood stop running down my back, I would have.

"Sold!" Master Azur shouted.

Oh, Goddess! It had finally happened! I had been bought!

A sob of relief escaped my chest. I nearly broke down in tears. Master Azur turned toward me and ordered me to stand. I did so, and quickly, only then realizing the toll the flogging had taken on me. My back thrummed with searing heat in long lines over my flesh. My head spun and the pain in my back pounded as my heartbeat elevated. A rushing sensation flooded my ears as the world pitched over on its side, enveloping me into the soft merciful black of unconsciousness.

"It is said that a slave owns nothing for which they can offer as payment to the world. I could not disagree more. The oldest currency for all things alike is blood. The proof of payment is sweat. And the greatest treasure a slave has, obedience."

Riquora, *The Scrolls of the Goddess*

CHAPTER 2: STITCHES

I woke screaming. Piercing white hot pain shot through my back. I tensed, gasped and thrashed wildly. My eyes opened wide with confusion and agony.

A wet cotton pad soaked my back in the unmistakable clean, sharp feel of alcohol. I didn't get very far with my flailing, as my body lurched to a halt. I was laying face down on a small bed. My arms were bound at the wrists above my head to the bed frame. I looked around and saw two slaves in white robes next to me. My brain registered faintly that they were healer slaves. The room was too bright and I had trouble focusing for a moment.

"Hold still!" one of them said with urgency. "We're trying to stop your bleeding!"

Their words got past my shrieking senses and I stopped struggling. With my face pressed to the bed, I began to focus on a shape as my eyes adjusted. A woman stood across the room near the door, staring at me. Concern and surprise flickered in her features. Even through the pain and brightness, I realized immediately the beauty and poise of a household slave.

Every estate had one household slave. They were not raised with the rest of us in the training house. Household slaves were bred with high specificity for their purpose. They were always the offspring of two other household slaves. Because of their breeding, household slaves were naturally of above average intelligence, grace, and charisma. They were the personal assistant to their King or Queen, worth far more than any of us common slaves. Which is why they are taught advanced skill sets that the rest of us are not trained in.

Mathematics, reading and writing helped them keep the daily schedules and budget for the entire house. They exuded charm and poise since they had to be respected as an extension of their owner. This usually meant that they were also good entertainers, quick with a song, a dance or a well-aimed smile while wielding razor-sharp diplomacy. They knew how to negotiate for everything from business deals to trade in the marketplace, since they frequently made purchases and acted as the monarch's proxy. They were the only slave entrusted with money and made sure all slaves were scheduled for shifts each day on the estate. They were called the Voice of the Master. Up until this moment I had never personally been within thirty feet of a household slave. For many years I wondered what was so great about them. What made them better than the rest of us? I no longer wondered.

To say she was beautiful seems too mild a word. She was a tall woman. In addition to that, everything about her seemed elongated. Her limbs were slender and delicate while boasting pert breasts and a seductively round ass. Her neck, too, was longer than most by nearly an inch. Her dress was a regal blue, accented with sheer draping fabric at her arms and back. She wore satin stiletto high-heeled shoes that perpetuated the regal vertical nature of her appearance. Her hair was a brilliant, coppery red that hung in long, loose waves around her face, framing her aqua blue eyes. Long feathery eyelashes lapped around smoky liner, and her glossed, pink lips parted in surprise at my outburst. What caught my attention the most, however, was a set of silver and diamond cuffs cast in the shape of little swimming fish that circled her wrists. The cuffs were chained to a solid silver collar around her neck and they all glittered, creating shimmering flashes of light around her face and hands. Only a household slave would be bound by diamonds instead of iron. She was, in a word, magnificent.

"Gaaaahhhh!" I shouted and lurched up as pain stabbed through the skin of my back. My wounds had been doused in a liquid that burned terribly on the proud flesh.

"You're all right! I know it stings." Said a soothing male voice over my shoulder. "It'll feel better in a minute. Just breathe. That should dull the pain a little for you."

I held still as best I could, dazzled by the beauty before me. The pain began to fade into the background of my senses from whatever medication they had used on me. I wish I could say that I looked as glamorous as the lady before me. Alas, there may have been some drool involved for my part.

The heavy metallic smell of blood and disinfectant stung my nose and I suddenly remembered everything about the auction. They were cleaning my lash wounds. Clearly, the healers had done this before and had the forethought to tie my arms down. I would have taken a swing at them otherwise. It was difficult, but I tried to focus on my breathing and relax on the bed. The male healer appeared over my shoulder with soaked pieces of cotton stained red and threw them into a nearby metal bucket.

"Well, he's awake," he said to the red-haired woman and smiled at me with apologetic eyes.

"Thank you, Jaideen. I can see that." She said with humor in her tone. She scribbled some notes with a blue-green feather quill in a leather bound ledger.

"I...I'm sorry," I muttered to Jaideen. "That...was not my most graceful wake-up."

"You're all patched up, new slave." He said to me as he unbuckled the restraints that held my wrists.

Jaideen was of medium height with an average build, but I suspected impressive functional muscle in his arms and shoulders. He had shiny black hair and caramel colored skin with compassionate brown eyes. Well-groomed facial hair encircled his full mouth, attached to a thin beard that lined his jaw. It was his eyes that I trusted the most. I could tell this was the type of healer who genuinely cared for the wounded.

"Happens all the time," he said with a hand on my shoulder. His voice was a rich baritone, soft and calm. "Lay there for just another minute. We're all done stitching you up, but we need to put a bandage over your back."

"Stitches? Hey, can I…take a look before you put on the bandage?"

"I don't see any reason why not," he shrugged. I sat up slowly, feeling the pull of injured skin on my back. It felt tight and swollen, but no longer painful. A tall mirror hung on the far wall and I shuffled over to it.

"Here." The healer said. He handed me a small mirror so I could look over my shoulder without twisting. "I just put those in, I'd really like for you to not tear them out."

"I'll be careful."

I took the mirror, turned around and looked over my shoulder. It wasn't pretty. My back was riddled with long sutured wounds from the flogger. A few had gone extra deep and those were the ones that had been stitched. They were on my upper shoulders where most of the force from the hit had landed first. I frowned some at my now thoroughly destroyed silver pants. They were stained around the top band in browning, dried blood. I grimaced and gave the mirror back to the healer.

"What are you smiling about?" the household slave asked.

"Nothing."

"Nothing indeed. You shouldn't be proud of being disciplined," she said, with an admonishing wave of her feather pen.

"I'm not proud," I said, then returned my gaze to my own back in the reflection of the mirror. "They make me look somewhat tough, don't you think?"

"I'm sure you looked very tough bleeding all over the floor of the auction stage," she commented with little inflection in her voice. I involuntarily frowned and moved away from the mirror. "You have some deep wounds there. It will take some time to close them properly. I will add one hour a day to your schedule to receive treatment." She scribbled in her book for a moment. She looked back up at the healer. "Jaideen, how long would you say until he is...*fixed?*"

I winced a little from the word "fixed" for some reason. As if I was some object that had broken that needed repair.

"He should need about a month of recovery," Jaideen estimated. "In a week, though, he'll be able to function without the bandages. He should clean them regularly and leave them open to the air after that."

"Excellent. That shouldn't be a problem for him to keep clean. He's the Mistress's new bath slave," she said and continued to work on whatever she scribbled in her book.

I was excited to hear that I had been purchased by a Mistress. Yes! I'd much rather service a woman. But a bath slave? The bath slave was notoriously known as the position for talentless pleasure slaves. It was where you were put when you know about aromatherapy and pressure points but weren't worth a fuck.

Literally.

I was led by the household slave out of the healers' wing. On our way to the door, we passed a few other slaves lying in beds. There were muscular men and women that looked bruised and slashed by animals. I figured they were guard slaves. This then made me wonder, what manner of creatures could do that kind of damage?

My brain was still a little hazy, and I had no idea where I was or who had purchased me. I wanted to ask the household slave. She didn't speak for a while, so neither did I. I figured it was best to wait until I was addressed rather than get myself into trouble. She seemed focused and not horribly interested in chatting. Instead, I followed that beautiful, bouncing, blue satin draped ass of hers down one corridor and up another. I'll admit, I was enjoying the view. As I followed those gliding, satin heeled footsteps, I realized this woman had the most luscious and bouncing curved backside I'd ever seen. Even through the material of her dress, I could see the rounded top crest of two thick ass cheeks that I could come up with scandalous uses for. It was possibly the most bouncy and fun part of her since her personality was a little intense. That lovely ass led me around for an hour while I struggled through a haze of exhaustion and hunger. In the midst of all that, though, I looked around the estate I was in.

The training house I'd lived in my entire life was made of black iron, wooden walnut doors and unpolished stone. Candles lit the halls and there were always fires lit in the humble structure of the main hall. It wasn't gloomy, but the training house was dark. Dark wood with dark metal shrouded in dim lighting. It was comfortable enough but fairly plain.

The castle was the antithesis of darkness. Everything was white light and shining gold. Immaculate, white marble ceilings held high by thick stone pillars. Veins of gold seeped through the pale stones and glinted in accent off of everything. There were layers of sheer ivory fabric draped from ceiling to floor over tall, crystalline-cut windows. Their beveled glass panes refracted tiny rainbows through the air of each room.

We passed three interior slaves in a lavish dining room as they worked on an extravagant arrangement of blossomed red roses. I noticed that when they saw the household slave, they immediately stopped smiling and talking. They all looked down and focused on their flower arranging.

We passed through a large archway that led outside to a verdant, well-tended courtyard. White slate stones formed pathways through the gardens, all of them lined with mature, blossoming scarlet rose bushes. The path of stone and roses led around a huge, ornate fountain in the center of the garden. The water from its bubbling falls created a shimmering halo of mist all around the area. A number of grounds slaves casually talked and trimmed the rose bushes that lined the walkway. Upon seeing us, or more appropriately, the household slave, their talking hushed and they all appeared to work more diligently. Their sudden silence made the bubbling and spray of the fountain the only sound left in the garden.

We passed the courtyard and came to a simplistic rectangular wooden building. The tall doors were braced open, giving me a full view of the inside.

Tables ran the length of the building. From the ceiling dangled metal chandeliers circled in white candles. At the far end were more tables holding large plates of fruit and fresh baked bread. A young guard slave lifted a lid on one of the large copper pots and began dipping out a rich-looking stew into his bowl. I felt my stomach rattle but decided not to indulge my appetite in the middle of my first tour of the castle. Two long fireplaces with massive hearths ran the length of the hall on either side. Both were filled only with flickering embers now, having died down from the morning's warmth. There were about twenty slaves eating at the tables together as we walked in.

Like before, the sight of the household slave inspired sideways glances and whispers from the others. I wondered if it bothered her at all, the hushed talking and wary side glances. Obviously, the other slaves did not consider the household slave a sister to be chatty with.

"This is the slave dining hall." She gestured with a pale hand that made the silver chains at her dainty wrists jingle pleasantly. "There is always food available, so you are welcome to help yourself whenever you are not on duty. But come, come. There's much more to see. This way," she beckoned with a hand on her hip.

I stowed my complaining stomach and followed her out of the hall. As we exited the dining hall, she pointed to an expansive mottled stone building across from the dining hall. "Those are the slave quarters. However, you will not be staying there. Just so you know where they are." She turned and headed back toward the courtyard.

"Wait, where do I sleep if not the slave quarters?"

"You will see."

Back inside the castle, I tried to pay attention to where things were. Mostly, all I could think of was how I would never be able to find my way back to the dining hall. I was convinced I would starve to death before this tour ended.

We approached a grandiose room with a golden throne at the back of it. In the throne room hung fanciful gold and crystal chandeliers. Behind the throne was an intricately detailed metal sculpture laid into the wall. It depicted a phoenix flying toward the viewer.

"Wow…" I exhaled into the massive throne room and heard my breath echo. "Greetings, my lords and ladies!" I bellowed, my voice resonating in the well-built acoustics.

She smiled and nodded copper curls at me. "This way."

I followed her to a doorway behind the throne that led to an ascending circular staircase. We made our way up. At the top of the stairs was another archway that opened up, leading to the Mistress's bath chamber.

"By the Goddess!" I voiced, far too loud. My words bounced off the tile and marble surfaces of the room.

The household slave turned and smiled at me. "Everything you need will be in here," she said.

I was running out of words to describe everything I had already seen. Beauty. Wealth. Magnificence. But the word I would reserve for the bath chamber was fucking luxurious.

It was easily four times the size of the bathing chamber at the training house. We were at the top of a tower in the center of the castle. Four decorative pillars stood around the room and between each of them ran long windows that circled the entire chamber. Rays of afternoon sunlight filled the room. Glass oil lamps with hanging crystals extended from the walls to light the room at night. Opulent gold sconces boasted ivory colored candles along each wall. There were latches with a small chain at each pane so that the windows could be opened for full air flow, keeping the place from mildew or stuffiness. Sheer white curtains hung at each pillar and gold rods ran the length of the windows. On the wall to my left was a three-paned, floor-to-ceiling mirror so one could see themselves from every angle.

There was a gilded vanity with a smaller mirror in front of it, as well. It was framed on either side with gold doors set into the walls. On the right side of the room was a glass-housed shower. Large, fluffy towels hung from a series of golden hooks along one wall. There were shelves and shelves of scented bath additions and grooming tools. Next to that was a pristine porcelain sink. There was also a free standing metal rack with bottles of wine and crystal glasses. Sitting on top of the rack was a jeweled box that seemed placed with some kind of significance. The center of the room was taken up by the largest bath I'd ever seen. A pool would be a more adequate descriptor than a bath. It could easily hold ten people comfortably, rectangular in shape and lined with an opalescent blue tile. There was a silver handle at the front of the bath with what looked like something that would flip the drain to empty the tub. Yet, as I looked around the bath, I didn't see any water pumps.

"Where does the water come in?" I asked.

"Right here," she moved over toward the shelves.

I saw another silver knob there. She turned it at few times and a shower of hot water flowed from pipes at each corner of the pool. She then reversed the knob, turning the water off. Steam puffed into the room immediately and I imagined that the water was probably scalding to the touch.

"The next knob to it will temper it with cold water if you need." She pointed to an identical circular dial beside it. "You'll get the hang of it." She moved toward a closed door near to the staircase.

"And over here is the Mistress's personal quarters." She opened the door to the Mistress's chamber and I was hit with a wave of rich smells. I could identify some, others I couldn't. Vanilla and amber were among the ones I recognized. There was also an intoxicating musky scent that made my heartbeat quicken.

White marble floor stretched out into the room. An enormous bed in the center was surrounded by white furs at the base. A white down blanket covered the mattress and white drapes hung from the ceiling, creating a canopy around the bed. I took a step forward and felt the household slave press a hand to my shoulder. Her fingers were cool against my skin.

"No. That's far enough. You will never enter the Mistress's chambers unless given her expressed permission. Do you understand?"

"Yes. Yes, of course." I nodded, feeling stupid. There was no way I was going to just be given free reign to go where I wished on my first day on a new estate.

"This way." She tilted her head for me to follow again.

On the far side of the bath chamber, I was led into an empty corner. There was an oak door that led to what appeared to be some kind of storage room beyond. No marble had been used in this room. The walls and floor were plain, grey stone. A small brown knitted rug had been thrown down on the stone floor to make the temperature on naked feet more bearable. A small window, about two feet across with wooden shutters, stood open to give some light. Against the wall near the door was a small, but comfortable-looking bed. It was dressed with clean linens and a few thick blankets at the foot. The pillow looked soft and inviting. Beside it was an oak table with a small oil lamp and a matchbox. Against the wall under the window rested a large table and a wooden chair. I noted all these things quickly, but my attention was drawn to two items in the room most prominently. The first was a tall wardrobe on the farthest wall from the door.

She walked to the wardrobe and opened its doors. Inside were various garments. Three drawers were set into the right side of the wardrobe and in the bottom were two pairs of soft leather shoes and one pair of hard leather boots.

"I think you'll be able to fit into any of these if you are asked to go somewhere public. You are welcome to wear any of them when you are not giving a bath. However, you'll spend most of your bath time wearing these." She pulled one of the drawers open and produced a pair of red briefs that she laid on the bed.

My mind suddenly wrapped around all that was being shown to me. And though I had somewhat interpreted the significance of this room, my mind hadn't formulated the full spectrum of my situation. I suddenly realized.

"Wait, am I staying here? Do you want me to sleep in this room?"

"Of course. These are your quarters."

"Oh!" I smiled.

"The Mistress may want to take baths at odd hours or be attended to at any given time, so the bath slave sleeps close to the bathing chamber."

My own room? I'd never fallen asleep by myself before. I'd always shared my sleeping space. I suddenly got excited at the concept of having my own bed! Something that was for me alone.

Well, sort of alone.

"And, um…is she here to keep me company?" I nodded toward the second thing that had grabbed my attention upon entering the room.

A large painting in an ornate black frame hung on the wall across from the foot of the bed. It depicted a Queen sitting on the same golden throne I'd just seen downstairs. She was dark and lovely. Long black satin curls hung over the pale white skin of her shoulders. Her smile was a wicked smear of deep cherry red that matched the gown she wore. And that smile that penetrated through the years and art, was full of a rich sensual charisma. Her eyes had a doll-like quality. Perfect sharp-bladed lashes encircled her predatory purple eyes like an open bear trap. She sat off center in the throne. One perfect bare leg with its black spiked heel pierced the arm of the chair. She held in one hand a small, jeweled knife and appeared to be running the tip delicately over her bottom lip.

"Who is she?"

"This painting is of Queen Crystavieve, the Mistress's late mother." She said plainly.

"She was beautiful."

"She was."

"Is there some reason this is hanging in here?"

"Maybe the Mistress wants someone to keep an eye on you," she shrugged.

"Uh huh." I bit the side of my lip, becoming increasingly more aware of how the eyes of the painting seemed to follow me if I moved.

"Don't let her bother you. It's just a painting."

"Right..."

I followed her out of the room back into the bath chamber with a glance over my shoulder to make sure the subject of the painting hadn't moved.

"I think that concludes our tour of what you should concern yourself with. We will start your personal training on what the Mistress likes tomorrow after you've had a good night's rest. Do you have any questions for me before I leave you to get settled in?"

"Yes, actually. Which Mistress was I bought by?" I asked.

Her eyebrows raised. "You don't know?"

"No, I was taking my little pain nap half-way through the auction. I missed the part about who I belong to finally."

She straightened up a little, pride shining from her aqua eyes.

"You have the honor of being the property of Mistress Isavyne. Queen of Cane, and also called by some..."

"The Ivory Mistress." I finished.

Oh Goddess...

Mistress Isavyne was known for being the only Mistress in the Kingdom who didn't have sex with other monarchs. It was common practice for the royalty to seal business deals with sexual joining, but she was said to never sleep with her peers. All deals with Mistress Isavyne were said to be struck by sword. Apparently, she found the notion of fucking other Kings and Queens for business, distasteful. This caused the rest of the royalty to see her as either an object of admiration and desire, or contempt and disdain. Many wanted to be the first to conquer her lust. Many more saw her instead as a stuck up bitch who didn't want to play by the rules. Her reluctance to share her body had earned her the glib titles of "Virgin Mistress" by some, and "Ivory Mistress" by others. I'd heard from other slaves in the training house that she only ever dressed in white and owned more diamonds than any other monarch in the land. She was rich beyond even the common standards for monarchs. Her business kept her wealthy since every monarch in the land, including the Emperor himself, wanted cane, the pink crystalline pleasure drug so widely used in Atlaind. Because of its demand, Mistress Isavyne had no need to barter by standard means. I had been purchased by one of the most notoriously beautiful and powerful Mistresses in the realm.

Though all I could come up with to say after hearing it was,

"Oh."

"Is there anything else I can help you with, Zsash?" The household slave gave me a warmer smile than before.

"Yes. One last thing. Can I ask you something personal?" I leaned in a little toward those languid blue eyes.

"Yes?" She looked down at her feather pen for a moment to break my eye contact.

"What's your name?" I asked, raising my eyebrows.

She gave a short, almost nervous laugh.

It was the first time I'd seen her smile. I decided immediately that it needed to happen more often.

"Oh! My apologies. My name is Khessi. I am household slave to Mistress Isavyne."

"I figured out the household slave part." I took a step in toward her. "And I'm a bath slave, huh?"

"*The* bath slave. There's only one on the entire estate."

"Do you think the Mistress will be using my other talents? I have been told that my pleasure skills are quite enjoyable."

Her smile faded and was taken over by wry diplomacy as she casually gauged my intended seductions.

"I would not presume to know what the Mistress desires from you." She eyed me coolly, meeting my gaze and lifting her delicate eyebrows.

I moved in another step. Then I ran my hand lightly down the cool skin of her arm until my fingertips rested against the metal of her silver wrist cuff. This was a terrible idea, of course. I knew it was way too soon to be trying to charm any girl, let alone the household slave. Sadly, the fact that something is an awful idea had never been enough to stop me from doing it.

"Well, you must know her better than any other slave here. I'm sure you know what she likes. How she...likes it. So, yes, I would greatly appreciate your advice on that and any other subject you feel is relevant."

"Absolutely," she said, with feathered lashes fluttering her cheeks, "As household slave, part of my duties are to advise and train the slaves of the estate in how to stay out of trouble. So, here's my advice, Zsash." She ran the feather end of her pen over my shoulder. I swallowed as she leaned in toward me slightly and spoke in a hushed tone. "Be grateful for your position. That's my advice."

"Well, how do you think I stack up compared to her other pleasure slaves?"

She paused for a moment and pressed her lips together, in thought. "I think you are the best pleasure slave I can imagine buying for one gold."

I winced a little and took a step back. "I see," was all I could manage.

She was still smiling, so at least she thought I was an idiot more than a bastard.

"Get some sleep, new slave. Your training starts tomorrow after breakfast. Come to my office by sun-up and don't even think about making me wait." She turned and swished away, waving her feather pen at me over her shoulder. Khessi disappeared down the stairs, leaving me alone in the bath chamber.

Which one of those rooms was her office? Eh, I probably should have been paying more attention to the tour and not staring at her ass so much.

That ass, though. *Whew.*

"The second code, submission is peace, spoke most prevalently to me during these years. I know in their hearts some slaves don't truly embrace the eight codes. Some cling to petty egos and don't understand the simple grace in submission. It is not a relinquishment of self, nor a dismissal of one's personality. It is the joy of serving and bringing joy to your owner. To devote your life to the will of one greater than yourself. I don't understand how men found fulfillment before it. How bleak to not know your life's purpose. I cannot imagine how our race bounded aimlessly around their existence before we knew the joy of domination."

Thralldrix of the Eight, *The Scrolls of the Goddess.*

CHAPTER 3: LESSONS

No slave is capable of sleeping in late. Since childhood, we are taught to rise with the sun and sleep when our duties are complete. We are all used to running on little to no sleep if need be. That being said, I was well rested the next day, having passed out from exhaustion the night before.

My body woke me with the first light of dawn. I gritted my teeth in pain as I sat up too quickly in bed. My back reminded me of the flogging it had received the day before; the fresh wounds felt sore and tight. The muscles beneath them felt bruised, as did my ribs.

I gingerly sat up while keeping the blanket wrapped around me to fend off the morning cold. I kept my feet on the rug next to my bed and used it to shuffle over to the wardrobe to avoid stepping on the cold stone floor with my bare feet. I knew I would be expected to wear my red briefs for bathing lessons, but it seemed a little chilly in the brisk morning air to walk around wearing nothing but those. I put on the red briefs, then pulled on a pair of black slacks and a simple but elegant white button up shirt. Also, one of the pairs of black riding boots I'd seen the day before.

The dining hall was packed. I didn't know everyone yet, but I was pretty sure the entire estate of slaves was there when I showed up. A fire burned merrily in the hearth and a choir of pleasant conversation filled the room.

I poured myself a heaping bowl of oatmeal from one of the large copper pots. I sprinkled cinnamon on the top, as was my favorite way to eat it, and then added a splash milk for good measure. I then grabbed a large plate and filled it with grilled pork, diced seasoned potatoes, fresh tomato slices, and some whole grain bread. Lastly, I plucked a large juicy-looking apple and a sprig of green grapes from the fruit bowl. With my plate already overflowing, I placed some of the grapes into my mouth, the rest dangling over my chin. This earned me a look from one of the cooks who was bringing out more food. I gave him my best grapey smile and then turned away. My stomach rumbled as I searched for a place to sit down. I passed by a group of scowling guard slaves dressed in well worn heavy leather armor and made my way toward some slaves dressed in various colors of silks. The way they dressed likely meant they were pleasure or artesian slaves. They hardly noticed me as I sat down and continued their conversation with the tone of squawking seagulls fighting over a dead fish.

"It's terrifying. Imagine if they ever got close to the estate."

"The Mistress would never allow that."

"You don't know that."

"Of all the estates, ours is the closest to...."

"Indeed! They could be on us before…"

"We need more protection than this!"

"I've heard the guard say that they're all disfigured."

"Yes, they start to take on traits of the beasts."

And suddenly I understood what they were talking about. There must be wyrlings somewhere nearby.

Well shit.

Wyrlings are slaves that can bind their thoughts to animals to gain benefits of the creature. It's called channeling. When channeling an animal they become more beast than man. I've heard tales how a few slaves have managed to channel something docile like a squirrel or a butterfly and keep their minds intact. Channeling is forbidden for slaves as it is against the fifth code of the Goddess. Most slaves who channel want to take on traits of powerful animals to gain strength. Rumor has it that when a slave channels a creature like a wolf or bear, the traits of the animal aren't compatible with our true nature and it shreds their mind. They lose themselves to the beast. They become a wyrling.

The other trait of wyrlings that channel aggressive creatures seems to be a wild, insatiable appetite for human flesh. It is a very real concern to find oneself surrounded by a number of wyrlings. They are likely to do more than kill you. Rape, torture, savage cruelty, and cannibalism are part of what awaits any slave who channels the meat-eating beasts of nature.

Bonding with an enchanted creature is something only the monarchy are capable of doing. It's what gives them their magical abilities. I'd heard a rumor that Queen Isavyne was the only monarch in a thousand years to channel a phoenix. I didn't know how that would manifest in her but I figured fire was probably a good guess. Not that I was interested in a demonstration. I was good without dabbling in the world of monarchy powers. They're so much stronger than us they could kill you by accident and hardly notice.

As I shoveled food into my face, I checked out a few other groups around the room. A flock of interior slave girls sat across from the fire, warming themselves and laughing. There were some cute girls there that I figured I might want to meet someday. All the other slaves were caught up in their own conversations. I was suddenly startled when I met the eyes of a slave who stared directly at me. I made an attempt to stare through him and away. He was a muscular man, with shaggy dark silver hair and a thick black beard streaked with lines of silver in it. He was sitting in the corner away from the other gossiping groups. He wore a charcoal colored shirt that had once been white, its sleeves rolled up to his elbows and a blue roll of fabric tied around his neck. He wore brown leather pants with various stains of ash and dirt. His feet rested on a short wooden stool nearby with his worn leather boots crossed at the ankle. His steel blue eyes followed me through tendrils of pink smoke coming from a pipe he had between his lips. Because of his dress and physique, I assumed he was some kind of grounds slave. Grounds slaves were built for manual labor. Hard physical outdoor work. Trades slaves and craftsmen fell into this group as well. Metal workers, blacksmiths, masons. I could tell this man was one of those. He had those thick calloused hands that boasted fingers dense with muscle. The kind of hands that came from gripping tools every day of his life.

I chanced a glance up again and found that, yes, he was still staring at me. This time, I decided to meet his gaze. His face was an interesting mix of youth and aged wisdom. He was older than me by about twenty years. His features were undeniably jovial with round cheeks and a warmth to his eyes. He carried enough muscle on him that I imagined he could be intimidating if he wanted to be. He leisurely blew a pink cloud of smoke out and nodded my way. I nodded back with a forced smile and raised a piece of bread in the air before gnawing off another bite. I stared back at my food with earnest. It was almost sunrise and I didn't want to start off on the wrong foot with Khessi.

Through some miracle of the Goddess, I managed to stumble my way up one hall and down another and somehow located the red-haired beauty's office.

The office had a different tone than the rest of the house. The entire room was encased in a giant aquarium. And I mean everything. Well, except the ceiling. The ceiling had an ornate crystal chandelier dangling from it. The walls and floor created an enchanting miniature ocean. Fish schooled through the walls of the vast room in every color imaginable. I was suddenly overcome with a feeling of claustrophobia. I fought the urge to leave as I felt I was going to be crushed beneath the weight of the ocean. All I could think was how bad it would be if the walls broke with the door locked. I started to debate the stability of the massive chandelier versus the strength of the glass floor. My eyes widened as I saw what was easily a ten-foot shark swimming below the glass floor. He glided lazily without disturbing the many colorful fish. They didn't seem to mind him either, so I figured he must have eaten recently.

There was an overstuffed black leather couch next to a rectangular glass table with no other chairs around it. This made me wonder where one would sit at this expansive table. A crystal pitcher full of water with matching glasses sat on the table alongside a vase with calla lilies in it. A cerulean blue fish with long elegant fins swam around the flower stems. On the other half of the room was a desk made of intricately carved black walnut. That is where I found Khessi.

She was counting gold coins and putting them into a velvet bag. She wrote with that feather quill she'd been using yesterday. She still wore her silver collar and cuffs, which I now assumed was something she was instructed to wear all the time. One delicate cuff clacked softly against the desk as she wrote. Her hair was loosely piled up on top of her head with little wisps of hair dangling in her face as she counted each gold piece with a sculpted, sparkling nail.

Khessi was occupied with her numbers, so I gently cleared my throat to let her know I was there. She looked up at me with wide, surprised eyes as I broke her concentration.

"Oh! I didn't hear you come in!"

"Sorry. I kind of lurk." I smiled and hoped that didn't come off creepy. Khessi was wearing an even more alluring outfit today than she had the day before. She wore a short purple petal skirted dress that plunged low enough to show off the perfect rounded sides of her breasts. It was also short enough to reveal her luscious legs all laced into a knee high pair of silver boots. She smiled at me with violet lips. I tried to hide the lust in my gaze as I smiled back.

By the Goddess, she was beautiful.

"I made sure to be extra dirty for you." She said, putting her pen down and closing her log book.

"Excuse me?" I stammered.

"For you to practice on before serving the Mistress tonight." She said, standing. "You're going to be bathing me so you have an idea of what is expected of you in your duties."

"Oh! Of course." I felt myself blushing at the idea of seeing the household slave naked. I didn't know why. I've certainly seen my share of naked women. Nervous butterflies fluttered around my insides. I tried to squish them beneath the boot of my masculine self-confidence. I was unsuccessful.

Khessi led me back to the bath chamber. We stopped at the edge of the pool where the faucet knobs jutted from the wall.

"The bath takes a while to fill, so you should start it early," Khessi said once we were filling the pool in the bathing chamber. "Better to add a little extra hot water than to leave the Mistress waiting." She turned the hot water all the way up, then turned the knob for the cold water to balance the temperature.

Our next stop was the shelves of bath soaps, salts, and oils. Jars and bottles of various shapes, colors and sizes lined them. Each one was marked with a small gold plaque, the fragrance type delicately carved on it.

"The Mistress likes all of these. But I would suggest starting simple before you start mixing fragrances too much," she said while she repositioned each and every individual bottle to make sure they stood in the exact center of their nameplate.

"I do have at least one gold's worth of skills in aromatherapy." I said with an amused grin. She smirked and shook her head a little. I added, "I'd like to make a good impression on the Mistress and this does happen to be something I know a fair bit about. I'll do a little scent mixing unless you're strictly forbidding I do so."

She sighed. "Suit yourself. But I would stick with something simple. Amber or vanilla perhaps. The Mistress is fond of rich fragrances," she said, furrowing her brow as she moved and idly repositioned the lavender oil a few times.

"Ah, well, this is not the Mistress's bath right now, is it? This is *your* bath. So what fragrances do you like?"

She turned to me with an arched eyebrow. She blinked a few times before answering. "I will defer to your superior knowledge on the topic," she shrugged.

"Hmm. Well, let me see." I took a closer look at the bottles, glanced over at Khessi, then returned my attention to the bottles again. Reading the labels, I picked up the strawberry salts.

I took a step toward her while I uncapped it and held the jar close to her shoulder. I closed my eyes and inhaled her scent mixed with the strawberry. I recapped it. "Too sweet. Doesn't mix with you."

"I'm plenty sweet, thank you very much," she chided with fake insult. At least she had a sense of humor in there. I reached for the lily salts next.

"Maybe something floral?" I opened it and again closed my eyes to test how the fragrance worked with her. "Hmm. Not bad. I think I was closer with the strawberries. Something fruity but lighter..." I looked around the jars again until I saw what I was looking for. As soon as I opened it and breathed it in against her I knew I had the right one.

"Mmm...peach. That will be nice." I held onto that one. I hate only putting one fragrance in a bath. I needed at least one more to temper it. Also, I may have been showing off a little.

I know, I know. Pride is an awful trait in a slave.

I grabbed the rose scented salts and tested that one with the mix of the peach. I closed my eyes again, inhaling. I licked my lips. The combined smell of peach, rose, and her natural scent made me salivate. It all smelled like something I'd want to spend time wrapping my tongue around.

"Lovely." I said as I opened my eyes. I doubled that sentiment as I looked up at her. I stood a bit closer than I had intended. I guess I had just kept moving in more each time I had tested the scents. She looked at me with an expression I couldn't quite place, something between intrigue and amusement.

"You should...um..." Her voice hitched a little and she cleared her throat. "You should put them in the bath now, so they can be fully dissolved."

"Yes....Yes, I should do that." I nodded, far more awkward than I usually am. I carried the two jars clumsily to the edge of the pool. I added two scoops of the peach salts and one of the rose. When I turned around I nearly dropped the jars.

Khessi was getting naked.

I turned around just as she worked her dress down over her hips and stepped out of it, hanging the purple fabric on a nearby hook. My mouth hung open slightly at the sight of her pale gorgeous breasts. They fit her slender frame well. Maybe it was the bath salts working their way into the air but her perky tits suddenly reminded me of peaches. Each tipped with a perfect pink nipple that boasted a glittering diamond piercing. Her bellybutton was also pierced with a sparkling pendant that dangled down from it. Her body was completely smooth; not a hair on it. And I do mean *everywhere*. Long legs and curvaceous thighs led up to that amazing ass that begged to be slapped and have teeth run across it. She was clearly comfortable with her nudity. I had figured she'd be the one to blush once the clothes came off. But I found I was the one feeling my temperature rise while she looked calmly back at me. Clearly, the Mistress had bought her for more than her writing skills. Not that I blamed her.

I realized I was staring and not so casually. I quickly busied myself with replacing the salts on the shelf, then went to shut off the water. Turning my back to Khessi, I began to undress down to my briefs while making great efforts to tuck my half stiff cock under the fabric and turn off my brain. This was going to be my job. It just wouldn't do to be getting hard at every flash of skin. I was also silently happy for the briefs. They did a decent job of holding me in, which I figured was a secondary function since I couldn't have been the first bath slave to become aroused.

She approached me with a curious look on her face as she stared at my chest. I hadn't had anyone new get a good look at me in a while. The butterflies began to rise again in the pit of my stomach. I got nervous whenever someone saw my chest for the first time and asked me about my scar. She reached out instinctually but stopped herself just before touching my chest.

"May I?" She asked. I nodded. She ran her fingers tenderly over the scar across my ribs. "How do you manage to get yourself so injured, Zsash?"

"It happened during my skill placement. I didn't do so well during the combat tests."

"It's not that noticeable really. The healers did a great job with their stitches."

"Well, it's enough that you noticed it." I shrugged.

"I read your purchase papers so I knew what to look for. It's really hardly noticeable."

"Well, that's nice of you to say." I grimaced, wishing we were talking about something else.

She pulled her hand back and stood up a little straighter, clearly getting back to business. "Things to keep in mind during a bath," her instructor's voice continuing. "This is about relaxation, not arousal. Unless the Mistress orders you to pleasure her, you are here to wash and relax her. That is all. That means no lingering on body parts for your own gratification. It also means not greeting her with an erection every time she takes off her clothes."

"I'll do my best, but there are some parts of me that just react on their own," I shrugged.

"It will probably happen the first couple times. That's why your briefs always stay on. I promise you though, after a while it will become very mundane and hardly something to get excited about."

"I doubt that, somehow." Obviously, she had no idea what being close to a beautiful naked woman did to me.

She ignored my last comment and moved on with her lesson.

"The first thing you'll do is shower her when she comes in." Khessi moved toward the shower. We stepped inside the glass enclosure and upon closing the door, she immediately turned on the water full blast without testing it. Freezing water sprayed down on me, fracturing any charm I had somewhat maintained in front of her. I retreated as far as I could against the glass and away from the icy blast. I'm sure I made some sort of high pitched exclamation. I can't really be sure. It could have just been the sound of my penis screaming and hiding as far inside my body as it could, thus relieving me of any pesky arousal, potentially forever.

Khessi let out a snort and laugh, flashing her pearly white teeth for a moment before trying to regain her composure.

"I'm sorry, the water is usually cold at first." She adjusted the knobs until the water warmed. Her cheekbones were tight with suppressed laughter. I glared at her while hiding my own embarrassed smile.

"It wasn't that funny."

"It was pretty funny," she said without looking at me.

The water quickly warmed up my skin. It felt good on my chest and the front of my body. My manhood also resumed its usual position now that it was not being affronted by frosty temperatures. I was reminded of my injuries as the hot water ran over my shoulders and down my back. Khessi put her face under the stream of water and held it there for a long moment.

"Don't drown yourself, please. It would look bad for my first day."

Laughing, she brought her face back out of the stream of water. Her eye makeup slightly smeared and a little ran down her face in a way that should not have been sexy. Yet, it was.

"So, you will want to wash her hair first. Let's start with that." She pulled the clip from her hair and long, damp red curls fell around her shoulders. She gestured to the bottles against the wall on my side of the shower, then turned around, putting her head back under the water. I stepped in toward her and ran my fingers through her hair, making sure it was wet enough. Then I began gently lathering her hair with shampoo. I took care to massage her scalp which elicited the tiniest of moans from her. As I rinsed the soap out, I ignored the white foam that traveled down the supple skin of her breasts, making its way across that flat luscious tummy and onto those hips. I noticed how a group of bubbles lingered in the cleavage of her ass before being banished in a spray of water down the drain. My jealousy abounded.

Oh, how lovely to be a bubble, I thought.

I rinsed her hair until it was free of shampoo. I added a conditioner which was decidedly less interesting than the shampoo bubbles had been. I left it in for a few extra minutes, then washed that out, too.

"Good job," she said while running her hands through her hair. "Now wash my body."

"Right." I picked up the bar soap and started creating a lather in my hands. She turned to face me. I thanked the Goddess under my breath for the pain in my back. My physical discomfort was the only things keeping me from being fully aroused. I started lathering at her neck and ran soap over her long slender arms. It took some effort to make sure not to become entangled in the chains of her restraints. I found myself massaging her limbs a little.

"Just wash," she instructed. "This is not the relaxing part. Keep your massaging for later. The shower should be the quickest part of your duties."

"Right." I tried not to linger as I washed her breasts. I tried not to squeeze any extra. I couldn't help myself from rubbing my thumbs across the nipples a few times. Khessi did not seem to react, but her nipples stood out. I dismissed this, thinking that it was probably just her piercings that made them appear more ridged. The more I tried to ignore her body the more I realized the silence in the room was suffocating.

"So, when were you purchased by the Mistress?" I asked as casually as possible while my hands ran down the length of her torso.

"When I was eighteen," she answered. I knelt down to run my soapy hands over her legs, carefully not looking any place specific.

"That must be nice." She shifted her weight to one foot so that I could wash the bottom of it.

"It is."

"So, you've mentioned a few times that you know I was only purchased for one gold. How much did you cost?" I asked as I ran my hands as far up her thigh as I dared.

She smiled. "You have a difficult time minding your own business, don't you?"

"Sorry, I just don't know what the going rate for a household slave is. Figured it had to be a fortune."

"It was. It's an embarrassing amount that I will not be telling you. Suffice it to say that I spend every day trying to earn my cost. To let her know she did not waste her gold."

"I hope to do the same. I want the Mistress to know I'm grateful. She saved my life. I'm not suited for the Cheritoth. I probably I would have died."

"Probably," she agreed.

"Couldn't you have pretended to debate that for a second?" I finished with the first leg and she shifted so I could continue with the other.

"I don't mean that in an insulting way. I wouldn't fare well in a combat scenario either. Most slaves who are sent there don't survive long. It takes a ruthlessness not many have in order to survive the Cheritoth. Doesn't mean anything bad about you. In fact, it's a compliment that I think you're too nice to survive there."

"You think I'm nice?"

"Nice enough."

"Hmm. Have you been there? To the Cheritoth?"

"Yes. The Mistress goes there a lot. She is good friends with Master Lovol who owns the Cheritoth. Oh! Don't forget to get between the toes," she said suddenly back on duty. I laced my fingers gingerly between her toes. It felt kind of strange to do it to someone else. But I didn't want to miss anything once I had to do this for real with the Mistress. Thinking I was finished, I stood next to her waiting for my next order.

"What should I do next?"

"You're not done yet," she shook her head.

"Oh? Where else do I wash?" I asked, seriously unsure.

"I'm sure you were trying to be respectful, but there is no need. Don't neglect *anything,* Zsash. I'm sure with your experience you're far from shy."

I then realized the parts I'd been neglecting. Suddenly I was overcome with embarrassment. I guess I was just a little intimidated by touching Khessi.

"So…you want me to…" My voice, as well as my eyes, involuntarily lowered and it became difficult to inhale. I blamed it on the steam pushing out all the good oxygen. I didn't exactly know what was required and didn't want to offend her by guessing and touching places I shouldn't. She gave me a small, placating smile.

"You want to make sure to clean thoroughly."

"How…thoroughly?"

"Very."

"All right." I lathered my hands with soap again and moved closer to her. Her stance was just wide enough to allow me to slip my hand between her legs. It took great effort to make the action about cleaning. I tried not to touch her in a way that was sensual. Although I'm not sure how well I succeeded. I couldn't tell if she was aroused at all. The soap and water made everything down there about the same texture. I wanted to grab her by the waist and slip my fingers into her. I wanted to see how she reacted to my thumb against her clit. But, I didn't. However, as I ran the flat of my palm over her folds, just enough to clean, something scraped against my hand and I paused. I looked down at her clit and realized what I had touched. I looked at her with surprise.

"You're pierced there, too?"

She blushed and looked away.

"May I? I've never seen one."

"If you must," she sighed and set one foot up on the tiled ledge at the front of the shower. She angled herself to show me the sparkling piercing in the hood above her clit. I ran my tongue over my lips absently.

"That's gorgeous," I muttered.

"Thank you. The Mistress is rather fond of it as well."

"And you? Do you enjoy your piercings?" I asked.

"You mean if it mattered what a slave thought?" she said with a smile that told me how proud she was of them. When I'd rinsed her off in front she turned around, giving me her backside. I lathered more soap in my hands and felt a streak of boldness. I ran my hands over her round, thick ass cheeks. Goddess, they felt good. I imagined sliding my hard cock against the crease where they met at the top. But, I focused on washing rather than letting my imagination wander.

Thank Goddess for the briefs.

I was doing fairly well until my hand found a familiar position with my fingers at her pussy and my thumb massaging the tight pucker of her ass. I must have stopped washing and sort of lingered there. She turned her head toward me and raised an eyebrow.

"Zsash, you are aware that it is a severely punishable offense to use a household slave for your own pleasure."

"Is it?" I said, still rubbing ever so slightly.

"It is."

"Good thing you were here to educate me then."

"Indeed," she sighed. "Household slaves are only allowed to be mated with other household slaves to create superior offspring." She sounded sad when she said this and turned her gaze away from me. I stopped with my teasing her and took my hand away.

"That sounds lonely for you," I said genuinely.

"That is irrelevant," she said dismissively. "That's enough soap. You can rinse now."

I rinsed her off, then shut off the shower.

So, household slaves were off limits. Why did she have to be so fucking gorgeous? How sad for her that she couldn't even enjoy herself with another slave. At least I could go get release or perhaps find affection with another slave. And why, why, *why* did that make being with her even more attractive? Why was the forbidden so enticing? The Goddess had a strange sense of humor.

We got out of the shower in silence. The aroma of peach and rose steam hung in the air and I was instantly happy with the effects. Light and sweet. I started to head toward the bath but she walked back toward the bath salts area. I followed. She grabbed a silver hair clip and put her hair back up, piling it all on top of her head. I followed her to the front of the rack of wine bottles and crystal glasses. On the top of the wine rack was a pink jeweled box.

"Nice rack," I said with as straight a face as I could. She narrowed her eyes and hid her smile through pursed lips. With my best faux serious tone, I gestured and said, "The wine rack. It's really nice. Very, uh…perky wine."

"Are you ever serious?"

"Not if I can help it."

She rolled her eyes. But I'd gotten her to smile again.

"The Mistress will usually want wine with her bath. Do you know how to open a wine bottle?" She pulled a black bottle from the wine rack and a silver corkscrew, then handed them to me. "And please, spare me the screwing related puns."

"Pfft, please. I never joke about alcohol." I took both items from her and with practiced precision, uncorked the bottle in a few seconds. "Do I know how to open wine, she asks. Ha!" I raised a cocky eyebrow at her then took one of the crystal glasses and filled it high enough for the wine to breathe and handed her the glass. She smiled approvingly, pleased with my performance. I then filled a glass for myself.

"Well done. Now, this…" She laid a hand on the sparkling, jeweled box that sat on top of the wine rack. "This is cane. Sometimes the Mistress will want some in her wine. You should add one level scoop to the glass and mix it until it dissolves."

"Cane? You have cane in here?"

"You belong to the Queen of the cane fields. Of course, we have cane here."

"Can I look?" I edged toward the glittering pink box.

"I suppose." She shook her still wet, vibrant hair at me. "You act like you've never seen cane before."

"I've seen it some. I've never tried it."

"Are you serious?" She exclaimed, genuinely shocked.

"I was instructed on how to employ it to maximize pleasure, but no, I've never been permitted to try any. It was too expensive. Closest I ever got was kissing a Master or Mistress after they'd been drinking something with cane in it. Gave me a little buzz."

"Really?" Her aqua eyes blinked at me in disbelief. Then her mouth pressed into a hard line of decision. "All right, there's enough time for you to sober up before bath time tonight. You should know how it affects you so that you don't have any first-time screw-ups in front of the Mistress. Add one scoop to each glass of wine." She then opened the box carefully. Inside was a sparkling pink powder. A small gold scoop was latched into the lid of the box. She made one level scoop and added it to her glass and then did the same to mine.

"Understand something, Zsash. Just because this is in here, it would be unwise to take any of it for yourself without permission. Do not fool yourself into thinking that the Mistress would not notice some missing. She knows I am training you this morning, so it will be acceptable. But, I'm telling you right now, some of the slaves at this estate have tried to smuggle cane for themselves when they harvest it in the fields. It does not go well for them."

"I understand." I nodded.

"Good." Then she licked the tip of her pinky finger and placed it in the pink crystals before moving it toward my mouth. "And taking more than this would be a very bad idea for you. Do you understand?"

"Yes."

"Open your mouth and lift your tongue." She said. I did as I was told. Her finger moved under my tongue coating the underside of it with the grainy pink powder. "Now close your lips and lick the rest off."

I tried to ignore the obvious sensuality in the action but did as I was told. It was not exactly a pleasant taste. Somewhat dry with a harsh, bitter tang to it. I could see why tempering it with something sweet was popular among the royalty.

"Good job. Now bring the bottle with you." She ordered and turned toward the bath. The moment her back was turned I took a fast drink from the bottle to wash the taste of cane out of my mouth.

Khessi stepped gracefully into the bath. She suddenly looked quite small in relation to the size of the pool. There were a few marble seats in the bath and she went to the centermost one. I also noticed there were some smaller cylindrical pillars throughout the pool that stood higher than the water. Khessi set the wine glass on one of them.

"There is a marble bowl there that will have ice in it by tonight. You'll usually set the wine in there to chill. But, for now, we'll have to drink it warm. Just set the bottle there." I did as she instructed. Then I lowered myself into the steaming water to join her. The water was hot at I waded in up to my waist. Khessi sat back in the stone seat. She stretched her neck a little before taking a sip of wine.

"What now?" I asked, positioning myself at her feet. "Would you like me to massage your neck?"

"Yes. That would be wonderful. The Mistress is also fond of massage. It would be good practice for you."

The water swished around my hips as I moved behind her.

"Pfft, practice. You know, not everything has to be a lesson. It's okay for you to just enjoy something."

"Wrong. Everything must be in accordance with the Mistress's wishes. Now, if I happen to enjoy something as a result of her commands, then it's just a happy accident."

"Ah, I'm starting to understand how that works." I moved the wet delicate wisps of red hair away from her neck so I wouldn't pull them. I worked my fingers around the silver collar and under it, massaging the tight muscles there.

"Goddess, you have strong hands." She moaned.

"You should see what else I can do with them," I purred close to her ear. She didn't answer but a soft smile rested gently on her lips. I lengthened the muscles of the neck with my thumbs and massaged down to her shoulders. She was incredibly tense, which I expected. In the short time I'd known Khessi it was obvious that she probably didn't relax much.

"What if the Mistress doesn't like me?" I asked after a few minutes of silence.

"I doubt she would have bought you otherwise. Do you?"

"I suppose not."

"Don't worry so much."

"Someone with this many knots in her back doesn't get to tell me about not worrying."

"Well, I'm a household slave. We excel at worrying. That's why we're good at what we do."

As I worked her upper back and shoulders, she started to let out long breathy moans that echoed against the tile. I'm good at what I do but that was much more of a response than I was used to.

"Are you all right? I'd really love to take credit but I don't usually get such a vocal response from a massage."

"It's the cane. It makes everything more intense."

"Must be nice. I'm not feeling anything different."

She looked at me through a red curl that had fallen between her eyes. Sweat had beaded up on her forehead from the heat of the bath making her glisten.

"Are you serious?" she said in exaggerated disbelief.

"Yeah, nothing. Sorry."

"That's odd." She said and pulled away from me to reach for the wine glass. She picked it up and handed it to me. "Finish your wine. Maybe you're just the type that it takes longer to get into your blood stream."

I drank from the glass and finished it. A moment passed. I shrugged. "It's not that important. I'm sure I'll feel it at some point."

"You are a strange one, Zsash." She laughed, flashing me a broad grin.

"By the Goddess…" I shook my head.

"What?"

"How on earth are your teeth so white?" I asked. To which she laughed more and looked away with a blush. I found myself smiling, too. Seriously though, it was unreal how white her teeth were. They practically glowed.

"The Mistress has me tend to my personal hygiene more than most." Khessi said, still smiling.

"That makes sense." I added. "You have to make her look good, right?"

She gave me a sideways glance and shrugged. "The Mistress looks good all on her own without any help from me. But yes, I do try to represent the estate well." She brushed the lock of hair from between her eyes to behind her ear. "Could you refill the wine, please? No more cane for me, though. My head is already buzzing."

"Can't handle your drugs, huh?" I laughed and grabbed the glass.

"Oh hush. It's the hot water and wine. That's all. "

"I don't seem to be affected."

"That's because I'm a delicate flower and you're a horse."

"Did you just call me a stud?"

Laughing as I walked up the stairs and out of the bath, I reached for the bottle to refill the glass. I was about to make another joke but

     I

        didn't

            get

                the

                    chance.

Euphoria.

Thick pleasure swept over me like a wave overtaking the surf. Every sensation reverberated through my brain with a ripple of pleasure and color that submerged my body and senses. My pulse raced. I started inhaling and exhaling in long labored breathes. Each inhale brought a wave of peach rose ecstasy sizzling through my nerves. I could feel each droplet of water that clung to my skin as it rolled off of me and the cooling of its trail against my flesh. Processing so many sensations at once, it made me feel like my brain was vibrating. Simultaneously, I felt like I was floating away while falling down a flight of stairs. I licked my lips, salivating as my brain processed the assault on my senses. I moaned a little with each breath. I was so caught up in the pleasure of it all that I didn't see Khessi cross the bath to me. Her hands were just suddenly on my shoulders. Her skin against mine burned and soothed at the same time. I couldn't hear her over the sound of my own heartbeat.

"….sit…" was the most I retained from what she was saying. I lowered myself to the stairs of the bath with Khessi's help. She took the glass out of my hand and set it aside. She then placed a hand on my face and lifted my chin to look into my eyes. I'm sure they were dilated to the size of serving platters. She shook her head slightly with raised eyebrows.

"Now, who can't handle their drugs?" she teased.

I would have at least made an attempt to conjure a witty response, if my brain had been capable of processing anything other than the pure undiluted pleasure pouring into my skull. I instead let out a string of moans and breathy pants in response. My hands pawed uselessly into the air until I found her waistline. Her skin was so soft. I became enthralled with how the curve of her hip felt against my palm. I just kept running my hands over her smooth silky body while the sensations reverberated through my skin.

"You're going to be fine. Don't try to move too fast for a while, all right?" When she took her hands from my shoulders her warmth was replaced with a painful fracturing cold. My skin complained loudly to the distinct absence of her touch. I grabbed her hand and pressed it against my cheek. Her touch felt like tiny bursts of velvet fire everywhere her hand pressed against me.

"Oh, Goddess..." I slurred as I looked at her. The vibrant color of her hair sent a thrumming chord of pleasure through my eyes. "Khessi...this is...incredible..." My fingers crept up to her lips where I traced their wet pink outline with a fingertip. Running my hand across her jaw, I let my thumb rest right next to her mouth.

"Now...Now, Zsash...Control yourself, please..." She protested for a moment before I covered her mouth with mine. Once I felt her lips, I couldn't stop kissing her. She tasted like peaches, too. She managed to push me away enough to speak quickly between kisses.

"No, this....so much trouble....we can't."

I lowered my lips to her neck, below her ear. Kissing and nuzzling there quieted her immediately. Well, she wasn't totally quiet, but she wasn't talking anymore. I trailed soft kisses down her shoulder to her collarbone, then up her neck and back to her lips. When I kissed her again, there was no resistance whatsoever. I licked between her lips and was met with her tongue eagerly moving against mine. Both of us were lost in the pleasure of the high. Her cuffed hands laced around my neck and pulled me closer.

Goddess, her tongue was so...

I'm not sure I can describe how good it felt. Delicate, luscious licking motions that consumed me in glossy peach desire. Everywhere her hands touched, searing pleasure sizzled my skin.

I wanted more.

My hands ran down her back, pulling her closer and she wrapped her legs around my hips of her own accord. Her breasts pressed softly against my chest with their diamond studded nipples taught with excitement. She moaned against my mouth in shuddering breaths. I laced my fingers into her fiery hair as our kisses became frantic. My cock throbbed with intense ripples of pleasure as she pressed into me, rolling her hips against mine in slow bucking strokes. The slick heat between her legs saturated the veil of satin between us. The red briefs I wore were the only thing that kept me from taking her right there in those moments.

I honestly can't tell you if we did this for minutes or seconds. Somewhere in the blur, I realized she was pushing on my chest. She pushed me away enough to slip in words.

"No…no…this is a mistake."

I released her from the kiss. I tried to snap myself out of the haze of desires running through me. Upon separating our lips, we both just sat there, wrapped around each other and gasping for air. Both our chests rising and falling in unison. Though, there was the creeping awareness that something had just happened that could get us both into a lot of trouble. We stared at each other for a few long moments of shocked tension.

"Uh…oops." I breathed.

She stared blankly at me for a moment. She then placed her hand over her mouth to stifle the laughter that followed. We both laughed. Loudly. Our embarrassed chuckling echoed around the spacious bath chamber and for a moment I was extraordinarily happy.

This was cut short by the sudden grip of arms around my shoulders pulling me back. Strong arms. I hit the tile hard. Pain registered through my back and I wondered if I had torn out my stitches. I also realized I had hit the back of my head pretty hard. Though I knew I was in pain, it strangely still registered as intense pleasure across the fiery injuries on my back.

Then there was a face above me I didn't recognize. The enraged face of a man came into my focus as he knelt over me. He shouted something I couldn't really understand through his fist crushing my face. Again, I knew it should hurt and that this was bad. Very bad. The kind of bad that I wondered if I still had teeth.

But again, all I could feel was that persistent hum of pleasure. Khessi appeared over the man's shoulder and I think she was trying to get him to stop hitting me. That was all I had time to register though before the final punch knocked me unconscious.

Again.

When I woke, there was no happy, thrumming pleasure. My body started to register the pain I was in. I tried to move, and I felt swollen and bruised everywhere. My head sang with pain. I was laying face down. However, I was not on the healers' bed as I had been before. I was laying on a cold stone surface.

I tried to move my limbs slowly. They seemed fine. The pain came from my face and back. I rolled onto my side, trying not to stretch the skin of my back injuries. I reached up to touch my face and heard the sound of metal scrape across the stone floor. I opened my eyes slowly.

It was dark. The room was lit by a single oil lamp, making it difficult to see anything. I looked down at my hands to find thick iron cuffs attached to long chains that threaded through a ring set into the floor. I still wore the red briefs. They were dry, though, so I must have been there for a while. Inspecting my face, I found my left eye was extremely swollen. I moved my jaw gingerly, feeling the bruising there and inspecting to see if I'd lost any teeth. They all seemed to be there. Thank the Goddess. I was thankful that my nose wasn't broken either. It seemed the majority of the hits had landed squarely on the left side of my face. The corner of my mouth was a little torn and a long wound ran along my cheekbone. Dried blood had settled down my face from my nose and mouth. I tasted blood and spit it out onto the floor.

"Don't you spit at me, you son of a bitch!" A man's voice came from the corner. The man who had been punching me moved out of the shadows. I had a better chance to size him up now.

He was my height and had a similar build as I did, only with bulkier muscles than me. He wore a tightly fitting white shirt that had flecks of blood on it, presumably mine. He too, was chained to the floor.

"I didn't see you there." I said. It was the truth. It wasn't exactly an apology. My voice sounded like how I felt. Weak and beaten. I really wished I could have been more intimidating, but it was the best I could do under the circumstances.

"No matter what the Mistress decides, if I catch you near Khessi again I'm going to slit your throat. Do you understand me? Khessi's mine!"

I was working up a witty retort when I became aware of a sound that made my heartbeat quicken.

Boots.

The sound of high-heeled boots echoed down the stone hall. A sharp click-clack that made my breath catch and adrenaline dump into my brain. The other man jumped to a standing position. I stood too, however, slower and with more pain. The door to the cell unlocked and swung open. I averted my eyes downward, so as not to accidentally look her in the eyes. A pair of flawless legs, sheathed in white leather boots stepped into the dungeon.

She wore a short, white satin skirt that flared around her hourglass hips and into a corset accented by diamonds. A necklace glittered at her throat, seated like a crown above the perfect rounded tops of her corset bound breasts. Without looking up, I could see golden hair draped over her shoulders. And when I say gold, I do *not* mean blonde. I mean *gold*, shining in waves of metallic splendor. Her fingernails were gold, too. They were long, slightly curved and pointed. She raised one hand to my face and tilted it up to get a better look at me. I shifted my eyes to the side, but with my peripheral vision, I could fully see her.

Her skin was pale and smooth. Fierce blue eyes with an opalescent fire reflected in them. She smiled calmly with a perfect bow of blood-red lips. So much magic to her beauty, it was staggering. Yet, there was something disturbing in her loveliness. Haunting, even. The elements of the phoenix made her gorgeous beyond compare but also terrifying. Even the smallest and gentlest of motions from her somehow blurred with a snap of speed.

A form stood behind her in the doorway. My eyes were adjusting still, but I could tell by that fluid graceful movement that it was Khessi. She did not raise her head to look at either of us and she stayed behind the Mistress.

Mistress Isavyne took my chin in her hand and ran her thumb over the cut at the side of my mouth. Though she did so gently, it took all my effort not to pull away in pain. Her sapphire gaze scalded over me for a few seconds. Then she forcefully released my chin and walked over to the other slave who had beaten me. The sharp sound of her slapping his face echoed in the small room.

"Corvas. What could you possibly have been thinking?" Her voice was calm but felt hot with disapproval.

"Please forgive me, Mistress." His tone was not the same as when he'd spoken to me. A tremor of fear rattled in his words. "I thought…I know how dear Khessi is to you. I just saw the new slave with his hands on her and I feared he was violating her."

"I see. You thought you would protect my property, by damaging more of my property?" She slapped him again. The sound gave me more satisfaction than I would ever admit aloud. I snuck a glance to my side and saw a line of blood trickle down his lip.

"I will do anything to repair what damage I have caused you, Mistress."

"Yes, you will." Her voice purred with silky cruelty. "I'm taking you off of your current position outside Khessi's office. You will report to patrol the front halls."

"Yes, Mistress. Thank you."

The Mistress nodded curtly to Khessi over her shoulder. The household slave came into the room with keys and unlocked the shackles at Corvas's wrists. The chains fell to the floor and he stalked out of the room. His eyes lingered on Khessi before he walked out the door. Khessi followed behind him with the keys and shut the door behind her. I only had a moment to realize that I was being left alone with the Mistress.

The quiet was suffocating until I realized it wasn't actually entirely quiet. She made a sound, something between purring and growling. It was actually much more unsettling than silence would have been. I stood there, feeling her piercing gaze on me while the pain in my back and head hummed with increasing intensity.

"Tell me, slave. Are you aware that household slaves are valued for breeding and therefore not to be used sexually by the other slaves? Not at least without expressed permission from me. If Khessi were to get pregnant by a slave of lesser blood it would devalue her significantly. The child of such a union would not be allowed to survive. You know all this, correct?"

"Yes, Mistress. I wasn't…" I stopped my stammering to think through my options for excuses. Unfortunately, I came up with mostly sarcasm. "I only kissed her. And I'm pretty sure I didn't kiss her hard enough to get her pregnant."

A slap sailed across my face. The cut on the side of my mouth started to bleed again.

"You're clever. That's cute," she smiled with tight lips. The Mistress raised her clawed hand over my shoulder and drew her nails down my chest, letting those gold talons drag across my skin. Not hard enough to cut, but enough for me to feel just how sharp they really were.

"I like clever." She continued, "I like slaves with personality. The Goddess teaches us that wasted potential is the greatest sin of all. When I saw you there at the auction, so desperate, pleading, begging for your mortal existence, I thought to myself, now there's a slave with potential."

"Thank you, Mistress." Unbidden, I had started to tear up a little. I don't cry, really, but I was both afraid and moved by what she had done for me. I hadn't realized until just then how grateful I was to her. The Goddess had heard my prayers. She had tested me with time so that I could be given to the most beautiful Mistress in the land. A single tear escaped and slid down my cheek. The

Mistress's fingers slipped behind my neck, pulling me forward to her mouth. I thought she might kiss my cheek. Instead, she licked delicately out to catch my tear on her tongue. Then her fingers slid through my hair, grabbing a handful and pulling me closer. Not painfully, but possessively, she pulled me into a rough kiss. Her lips glided over mine heatedly. I stilled my hands from reaching for her, as I knew that would get me in further trouble. When she pulled my head back away from her I found myself staring into those surreal, blue eyes. They were hypnotic. Her red lips crooked at the corners as her golden eyebrows arched in amusement. I looked away as fast as I could, apologizing for meeting her gaze.

"Oh, Goddess! I'm so sorry, Mistress."

She smiled.

"Your fate is still undecided, my fine young, Zsash. You have many lessons to learn yet. Painful lessons, I fear. But we shall see what it makes of you."

"Thank you, Mistress." She moved away from me and I felt cold all over. I shuddered slightly, realizing how warm it was near her.

"You will stay the night in the dungeon to fully appreciate the living quarters I have given you. Khessi will retrieve you in the morning and see to your injuries. I will be expecting my bath tomorrow after I go hunting." With that, she turned and left in a swish of satin and gold.

No longer in the presence of the Mistress, I laid back down on the floor. I was so cold. And the thundering pain in my head and back was screaming for me to pass out. My eye seemed to have swollen even more in the short time since I'd been awake. I was a mess. Pain, cold, and exhaustion were making everything in me ache. There was no way I was going to be able to fall asleep.

"There is no such thing as a flawless slave. We are, all of us, created to be imperfect beings. It is not in the Goddess's design that we should be perfect. Take comfort in this. All a slave can do is listen to the lessons of their Queen or King and hope to be better than they were the day before."

Misteryn, *The Scrolls of the Goddess*

CHAPTER 4: MISTAKES

To my surprise, I actually did end up sleeping some that night. Whether it was more passing out than sleeping, I couldn't really tell. The body hits a point of exhaustion with extreme injury that it just decides consciousness is not required, nor preferable.

I was woken by the sound of the lock opening in the cell door. Khessi crossed the room to me with a set of keys and unlocked the shackles at my wrists without a word. She looked upset. Her face was set back into the diplomatic stonework that it had been when I met her, and I found myself missing the cute, flirty slave girl I'd spent time with in the bath chamber. I felt this sinking feeling that I would not see that lovely smile of hers again anytime soon.

I followed her out of the cell and down the corridors through the estate. I did my best to keep up. She walked at a brisk pace. My legs were kind of numb and my whole body fought moving around so much.

"Khessi, are you..." I started saying.

"I'm taking you to the healers. Your stitches have been ripped and need to be fixed so you don't get any infections."

"I'm sorry for kissing you. I...it was the cane, mostly," I lied.

"It's fine," she said over her shoulder while walking quickly ahead of me.

"Were you punished?"

"We should probably talk as little as possible."

"Wait!" I grabbed her arm to get her to slow down, a little harder than I meant to.

She spun around, pulling her arm away from me. Indignation burned in her eyes. "Keep your hands *off* me!" she said in a hushed tone.

"I'm sorry. I just…Are you angry with me?"

She sighed. "No. I'm not angry with you. One cannot be angry with a fox for hunting a rabbit. However, you should keep your distance from me."

"Did the Mistress say something?"

"Zsash, you have been out of the training house two days and managed to screw up for most of that! You need to understand your position, get into a routine and take some time to figure out your new life here, which hopefully will include fewer beatings."

"You're not…Corvas and you aren't…?" I stammered about with an unfamiliar tension in my chest.

"Don't be ridiculous!" she spat. "Obsessions from the estate slaves are part of being a household slave. It's our job to be endearing and make others like us. It's not uncommon that a slave would think that there is something more between us than there really is. It happens all the time." And when she said *all the time*, she looked straight at me.

"Oh, I see." My attempts to sound indifferent were not successful. "I guess I'm just naive. I thought that you and I were becoming friends."

"Well, let me clear it up for you. I am not your friend! You answer to me as I employ the will of the Mistress and nothing more. The household slave doesn't run favor with anyone and we certainly do not entertain in notions as simple as friendship."

"My apologies," I nodded, devastation knotting in the pit of my stomach.

We made our way silently through the halls to the healers' wing, where we were met by Jaideen with a concerned expression on his face. He placed his hands on my arms and inspected my battered face.

"Oh, my! I wasn't expecting to see you again so soon." He winced when he inspected the left side of my cheek.

"Yeah, it wasn't my idea."

"Well, you wanted to be tough, right?"

"I may have overestimated the value of toughness. Not as fun as it sounds."

Khessi looked away with an exasperated sigh and then wrote in her book with her feather pen. "I have things to attend to. I trust you both know your duties and can keep out of trouble in my absence."

I didn't respond.

"Not to worry, I'll take good care of him," Jaideen said, getting out some bandages and thread. Khessi turned and left without another word or a backward glance.

I was in terrible shape. The stitches on my back had indeed been torn open. I had been unconscious when they were put in the first time, and I truly wished I had been the second time. Jaideen sprayed a cooling mix of something numbing on my back. It dulled the pain some, but it still hurt. Once finished he turned his attentions to my face and disinfected the injuries there. While he cleaned me up, he asked me about my chest scar. I explained how I got it.

"Does it still hurt?" He asked me.

"It only really hurts during the winter for some reason."

"That's not uncommon. Old injuries ache. It's what they do. They remind you not to make the same mistakes again." He applied a small dab of a minty liquid to my injured lip. I reached up to my lip and he slapped my hand away. "Don't mess with it." Jaideen said with a shake of his head.

"Sorry. It stings."

He turned from me and began cleaning up.

"I'll try not to be in here again so soon," I said, getting up.

"You can just drop in and say 'hello' if you like. You don't have to be dying to make friends," he smiled.

"I don't know. I kind of screwed up trying to make friends with Khessi."

"Khessi is a good friend. She's just an even better household slave. Don't take it personally. She has a lot more stress to deal with than the rest of us."

"Yeah…" I said dismissively. "Thank you for all your help, though."

"As I am commanded," he smiled, shrugging as he cleaned up.

After leaving the healers wing, I got myself some food. It may have been my imagination but I felt like everyone there was staring and judging me. There were two guard slaves that looked especially annoyed with my presence. Friends of Corvas, I would imagine.

When I got back to the bath chamber I finally had a chance to look at myself in a mirror. It was strange. The right side of my face was pretty much undamaged. The left side, however, was a fucking mess. My left eye was wreathed in a blackish purple that spread into a deep magenta. A halo of light blue grey shadowed down my cheek and up my forehead. The cuts on my cheek and lip were thick and deep red.

I spent the better part of the day arguing with myself over which scents to use in the Mistress's bath that night. Amber? Vanilla? Sandalwood? Or perhaps more fruity and floral? Apple and white lily? I couldn't make up my mind.

Once the sun began to go down, I decided to get the bath started. The last thing I wanted was to not have a bath drawn my first night bathing the Mistress. I made the water extra hot since I didn't know how long it would be until the Mistress arrived.

I went to the shelves and decided on amber with vanilla and tempered it with honey. The bath salts mixed with the hot water made the room steam with rich, sweet aromas. Once the bath was drawn, I lit the oil lamps and waited. The windows began to steam up with all the heat, so I opened them.

Dusk crept over the horizon. The sun burned orange at the base of the mountains, throwing hues of purple and magenta across the valley. It was so peaceful out there. Grounds and interior slaves were talking at group campfires near the slave quarters. Some were still walking back from the cane fields, holding baskets and ending their day's work. Laughter and conversation hummed with the bubbling of the fountain below in the courtyard. A content happiness drifted over me. The warm steam in the room and the cool evening air hitting my skin was just so relaxing.

My calm was broken when a pair of riders galloped past the cane fields toward the castle. A few slaves ran out to meet them.

The Mistress rode a magnificent white stallion and carried a bow of oak laden with gold. On her back was a quiver of golden arrows. She wore a white leather corset coat with a hood that billowed behind her as she urged the stallion on at a fevered pace. Her long, gold hair was braided off to the side and bounced behind her as she rode. Her luscious red lips arced up in a joyous flashy smile as she looked over her shoulder. Riding a sleek brown stallion only slightly behind her was a sculpted Master wearing a black tunic emboldened with diamonds. His eyes were lowered in determination as he rode hard to keep up with the Mistress.

As they stopped at the front of the gardens, the Mistress dismounted with a well practiced and graceful hop down to the ground.

"Oh...So close, Braxian," she said with her hands on her curvaceous hips. Braxian pulled on the reigns of his horse, stopping quickly. He dismounted with much more care than the Mistress had and looked at her with a sore expression. Goddess, he was fucking tall.

As much as Mistress Isavyne was known as the Mistress of the cane fields, Master Braxian was known for his diamond mines. It made sense, why he had so many decorating his wardrobe.

Beneath the glittering tunic, he wore a simple high collared sapphire blue shirt with its sleeves rolled up over his muscular forearms. I immediately felt inadequate about my body, seeing how his shirt pulled across his chiseled chest and bulging arms. Honestly, I felt sorry for the horse he was riding.

Master Braxian moved differently than any other Master I'd seen. There was purpose to his actions. The hunger I had observed in the eyes of monarchs, he had replaced with focus. Sure footing over showing off. He had an air of charm about him and a boyish smile that curled cockily at the corner of his mouth. His teeth sparkled white against the rich tone of his sun-kissed skin. Master Braxian was well groomed but with the tiniest disheveled roughness to him. He had short, spiked hair like a wild thorn thicket of bronzed umber and a bristle of facial scruff that told me he shaved frequently but not daily. When he smiled, it created a fan of wrinkles at the edge of his eyes that one hardly sees on a King. He approached Mistress Isavyne slowly. His gait dripped with velvet and vetiver, all tucked behind a mask of diplomacy that I had no doubt he had spent years cultivating. He maintained a haughty, but good spirited grin at being teased.

"You'd run that horse to death just to keep from losing a bet to me, wouldn't you?" he chuckled.

"Don't be dramatic. He's a runner. He loves it," she said, patting the stallion's snowy mane. Mistress Isavyne gave an affectionate slap to the side of the horse and nodded to a grounds slave nearby to take the reins.

"And what of our other bargain?" Braxian leaned in and wrapped his arms around Isavyne's corseted waist.

"You did *not* win that bargain."

"Didn't I?" His eyebrows raised as he leaned in closer to her. They spoke so quietly I couldn't hear what they were saying. After a few moments, Mistress Isavyne unhooked his arms from around her and playfully pushed him back onto a stone bench in the garden. The Mistress placed one muddy boot suggestively on the bench, on the outside of Braxian's leg. She bent down towards him, running her gloved hands over his shoulders. Mistress Isavyne ran her fingers around his collar and pulled him into a kiss. She gently worked her lips against his in a slow building passion. Braxian's hands did not remain at his sides for long. His strong fingers slithered up one thigh till they rested on her hip, while his other hand crept around the back of her neck to deepen his hold on her. She let out a breathy moan against his mouth and opened her lips wider to his advances. His tongue slipped between her lips briefly. Then, just as quickly as it had started, she released his collar and moved away from him.

"There! I've fulfilled the bargain." She sauntered away from him with a grin. Braxian scoffed and jutted his chin at her.

"You're cruel, you know," he said through gritted teeth.

"I thought you would have realized that by now and given up on your pursuit of me."

"Oh, I don't plan on giving up on you anytime soon. Besides, you'd miss me too much if I did."

"Hmm, true." She admitted with a tilt of her head and a hooded glance. "I do find teasing you infinitely entertaining."

She started to unlace her corset coat in front of him and his eyes sparkled with desire. He confidently but slowly stood up from the bench, moving toward her. As she continued to undress, she took steps backward to keep her distance, never breaking eye contact with him. Her corset slipped over her shoulders to the ground. Underneath, she wore a chemise. Once uncorseted, the chemise hung around her in a swish of white fabric that stopped mid-thigh.

"The evening is just beginning and I've yet to see your estate beyond these grounds. A gracious hostess would invite me in and let me see what's inside." He suggested.

Mistress Isavyne widened her stance a little, swaying from side to side like a cat sizing up its prey.

"This has been fun, Braxian. I do enjoy your company. Much more than when we were younger."

"Well, that's not saying much. Anything would have been an improvement to the way I acted before."

She shrugged, nodding.

"That being said, you have become a fine King. Worthy of my friendship."

"That I will take as a compliment." He closed the distance between them and leaned down taking her chin between his finger and thumb to place a sweet lingering kiss on her lips. A raspy sigh escaped from him as he struggled to control his lust. He moved back from her ever so slightly to gaze into her eyes. "You are the most enchanting beauty. Do you know this?"

She looked away from him, biting her lip.

"Do you blush so easily, Isavyne?"

"Your flattery is very sweet."

"I mean it. Vehemently."

" And you are moderately good at kissing." She shrugged.

"Only moderate? Well, surely, I need more practice." He leaned in to kiss her again, but she took a few steps back from him.

"Perhaps another time. After such bracing activities, I require a bath."

"Ah, yes of course." He tilted his head in amused thought. "We could take a bath together," he suggested.

"Oh, I don't think so. I'm pretty sure that would just lead to us getting dirtier, rather than cleaner."

"You say that like it's a bad thing." He crossed the distance between them in a heartbeat. As he reached to place his arms around her once more she lifted one leg in a high front kick with such control and agility. The position made the muscles of her calf and thigh stand out. She didn't kick him, really. She just pushed the toe of her boot into the center of his chest, leaving a little smoosh of mud at the part in his shirt where his chest lay bare.

Braxian slid one hand over her ankle, holding her foot to him. Then he tilted his head to peek down the length of her extended leg. He laughed and bit his bottom lip, nodding.

"You're infuriating." He smirked.

"You love it," she said, lowering her foot back to the ground. She then turned with a snap of her golden braid.

"Good night, Braxian!" She sang as she walked away without looking back. In that moment, she also pulled her chemise off and tossed it behind her. Braxian watched the sassy swing of her naked ass while she walked away from him, wearing only her muddy riding boots. An interior slave scurried from the shadows and began picking up clothing as the Mistress walked into the castle.

Braxian stepped into his saddle and slung a leg over his horse. I didn't envy him having to ride a horse back to his estate given the condition I'm sure was afflicting him in his pants.

"Fuck," he spat, shaking his head as he mounted his horse. After a moment more of watching the Mistress, he kicked his heels into his steed and rode away.

As I watched the King of Diamonds disappear into dusk, I suddenly realized that Mistress Isavyne was on her way up right that second! A lazy slave sitting on the windowsill did not exactly send the message I wanted. I rushed to the front of the chamber to meet the Mistress when she entered the room. I did not have to wait long.

A few minutes later, the Mistress came up the stairwell of the tower. She tracked mud on the stairs with every step. I could imagine all the slaves rushing to clean the house after her. Her eyes met mine and I felt my heart jump as blue ice stabbed into me. I was brought motionless seeing her up close and naked for the first time.

I may have mentioned before how lovely her cleavage was. Seeing her full naked breasts was an entirely different and incredible experience. I have seen many women undressed and have enjoyed every set of breasts I've had the pleasure of meeting. With the Mistress though, the size and curve seemed to defy gravity itself. They remained proportionate to her body, matching the width of her hips. Her breasts were not only full but beautifully rounded perfection with rosy pink nipples at the center in just the right scale to their mass. I wanted nothing more than to draw them into my mouth and run my tongue wantonly across them over and over.

While my mind wandered, she kicked out a leg, tilting one curved calf muscle towards me, and looked down at her boots. She raised her sharp golden eyebrows in expectation.

"Oh," I stumbled and knelt down to unlace her boots. My fingers fumbled with the laces for a second.

"No," she scolded. "Don't use your hands. Place your palms flat on the floor on either side of my foot." I did so. The marble of the floor was surprisingly cool compared to the humidity in the room. "Now, unlace my boots with your mouth."

"Yes, Mistress," I paused and looked up at her leg for a moment. I then lowered my mouth to the knot at the top of the white leather. I took the knot between my teeth and began pulling at the middle. It took a few moments but eventually the knot came undone and I was able to undo the bow there. Carefully, I took a lace in between my teeth and pulled it from the grommet it ran through. Slowly, one by one I pulled the laces out and untied her boots. When I had unlaced them both, I sat, bowing my head and awaiting instruction. She had undone her braid while I worked on her boots. Her hair now hung down around her breasts like a golden cloak.

"Now you may remove my boots." She ordered.

I slipped one hand around her calf and used the other to pull the boot off from the heel. I repeated this with the other foot. Now completely naked, she walked to the shower. I followed. Khessi had never mentioned anything about removing the boots like this. Yet, the Mistress had reacted as though I was supposed to know. Had Khessi been setting me up for failure, not telling me everything I needed to know? That concerned me.

I entered the shower behind the Mistress and closed the glass door. Remembering my cold splash from before, I made sure the water was toward the hot side. She seemed to find the temperature to her liking and moved to stand under the running water. Dirt streaked down her skin and swirled in the drain, leaving her flawless skin glowing radiantly. This close and in the light, I saw her face maintained both youth and wisdom simultaneously somehow. Her lips were a shade of deep red, like the roses in the courtyard. She stepped back under the water and I began running my hands through her long hair. It looked like strands of melting metal between my fingers. The well-trimmed curls at the axis of her legs were the same metallic gold.

The Mistress was not a skinny woman. This is not to say that she was overly muscled or fat. Her body was a perfection of the female form. Wide hips that rounded into a thick, firm ass, and thighs that boasted strength. Her arms and forearms bore definition without appearing sinewy or hard. Her whole body was soft but strong and built for action.

"Slave?" she said, sounding irritated.

Damn it. I needed to learn to pay more attention. I realized she was waiting for me to wash her hair. Instead, I'd kind of just been playing with it under the water. I leaned down to the shampoo I'd used the day before on Khessi. Though, as I started washing it I realized the Mistress had a lot more hair. I tried to be thorough, but also gentle. The warm water made my back stitches sting. Between that and my nervousness, I was nowhere near turned on, which was probably best so I could focus on my work.

When the golden mass was bubbling with white suds, I decided to rinse it out. Once I had cleaned her hair of all the foam and bubbles I turned off the water.

"You are forgetting to wring my hair out," she said without looking at me. I swallowed and tried to figure out how women ring the water out of their hair. Like a towel or laundry, I supposed. I took her hair in both hands and twisted it to get the water out. The slap across my face shot out so fast I didn't see it until the stinging in my cheek began.

"Not like that!" she scolded.

"I...I'm sorry Mistress. I've never had to..." I tripped over all my words. And then I said that first thing that came to me. Though it was true, it was not anything I should have ever said. "Khessi didn't tell me how to do that."

As soon as I said it I knew I'd broken one of the silent rules of all slaves. Which is, don't blame others for your fuck-ups.

"Oh! Well, I'll make sure to punish Khessi for you not knowing how to get water out of my hair, then," she said shortly, and I winced. "It's done like this," she said and held her hair near the top grasping it with the other hand and squeezing while she pulled her wet hair through her closed hand. "Now you try." She said with slow emphasis as if I was a small child.

I did so successfully four times, watching water squeeze out of her hair. I went to do it a fifth time and she slapped my hand away. I was failing at this, miserably.

"That's enough!" She snapped. "I'll have to punish Khessi for not telling you how many times to wring my hair out. She must have been..." She looked me up and down slowly. "...distracted. You should wring it out four times."

This was bad. Khessi was already not my biggest fan and this was going to make everything so much worse. I kept my head bowed as I opened the door and stepped out first, holding the door open for her. She left the shower, and instead of heading to the bath, she walked to the vanity. The silence started to crush me again. I didn't know if asking her something would make her angry, but I decided to try. Maybe she would be less irritated if she had a drink. I cleared my throat, trying to sound confident and charming.

"Mistress, would you like a glass of wine?" I asked with the voice of an eleven-year-old boy whose balls hadn't dropped yet.

"Only every night," she sighed. "I will be speaking with Khessi tomorrow."

I couldn't help the babbling concern that suddenly erupted out of me. Feeling I had betrayed my beautiful new friend, the idea that I'd done something that would make her dislike me more was terribly upsetting.

"Oh no, Mistress, please! She did train me. I'm just so nervous. Don't punish Khessi for my ignorance."

"Silence!" she hissed through clenched teeth and I immediately regretted saying anything. Anger flashed quietly in the fire of those blue opal eyes. When she pressed her lips together they looked like a rose bud tightening closed in the shade.

"How dare you tell me what to do with my slave! If you did not want her punished, you should not have brought her name into your shortcomings."

"I know. I didn't mean to...I only..."

"Silence!" She repeated again. "Are you incapable of following even the most basic of commands?"

I managed to gain control over my mouth again and remained silent. The Mistress took a long metal pin from a drawer. She piled her wet hair on top of her head. Lacing the pin through her hair, it stayed up in a perfect tousled bun on top of her head. I opened a bottle of wine and poured a glass half full so it could breathe. Water sloshed in the pool behind me as she got in. Hurriedly, I followed her into the water, setting the bottle into the stone bowl that was full of ice. She sat in the same center bench Khessi had. I tried to look graceful and obedient as I crossed the water to her. I bowed my head as I handed her the glass, trying for all I was worth to look humble. To show her how much I wanted to serve her. She took the glass from me and took a sip. I wished I could have inspired the sweet giggling charm I'd seen her display outside with Braxian, but I was apparently more irritating than charming.

The silence in the room was miserable. I stood in the water with my brain eating me alive debating if I should do something more that I wasn't thinking of. Regardless, I was silent. She sat with her eyes closed as she soaked, breathing in the rich scents of amber, vanilla, and a dash of honey, occasionally drinking from the glass. I stood, watching her naked form float in the water while my fingers and toes pruned.

After twenty minutes of silence, I decided I would offer to do something relaxing. Maybe I would find a way to endear myself somehow.

"Would you like me to rub your feet, Mistress?" I said timidly.

"Goddess, you talk a lot," she said, taking another long drink. I gritted my teeth.

"But I want to be a good bath slave."

"That's your problem right there. *You want.* For example, you want to talk right now. So, we'll talk."

"I only meant to…oh, Goddess…" I sighed heavily.

She finished the wine in her glass with a final gulp and set it down noisily on the stone side table. For a moment I worried it might shatter, but it didn't. She leaned back and rested an elbow on her bent knee.

"Do you know why I bought you, Slave?"

"No, Mistress." I hung my head, shaking it, unsure as to why anyone would have bought me at this point. "Because wasted potential is the greatest sin of all?" I guessed, thinking of what she'd said to me in the dungeon the night before.

"Hmm. At least you are listening."

I gave a small shrug and a slight smile, happy that I had a good memory for such things.

"Do you imagine that I bought you so that I could hear the sound of your voice prattle about your insecurities while I attempt to relax in my bath?"

"No, Mistress."

Ugh. I'm the worse slave ever.

"Do you think it is because your muttering to yourself is somehow enlightening or insightful?"

"No, Mistress." This was not going well at all. "I only thought…" I started but stopped when she talked over me.

"*Potential*, however, is only just that. It is not practicality. I have no use for blank, passionless slaves. And from what I saw at the auction, you clearly have passion."

"Thank you, Mistress."

"You also have excessive pride and disobedience. For which I also have no use."

I shifted uncomfortably. The warm water suddenly felt much too hot as my face flushed. She continued, "I read your papers when I bought you. A pleasure slave in his thirtieth year. Tell me, Zsash…"

I jumped a little at her saying my name.

"Do you consider yourself a skilled pleasure slave?"

I didn't know what to say. I guessed honesty was the best policy. As per my usual, I guessed wrong.

"Would it sound vain to say yes?"

"It would," she nodded. "It may be true. But the saying of it lacks humility and more importantly, perspective. The correct answer would be that if *I* think you are a skilled pleasure slave, then you would be so. Do you understand?"

I searched for words but they were all slipping from me. "I would be happy to pleasure you in any way…"

She cut me off again and clicked her tongue with a tsk tsk tsk sound. "That is a suggestion to comfort you. Of course, *you* want to pleasure *me,* as you would enjoy that. But how can you possibly please another, let alone a Queen, when you are so concerned with what you want?"

"I don't understand."

"The way you form your words, your thoughts even, is disrespectful. How can you hope to be good at pleasing a Queen when you are so motivated toward your own willful desires? You could learn a thing or two from Khessi, if you bothered to listen to her lessons."

"I want to be different. Tell me what I can do to…"

She stood and moved toward me with a predatory ease. I flinched my head to the side as she ran one of those gold nails up under my chin. Her movements were perfectly balanced and eerily beautiful. I averted my eyes, while hers bore down on me. Her breasts pressed warm and soft and completely intentionally against my body as she closed the space between us. I stifled a groan as she spoke quietly, just inches from my face. Her sharp claws ran softly over my throat and lips.

"Tell you, you say? You presume to command me? To get me to tell you something? It is *you* who answers to *me*. Not the other way around. You will ask when you speak to me. Or better yet, beg. Every word that passes your lips should be a request. Demands are not an attractive trait in a slave. You also said 'I want'." She forcefully grabbed my jaw between a thumb and finger. I felt her unnatural strength. How effortlessly she could crush my bones. She wasn't hurting me, but there was no way I could have moved my face from her either.

"But...I do want to..."

"Ah, ah, ah. Shhh." She stopped me. Tears slid down my cheeks in frustration and shame. "The word want should be struck from a slave's vocabulary when addressing a Queen. The most desirable words from a slave are 'will' and 'please'. There is never what you want to do. There is only what you will do. What will you do for me, Zsash?" Her anger turned to a purr.

"Anything." And I meant it.

"We will see."

"I would do anything for you. You are my Mistress..." This statement earned me renewed strength into her grip as she moved my face closer to hers.

Her touch heated, edging on a burning sensation. "And *that* is the biggest part of your flaw, Zsash." She drew my face close to hers. "Look at me," she commanded.

I lifted my shame-filled eyes, filling with unexpected tears. My chest felt tight and the muscles in my gut clenched.

"I am not *your* Mistress. The word 'your' implies ownership and used in connection with my title is offensive. Watch your wording more carefully as to not offend my sensitive nature. I know this is a lot for you, my pet. So I will be clear." She moved past my face to whisper in my ear, her voice soft and rich as it wrapped around my heart. "I am not *your* Mistress. You are *my* slave. You cannot *make* me happy because there is nothing you could make me do. But, you *will* do what I command and that will please me. Obeyed orders are far sexier to me than your prick could ever be. Understand?"

I nodded numbly. She released my face, leaned back and smiled with approval at me. I stared into her eyes as more tears escaped to streak my cheeks.

"I will have your punishment arranged by tomorrow. Go see Khessi for it in the morning." She took a step back from me, walking out of the bath.

"Thank you, Mistress."

"And in the future, I don't ever want to see the bottom of my wine glass ever again. I will stop you if I don't want more," she added.

"Yes, Mistress," I said with defeat.

She pulled the pin from her hair and a cascade of half dry locks tumbled down her flawless back. She walked toward her bedroom as I stared at the empty glass. I felt it reflected everything about myself. A sparkling shell with no substance.

"Oh, and Zsash," she turned back toward me.

"Yes, Mistress," I said with my head hung low.

"The honey in with the amber was a nice touch." She turned and closed the door to her bed chamber, leaving me alone in the bath feeling extremely stupid and even more confused.

"There are very few codes between slaves. It is understood among the slave castes that loyalty begins and ends with the commands of their Master. That being said, there is one rule that is obeyed among the lot, from common to household slave. That it is a coward's move to blame another slave for your inadequacy. If you paint your feet red because another slave told you, it pleased the Master. If you then received punishment for it do not blame the slave who gave you false information. For it was your choice to heed the advice of a slave rather than obtain the will of your owner."

Loash, *The Scrolls of the Goddess*

CHAPTER 5: SILENCE

While eating breakfast the next morning, I was happy that none of the slaves seemed to pay much attention to me. I kept an eye out for the guards and Corvas in case anyone intended to continue my beating streak into day three. Breakfast passed without incident.

After checking in with Jaideen and having my injuries cleaned, I headed down to Khessi's office. When I arrived, I knew something was off.

The oceanic scene that was the office had been covered. Swathes of black velvet curtains had been pulled over every wall making the glassy floor the only part where I could glimpse sea life. My heart began to drop as I realized this was some form of punishment for the household slave. To be deprived of seeing her sea creatures.

Leading up to her desk were pieces of parchment, crumpled into balls and littering the floor like small blooming flowers. She had clearly been working on writing something for a while and these hadn't made the cut. Khessi leaned over the desk with her face close to a piece of parchment, the palms of her hands holding the parchment flat and steady. She moved her neck and head with slow deliberation. I stepped closer to see what she was doing. A black satin strap held a silver gag in place in her mouth. It was bejeweled with diamonds, like every other piece of jewelry she had. Protruding from the mouthpiece about an inch, however, was a silver quill nib.

She was so focused on her work that she had not noticed me yet. I watched her move with practiced precision to dip the tip of the quill into a nearby inkwell. Dragging the tip over the edge of the well so it would not drip, she then continued writing whatever letter or paperwork she was busy with. And I knew instantly that this was my fault.

83

I attempted to quietly slip back out of the room. When I took a step backward, I knocked hard into the corner of a table. The table leg screeched on the glass floor abruptly. Khessi's eyes flickered up, startled. In this second of distraction, a single drip of black ink escaped the quill tip and landed on the parchment. Her aqua eyes snapped back down at the paper, followed by the most exasperated cry of frustration. She glared at me with icy shards while she lifted the parchment and crumpled it into a tight ball with her finely manicured fingers. She threw it down into the pile on the floor with the other failed attempts. Khessi let out a long huff of irritation. Sitting up straight to look at me she shook her head in slow disapproval.

"I am so sorry. I was just so flustered when I got around her."

She stood and opened a drawer in the desk.

"What's that?"

She took something out of the drawer that was made of black leather, accented with metal. It was large and looked almost like a piece of armor.

"Oh shit…" I said, getting a better look.

She nodded with raised eyebrows and showed me the gag I would be wearing. A face corset was really a better description for it. She then stepped behind me to fit me with the corset collar. It opened at the back, the front piece made of solid leather traveling from my collar bones up my neck and over the lower part of my face, just under my nose. It fastened behind my head and neck with silver buckles that then locked, so that I would be effectively silenced while wearing it.

She gestured for me to follow her and I did. We walked all the way back to the bath chamber. When we got there, she showed me to a closet that held a wooden bucket, a rack of soap and various brushes, brooms, and mops. She pulled out the bucket and soap and set them on the floor in front of me, then gestured to the room around us. I nodded, understanding. She handed me a piece of parchment with writing on it. It said,

Your time bound will help you learn to think before you speak. Your punishment will continue until everything in the bath chamber is thoroughly cleaned.

- Mistress Isavyne

I nodded again. Khessi turned and stuck the piece of parchment on the edge of the mirror in front of the sink. That way I would be able to reread my punishment over and over throughout the day. She then turned on her heel and left without a glance back.

For the rest of the day I cleaned. I opened the windows wide to allow a nice breeze to work its way through the room. I swept every corner. I ignored the pain in my mouth as I scrubbed every tile thoroughly. I ignored the pain in my back as I washed all the glass and mopped the floor. Pain I could ignore. The part I had trouble ignoring was the thirst. I wanted a drink of water. Badly. I was sweating from the physical labor and surrounded by water that I couldn't drink. All I could do was keep working and push it all to the back of my mind.

When it got closer to sunset, I drew the bath. I took a moment to think about the bath fragrance. Should I play it safe since the Mistress seemed to enjoy the one from the night before, amber, vanilla, and honey? I thought about it for a moment. She liked creativity and initiative. Also, Khessi had said that all the fragrances were ones that the Mistress had approved of. Then again, I'd had rotten luck lately. It was probably best to stick with what I knew was good. I scooped in amber and honey. Then I readied a glass and bottle of wine, placing them near the bath.

When the Mistress arrived, she wore a short satin robe in white, of course. She dropped the robe onto the floor. I picked it up and hung it on a nearby hook. I followed her into the shower. Her long hair was in a braid that hung over her shoulder. Before starting the water, I unclipped her hair and unbraided it. I no longer noticed her raw beauty, or at least, no longer acknowledged it in my thoughts. I focused on my task. I washed her body gently but thoroughly. Then her hair. I remembered to wring it out one, two, three, four times.

When she went to the vanity to put her hair up, I took that moment to uncork the bottle of wine and pour a glass. When she walked to the bath I bowed my head and handed it to her. I wasn't sure because I was keeping my eyes down, but I think she smiled a little. She soaked in the bath for a while before finishing her first glass of wine. I was poised and ready to refill it before she swallowed that last of it.

Three glasses later, I was surprised when she motioned me over to her.

"Massage my shoulders, slave," she ordered softly.

I did so, using long strokes over her muscles to work the tension from them. I watched her glass carefully so I wouldn't get so preoccupied with massaging that I forgot to pour her more wine. When she finished the next glass, I stopped massaging to grab the bottle but she waived me off.

"That's enough for now."

Lowering my head again, I gently set the bottle down and returned to her. She was standing though, and heading for the stairs leading out of the bath. I moved quickly to follow her as I grabbed a towel. She paused and lifted her arms so that I could wrap it around her.

"You did well tonight, Zsash. Keep up the good work. There's hope for you yet."

I bowed deeply, hoping that this would be followed by my release from the leather.

Instead, she walked toward her bed chamber. The Mistress stopped by the mirror that held the piece of parchment. Then looking at me in the mirrors reflection, she tapped a gold claw on the parchment.

"I am surprised at your inability to complete a task list of one item, however. Perhaps tomorrow night." She shrugged slightly and turned to head into her room. The door shut behind her.

My heart sank into the pit of my empty stomach. What had I missed?

After a poor night of sleep trying to breathe and not bend at the neck, I woke and headed down to the healers' wing. Jaideen didn't smile when he saw me this time. He shook his head.

"Seriously?" he cried out, throwing his hands up. "Already? How is possible to get into so much trouble in such a short amount of time?"

I shrugged, shaking my head. I wanted to say *I'm just that good* or *At least I didn't tear my stitches out*. There were a number of clever phrases that came to mind. This pissed me off. The gag was getting in the way of my being clever.

Jaideen cleaned my wounds while continuing to express his shock at getting myself punished again so soon. I sat and listened while feeling light-headed from physical exhaustion, and lack of water and food.

As I headed back to the bath chamber, I decided to see if Khessi was still gagged. I also wanted to see if she was still mad at me.

I didn't make it to her office, however. As I entered the main entryway I saw some familiar faces I wasn't looking forward to seeing. Ever again. Posted by the main stairwell were Corvas and some of his fellow guards, all of them meat castles of strength and intimidation. The surprise on Corvas's face told me that he hadn't heard of this new punishment of mine.

"Oh hoo!" Corvas hooted. It echoed obnoxiously in the high ceiling of the entry hall. I changed my course to visit Khessi immediately and walked toward the stairs. My eyes closed and I huffed in frustration as Corvas stepped in front of me, blocking my path.

"That's a pretty accessory you've got there, new boy. What did you do now?"

I stared at him. They all laughed. I moved to walk around them again and Corvas moved again to block me. I wanted to answer him with my fists. I'd had about enough of this bastard bullying me. The last few days hadn't been the most glamorous or comfortable for me. I was hungry, thirsty, in pain, tired and all around sick of being fucked with.

"Come on, speak up!" He leaned in toward my face and I steadied myself to dodge if he threw a punch at me. He took in a deep breath and laughed. "You fucking stink like a whore's bed, you know that?"

The guards all started making little side comments about my sexual performance and overall appearance. Corvas was in my ear doing some kind of bragging. I'm not sure of everything he said. Something about,"...This rank bitch thinks he's going to bag himself a household slave."

The sound of blood screamed through my veins, preparing for a fight. Sweat accumulated on my furrowed brow. My hands shook at my sides as I balled them into fists. I hated how his face sneered when he smiled at me. I hated how attractive he was for a guard. How unscarred he was. I had more scars than he did. The healing wounds on my back suddenly pulsed with the surge of my heartbeat. I wanted to crush out those white, mocking pearls between his lips. If he touched me in any way, I was going to break his face. I didn't even care what the other guards did to me. I was going to make him bleed. More so, I wanted him to regret having ever spoken to me.

"What in the name of the Goddess is going on out here?"

The tone of Khessi's controlled delicate voice splashed over me like cool water. Relief melted my hatred, letting reason creep back in. My fists relaxed some at the sound of high heels approaching.

"This is not a Cheritoth ring. If you act in any way contrary to how you would when the Mistress is present, it is not permissible. And she will hear about it from me!"

All the guards stood upright at their posts silently. Corvas moved out of my way, the smile still not sufficiently gone from his expression for my liking. I continued up the stairs without looking behind me. I should have waited for Khessi to dismiss me. But I was anxious to get out of that place. I slowed my walk a little to overhear some of the conversation behind me.

"Corvas, you will cease this antagonistic behavior with Zsash immediately," Khessi reprimanded him.

"Oh, I'm sure poor sweet Zsash can take care of himself. Are you two so close already that you feel the need to protect him?"

I pretended to take a look at an extravagant floral arrangement in the hallway to let myself linger and listen. I smiled at two interior slave girls dressed in short black form fitting dresses and functional black high heels. They stood across the hall folding linens and also eavesdropping. We shouldn't fool ourselves. All slaves are gossip mongers.

"The new bath slave is still in training. His punishments are for the Mistress to decide. Your first *misunderstanding…*" she said slowly with deliberate emphasis, "has been dismissed by the Mistress. However, any further actions against him by any of you," her voice raised as she looked at all of the guards. "…will be viewed by me as hindering his training and will be reported to the Mistress immediately. I trust you all understand the weight with which the Mistress heeds my words."

"Of course," Corvas answered with a sweet tone and a bow of his head. "We were just teasing. He's had a rough start is all. I've already apologized to my brother Zsash for our previous misunderstanding, which was just exactly that. I thought he was hurting you. My only desire has been to protect you."

"The desires of a slave are meaningless and therefore not actionable. Was it the foreign sound of my laughter, of which you are so unaccustomed to, that confused and impassioned such violence?"

A murmur of stifled laughter rose from the guards. I smiled behind the leather collar. Then Khessi's voice became softer as she leaned in to speak to Corvas in hushed intimate tones.

"Or was it instead, the sound of my pleasure? Of which, you are also so unfamiliar?"

Corvas was left speechless.

"I do know guard slaves are encouraged to solve problems with violence. Indeed, it is what you are trained for and best at. I would suggest, however, that you develop additional intellectual skills. As much as such abilities are possible, anyway." There was a pause as she let her words resonate with him. She then said to all of them in a sharp tone, "Get back to your posts!"

Her heels clicked briskly up the stairs behind me and I hurried along, trying to appear as though I hadn't listened the whole time. The interior slaves also busied themselves with their linens again.

"Zsash!" Khessi called out. I turned towards her with my best surprised face. From the nose up anyway. "Did you clean the bath chamber yesterday?" I nodded. Her eyebrows knitted in confusion. "You must not have done a very good job."

My eyes rolled on their own.

"Get back to the bath chamber and clean for the rest of the day until bath time."

I nodded again and gave a muffled "Mmhmm."

That's what I was going to do anyway. I thought as loudly as I could. Goddess, I missed being able to talk.

"I will visit the bath chamber later today to make sure you don't miss anything this time." Khessi jotted down a note in her book, the feather of her quill bouncing fluffily. "Well? Don't just stand there staring at me. Get cleaning!"

I nodded again with a muffled "I'm going!" Though, I'm not sure anyone could have understood me and turned to return to the bath chamber.

"I used to mess up all the time because I was never quite sure if my Mistress was teasing me with her outlandish commands or if she was serious. I would run myself in circles trying to make her happy and never seemed to accomplish anything the way she wanted it done. It took me years to realize that she *liked* it when I obeyed her every command. But she *loved* it when I fell short of my orders. So now, I mess up all the time because I realized that's what she likes best."

Dornic, *The Scrolls of the Goddess*

CHAPTER 6: DIRTY

What had I missed? I stood in the center of the bath chamber and looked around the room. I thought I'd done a pretty good job yesterday. Obviously, I'd missed something.

I went to the cleaning supplies closet and got out the bucket and brushes. I decided to clean the entire place over again. I cleaned the bathing pool first since I figured it was technically dirty since last night's bath. I cleaned everything I'd already cleaned the day before. After combing the place over, I did eventually realize there actually were a few more spots I missed. I polished the metal and crystal. I dusted all the bottles and jars. I even cleaned the under surfaces of everything I could find.

When I finished with the bath chamber, this time, it sparkled. And I do mean that literally. With the windows open and the sun catching the crystals and reflective surfaces. The whole room took on a brilliance. There was nothing more I could go over without going over work I'd already done.

Even so, I kept cleaning.

It was around this time that a strong breeze blew through the open window and I smelled something bad.

"Ugh." I actually said out loud into the gag. I was wondering what smelled so rank and horrible, and right about the same moment I realized what it was.

It was me.

That's when it all came together.

I had taken Corvas's insults to be just shit talk but, yes. I actually did stink. I reeked of medicine and blood and sweat and just kind of an all over funk in a barrage of weird smells. I had been so focused on the problem around me that I wasn't thinking of myself as part of the problem. This, in grand retrospect, could be the source of many of the issues I had gotten myself into in my life.

The realization was so abrupt that I dropped the towel I had been scrubbing with and got into the shower immediately.

I let the water wash my body and clear my thoughts. The hot water against the cool breeze outside felt beautiful. And I thanked the Goddess with leather-smothered lips for sending me the breeze that brought my realization.

I was the unclean thing in a room of vigorously cleaned things. I had also made myself more dirty, sweaty and gross in the process. *Of course,* that was one of the duties of a bath slave. The Mistress didn't want some filthy man bathing with her and touching her clean skin. I needed to take care of my body if I was to have it in proximity to the Mistress. It also occurred to me that perhaps I needed to change how I listened to what the Mistress said. I had to learn to think beyond the obvious meaning of things.

Finishing my shower, I splashed myself with sandalwood and vanilla. I cleaned under my nails and trimmed them. As it approached dusk, I poured the bath for the Mistress. Tonight, I wanted a fragrance that would represent freshness. I went with crisp apple tempered with lily. I was starving and it almost made me feel like I was eating an apple to be standing in the steaming room.

I had been going around the bath chamber naked since my shower and was about to put my red bathing briefs back on. I realized that they, too, were probably dirty. So I made a choice. The briefs were really to maintain the veil that male bath slaves don't get erections or to keep some privacy. I hoped I was making the right choice.

When Mistress Isavyne entered the bath chamber, I was kneeling and naked, my head hung low in submission. She approached me with gold and diamond-heeled stilettos that came to rest in front of me. I didn't look up. She leaned over and inhaled.

"Very nice," she murmured as she ran a clawed hand through my hair. "Khessi," she said behind her.

I felt Khessi's cool touch on my shoulder while she lifted the lock at the back of my head. Then the beautiful sound of a lock clicking open echoed. The leather was taken from my neck and mouth. I groaned in relief as I worked my jaw and touched my face to get sensation back into it. I found two days of stubble on my face. I hadn't even thought about that! I hoped the Mistress didn't count my unshaven face as part of it being unkempt.

"Thank you, Khessi. That will be all."

"Yes, Mistress," Khessi said and I watched her voluptuous ass head toward the spiral staircase.

Now alone with the Mistress, I stood and walked toward the shower. But the Mistress motioned toward the bath.

"I do not require a shower tonight," she said over her shoulder as she stepped into the steaming water. "Bring shaving supplies and my wine, Zsash."

It only took me a blink to comply before I joined her in the bath.

"Sit." She pointed to the stone seat in the center of the bath. I crossed the water to sit down, but not before handing her a glass of wine. I continued to keep my eyes down. This kept them aimed mostly at breast level, which was fine with me. The Mistress took a drink of the wine and sighed.

"You are not wearing your briefs, my pet." Her tone sung sweetly.

"They were dirty, Mistress. And I wanted to do my best to follow your instructions. If it displeases you I will put them back on."

"Nonsense. Seeing you this way is actually very pleasing to me."

My skin tingled and a thrill of blood surged through me. I couldn't exactly tell, did my trained ear detect flirting?

"You have done very well, slave. Everything in my bath chamber looks wonderful."

"Thank you, Mistress."

"Except for this one last thing. Which, of course, you couldn't help." She ran her palm over the scruff on my face. Then reached for the honey soap and made a lather in her hands. She began smoothing the foam over my stubble.

"I am happy you are learning to follow directions. Nothing is more appealing than an obedient slave."

"Whatever I can do to please you, Mistress."

She cleaned her hands off in the water. The apple, lily and honey scents drifted over my senses. I expected her to reach for the razor I'd brought. But she didn't.

"I'm so glad to hear you say that. Now, hold…very still," she said.

Confusion wrinkled my brow a second before she brought one gleaming gold claw to my face. Tilting my chin, she ran her nail down my cheek, shaving away the scruff I'd grown there. I sat motionless while she shaved my face with her golden claws.

Can I just say that again?

Her golden, fucking, razor sharp claws!

The metallic talon ran slowly over my cheeks, then down my chin. I swallowed cautiously as she lifted my jaw to reach the tender part of my throat.

She was so close to my face that I found myself staring at her features. Her blue eyes with crystalline striations focused on not cutting me, narrowing from time to time. Occasionally her pink tongue perched on the edge of those ruby lips in concentration. Though focusing, her expression always appeared casual. The long feathers of her eyelashes batted lazily every once in a while. Surprise caught me when she eventually glanced up to look at me, causing me to jerk backward ever so slightly.

"Oh, now you've done it." She said looking down at my neck. "I told you not to move." I registered a slight pain in my neck and felt a trickle that I would have mistaken for water. It dawned on me that I must be bleeding a little. My jostling motion had caused a cut. She ran her hands through the water to clean them off, then brought a handful of water up to my neck and rinsed my skin. I didn't feel any pain. The cut must not have been very deep.

She reached for her glass and finished it in one gulp. Only moving my arm and without breaking the Mistress' gaze, I leaned to the side of the bath to grasp the wine bottle. With the other hand, I wrapped my fingers around her glass to steady it while I filled it. Somehow I pulled it off without so much as a glance to what I was doing. The Mistress arched a golden eyebrow, impressed. Honestly, I was impressed with myself as well. I can be smooth sometimes.

"Now, let me see you," she commanded and moved back from me a little to admire her work. I touched my face and was shocked at how close the shave was. It made my skin feel so incredibly soft. The Mistress ran her hands slowly over my face and neck. She nodded approvingly.

"Stand," she ordered. I did so, realizing only within seconds of the motion that this put her sitting at my standing hip level. She ran her hands over my chest, slowly, like she was taking in the texture of my skin. Her fingertips glanced gently down my body until they rested on my hips for a brief second, then lowered still to the hair between my legs. She stopped her hands, I'm sure quite on purpose, just above the base of my cock. It caused me to stiffen with embarrassing speed. She ignored this and continued to focus on the thatch of dark hair there.

"This too, I do not care for." She reached for the honey soap again. Assuming that I was about to get a similar treatment as my face, I steadied myself. I had been concerned about her nails at my throat before. Now I was well beyond concerned.

As she moved her hands together creating the lather I realized two things. First, how small her hands were. For a creature of such power, they were delicate beyond compare. Long and slender and deceptively fragile looking.

The second thought was that the Mistress was about to lay her hands on me and how I needed to think about something else in order to not move or thrust or twitch or climax from this.

As her hands smoothed foam between my legs, I felt my pulse surge through my groin. I inhaled deeply, grasping at all my self-discipline. Don't laugh at me. I have self-discipline, damn it.

"Open your legs more," she said without inflection. I took a step out and was met with her hands running the warm, soft suds near the base of my cock. A moan escaped my lips and I immediately pressed them tightly together. I clenched my jaw and tried my best not to move.

"Did you say something, slave?" the Mistress asked, her hands still fondling me. I swallowed, trying desperately to moisten my drying mouth.

"No, Mistress."

She smirked and looked back down. Her claw ran long and smoothly against my skin. I stared blankly at the walls in front of me fiercely counting the tiles.

One, two, three, four...shit, what comes after four?

Her nail scraped down in long motions, narrowly missing my erection. But without ever actually touching it, again and again. Every once in a while, she would swish her hand in the water, cleaning it off. I didn't dare look down. My breathing grew heavy and more labored with each exhale. I was getting so hard I could feel my cock standing straight up. It made me worry that its new position, so close to my body, might get too near her claws.

"Put your leg up on the seat," she ordered. I did so without looking down, guessing what was coming next. I had expected she would shave me completely at this point. I didn't expect at that moment for her to wrap her hand around my shaft.

I gasped loudly, followed by a moan that echoed around the bath chamber. Her grip was strong and slick with the soap. I couldn't help but look down. She held my swollen cock in that lovely delicate hand. She wasn't jerking me off, but the pressure of her hand around me was creating a wonderful, awful urge to lift my hips.

Don't move. Don't thrust. Don't twitch.

I exhaled a moan again and resumed staring at the wall. Amidst the hot, light friction of her palm and the pleasure it caused, I dimly realized that she was continuing to shave me. I tried to breathe but the air caught in my lungs. I bit my lower lip, pushing away all natural instincts. I hadn't had sex in days. I was so hard I was worried that if she cut me I might completely bleed out.

"Mistress…" I begged finally. "I don't know how much longer I can hold still. Please…"

"Now, Zsash. You've been doing so well. Don't make me punish you again."

Having finished shaving me clean, she ran her soft hands over the newly smooth skin. Then, one stroke up my shaft that caused me to hold my breath.

"Making messes again, Zsash?" Mistress Isavyne teased. I looked down to make sure I hadn't accidentally released some into her hand. I hadn't, which made me confused by her words. She moved away from me and up the nearby steps, then sat down and parted her thighs. I could see what she meant now by *making a mess*. Her pussy was slick with excitement.

"Let's see if that mouth of yours is good for anything more than getting you into trouble." She beckoned me to her.

I didn't even think about it. I knelt down on the steps of the bath and lowered myself between her legs. *This* is what I knew about. I was finally back in my own arena. My hands traveled slowly from her ankles to her calves, then up her thighs, building deliberate tension as I did so. My face rested a few inches from her glistening sex and I exhaled a hot breath against her. Her hand ran through the back of my hair while I delicately raised her legs up onto my shoulders. My hands rested on the backs of her thighs. Using my thumbs, I opened her wider to reveal her clit, then lowered my mouth and began licking with long wide strokes.

"Mmm…that's right. Let me see what you can do." She purred, biting her lip.

Her first gasp echoed around the room and into my ears. It created a hunger in me to bring that glorious sound from her again. I lapped slowly, treasuring the scent and taste of her musky, sweet juices mixing with the apple bath water. I waited until her hips rocked ever so slightly in my hands to change my technique. I braced her clit with my upper teeth, not biting, mind you. I trapped it between my teeth and the bridge of my tongue and began a series of quick, rubbing strokes on the swollen bud of her pleasure. Her breathing quickened. So did mine. I wanted so badly to be inside her. I felt her hips raise to press herself closer to my mouth. Her moans were slow and breathy.

"Yes…Mmfmm…That's it, slave. Keep fucking me with that pretty face of yours."

I slipped my tongue lower and began licking as deeply as I could inside her. Repeating the motion while I squeezed her thighs. I pressed my face into the warmth of her flesh, getting lost in the rhythm of that licking motion. She rocked against my mouth, moaning sensuously.

I chanced a look up at her. A few golden locks hung on her lightly sheening brow while her hooded blue eyes followed my movements. She cupped her breasts slowly, teasing her firming nipples between her fingers. Lusty words formed on her scarlet lips, commanding me to continue.

"Oh yes, just like that, slave. Lick me deeper!!"

I held her hips stationary while I licked further inside her, increasing the rhythm. When I chanced to glance up, she no longer watched me. Her eyes were shut tight while she squeezed one breast. Her other hand lowered to the back of my neck to hold my mouth against her. Her legs on my shoulders, she opened her thighs wider to me. I panted and moaned loudly against her soft, wet pussy, each lick driving me wild. Her thighs began shaking and she played with her nipples roughly between her fingers.

"Oh, Yes! Yes, that's fucking perfect. Just like that! Goddess, your tongue's so fucking good! Fuck yes, that's it! That's it! I'm gonna cum!"

She was incredibly sexy cumming into my mouth. Fiercely beautiful cries pierced the bath chamber's stillness while I lapped up her sweet juices until her cries became sighs of pleasure floating alongside the lightly slapping waves of water in the bath.

She sat up and grabbed me by the back of my hair. Pulling me roughly up to her mouth and into a kiss.

"Nicely done, Zsash." she said breathily after she pulled away.

"Thank you, Mistress." I panted. I was so hard that I ached to finish with every hopeful throb that pulsed through my groin. Her sapphire gaze drifted down to my pleading cock as it strained away from my body, then her eyes rose back up to look at my lips.

"My goodness, you're so aroused my pet. Did you enjoy having your face used like that?"

"Yes, Mistress."

"You do what I say, slave. That includes cuming if I tell you to. Understand?"

"Yes, Mistress." I shuddered.

She took another step toward me. Her water-warmed flesh was so close I could feel the heat radiating off her skin. She kissed me again roughly, making sure to keep her hips far enough from mine. The tips of her breasts, though, glided softly against my chest. Unbearably soft.

"I like how I taste on your lips. Can you still taste me, Zsash?"

I licked my lips and tasted her sweetness there. The pressure in my body rose as my heart began to beat faster.

"Yes, Mistress," I answered.

"Keep your hands at your sides." She commanded. I nodded as she closed, even more, distance between us. I stared straight forward, trying desperately to think of something else other than the beautiful naked Queen inches from my erection.

"Do you desire me, slave? Do you dream of worshipping my gorgeous tits while I fuck you and take you for my own pleasure? I want you to think about what it would be like to slide that thick fucking dick of yours into my tight little cunt, right now?" I moaned, trembling with the effort it took not to move. The Mistress ran her hands up my sides and across my chest. "I want you to imagine how it would feel if I let you inside me. My silky, warm cum dripping between my legs. So wet from your tongue licking me. That if I let you fuck me right now, how easily you'd slide inside..."

"Mistress..." I begged.

She ran her fingers softly through my hair. With a few gentle caresses, she drew her claws over my scalp, causing goosebumps to travel down my arms. She began to pull my hair in her grip, bringing my cheek against hers till her lips rested at the edge of my jaw. She whispered.

"...Imagine how hard you'd fuck me, Zsash. How if I let you, you'd bury all of that beautiful cock deep inside me..."

"Oh, Mistress, please..." I gasped.

She was moaning softly between kissing and lightly licking my ear. Whispering how good it would feel if she ever decided to take me.

Goddess, if only she wanted me to...

My eyes were squeezed tight and my hands clenched open and shut. I was breathing hard and shaking with effort.

"...pumping it in and out while I take you. I'd squeeze you so tight until you were begging for it. Until you couldn't stand it anymore. Taking you so good and so hard and fast till I'm quivering in pleasure all around you! Forcing you to cum deep so I can feel that cock throbbing and spilling inside me. Fuck yes, slave! That's all you're good for. Giving me what I want. And what I want is for you to cum for me, right now! Do it! Let me see you fucking cum!" she whispered, panting and pulling at my hair with her moans pushing me unbearably toward release.

I cried out as I came, pushed beyond the bounds of my control, triggered by only her words and her breath against my ear. I released the tension that had been building inside me. Clenching my hands at my sides and thrusting into emptiness as the pounding pleasure shook through me. My cock jerked and shot with each wave of crushing ecstasy. It left my head spinning as I moaned against the Mistress's shoulder. I had lost track of myself and my forehead now rested in the crook of her neck.

"Very good, my pet," she purred.

"Thank you, Mistress," I nodded, still catching my breath.

"You must be hungry after being locked in that device the last few days," she said backing away from me and getting back into the water. She was right.

My stomach grumbled a little now that it had been reminded of its emptiness.

"You are dismissed. Go downstairs and have Khessi feed you dinner. I'm going to stay in here for a while longer. You can drain the bath when you come back later tonight."

"Yes, Mistress." I bowed my head and left the bath, heading for the stairwell.

"Zsash?"

"Yes, Mistress?"

"Put on some pants."

"Ah." I looked down, then gave a little bow again. "As the Mistress commands!"

She shook her head and the most wonderful thing happened. She laughed. A charming, endearing sweet laughter. I could get used to this.

"To be touched by the Goddess is unlike any other feeling in this world. A sensation beyond pleasure that crosses the planes of existence. It is joy, lifted in the pure searing pleasure of your complete submission. Like looking into a circular mirror at your reflection a million times, refracted in the pure white soul light of her love. I have dedicated my life to becoming the slave I saw in that mirror, to admitting my own imperfections and purging them from my flesh. Many do not have the strength to look so far within with such naked sight. There, you will find monsters of your own creation bound to your heart by chains of pride and sin. Monsters that do not die quietly. "

Misteryn, *The Scrolls of the Goddess*

CHAPTER 7: CLEAN

I *might* have been skipping down the halls to Khessi's office. My giddy steps reminded me of my last morning in the training house with Basz and Trylith. For a moment, I wondered how my sisters had fared after I'd passed out at the auction and if they had gone to good homes with kind owners. I brushed the darkest possibilities from my mind and assured myself that with their beauty they had certainly made their way to somewhere fantastic. I also thanked the Goddess for my own situation and marveled at how bleak things could feel in life, right before they get wonderful.

On my way down the stairs, I saw a familiar face standing guard in the entryway. I believe I've mentioned that from time to time, I cannot keep my mouth shut. This qualifies as one of those times.

I slid down the last three feet of the banister and landed with a spring in my step as I walked over to Corvas. He was already glaring at me. *Excellent.*

"Good evening, brother!" I bellowed. "Yes, indeed. Such a fine, fine evening." I repositioned my crotch casually. All right, not so casually. "It is so good to get out of that gag. Whew! I am hungry!" I squared my shoulders and stood in front of him, fanning myself at him a little. "You smell that? Apples and lily from the bath. I was indeed very dirty." He opened his mouth to shoot out some snide little comment, but I spoke over him instead. "Well, I don't want to bore you with the details. I know you have lots of important things to do. The busy life of a guard slave that you lead. All that standing, and…hmm." I paused, taking a long breath in through my nose. "…watching. Too bad you don't get a chance to use your sword in the service of the Mistress more often.

I mean, this bath slave title has a really negative connotation for something so, intimate with the Mistress." And now I leaned in to whisper in a hushed tone like it was a secret, "Have you ever ran your fingers over the naked skin of a Queen before? Or tasted the luscious golden honey she releases in pleasure?" He didn't say anything. Or at least, not fast enough before I responded to my own question. "Oh! What am I saying? Of course, you haven't."

Goddess, he hated me. He flinched a little and I turned away with my smile, which I'm sure could only be described as dripping with rank arrogance.

"Sorry, I can't stay and chat with you longer. The Mistress was very specific that Khessi is to feed me dinner. I don't know what it is, but being around our beloved household slave always makes me hungry."

I left, feeling his eyes on me, my back warming with his pure, undiluted hatred. I should have known better than that. Scratching at a wound will only cause it to bleed and fester. The same is true of enemies. The best policy is to always leave it alone. Let it heal until it's just a scar. But, I've always had to learn things the hard way.

Entering Khessi's office, I immediately knew something was terribly wrong. She sat on one of the couches, her bright hair hanging over her shoulders. She held something small in her hand. She looked up at me, her eyes swimming with tears. Her makeup had been something elaborate as it usually was but her tears had created blue and pink streaks down her cheeks. Her shoulders shook with visible tremors as she sobbed.

"Oh, sweetheart…" I breathed softly and went to sit next to her.

"I'm sorry. I wasn't expecting anyone this evening," she said, trying to wipe the tears off her cheeks.

"No, no. You don't have to apologize to me. Should I leave or…" I searched for the right thing to say while she was so distraught. Her hands were folded delicately in her lap while she cried silently.

"Is there something I can help with?" I offered.

"No," she said and looked down at her hands. She opened them and I saw what she held. Delicately laying in her palm was the small pink fish that I had noticed living in the plant vase before.

In an attempt to make her feel better I rubbed her shoulders and said, "Oh, honey, it'll all be okay. It's just a fish."

She stopped crying and looked at me. Outrage and disbelief traveled across her lovely, color-stained face.

"Just a fish?"

"Well, yeah. What I mean is, it's nothing worth getting so upset over."

Those were not the right words.

"What is wrong with you?" she shouted in a tone far above the carefully checked mode of speaking I usually heard from her. "What exactly did you do in the training house for thirty years? It certainly wasn't learning how to keep your mouth shut. Or anything involving sensitivity for another living being!"

"I'm confused. Am I being insensitive to you, or the fish?"

"To her!" she shouted, cradling the small creature, pulling it tightly to her chest.

"How can she be upset with anything I say? She's dead."

She opened her mouth to yell at me but then just started to cry harder. Goddess, why was I such an asshole sometimes?

"Hey, hey. I'm sorry. I…I was just trying to make you feel better."

"Well, you have failed miserably!" she snapped through soppy tears. "I'll have you know that this is not *just* a fish! She was my friend and I was hers. I was her only friend, Zsash, and now she's dead."

"I'm sorry. I'm sorry." I repeated. "I didn't mean to… speak poorly of the dead." It sounded so stupid the moment it came out of my mouth.

Let's be clear. It's a fucking fish.

This is the type of fish you use as bait for real fish.

I was acutely aware that was not how Khessi felt about it. Even though I didn't care about this little dead creature, I did realize something new. I actually did care about Khessi.

My new reverence for the death of her "friend" seemed to buy me a couple seconds of rational thought. So I continued with, "Should we...bury her?"

"I don't know. It doesn't seem right that she should be laid in the earth," Khessi ran her index finger in a small, affectionate motion over the small pink back fins. "She really loved to swim."

"Yes, fish. They do that." I was fortunate that her grief seemed to filter out how much sarcasm actually made it into that statement. "Uh, perhaps a burial at sea?" I suggested hopefully. She looked up at me with glistening doe eyes and gave a little nod. "Hold on for a moment." I told her.

I ran down the halls and around corners until I found what I was looking for.

In the kitchen were two interior slaves. One was young and attractive with dark, chocolate-colored hair and deep brown eyes. The other was an older slave woman with dark leathery skin and graying hair. Both were pressing and kneading bread dough on a wooden table.

"What in the Goddess's name are you doing barging in here?" the older woman asked in a commanding voice.

"I'm sorry! I was wondering if I can take something from the trash? It's not for me. It's for Khessi. I just need a small box of some kind."

"I've got a small box you might be interested in," the brunette suggestively laughed.

"Sira! Mind your work, child!" the older woman scolded. She turned back to me. "We've got some raspberry crates out there in the trash that might suite your needs. Out that door," she pointed to the back of the kitchen.

"Thank you, mother." I said, trying to be charming and polite.

"Don't mother me, pretty boy," she said, pointing her finger at me now. "I'm Nilda, the interior matron here. I'll be keeping an eye on you, pleasure slave. You hear me?"

"Yes mother, er...thank you, Nilda. I'm Zsash, the new bath slave," I said as I made my way to the door.

"Oh, we know about you, Mister One Gold slave," Sira smirked.

"Uh, right." I said, unsure of what that meant as I headed across the room. Nilda slapped Sira on the ass of the little black dress she was wearing. It left a hand print in white flour. I smiled at their banter but continued out the door to the trash.

As I was I leaving, I heard Nilda scold with humor in her voice, "Goddess's tits, am I going to have to pour a bucket of ice water on your twat to get you to stop flirting?"

In the trash bins, I found what I was looking for: a small wooden box. I ran back to Khessi's office as fast as I could with the tiny coffin.

When I got there, Khessi was much more composed than she had been. She now held the tiny body in a little bundle of fabric, which I assumed was the burial shroud. I provided her with the open box and she laid the little bundle inside.

I hadn't been to the beach near the estate yet. It was a long walk past the gardens and the fountain, far out past the cane fields. I started to grasp that the Mistress owned a gigantic property. I didn't say anything for most of the walk down. I dreaded saying something offensive that would send her into tears again. The safest question I could come up with was, "Do you want to tell me about her?"

"Her name was Glo. I found her in the shallows a few years ago when the tide was going out. Her kind do that, though. They come into the shallow water to find food and sometimes get caught on land in a puddle for a while. They are built for breathing air too, though, so they can survive in a tiny amount of water if need be. Just enough to keep wet. She really loved living in the plant vase. You should have seen her playing around the roots.

When they spend half their life in so little water it's a really nice treat for them to have so much space all to themselves. She really loved living in the castle…"

She went on like that all the way to the beach. As she regaled me with tales of her fish friend, she lost track of propriety and wrapped her arm around mine as we walked. I started to get a picture of why the fish had mattered so much to Khessi.

Household slaves have a lonely life. They aren't supposed to take lovers. They hardly have friends. To be the Mistress's proxy is to be superior and set above all other slaves. However, in the end, they are still just a slave. I suddenly felt incredibly selfish and spoiled in my life and many sexual companions. I listened to her speak of Glo, and felt compassion for Khessi.

When we got to the ocean, we stood there in silence for a long moment looking out towards the sunset. As she knelt to set the little raspberry box into the water, she laid a gentle reverent kiss on the top of it. Then she let the waves take it away.

It broke my heart to see Khessi so sad. Watching her eyes glistening with tears in the evening light, I wrapped my arms around her with her brilliant hair on my cheek. We watched the tide go out against the setting sun. Purples and pinks claimed the burning orange skyline as Glo was laid to rest. Khessi and I spent hours on the beach talking into the night.

The next morning I awoke to the unfamiliar sensation of water lapping at my toes. The first thing I saw was a veil of deep orange. I soon realized I was seeing the morning sun through a lock of Khessi's hair. With years of experience trying not to wake someone who slept next to me, I raised my hand to slowly move the hair from my face. Khessi was curled against me, stealing my body heat, the way women do. She looked incredibly disheveled from her normal appearance, though still beautiful. Her makeup was all smeared from crying the night before. Her normally painted lips were now slightly rough but pink with their natural blush. Her hair was messy, well, messy for her anyway. A smile curved slowly up my face watching her. I ran my fingers lightly over her hand that rested on my chest. My fingertips traced little patterns down her forearm, then up her shoulder. Her pink lips parted slightly in a sleepy murmur. I wanted to kiss her again. My fingers trailed up her neck to her face, just in time for her aqua eyes to flutter open. They were so clear and blue in the sunlight, and I saw their centers shrink to pinpoints. She took a slow deep breath in, not quite aware of where we were. It was all so beautiful.

For a second.

Her eyes widened with realization of where she was upon seeing my face. Her startled oceanic eyes trailed lower to her hand on my chest and finally down to her feet tangled against my legs. She pulled away from me so quickly I shuddered at the sudden cold in her absence.

"You let me fall asleep?" Her tone was accusatory.

"What? I didn't let you do anything. We were talking and we both fell asleep."

"This doesn't look good, Zsash! Everyone knows you kissed me before, and now if people saw us asleep here it looks like…" She shook her head and started walking briskly up the beach away from me.

"So what if that's what it looks like? That's not the truth. And even if it was, it's nobody's business."

She scoffed at me in disbelief.

"You are so simple! You have no idea how things work. How things seem and how they are perceived is a thousand times more important than the truth! This is how rumors get spread that a household slave is devalued and how we get sent to the Cheritoth. Stay away from me, Zsash!"

I watched her pale shoulders walk in front of me. My brow furrowed and I felt hot in the face. Embarrassment mixed with my own indignation. She talked like I was some fevered boy that wouldn't take no for an answer. Like there was something wrong with me.

"In the bath with the cane! You kissed me back!" I said over her shoulder.

"That hardly matters!" she shouted. Catching up to her, I grabbed her arm and spun her around.

"It matters to me. I'm getting a little sick of you talking to me like I'm a mistake. You clearly like me, at least enough for friendship. I mean, would that be so bad?"

She sneered at me and it twisted her face into an ugly, cynical smirk.

"In case you didn't pick up on it before, bath slave, I don't mix with others. I'm better than you. Better than any slave here. That's what household slaves are bred to be. Lower than Mistress but better than you. It means I have no peers. No friends. Find yourself some interior slave girl to pump your needs into. It will not be me! You couldn't possibly understand the responsibilities I bear, nor the pressure I'm under to perform my duties. I don't have time for an infatuation!"

"Infatuation?" A disbelieving laugh escaped me. I let go of her arm and she continued to walk up the beach. "That's awfully presumptuous! Just because I felt bad for you doesn't mean I'm infatuated."

"I didn't mean you!" she called over her shoulder.

I stopped, throwing my hands in the air. "What does that even mean?" I shouted after her. "Shit," I cursed, kicking sand.

I turned back toward the water and sat down on the beach, thinking, pouting. As the sun rose, hoards of small, white birds ran up and down the beach with the tide. They pecked their beaks into the sand, hunting for bugs or small fish.

I felt like an idiot. Maybe I was infatuated. I liked Khessi, but she was right. A household slave wouldn't be attracted to me. The whole notion of her even being interested in someone as simple as myself, sounded unlikely. It wouldn't be the first time I misread a woman. I may be able to get a woman to climax but their motives are a complete mystery to me.

The Mistress was a mystery to me, too, but that was expected. At least she was straightforward. Command equaled action. I could follow directions all day. Khessi's cryptic, accusatory words colored with so much emotion made no sense. I guess she was pretty clear about one thing, though. She wanted me to leave her alone.

As I sat there, I realized the birds hunting on the beach were carrying small brightly colored things in their beaks. They were the fish that had washed up and gotten stuck in water holes in the uneven sand. The same type as Glo had been, all beautiful and brilliantly colored. Suddenly, I had an idea.

It took me about an hour to find a small clear bowl from the bath chamber. It held some rose petals. I put them into the bath and rationalized this by deciding that I would use them tonight, so the jar would be empty anyway.

When I got back to the beach it was well into the morning, almost midday. I put some ocean water in the jar and then started to comb the beach. After a while, I found one that I liked. A lovely pink fish just like Glo. I scooped her into the jar and ran down to the waves to add more water. Once full, I held the jar up to the sun to see my prize. The pink fish wiggled frantically in the jar, clearly not happy about being my captive.

"Hah! You're mine now!" I said to the tiny eyes that stared fearfully at me through the glass. It was only a moment later when it jumped from my jar in a speedy pink arc back into the ocean. "Damn it!"

I learned some lessons about fish. After the lesson of "put a lid on the jar because they are jumpy little fuckers," there was the lesson of "birds will grab them out of your hand if you're not careful." I also had the lesson of "fish aren't the only things that wash up on the beach, and some of them sting" and the lesson of "don't grab a fish with your bare hand while you're frustrated because you'll squish it and kill it." There was no need to ever tell Khessi about that last one.

After all that, I started walking down the beach, looking into the sand when I saw it. A beautiful fish with long, graceful fins of blue and red lay in a shallow sand dip. There was so little water that she was laying on her side to remain submerged. She was slightly bigger than Glo and had much longer fins. I scooped her up into the jar along with water from the hole and ended up getting some sand in there are well. She flopped around some, swishing her tail violently. I closed the distance to the surf a moment later and added more water to the jar, then closed the lid, as per lesson number one. I would give Khessi a new fish. Maybe then she and I could be friends.

I was so elated by my victory that it took me a moment to register that a noise came from the water near me. It was a strange sound that trickled through my thoughts until I became aware of it. The water lapped at my calves and I looked around to find the source of the gurgled hissing noise. It was almost like laughter but with more desperation in it. I looked around, up and down the long distance of the beach and saw nothing. A soft flicker of something against my ankle under the water caused me to look down. I swallowed a surprised yelp as a face floated in the water between my legs.

I jumped back in fear before falling into the water. I pushed back with one hand and held the jar in the other.

It was a woman. Sort of. She had green gray skin and reptilian eyes. Her hair was extremely long and the dark green color of seaweed. It floated in the water around her face and over her bare shoulders. She swam toward me slowly, looking me up and down. I was so startled I didn't know if she was a threat or not.

"Will...you...eat?" she asked in a high, sing-song tone. Her words were slow and broken as though she had to search for what to say to me. Like someone who has just learned to speak. Or someone who's forgotten how.

"What?" I stammered.

She moved closer to me until her face was a foot away from mine and her cold hands rested on my shoulders. I sat in the soft sand with the surf up to my waist. Her legs rested on either side of my thighs and I groaned a little at the new pressure her body offered against me. She narrowed her gaze and ground her pelvis intentionally into me. Wild, animalistic grinding against me with no self-awareness to the wrongness of it. Her reptilian eyes followed me without empathy, reflecting nothing but hunger.

I shook slightly with adrenaline and fear. This slave girl was a wyrling. She had traits of the ocean life she channeled, which meant she was undoubtedly a runaway slave. Depending on what beastly characteristics had consumed her she could and might kill me. She spoke again, pulling me from my fearful speculation.

"Will you eat?" She repeated and brought a webbed hand to the jar I held. She wrapped her long cold fingers around mine and the jar. I noticed each was tipped with a white and jagged claw. She brought the jar closer to my mouth and I figured it out. She'd watched me making an ass out of myself for the better part of the last hour to catch a fish. She must have figured I was hunting for food, and doing so poorly.

"Eat," she nodded again.

"Oh! Uh, no. I'll, um, save it for later." I pushed the closed jar up the beach behind me.

As I shifted, I felt something sharp under my other palm buried in the sand. I tried not to show that I was searching under the water as she licked her lips, watching me. I was pretty sure what I felt was a long shell. Something pointed and sharp lay under my hand.

The wyrling girl brought her other hand up to my cheek and stared at me with wonder. I swallowed hard and tried not to flinch as she caressed my face with her wet, webbed hand. Her black tongue trailed over her top lip for a moment before she gave me a smile that showed multiple rows of tiny sharp teeth.

"Shiny," she said before kissing me. I expected the kiss to taste terrible. She certainly looked like kissing her would taste like eating a raw eel. It didn't. She tasted like a woman, though I caught salty traces of seawater at the edges of her mouth. I closed my eyes and went with it. The kiss felt nice, so I didn't fight it. I hadn't seen her fully out of the water but I was suddenly painfully aware of how naked she was. My hands went to her hips as she locked her feet behind my lower back and rocked her body against mine. My hands felt down her back over nubs of a protruding spine that ended at her tail bone. I felt the soft flesh of her ass and pulled her into me. She wore some kind of belt fashioned with bits of shell and metal. She slid her hands up my chest and I was vaguely aware that she was tearing my shirt. I reached lower past her thigh to rub my fingers between her legs. She whined with desire into my mouth.

I gasped in surprise as a second mouth was suddenly on my neck. I broke the kiss, only to find another wyrling kissing my shoulder. This one had blue hair and pearly black stripes across her skin. She glanced at me only for a second, then grabbed the back of my hair to expose my neck. I closed my eyes and felt dark tongues travel down my throat. Their wet hair clung to me and dripped across my skin.

Then there were more hands. And more mouths and licking tongues. They seemed to surround me. I didn't know how many there were and I didn't care. I didn't open my eyes. I just felt. I kissed one mouth, then another, and another. Hands pulled at me and their nails left little scratches. Their cold bodies rubbed against my warmth until I was unable to distinguish my own breathing from the panting breaths around me. My fear had utterly gone and was replaced by a swirling sea of lust.

The thought I had before the first bite to my inner thigh was, *Maybe wyrlings aren't so bad.*

Pain shot through me and my eyes opened to a mass of dark hair and bodies in front of me. I cried out in pain and began to push them away. There were at least ten wyrlings around me. I pushed away from them as best I could. As my hand pressed into the wet sand below the waterline, I grabbed for the sharp shell. Feeling the edge beneath my hand I raised it at the nearest body. I slashed a purple-haired woman across the neck and pushed the green-haired woman away. Standing clumsily, I backed up onto the beach. Pressing a hand into the wound on my thigh, I tried to stop the blood that streamed from it. Scaly limbs and mossy-haired creatures followed me up the beach as I struggled to get away. Some of them snapped their teeth at me in a fast biting motion. I didn't think I could outrun them, so I gripped the weapon in my hand and readied for their attack.

They all sprung at me. I slashed at them frantically. I hit flesh and brought a screech from at least one of them. One came at me from behind and I was knocked to the ground. More bites came. Strong arms held my limbs too tightly. I felt my joints pulling. Muscle and tissue stretched to the point of breaking and I heard my shoulder render a grotesque popping sound, followed by a sharp hot pain that burned like lightening down my arm. I had a brief moment to inhale, readying my lungs to scream as I realized they were going to tear me apart.

A heartbeat later, arrows and shrieking pierced the air. I was dropped to the sand as Corvas and some of the guards rode up on horses to my rescue. In the next moments, four wyrlings were killed by the guards and the rest escaped into the sea. Corvas rode up to me and looked at my wounds.

"Oh, it's you. If I'd known, I would have let them finish," Corvas said, giving me an ugly smile. "That would have made my day to find you all torn apart and food for the birds."

I stood up gingerly, putting pressure on my bleeding leg to see if I'd be able to walk on it.

"Look, what is your problem with me? I didn't do anything to Khessi. I've never done anything to you. There's no reason you have to be a dick towards me."

Corvas laughed a little and haughtily dismounted his horse. He strode over and I palmed the weapon I had found in the sand. I wanted to keep it a secret if he suddenly attacked me.

"Well, I appreciate you being so straightforward about that, so I guess I'll do my best to reply in kind. You're a fucking worthless pleasure slave and you thought you could put your hands on my prize? I don't put up with that kind of disrespect."

I squinted, confused. "What are you even talking about?"

"Shit, no wonder you weren't bought until auction."

I looked away, suppressing the urge to punch him. I was in no shape to fight him so I just let him carry on as my blood trickled into the lapping waves.

"The guard captain is the highest ranking slave after the household slave. If anyone is going to fuck that fire red pussy it's going to be me. And after she finishes squeezing out a baby or two for the Mistress to sell to the household school, she'll be with me. That is why I don't like you looking at her the way you do. The way you pleasure slaves look at any hole and think it's fair game for you. I don't care who else on this estate you fuck, but you stay away from Khessi. She's mine."

Countless things ran through my brain to say to that smug son of a bitch. There were so many holes in his flawed and narcissistic logic, that I now understood what type of idiot I was dealing with. And it might have been the loss of blood. Or it might have been how deadly serious he took himself. But I couldn't help it. I started laughing. I thought he might hit me for a moment but his eyebrows knitted in confusion as I turned, reclaimed the jar with the fish in it and began to walk away.

"Was that fun for you?" I asked the fish sparkling in the light rays through the jar.

I actually managed to walk all the way to the healers by myself, leaving a minimum blood trail. I made sure not to bleed on anything inside the estate that couldn't be easily mopped.

Upon my arrival to the healers, the first thing Jaideen said to me was, "This is getting excessive, you realize."

"Oh, believe me. I realize."

He treated my wounds and bandaged me up. All the time swearing and huffing under his breath about how I was the most injury-prone slave he'd ever met. Since I was still scheduled to do the bath for the Mistress that night, he disinfected my injuries and told me to let them breathe in the open air as much as possible.

Walking was easier now, but I still moved gently so as not to start anything bleeding again. I made my way to Khessi's office and found her at her desk, her feather quill plumed and bouncing as she wrote. I cleared my throat to alert her to my presence. She looked up at me and concern flooded her features as she saw the state I was in.

"Oh, Goddess! What has happened to you now?" she exclaimed.

"Did you know there are wyrlings down by the beach who like to eat slaves?"

"I do," she looked away, then added, "I don't go in the ocean by myself much anymore. It's getting too dangerous."

"That would have been good to know earlier." I shrugged, "Look, in any case, I don't have much time before the Mistress's bath but I wanted to give you this." I set the jar with the little fish swimming around in it on her desk in front of her.

"I thought I'd name her Gem because she sparkles like a jewel. Of course, you can name her whatever you like." I tapped on the glass of the jar, waving my fingers at the fish and smiled. Khessi gave me a wince veiled in a smirk.

"They don't actually like tapping on the glass. It sounds like thunder to them."

"Oh!" I mumbled. "Sorry little lady," I said, looking at the tiny eyes darting back and forth at us.

"It's a boy, Zsash."

"What?"

"Gem is a male fish."

I stared, confused at his long, colorful fins. "But he's so pretty."

"Of course he is! The males have the longer, more elaborate tails than the females. It's part of their charm. What brings the ladies to them."

"Oh. Yeah, I guess you should rename him."

"No! I think Gem is a very fitting name. He seems to like it. Don't you, my pretty boy," she smiled into the water. I was distantly jealous of the attention the fish was getting from Khessi. She took the lid off the jar, speaking to the fish in a motherly tone. "That's better, isn't it? Were you all shut in there for a long time?" She said to the fish.

"Careful. They're pretty jumpy."

"Well, he'll like it better now that there's more air. Besides, maybe you'd like to stay here with me?" Khessi said to Gem. It didn't jump. The damn fish just swam in a happy little circle. Khessi turned to me and said, "Thank you, Zsash."

"You're welcome." I smiled with a nod, then began to hobble out of her office.

"Zsash," she set the jar down on the desk and followed me. I stopped, looking into her lovely eyes as she decided what to say. She declared gently, "I meant what I said earlier today."

"Great. Is that all?" I felt the heat of rejection returning to my face from the morning.

"No, that is not all. I wanted to say I was sorry about how I said it to you, though. I didn't have to be so mean. I can't be alone with you anymore or people will talk. However, I would like to be friends. As much as such things are possible alongside my duties."

I smiled. "I'll take that."

"And get some rest. I'll take care of the bath tonight so you can heal some."

"Are you sure? I don't feel that bad anymore. I can do it."

"Mmm…" She tilted her head and looked at my seeping leg bandage. "I don't think the Mistress will feel so clean with that much blood in her bath."

"Thank you." I nodded, grateful.

I grabbed food and took it back to my room. After the day I'd had I just wanted a little time to myself to get my thoughts in order. I set the plate of food on the table in my room. The door had no lock, so I pushed my bed in front of it in case anyone should try and open it. I didn't want any surprises. I then pulled the weapon from my belt to get a better look at it.

It was no shell, but a small dagger. A lovely graceful spike of metal is what I had found. It was sharp and perfectly weighted. I found that I could twirl it through my fingers with little effort. I threw it a few times into the table from across the room. I found that it always tumbled true and pierced the flesh of the wood.

But the question remained, what do I do with it? Something like this belonged to either the Mistress or another monarch. I had no business considering it mine.

And yet...

I could not bring myself to turn it in. If the blade was not mine, at least the secret was mine. This was a concept that convinced me not to tell anyone about it and more importantly, became my first real punishable offense. The thrill of that alone was so potent that even if I'd known I was going to get caught, I still wouldn't have given it up.

"Live for your duties, day in and out. Always strive to be more than you are because no matter how much you try, you're still never there. I cannot abide slaves with idle hands. It makes them sloppy, lazy and worse, willful to their own flights of fancy."

Thralldrix, *The Scrolls of the Goddess*

CHAPTER 8: TROUBLE

I guess it happens to every slave at some point. Eventually, the newness of being purchased wears off and you fall into a routine. Every night was full of several hours of bathing and taking care of the Mistress. She grew fond of teasing me and occasionally let me go down on her. However, I was never allowed to have sex with her. Every night I would brush against her naked, beautiful form. And every night it created even more unbearable sexual tension, but I still hadn't had sex in months.

Many of my evenings were spent playing around with the slip knife I'd found on the beach. It was so beautifully weighted it begged to be thrown. So I did. In fact, it sort of became my nightly ritual. I'd sit on the edge of my bed and throw the knife into the wood desk, usually while distracting myself from the enthusiastic moans from the Mistress's chambers. All the same, it was such a routine of mine that I realized I was actually getting quite good at accurately throwing and hitting where I wanted. After a while, I realized I was destroying the side of the desk. So I brought my food up to the room with me at night, including a few apples. I practiced throwing the knife into the apples. When I got good at that, I threw the apples in the air and tried to hit them with the knife before they fell. It took me a while, but I finally got it down. The rest of the furniture suffered a few marks during my practicing. I was always very careful not to aim in the direction of the painting in the room. The Mistress finding the furniture damaged seemed much less frightening than the Mistress finding that I'd destroyed an irreplaceable painting of her mother.

For a few months, that was my life. I played with my knife, played with dick and gave baths. I wanted to go talk to Khessi. Every time I tried it seemed she was very busy. The last thing I wanted to do was irritate her.

Let me tell you right now that bored, lonely, and sexually frustrated is a sure combination for a man getting himself into trouble.

I don't remember exactly when I started bending the rules, but it was a gradual thing.

The first rule I broke was that I started using cane whenever I felt like it. At first, I regulated how much I took, telling myself that I didn't want to get caught so I would only take a little. My restraint soon dissolved like so many grains of cane in a glass of wine. I would use it early on in the day so that I was never under its effect while I had to give the Mistress her bath. I just wanted to feel something, anything to break up the monotony of my listless string of days.

Sometimes I would sit naked in the empty pool and touch myself while the cane set my senses on fire. When I got too bored with that I started using the oils. It was amazing how smells transferred into physical pleasure with cane. I would drizzle honey onto my tongue, then use amber oil to jerk myself off while I imagined the Mistress's slick pussy riding me.

Orgasms on cane are *un-fucking-real*. They somehow seem to last forever. My cock would twitch for an hour after I came and made it painfully sensitive, none of which was enough of a deterrent to get me to stop. It lacked somewhat compared to actual physical contact, but it was the best option I had at the time. It was during these days that I decided to explore.

I looked everywhere for Khessi's room so that I could snoop around and look through her things. I admit, I'm creepy and wanted to look through her stuff and see where she slept. Don't judge me. Here's the thing, though. I never found it. That led me to believe that Khessi must have had a secret bed chamber known only to the Mistress.

One day I was bored and, to be honest, pretty intoxicated. At this point, I figured that as long as I didn't miss bath time, no one would check up on me. I was drinking a glass of wine that was laced with cane, which I had, of course, helped myself to. I rubbed my chest pleasantly as I wandered idly toward the forbidden door to the Mistress's quarters. And I just remember thinking...

It's not like anyone is going to know.

I ran my fingers over the smooth golden metal of the doorknob for a moment, letting its cold, hard texture ripple through me. Then I twisted it open and wandered inside the most off-limits place in the entire castle. Frankly, I'm surprised my curiosity held out three months.

The room was huge. The bed in the middle of the room could comfortably fit four people. A canopy of sheer white cloth hung down each cherrywood pillar at the corners of the bed. Hanging from the two pillars at the foot of the bed were two gold rings. I ran my hand over one, and I looked down to see two identical rings in the floor.

"Uh huh," I smiled, wondering if the Mistress preferred chains or ropes to hold her slaves. I shuffled around the stunning bed chamber, drinking my glass of wine. The white furs around the bed were warm and soft on my bare feet. I ran my hand over the ivory satin comforter and thought that the bed felt like it would be extremely comfortable.

It was.

I laid there in the Mistress's bed and by the Goddess I wished I could sleep in there every night. Her scent clung to the pillow and I turned my head to breathe it in deeply. Wrapped in cane and satin, I laid there for a while until I saw something that caught my attention. A set of cherrywood slatted double doors were set into the wall across from the bed. Bars of light showed through the slats making soft patterns on the floor,.

Beyond them was another small room, about the size of my quarters that was filled with the Mistress's wardrobe. The smell of sex and leather rolled through my senses. Practically everything was white or gold, which was not a surprise. A large rack to the left was filled with pairs of heels and boots and next to those was a large dresser. I wondered what was inside, so I opened it.

The first two drawers were filled with jewelry. I moaned a little as the gems inside caught the light, sending flashes of pleasure through my vision. I'd never seen so many diamonds in my life. I marveled at their flawless brilliance and wondered how many of them had been gifts from Master Braxian. Clearly, this was one of the advantages to courting the Master of Diamonds. The third drawer brought an instant smile to my face. I think I actually said "Oooo…"

Before me was an entire drawer of finely crafted sex toys. Gleaming gold and glittering with jeweled accents. Various phalluses, plugs, beads. I set my wine glass on the top of the dresser and lifted out an L-shaped phallus to inspect it further.

"Oh my…" I said to myself.

The jewels for this one were at a nub set at the bend of the metal and I wondered how many women the Mistress had fucked with this or men for that matter. Or maybe she had them wear it and fuck her?

I wonder if the Mistress has used this on Khessi? My brain said without permission.

What I wouldn't give to see that. The only thing sexier than the Mistress and Khessi tangled together in pleasure, was if they decided to somehow include me in it. I set the phallus back in its spot as something glowing caught my attention.

I knew what they were the moment I saw them. Eight blue crystals that glowed softly in the dim light. As I picked one up, it began to slowly vibrate. These were resonance stones. The warmer they were, the more they vibrated. If they are set against the skin they continue to vibrate more and more until they are removed. I had seen various undergarments and halters made with spaces for resonance stones. We got to experiment with them during my training house days, but I hadn't seen one in years. They were outrageously expensive and I was informed that not all royalty can afford them. Somehow it made perfect sense that the Mistress had four sets.

The fourth drawer contained an assortment of tools and bindings, some of which I was familiar with and some I actually wasn't. Cuffs, collars, bars, rope. Various tools for holding a slave in whatever position she wanted.

Below that was a drawer full of neatly folded scraps of satin that turned out to be the Mistress's underwear. I pulled out a pair of white panties and inspected them. They smelled nice with the clean, fresh smell of newly laundered linens. But that's not what I really wanted to smell on them. I wanted that sweet musky scent I'd licked off my fingers after the baths when the Mistress had used me.

Though I'm not proud of this, I decided to take the panties. I also decided to not press my luck and began leaving her chambers. As I did, I heard the sound of the bedroom door opening. Quickly and quietly as I could, I shut the door to the closet almost all the way, leaving a small crack to peek through.

A sigh of relief escaped me as I saw that it was not the Mistress. Through the crack in the door, I watched two women wearing the simple black dresses of interior slaves enter the room. One was Sira, the interior slave who had given me the raspberry box to bury Khessi's fish, and another beautiful interior slave with strawberry blonde hair set into braids.

"We shouldn't be in here again!" the strawberry girl said in a meek voice. "We're gonna get caught."

My eyebrows raised in shock as Sira kissed the girl's pink luscious lips into silence.

"Hush now. The Mistress won't be back for hours. Besides, you're already so worked up." Sira said and slid her hand under the girl's dress, making her exhale heavily and moan. She bit her lip in the most deliciously cute way as Sira led her to the end of the bed and pushed her onto it. Strawberry's green eyes watched with lusty fascination as Sira ran her hands up pale legs to reveal the apex of ginger curls. Sira kissed her way up her lover's thighs. She left a shining wet path as she trailed her tongue upward over sensitive skin until she got to the petite ginger sex. Moans and breathy sighs encouraged Sira on. Losing all sense of caution, the girl lifted her knees up to the outside of her shoulders and wrapped her hands around her ankles. Apparently, she was very limber. She opened herself as wide as she could to Sira's seeking tongue. The back of Sira's head kept me from fully seeing what she was doing with her mouth, but not what she was doing with her fingers to herself. She was stretched out flat on her stomach with her face between Strawberry's thighs. Sira's right hand rested at her own pelvis, swirling her fingers around her pussy for a while to get them slick, before sliding them inside. She was working three fingers in and out and moaning.

I wanted to give her something better to moan about. I wanted to come up behind her and push inside that juicy, pink slit. Make her moan into her lover's body while I fucked her from behind. Goddess, I just wanted to cum inside a woman again.

With so much moaning in the other room, while I was drunk and on cane, you better believe I was hard. I don't even remember giving my hand permission to start jerking me off.

The strawberry blonde tossed her head back and forth in pleasure on the white pillows. She gripped her ankles tighter as her thighs began to tremble. Her moans became a quick pant. I saw her clenching her eyes closed as she neared climax. Sira's tongue worked feverishly over her lover's clit as she screamed her release in the throws of ecstasy.

I hadn't realized I was grinding my teeth until I relaxed. The two interior girls laughed quietly in the other room.

"Yeah, I needed that," Strawberry sighed.

"Mm hmm. You know I take care of you," Sira said, moving up over the girl's body to kiss her. They kissed passionately for a minute and I started to wonder when they might leave so I could get out of the closet. For a second I thought about putting my hard-on away and taking care of it later.

But then Sira straddled Strawberry's waist as they were kissing. It was a move I was familiar with and I felt myself swell impossibly further. Strawberry ran her hands down Sira's back until she could grab her ass. She tilted her hips up until their pussies touched and they started to grind against each other. Sira took Strawberry's small breasts in her hands, massaging them, pulling roughly on the nipples until they stood out firm. Strawberry arched her back as Sira lowered her mouth to the other girl's breasts. Both women curled around each other, rubbing their pussies together.

I closed my eyes and clenched my jaw, trying desperately to keep quiet. Soft sounds of warm, wet flesh moving together in rhythm pushed me further toward the edge. My hand moved faster up and down my shaft seeking release. They moaned through passionate kisses as they rubbed against each other's clits. Sira pressed down into Strawberry as she found the spot she wanted and bucked into her harder.

"Oh, fuck! Yes, right there," Sira whined. "Stay just like that. I'm so close, don't stop!"

"Cum on me, sugar. Cum all over my pussy!" Strawberry moaned breathily. Sira threw back her hair, panting desperately to get air. She fucked against Strawberry hard and let out a long cry of pleasure, grabbing the other girl's hips as she came. I was pretty sure they didn't hear me cry out a little when I shot my load into the pair of satin panties in my hand. Moans turned into whispers as they cradled each other for long minutes.

When they stirred again, it was to change the sheets on the Mistress's bed. They removed the ones they'd just disturbed and remade the bed with clean linens. I smiled a little internally. No wonder they'd gotten away with this for so long. They just messed up the Mistress's bed and remade it, thus removing all evidence of their punishment-worthy tryst.

I dropped the now soiled panties into the basket of dirty laundry and waited for them to leave the room. They finally left a few minutes later. I let out a sigh of relief as I heard the bedroom door close and their feet walking away. I opened the closet door and took a cautious step out into the Mistress's bedroom.

Sira turned around and let out a short scream of surprise as I stepped out of the closet. Apparently, Strawberry had left her to finish cleaning up.

"You!" Her eyes were wide with embarrassment and disbelief.

"Uh…" said my witty, witty brain.

"Were you in there watching us the whole time?"

"Uh…" was repeated.

She crossed the room to me, holding her hands over her mouth fearfully. "Oh, please don't tell the Mistress! Please! We would be in so much trouble."

"Of course not! Calm down, I'm not going to say anything."

She nodded her head, rationalizing. "Okay, thank you."

"We should probably go before the Mistress gets back, then." I gestured toward the door.

"Yes. Yes, of course," she nodded. We left the bed chamber and she scurried on her way back down the stairs. I shook my head clear and laughed a little. That was the most interesting thing to happen to me in a while.

The rest of the night went by fairly normally. I gave the Mistress her bath. It seemed as though she'd been preoccupied lately, so I scented it with milk and lavender to help her relax. She didn't seem horribly interested in talking or tormenting me. I kept her wine full, though she did not take any cane. Her brow maintained a constant expression of concern. I wanted to ask her what was wrong but thought better of it. It wasn't as though she was going to ask advice from a bath slave. I moved to massage her shoulders like I usually do, but she waved me off.

With the exception of watching two slave girls fuck in the Mistress's quarters, that day was pretty much the same as all others.

Until that night.

I was awakened by the sound of the door to my room opening and a figure slinking inside. The figure closed the door quietly behind them and moved toward my bed. I sat up to find Sira tiptoeing across the cold floor toward me. She wasn't wearing much, just a simple shift dress of sheer pink fabric. Based on the points of her nipples, it was cold outside my blanket.

"What were you doing there?" she quietly asked straight away.

"What? Well, what are you doing *here*?" I countered in a whisper.

"I wanted to talk to you," she said, wrapping her arms around her and hopping to each foot every few seconds.

"You could have talked to me tomorrow."

"I wanted to talk to you now." Her jaw shuddered a little around the words.

"By the Goddess, at least get on the bed so you don't freeze to death." I pulled my legs toward me and freed up the foot of the bed. She sat down and I put one of the blankets around her shoulders. We sat cross-legged in front of each other on the small bed, blankets wrapped around us.

"Thank you," she said, warming up.

"So what was so important that it couldn't wait until morning?" I said in a hushed voice.

"What were you doing in the Mistress's closet?" she asked.

I paused, thinking. "Why do you care? I certainly wasn't in there to have sex on the Mistress's bed like you two, if that's what you mean."

"I just meant, were you in there because you knew we'd be in there?"

"No! I had no idea that was a hobby of yours. I was just..." I had to think of what to say. "I was just curious and looking around. I'd never gone into the Mistress's room until today."

"Really?"

"Yes."

"But, why didn't you say anything when you saw us come in? Did you...enjoy watching us?" she asked, slowly leaning closer to me.

I pressed my lips together, thinking about if I should answer her truthfully. Her eyes were wide and dilated, her lips slightly parted. Her breasts rose and fell with her excited pulse as she waited to hear my answer. I tilted my head slightly.

"Yes." I said softly, beginning to understand why she was here. "At first, I thought I would just hide until you left. But...you both stayed a little longer than I expected. Not that I'm complaining. You put on quite a show and I certainly enjoyed watching you both."

"How much were you enjoying it?"

"Very much."

"How much is very much?" She teased.

"Thoroughly." I raised an eyebrow.

"And you are a pleasure slave, right?" Her hand found its way slowly inside my blanket. Her cold fingers pressed into my chest, stealing my heat. She stared at me with large, brown eyes and blinking, feathery lashes.

"I am," I said, trying to keep my breathing even.

"You know about pleasing a woman?" she asked, unable to look me in the eyes. Her mouth opened and closed for a moment as she tried to figure out how to request what she wanted. I closed the distance between us slowly. She wrapped her arms around my shoulders and kissed me. She smelled wild and delicious, like cinnamon and oranges. As the kisses deepened, so did our desires. She kissed me frantically while I grabbed her firm, lovely ass and pulled her toward my waist. She gave a little hop up onto my lap and wrapped her legs around my hips, pressing her breasts into my chest. The sudden pressure of female flesh against me created a sharp pang of desire throughout my body. I realized I had needed so much more than just getting off. I was tired of masturbating. I needed the pressure of a woman moving against me. I'd missed it so much.

She kissed me hard with her arms snaked around my neck, my warm skin heating her cool flesh. I pushed her back onto the bed with her legs firmly around me. Leaving a trail of kisses down her throat, I listened to her moan quietly. She pressed her hips forward to rub against the bulge in my pants. I met her rhythmic motions rocking against me, driving me wild with need. I squeezed one of her breasts through the pink fabric as I licked and kissed lightly down her neck to her chest, before taking the other fabric-covered rosy peak into my mouth. My tongue flicked over the fabric trying to reach the flesh beneath while taking time to bite softly as my hand massaged its partner.

When my fingers finally slid into her, she gasped loudly. I chuckled and hushed her. I didn't want to alert the Mistress to what was happening in the next room. Sira smiled too and put a hand over her own mouth to quiet herself. Her thighs parted wider as I pushed my fingers into her and rubbed her clit softly.

"Oh Goddess, that's fucking good," she whispered.

I pumped my fingers into her, increasing tempo until she was wet and hot in my hand. Her cries became more difficult to silence until suddenly, she pushed my hand away.

"What? What's wrong?" I asked, pulling away from her. She grabbed the front of my pants and pushed them down. I groaned as she wrapped her hand around my cock.

"I want you to fuck me with this thing. I've never been with a pleasure slave before. Is it as good as everyone says?" she smiled.

"Goddess, I hope so." I said under my breath, wondering how long I was going to last in my current state.

Everything about this felt dirty and rushed and full of need. And I was totally fine with that. She pulled me down to her and I ran my hands over her legs, bending them to where her ankles rested at my hips. Her body lay open and ready for me. I rubbed against her entrance a few times. She was so slick and throbbing already. There's nothing better than a woman who wants to be fucked when she's dripping and hungry for pleasure. I held Sira's hips firmly when I found the right angle and sank into her without resistance. I filled her as deeply as I could with a single thrust and groaned between my clenched teeth.

"Fuck..." I moaned against her throat as she whined beneath me.

I sighed and didn't move for a few moments, clearing my mind so that I didn't climax instantly. I relaxed my grip on her hips as I began moving inside her as slowly as I could manage. I pulled out enough to trail the head of my cock over her clit, then plunged slowly back in deep. It wasn't long before she was whimpering again, only louder this time.

"Shhh..." I said, smiling. She nodded and messily smiled back at me, pressing her lips together. The smile disappeared as I quickened my pace again. I thrust into her deeper, increasing the tempo of my hips. Her pussy gripped my dick with the same quickened pace. As we kissed and fucked with reckless abandon, she started to reach over the edge of orgasm.

"Please don't stop....please don't stop....Oh fuck! I'm gonna cum if keep fucking me like that!" She tried to whisper. With one final thrust, she came for me, drenching my cock. I grabbed the back of her neck and kissed her while her body clenched around me. I smiled against her mouth. Finally, feeling like my old self again. Like a pleasure slave.

I slowed down, letting her enjoy and ride out her orgasm. I did my best to prolong mine.

"Goddess tits, that was...." she continued panting.

"Thanks." I interrupted with a smirk, still rocking against her. I wanted her to climax at least once more before I finished. If I could hold out that long. I'd missed this so much!

She kissed me again. Then with a wicked smile and tousled hair, she said, "Let me up. I want to be on top."

"All right." I shrugged. That sounded fine by me. I was still so hard that it was easy to grab her waist and roll her over me without taking my cock out. I sighed satisfactorily, resting my hands behind my head. Sira kissed me softly, then backed away from me to sit back up on my hips. I moaned at this new angle her body provided. Her hips rolled slowly as she rode me.

"I want to try something," she said, then slowly lifted off of me before I could respond. She shifted her hips forward and I found the tip of my cock brushing the pucker of her ass.

"Whoa!" I said, startled but excited. "Are you sure?"

"I figured you'd know how to do this."

"Yeah, I do. Do you?"

She answered me by bringing her ass slowly down over my shaft and making me curse.

"I'm the dirtiest slave here, Zsash."

"Clearly."

"I want you to fuck me as hard as you can 'til you cum inside my tight little ass. Pretty please, show me what a pleasure slave can really do." she whispered, grinding slowly on my cock.

I'd hate to disappoint a girl. And she did ask for it.

I answered her smug smile by sitting up and pushing my fingers into her pussy. She gasped and cried out as I filled up both her holes. I rolled my hips to buck inside her. Her teasing smile melted into a lustful groan as I fucked her with more control from the bottom than she expected.

"Is this what you want?" I asked, wrapping my free arm around her waist to pull her into me faster.

"Ahhhh, yes. Oh, yes...like that..." She mumbled. Her eyes squeezed tight each time I entered her.

Pleasure gripped her mercilessly as I began pounding hard into her with my cock and fingers. All thought of staying quiet was gone. My fingers crooked upward inside her pussy while I fucked her, pressing the spot I knew would make her orgasm. My thumb was against her clit, stroking her in time with my thrusts. She started whimpering and biting her lip. The pleasure building inside her faster than she'd expected.

"I do know how to get you to cum this way. And I'm more than happy to give it to you," I panted as I lost myself in desire. "Is that what you want? Tell me! Is that what you want?"

Goddess, it was so fucking beautiful.

She kept crying out, "Yes, yes, more, please. Please fuck my ass. Oh Goddess, I want to cum. Oh, please fuck me and make me cum!" Her cries began to rise again and I didn't even care who heard. An expression of ecstasy held her lovely face while I thrust into her tight passages. Her eyes were fixed on my glossy fingers taking her pussy. Just a little more. Just a little more!

Oh fuck, Goddess, if I could hold out just a little longer!

She rode my dick hard and clawed at my back as she came. Her pleasure shuddered through her pussy as it squeezed my fingers and her ass tightened around my cock. I couldn't keep her quiet enough and I prayed the Mistress hadn't overheard us. A woman's orgasm has always been my undoing. The way her body pulsed around me, her hips rocking out of control to get more of me inside. I thrust into her a few more times until the tension in my groin focused into a white hot point beyond stopping. I cried out as the orgasm I'd been building for months released into her. My muscles clenched and my cock spasmed as I came inside her tight, throbbing ass.

It was incredible.

I laid there against her breast still inside her for a long while. We both panted and moaned in the aftershocks of pleasure. Finally, I pulled back from her and shook my head a little.

"Whew!" I panted.

"You must have needed that as badly as I did. I haven't had any good dick in a while," Sira sighed and kissed me again. "I told you. I'm the dirtiest slave here."

"Well, I like dirty girls. I'm happy to be of service," I said, feeling a little used but, whatever. I was not about to complain.

It was from that night on that I started getting regular visitors in the night. Sira must have given me a good review to many of the other interior slave girls. It brought an end to the frustrating nights of tears of boredom and celibacy I'd been working on. All of it right next door to the Mistress's bedroom. I was a bad, bad slave.

"The slave who thinks they can keep secrets from their Master is not just deluded. They're an idiot."
Loash, *The Scrolls of the Goddess*

CHAPTER 9: SECRETS

Life had gotten a lot better since that night. Bath time continued as usual. I'd begun routinely entering the forbidden chambers of the Mistress. I'd stolen a few more pairs of her panties in my spare time and had made a habit of using them in my nightly lusting. I would touch myself with the satin that had rubbed against the Mistress and imagine it was her pussy. I hid the stolen panties in with my dagger, which I had officially named "Secret". It seemed fitting that I would hide all my secrets in the same place. It was such a source of pride for me that my bladed prize spent its days in a nest of the Mistress's undergarments.

I was still practicing with Secret in the evenings. I've never been much of a fighter. But all alone in my room, where no one could see how often I dropped the knife or didn't hit the mark, it was a safe place to live out my fantasies of being a badass. Even if I wasn't man enough to wield a sword or pull a bow. I could be a lethal eating utensil assassin. Yes, if I ever needed to defend the Mistress while at the dinner table, I was fairly certain I could throw a dinner knife and make it stick.

My use of cane and wine had slowed to hardly anything, due to the fact that I needed to please the bevy of interior slaves who visited me. Sira and I or some of the other interior girls frequently made the sheets dirty on the Mistress's bed before they cleaned up. I'm happy to say that I had a steady stream of ladies to release my pent up sexual energy now. Actually, my stamina increased. I was satisfying so many girls a day it was exhausting. Not that I was complaining. I was entertained so much that I started to forget that I hadn't seen Khessi in a while. I started to wonder what the fair red haired household slave was up to.

One evening, I found myself heading to her office. As I entered, the blue-lit water illuminated a school of silver fish that passed by the far wall, causing a wave of shadows across the empty room. It felt really cold in there without her. I sighed and walked to her desk. The faint smell of her perfume still hung around her chair. A light and fruity floral mix. I ran my hands over the intricate carvings on the desk. The little fish, Gem, was in a vase on top of the desk. He was swimming merrily around a plant and seemed to be in good fishy spirits.

"How's it going little man?" I said to him.

Now, I can't tell if it was just a habit at this point, or good old-fashioned curiosity, but I'd developed a habit of going through things that didn't belong to me in places I wasn't supposed to be. So, I started going through the drawers to Khessi's desk. The first three weren't surprising. Quill pens, ink, paper, wax, seals, scrolls, books. Some tiny dried worms that I'm sure she fed to Gem. But in the third drawer, I found something I knew I shouldn't be reading as soon as I picked it up. It bore a metallic blue seal with the crest of a Gryphon on it. The letter enclosed read,

Dearest Isavyne,

His imperial highness has charged me to inquire with each monarch about an act of entertainment at this season's Blossoming festival. If you could make your assessments of what slaves would be the best candidates for such games at your earliest convenience, that would be smashing.

If you could also please plan on shipping me cane for the coming festivities. My same order as last year and our arrangement still stands. Champcane was so popular last year we used it all up.

Cannot wait to see you, love. It has been far too long.

Yours,

Lovol

I didn't fully understand what I read until I saw the name. Master Lovol was the Cheritoth King. The Emperor was asking for spare slaves to die in Cheritoth games during the Blossoming celebration, which happened every year when the first flowers opened in the imperial garden. It was a time of great excitement even among slaves since it involved masked dances, food, and parties while the Monarchy were away in the imperial palace.

I had just put the scroll back and closed the desk drawer when Khessi walked in.

"What are you doing in here?" she said in a much higher register than I'm sure she meant.

"I was looking for you." I tried to answer casually.

"Get out from behind my desk. You've no business back there." She walked across the room toward me in a swish of teal fabric.

"I'm sorry."

"What brings you down from the tower, Zsash?"

"Well, I haven't seen you in a while. I just wanted to see what you were doing these days." I cleared my throat and restated, "When I didn't see you here, I thought I'd leave you a note."

"Well I'm here now, so there's no need."

She seemed irritated with me, and not just because I was near her desk. I seemed to have pissed her off generally. I wondered what I had done now.

"I haven't seen you around and you haven't come to see me. I was getting kind of lonely without my favorite household slave." I flashed her a smile and tried to be charming. It didn't work.

"I am extraordinarily busy, Zsash. The Mistress has several large shipments for the upcoming Blossoming festivals. I have much to keep in order. Besides, I would have thought that you had plenty of entertainment. What with you servicing most of our interior girls."

Blood rushed to my face and I suddenly felt defensive. Also strangely guilty. Though, I knew there was no need. Slaves were permitted to have physical relationships as long as it didn't impede on their responsibilities. Well, all except household slaves.

"You know about that?"

She scoffed at me.

"Oh please, I know everything that happens on this estate. Least of all the conquests of the bath beast."

"Bath beast?" I laughed.

"Not my term for you. But the girls do talk. I hear all about the sexual exploits of our dear interior slaves."

"Are you jealous?" I shrugged boldly.

"Extremely. Many of our ladies are quite attractive. If I have more time after the Blossoming festival, perhaps I'll bed one myself."

"That's not what I…" I started. Then I changed my statement. "I didn't think you were allowed to have sex."

"Not with men. I can't ruin my breeding potential on something so trivial."

" I see." A huff escaped my chest.

"There will probably be new slaves purchased after next season. I completely understand you taking advantage of the situation while you have the chance."

"What does buying new slaves have to do with that?"

" Oh," she said with a feigned wince of pity. "They always do this. They get all excited about a new slave and have to try him or her out. They just like to play with the new toy on the estate. It's just what sluts do, I suppose."

"Wow." I was floored at how vindictive her tone was. I started walking away from the desk. "You know what, I'm going let you get back to…whatever it is you do here since, I know, it's far more complicated than anything my insignificant mind could grasp. I've got to get back to my sluts, anyway. You know, before they become too bored with me." I walked out of her office without looking behind me.

I stalked down the halls of the castle, fuming. Staring at the floor and I'm pretty sure, muttering to myself like a crazy person. It served me right for thinking she ever liked me. What was I thinking? There was no future in a household slave. They were all elitist snobby cunts. Especially Khessi! All of them thought they were better than the rest of us. I almost felt bad for the next interior slave girl who came to see me. I was pretty sure I was going to hate-fuck the shit out of her.

I was still staring at the floor as I rounded the lower staircase in the main hallway. I turned right into Corvas. He was as surprised as I was. Six other guards stood around in the main foyer and they all were suddenly watching us.

"Sorry," I said as a reflex. "I didn't see—"

"Get your head out of your ass!" he barked at me and pushed me, really hard in the chest. He hit me so hard it made my old chest scar ache, reminding me of the last bully who had hurt me. My hands opened and closed into fists as I felt my heartbeat rise.

"Don't. Fucking. Push me." My voice was quiet and through clenching teeth. I hardly recognized it. The person that voice belonged to sounded dangerous.

"Don't push you?" Corvas said, looking around and then back at me with narrow eyes. "Or what?" he snapped and raised his right hand to push me again. I smacked is hand away. He immediately countered with grabbing me by the throat. A graceful side-step later, a swift kick to the back of my knee and he was standing behind me, his hand crushing my windpipe. He laced his other arm behind my head in an attempt to hold me in place.

Blood red hate blazed up into my brain. I reached down and grabbed Corvas by the leg and pulled up. This sent us both falling backward. His grip on my neck released and I took the moment to send my elbow flying back. It cracked him in the nose and I heard the crunch as it broke. I stood and ran up the staircase, trying to get some distance between us. Corvas stood a moment later, holding his nose. Crimson poured down his face onto the breastplate of his armor. The six other guards joined him and I realized they were all about to gang up on me. I needed protection. I contemplated running to Khessi's office, but a little bur of anger made me dismiss that idea immediately. My only hope was to run to my chambers and hope the Mistress was there.

"Get him!" Corvas shouted through his hand. They were all wearing armor and had a lot more muscle than me. That made them stronger, but I was faster. Much faster. I ran at full speed down the halls and up the stairs to the bath chamber. I turned and ran into the Mistress's room. I wasn't even thinking about the fact that the Mistress would be angry with me barging in. I acted out of sheer fear as the guards chased me. I stopped short upon opening the door. The Mistress was not in her chambers.

But someone was.

The petite form of a female dressed all in grey stood before me. Tight cotton pants tucked into soft leather boots. Her tunic had a pointed hood on it and her face was covered with grey fabric. Her head snapped toward me as I barged in. She was as surprised to be seen as I was to see her. She tucked a piece of white satin into a pocket. A pair of the Mistress's panties, not unlike the ones I was fond of stealing.

"What are you...?" Was all I could get out before the mysterious grey woman ran toward the open window and leapt through it. She disappeared into the night. Just in time for Corvas and his guards to catch up to me.

"You're going to regret that," Corvas said smiling through blood.

"Hey, did any of you see that?" I asked, suddenly preoccupied with the vanished woman.

"Yeah, I saw you entering the Mistress's private chambers. We all saw that."

For the second time in so many months, Corvas beat me within an inch of my life. Except, this time, he had the help of six others to hold me down and join in. I still don't have full recollection of what happened. I hid in the dark of my arms over my face for most of it. I remember being surrounded by boots. I remember hearing parts of me breaking. Sickening thuds crashed into my body, making it difficult to breathe.

Through the blur of pain, I suddenly heard a woman's sternly shouting voice. Despite her usual bossy tone, she sounded pissed off. I lowered my arm from my face slowly to see Nilda, the interior matron, coming to my rescue.

"What is this ruckus in the Mistress's home?" She demanded.

"Just doing my job. This slave was found skulking around the Mistress's chambers."

"Your job is to bind him and take him to the cells for the Mistress's judgment. Yours is to enforce, not punish. This poor slave is nearly beaten to death. Mark my works, Corvas, you will not be Guard Captain for long. A hot head and desire to cause pain is the sort that ends up in the Cheritoth."

"As always, Mother, I hear and respect your words. I will take the disobedient one to the dungeon immediately."

"Don't be ridiculous!" She waved off the guards around me and knelt down by my side. She looked at me with kind, dark eyes. She inspected my body while I stared at the ceiling. "Broken arm. Broken fingers. All over flesh damage. Probably some broken ribs too. Goddess knows what else you broke on the poor boy. He needs to be taken to the healers."

"Indeed. We'll take him there straight away. Thank you for your help, Mother. We'll take care of the situation from here."

"You do not dismiss me, child! I will be ensuring this young slave is not badgered by you any further. Just go back to your post. And pray the Mistress has mercy on your punishments for this outrage."

"As you wish, Mother. I will explain it all to the Mistress upon her return."

"You do that," she spat.

Corvas and his guards turned and left down the long staircase, leaving me with Nilda. I looked down at myself. I was bleeding in a few spots. Scrapes, cuts. There was a dark, ruddy color to some of my skin where bruises would be emerging soon. It took me a moment to realize that my arm was no longer exactly straight. My left forearm was bent at a strange, unnatural angle. It hurt to breathe. My chest felt hot with sharp pain. I would have screamed, but everything hurt too much to make a sound. Moving was the worst, though.

Nilda helped me to stand and we slowly made our way down to the healers. I was wheezing and making the most terrible wet gurgling sounds when I breathed. Several interior slaves who had been lovers of mine saw us walking by. Looks of shock and terror crossed their faces.

"Nilda! What happened!" said one of the girls as we passed.

I smiled through blood on my lips and shrugged. "She kicked my ass."

The girl didn't laugh. But it got a chuckle out of Nilda and I let out a soft red splatter of laughter. I then spiraled into a disgusting coughing fit. My chest felt heavy.

"Come on, boy. You'll drown in your own blood if we don't get you help quickly."

I nodded and tried to move faster down the halls. Any adrenaline I'd been granted from the fight was dwindling. The pain was getting steadily greater.

"In case I don't get a chance to say it later, thanks for saving me. You're my hero."

"Well, if you die, I won't have saved you."

"I suppose not. How did you stumble onto my situation, though?"

"Oh, I was headed to the bath chamber anyways." She shrugged.

"What? Why? You never come up there."

"Figured I'd try out the bath beast all the girls are talking about," she said with as straight a face as she could muster and winked at me.

And the laughing from that nearly killed me.

The first word out of Jaideen's mouth when he saw me was,

"Seriously?" He took my unbroken arm and led me to a bed. "By the Goddess, Zsash! How do you get yourself in these situations?"

"Just lucky, I guess," I mumbled through blood.

"Don't lay down. You'll suffocate," he instructed. "Sit here and I'll be right back. I have to grab a few things."

Nilda nodded to me.

"Are you going to be all right? I really should go wrangle in my girls and boys. I'm sure they're doing nothing but gossiping by now." She said.

"Yeah, he'll take care of me. You've already helped me here." I grabbed her hand weakly before she left. "Thank you."

"Of course," she stated plainly. "Get better, you hear. My girls need their distractions."

Nilda patted me on the shoulder before leaving me alone to wait for Jaideen. I sat there and did my best to continue breathing.

The next few hours were exceptionally painful. Jaideen gave me cane to dull the pain, but everything still hurt. He set the bone in my arm and treated my wounds. The biggest problems were my broken ribs and a punctured lung. There was nothing he could do to fix them. He said that my lungs must have been damaged because of how much blood I was coughing up. Unfortunately, those were two things that he couldn't really treat. All he could do was give me more cane for the pain, bandage the ribs and see if I lived.

I sat on the bed in the dark hours of the night. The walls of the healer's wing were dimly lit by numerous oil lamps. A few hours into sitting there, the bruises started to show up. Purple and brown and blue all over me. My arm was cradled in a splint and a sling around my neck. I was a mess. I silently regretted taking so much cane in the last few months. It didn't affect me the way it used to when I first started. I'd built up a bit of a tolerance to it, so the pain was not dulled as much as it should have been. Of course, I couldn't say anything. I just took what Jaideen gave me and sat there quietly, hating how much I seemed to get beat up in my life.

I started to nod off a little when the scent of peach and rose drifted through the room. My eyes fluttered open and I saw Khessi standing at the end of the bed. She looked upset. I was starting to get used to that around her. She moved slowly and sat on the edge of the bed. She was holding her book and feather quill. She was also holding a small red box that had a gold bird carved into it.

"How are you feeling?" she asked. I thought about it for a second.

"Purple," was the best descriptor I could come up with.

She smiled softly and looked over my injuries, shaking her head. "I'm so sorry that he seems to have become fixated on tormenting you."

"It's not your fault."

"While it isn't my hand, it still feels like my fault. He hates you because of me. I'm also sorry for how I spoke to you earlier. I was just...Well, I shouldn't have spoken to you like that."

I tried to shrug but looked away.

She continued. "The Mistress returned a little while ago and has been told of the situation. She spoke with Corvas and Nilda."

"And?" I rasped.

"Corvas says that you invaded her private chambers. He says you antagonized him and his guards. That you broke his nose and then they got carried away with restraining you."

"Hmm, poor Corvas. It's a good thing he had those six other trained guards to fend me off." I put on a slightly theatrical air to my voice and continued, "How would he have defended himself against such a devious bath slave?" I scoffed and spit some of the blood in my mouth out onto the floor.

"Has anyone ever told you that your above-average vocabulary and ability to wield sarcasm is charming in a really self destructive way?"

"You think I'm charming?" I asked with red grooves in my smile. She ignored my last statement and pulled her quill out and opened her book.

"Can you tell me your version of the events from this evening?"

I nodded and tried to sit up more. I was not very successful.

"There's not much to it. I left your office and ran into Corvas. I apologized but he decided to take it personally and grabbed me by the throat. I then broke his nose and ran to the Mistress's chambers to try and find her. I saw...." I then remembered the woman in grey. I thought about it for a moment. Should I mention it? After everything that happened it almost seemed like I'd imagined it. I saw her so briefly. I'm sure it sounded like some kind of ridiculous embellishment that didn't belong in the story. So I decided to leave it out. "I...saw that the Mistress wasn't there. And they beat me nearly to death. The end."

Khessi wrote quickly, taking notes of what I said. "Is that all that happened?"

"Yeah. Just another night of Corvas trying to kick my ass for no reason."

"The Mistress is not pleased with the fights that have erupted between you two. She forgave the first one as it was obviously a misunderstanding."

"Misunderstanding?"

"Jaideen was uncertain if you would survive the night, so the Mistress sent me with something to help you heal faster." She opened the red box. Inside was a crystal vial that contained a glowing liquid of a golden opal hue. There was a tiny gold cup that I would have mistaken for a thimble in any other situation. Khessi took out the vial and the tiny cup. When she removed the stopper on the vial, a mist of shimmering colors emerged. I thought it could be some kind of special cane. I all but heard the sound of feathered wings and gentle wind in the light of the liquid. Don't ask me how, but there were extrasensory perceptions that came with looking at this stuff. It was clear to me that this was some kind of magic. With great delicacy, Khessi poured a small amount of the liquid into the cup. She then handed it to me and replaced the stopper.

I looked down at the liquid. It smelled something like vanilla and sugar. Again, images and sounds flashed across my mind. A deep blue sky, glittering with stars. Red shimmering cliffs made of ruby shards. An ocean of fire dancing with hues of orange and blue. I blinked a couple times just staring at the entrancing liquid in the tiny cup.

"Drink it." She said with a nod.

I did.

It's difficult to explain what happened next. I was in so much pain that it had started to bleed into everything I felt. As the medicine, or whatever the substance was, ran over my tongue I was aware of my tongue feeling better. In fact, it left such a dramatic feeling where it touched that immediately my tongue, throat, and stomach felt better. Khessi packed up the box, her book, and quill.

"When you are able, the Mistress would like to see you in your bed chambers."

She said nothing more. She left me there with only the scent of peaches and rose to keep me company. I wished she had stayed longer just in case the magic potion didn't work. If that was the last time I'd seen Khessi that would have been sad.

I sat there for a minute. I felt a little better, but I was still horribly injured. I anxiously began to contemplate how I was going to make it to my bed chamber in my current condition.

As I had this thought, I realized my breathing came easier to me. The weight that had been in my lungs dissipated. I wasn't entirely convinced of what was happening until I felt a slight crunch in my side. Then my ribs felt better.

"What?" I said touching my sides. The pain was gone all of a sudden. My broken ribs were...healed. Just like that.

The jubilee of purple and brown colors that had appeared on my legs faded in a few minutes. My arm was still tender, but after a while, it went from feeling better to mending entirely.

In an hour, I was completely healed of all injuries. I laughed in disbelief. I'd never even heard of anything that could heal someone like this. I'd been preparing my mind for months and months of recovery. To be back to normal only a few hours later was a miracle. Praise the Goddess! And praise the Mistress for taking pity on me.

I went as quickly as I could to meet with the Mistress as Khessi had instructed.

As I approached my bed chamber, I started to feel my chest tighten again, but for a new reason. The door was open. I entered to see the floor littered with all the pairs of panties I had stolen from her dresser in the last month.

The Mistress sat on my little bed, holding my glittering knife, Secret. She looked at me with blue fire in her gaze and rolled the knife in her fingers.

"We need to have a conversation, my pet."

"It is proud and spiteful for a slave to hold onto strong feelings, be they good or bad. Strive instead to let feelings pass through you like the flow of a gentle stream. All pain and pleasure, be it physical or emotional, is only temporary, and ultimately meaningless. However, the enlightenment you receive during those sensations, are priceless."

Misteryn, *The Scrolls of the Goddess*

CHAPTER 10: PUNISHMENT

Chained and naked, I stared blankly at the stone floor of the dungeon. I knelt like a dog on my hands and knees before the Mistress, with my head bowed in shame. The Mistress sat on a small gold chair with her legs crossed elegantly, while I knelt with my face down by her boots. She held a gold leather flogger and smoothed the tails of it through her hand. My injuries were fully healed, however, this did not make the stone floor any more comfortable.

I had already detailed to the Mistress how I had found the knife and that I had opted to keep it, rather than turn it over to her. Of course, I'd known it wasn't something a slave should have. But I hadn't taken it from anyone, so it wasn't exactly stealing.

The panties, on the other hand...

"It's a bold move to steal from me." She was saying.

"I'm so sorry, Mistress," My voice shook with effort as I tried not to cry.

"No, you're not." She lifted one boot and pressed the heel of it into the center of my back between my shoulder blades. "You. Are. Not. Sorry. You would have continued to sit pretty in the tower, fucking my interior slaves and enjoying the private chambers I've given you, not to mention *my* chambers! You would have kept on stealing *my* garments, *my* wine, *my cane*," she emphasized. A sigh of defeat escaped my chest and echoed on the stone walls without sympathy. "You have stopped, but not because you are sorry. You have been taking from me for quite some time, my sweet. We shall have to cure you of this flaw." She pushed me down with her boot until my chest was pressed against the freezing stone floor.

I expected her to crush me beneath her boot or perhaps stab me to death with the heel. But she didn't. She removed her heel from my back and took a handful of my hair, raising my face to the level of her lap. My wrists strained behind me as the chains were pulled taught against the floor, holding me back. She pulled me upward so she could see my face. I looked away.

"I'm going to give you a gift, Zsash. The gift of appreciation. You do not yet appreciate my generosity."

"I do! I do, Mistress."

She slapped my face hard and the cry I let out was little more than a bark of pain and shock.

"No, you don't appreciate your gifts. Not at all. But you will. I will see to it." She released my hair and stood. She walked over to the wall behind me and I heard a metal lever being pulled. The chains at my wrists suddenly hoisted me from the floor and toward the ceiling. They dragged me upward as I struggled to stand quickly on my numb feet. The chains stopped once each of my elbows was parallel with my shoulder, my arms effectively held away from my body and dangling.

"There are stages to appreciation. The first is pain."

I stared forward trying to steady myself. The heels of her boots clicked against the floor as she paced behind me, swishing the flogger in circles "For this phase of your punishment, Zsash, you will answer my questions and *only* my questions. And you will answer them truthfully. But you will never tell me 'no.' I don't want to hear that word pass your lips. Do you understand?"

"Yes, Mistress."

"Do you love me, slave?"

"Yes, Mistress."

"Do you find me beautiful?"

"Yes, Mistress. You're the most beautiful Queen I've ever seen."

"Do you touch yourself and think of me, slave?"

I winced for a moment, delaying the answer as long as I dared.

"Yes, Mistress. I do."

"Is that why you steal my undergarments? So you can jerk yourself off and pretend I'd ever let you fuck me?"

I sighed heavily. "Yes, Mistress."

"How many pairs of my panties did you steal?" she asked.

"Five," I answered truthfully.

Sharp pain slashed me as she brought the flogger down on my back. A shout of surprise escaped my lips. I managed to remain quiet as she brought the leather tails of the flogger down on my back several more times. This flogger was not tipped, just leather. It was not enough to break the skin, like the flogger that had been used on me the day at the auction. The strikes still stung though, in long hot strokes across my back. Her lash hit my left shoulder, then my right. Followed by each side of my lower back, her strokes creating the figure eight pattern.

While each strike of the flogger landed, I started to think about my answer and why it was earning me punishment. Granted, I deserved to be punished anyway, but I had told the truth. I had only stolen five pairs of her underwear.

"How man pairs of my panties did you steal?" she asked again, her words cutting through my thoughts.

"Five." I repeated. The lashes became instantly harder. Stinging became sharp slapping pain. I would certainly have bruising tomorrow under the skin. "It was five! Only five!"

"Silence, then! If you cannot tell me the truth, you will not speak at all!" she hissed. "I will break you for a while, instead. You will tell me the truth eventually, Zsash!"

"But I don't know what you want me to say!"

She struck me harder than before and I yelped in pain, squeezing my eyes shut tightly and clenching my jaw. When I opened my eyes, she was standing in front of me.

Her porcelain hand clamped around my throat and I felt how much stronger than me she was. I was nothing compared to her power. A cloth doll in the clutches of an eagle. She pulled me toward her by the throat. A thin wispy sound came from me as I struggled desperately to pull in air. She spoke so quietly it terrified me.

"I told you to be silent. When I require another answer from you I will ask you a question. Do you understand?" I tried to nod but it wasn't good enough.

"That was a question I just asked you! Is this really so difficult for you to grasp!?! I ask a question, you answer. I don't ask a question, you remain silent. Do you understand me, slave?"

"Yes." I gurgled through a strangled voice.

"Yes, what?"

"Yes, Mistress!" I added with urgency.

She released me and I stood back up, coughing and gasping for air. The Mistress resumed her stance behind me and the lashing continued. I don't know how long she flogged me for. At first, there was pain and it was sharp and bright across my skin. After a while, the strikes became a lull of pain and rhythm and I felt like I was living inside my breaths. Inhale, slap. Exhale, slap. Inhale, slap. Exhale, slap. It was a sharp heartbeat against my skin. A gentle rocking to sleep into a nightmare. I was a breaking ship on a sea of pain under a cloudy sky of fatigue. On and on, in a red, swollen figure eight across my body. When she decided she was done flogging me, she pulled out a piece of cane shaft. The blood red, reedy branch that cane grows inside. She flicked it from side to side once, letting me hear it whistle through the air.

"You like cane, Zsash?" She asked.

"Yes, Mistress." I exhaled, miserably. It's not as though I could tell her no.

"Good," she mocked. "Then I hope you enjoy this." She first patted the switch along the outside of my arms. The stinging pat of the reed was almost enjoyable at first. Like a massage over my skin on the first pass. She ran the smooth round surface somewhat gently, patting it along the tender part of my inner arms. The strikes became increasingly harder. Their report on my flesh was red hot and sizzling. I could not stay silent for the pain these caused. I hissed and contorted my body to try and diminish their impact any way I could. Nothing helped. The cane whistled down, again and again, its merry tune of torment continued until long red lined welts stood raised all over my arms and back.

It wasn't until she caned the back of my thighs that it brought something up in me that was both terrible and sensual. I moaned and grit my teeth with each snap of the switch. My cries turning into painful moans of pleasure under my breath. As she drew the strikes across my ass, I realized how turned on I was getting. Through the sea of pain, a thread of pleasure had hooked into me and began wrapping itself around my senses.

"Mistress...Mistress, please..." I begged.

"Silence!" she hissed and struck me just below my ass cheeks.

She alternated a while between the flogger and the switch while my cries echoed around the dungeon. My breathing was heavy as I became light headed. My skin was red and hot and becoming soundly welted.

I stood there, trying to hold still as the tremors in my muscles continued to make me shake. My skin was so inflamed and sensitive that I could feel the pressure of the air around me.

That is when she ran her hair across me. Her soft curls of gold satin ran unbearably over my all too sensitive skin, creating painfully edged pleasure. I gasped and pulled against my restraints as chills rolled up my spine. Her hands moved gently up the back of my thighs. Her skin was so soft against mine it brought me to tears. She squeezed my ass cheeks for a moment then continued lightly tracing her fingers up my back. My nerves were on fire. I felt every pinpoint of smooth contact of her skin against mine. My erection stood straight up, in clear betrayal of all orders from my brain. I had been hoping against hope that my arousal would go unnoticed by the Mistress.

She walked around in front of me and dawned a wicked ruby grin.

"Oh my," she said, looking down toward my waist as if she was surprised. She stood directly in front of me, an inch away from touching me, quite intentionally.

"It looks like you've been enjoying your punishment a bit too much."

I made sure not to meet her gaze as she raised the switch and ran it down my chest until it rested against my hip.

"Do you enjoy pain, slave?"

"I...I don't." I stuttered over the words.

"Oh, really? Is that lie for me or for yourself?" she purred, letting her head tilt to the side so that her long golden hair teased between my legs. My mouth dropped open with each silken caress that drifted over my shaft like the fluttering of a moth's wings dancing around a flame. I shuddered, holding my breath without meaning to.

"I didn't know you would get so hard with me beating you like this. Maybe...I should hurt you a little, here, so it can still be considered a punishment." she said, running the smooth rounded switch along the backside of my hard cock.

"Please, Mistress. Please don't...I can't..."

"How many pairs of my panties did you steal, slave?" she asked again. I sucked in a shaky gasp.

I did not want her to cause me pain there.

"Please Mistress, I'm telling you the truth. I only took five."

She slapped my cock with the switch, ever so lightly.

It still hurt.

"How many?" she asked again, with the switch of cane still toying with me. My chest felt tight and I didn't know if I could take a breath in to speak.

"If you tell me what you want me to say, I'll say it. I'll say whatever you want!" I pleaded.

She struck me again, a little harder this time. I grunted in frustration and pain as I ground my teeth together.

"Please, Mistress, please! I don't know the answer!"

"How many?"

"I'm telling the truth!"

She slapped my cock with the cane again and I cried out. The pain was sharp and intense with no way for me to escape it. My heart thumped percussively in my chest as unbidden arousal crept through the back of my thighs. Tears began to slip down my cheeks.

"What's got you so upset, my pet?" she asked with a casual tousle of her golden locks.

"I only took five..."

She slapped my cock again softly with the switch. I grunted through clenched teeth and more tears stung my eyes.

"That is not what I asked you about this time. Please try to keep up. I asked what's got you so upset?" she repeated and brought the cane across me again.

"I'm a disappointment!" I said without thinking.

"Go on," she coaxed. She moved closer to me, running her silken hand lightly over the length of my cock. I struggled to speak through the pleasure and sensitivity.

"I'm not even worth the one gold you paid for me." More tears escaped me.

"I'll be the judge of that. Are you enjoying your punishment?"

I trembled under the blue fire of her gaze and it made the chains at my wrists jingle almost pleasantly in the dark dungeon.

"No," I answered, with immediate regret as she removed her hand and struck me with the cane again. I changed my answer. "I mean, I think I like...." I fought to clear my mind. "...I think I like having your attention. Even if it's painful, Mistress."

"Hmm, that's interesting," she said and tapped the cane against her other open palm for a few moments in thought. A gentle smile touched her lips and she ran a soft hand over my tear-streaked face. I wondered if she was considering the possibility that I had told her the truth.

In a flash of realization, I suddenly figured out why the number didn't match up. The woman in grey! She had stolen a pair of the Mistress's underwear. I cursed myself under my breath for not telling Khessi about her when I'd had the chance, and then not mentioning her when the Mistress had asked me. Now, whenever I said it, it would just come out like I was making up some invisible stranger to take the blame. I knew it would look bad. But I didn't want to lie to lie anymore. Without thinking it through all the way I said,

"Six! Was it six panties?"

Her smile faded.

"Why change your answer now? More lies, my handsome pet?" she said in a frosty tone, her compassion pulling away.

"I'm not! Well, I am guessing because I don't know how many more were taken. But there was a woman in your room not a moment before Corvas and the guards showed up. I saw her take a pair of your panties!"

"Why did you not mention this to Khessi when she asked you what had happened?"

"Because I didn't know…" My sigh rattled off the stone walls. "I didn't think I'd get caught."

"And where did this thief run off to, without anyone else seeing her."

"She jumped out the window."

"Uh huh."

"It's the truth!"

"I see. So, a mysterious panty thief is caught in the act by the one *actual* thief who also happens to be stealing my underwear? And then, they disappeared out the window without a trace. Is that what you're telling me now?"

"What are the fucking odds, right?" I half laughed nervously.

The series of strikes after that comment, I actually deserved.

I gritted my teeth and regretted saying it immediately.

"I'm sorry Mistress. I wasn't…"

"Be silent!" she struck my cock again. I whined and grunted through the pain. My hips thrust against my will toward the pressure. Even painful pressure. Tiny red lines had developed on the shaft of my swollen erection. The Mistress took a step back from me, clicking her heel on the floor in thought.

"In fact, since you can't seem to exercise the fucking willpower to quiet yourself. This should do the trick." She took a step back and moved her hands under her skirt. She stepped out of the white panties she wore.

"Open your mouth!" she ordered while grabbing my jaw. I opened my mouth. She stuffed her panties between my teeth, filling my mouth with white satin. They were still warm from her skin. The scent of amber clung to the fabric along with the undiluted scent of her intoxicating wetness. I'm ashamed at the sudden thrill that passed through me to have them in my mouth, a thrill that was blurred by the sudden return of the flogger being brought down over my ass cheeks.

I stopped trying to speak. I relaxed into broken submission. Pleasure, pain, truth, and shame all melted together as I gave into my punishment. The lashing traveled up my thighs while tears slid down my face. My teeth worked into the soft fabric between them as I strained against the chains, crying out with each strike.

She moved to the front and struck my hips and thighs, letting the strokes drift over my cock each time. I moaned behind the satin, tasting her pussy in the fabric, while every fiber in my body betrayed me. The pressure built in my thighs, making me more aroused with each painful strike.

She began bringing the leather straps down against my cock again. I cried out this time, in moans of sharp pleasure. It was a terrible reaction that made me harder with every slap of the leather. She increased the speed of the hits. I arced forward on straining tip toes, hating and loving the scarlet smile my pain brought to her lips. I twisted in my shackles, moaning, needing the pressure, no matter how much it hurt. No matter how shameful. I felt myself begin to fall over the edge into orgasm. I started to cum with her flogger still punishing my cock. My muscles locked down tight while I pressed my hips forward into nothing. I moaned and cried out, my hips thrusting out of my control, gripping the chains desperately while my cock twitched in violent spasms. My cum spattered onto the cold floor in front of me, while my cries echoed meaninglessly off of both Mistress and stone.

I panted with effort, trying to find my way back to my mind. I realized I was hanging in the chains and struggled to get to my feet. I flinched slightly as I felt her delicate hand on my face. She plucked her panties from between my lips, then wiped tears and sweat from my face with the satin. I couldn't bare to look at her.

"Mistress..." I said, my voice shaking as the muscles in my arms and legs trembled beyond my control.

"Shhh..." she cooed, caressing my face.

I babbled, delirious with pleasure, pain, hunger, exhaustion. I tried desperately to be heard.

"I...I stole from you. I did. But I'm not lying. Please, please believe me..."

She then took my jaw in a crushing grip and brought my face to look at hers. I reluctantly looked up into her hypnotic blue eyes.

"Zsash. Shut up. By the Goddess, if you could just learn to control that mouth of yours, you'd be perfect."

"Yes, Mistress." I nodded. Well, she knew now. At least I'd gotten it out. I couldn't make her believe me. But I'd done my best. She released my jaw and walked past me.

The chains slacked and I fell to the floor like a sack of straw. The Mistress turned and walked toward the door of the dungeon.

"Get some sleep. We'll continue your lessons soon." She said as the heavy wooden door slammed shut behind her.

I laid worthlessly on the stone floor, letting it pull some of the heat from my burning skin.

Trying to sleep was nearly impossible. My first impulse was to sit in the golden chair in front of me. To my disappointment and I'm sure, the Mistress's design, it was too far for me to get to beyond the chains that held my wrists. I lay on the floor, freezing and in pain. I curled into a ball, wrapping my arms around myself. I tried to relax enough to fall asleep. Eventually, I passed out from exhaustion.

I felt as though I'd only just let my eyes close when I woke to the sound of the door creaking open. Fear raced through me and I struggled to get to my feet. I knelt and put my face to the floor expecting to see white boots before me. I was instead met with bare feet and a long blue skirt. Khessi knelt down in front of me, concerned pity in her beautiful face. She held a bottle in one hand and something wrapped in a white cloth in the other. I sat up slowly.

"Here," she said, setting the items in her hands before me. When I reached for the bottle, I realized that I was still shaking violently, either from cold or stress. I'm not sure. She steadied my hand and helped me raise the bottle to my lips. It was wine. I drank a large mouthful, hoping it would dull my pain. The other object, wrapped in a white cloth, turned out to be a piece of bread. I stuffed it into my mouth with more wine.

"You're freezing," Khessi said and unwrapped the large blue shawl from her shoulders. She wrapped it around me. It felt so much warmer inside the shawl and I made a vain effort to cover my nudity. Though even the soft fabric of the shawl felt rough against the welts on my body.

"Thank you," I said between the rattling of my teeth. "It seems like a waste, but still, thank you."

"A waste?"

"The Mistress is probably just going to kill me."

"Zsash, I am here because the Mistress instructed me to bring you wine and bread. I doubt she intends to turn around and kill you."

"She might as well have left me to my fate at the training house."

"Don't be dramatic. You didn't deserve to die in the training house. You do deserve everything you're getting right now, though,"she stated plainly.

"Thanks," I snapped vindictively, silently hating how gorgeous and collected she was as she sat there in front of my trembling, pathetic self.

"You know what? You're rude," I told her.

"Excuse me?" she scoffed, arching her eyebrows.

"Yeah. You are. All I have ever done was try and be nice to you. And you have, on occasion, treated me like shit. Whenever *you* started to realize that you might like me, you have given me nothing but fucking attitude. It's not my fault household slaves can't have relationships. I didn't make the rules. So, don't take it out on me!"

Her face hardened. She let out an indignant laugh with her jaw offset. "All right, some of that may be true. But speaking of taking things out on others who don't deserve it. I'm not the reason you're here! *You* got yourself into this mess. What could you possibly have been thinking? Stealing? From the Mistress?"

"I...I don't know. I guess I figured she wouldn't notice."

"You thought she wouldn't notice. Which part?" she said, pulling the wine bottle from my still drinking lips so that it caused a drizzle down my chin. "You mean when you stole cane? Or wine? Or because you were hiding a dagger you found on the beach?"

"I didn't steal that."

"Oh, right, because that couldn't possibly be the property of a monarch that might want it back? You thought what? That it wouldn't be missed? Should I even bring up you stealing the Mistress's personal garments?"

"No." I looked into the corner ashamed. I sullenly munched on more bread. "I guess I shouldn't be surprised. I always manage to mess up. That's why I was never bought. I screw everything up. I'm hopeless. Everything I touch turns to shit."

"Oh, by the Goddess! Give it a rest! Could you be more tragic with your self pity!?! I, I, I. Me, me, me. Oh, poor Zsash. Stop your complaining!" she said, pointing her finger at me. "Things are not as bad as you think."

"Oh really, how's that?"

She looked into my eyes and I noticed for the first time since she'd come into the cell how close her face was to mine. Her smokey glittering makeup sparkled in the dim light of the cell.

"The Mistress does not waste time on worthless slaves. If she didn't like you, she'd just sell you. Or kill you. Do you think she wastes food or time on a slave she intends to discard? She wants you to take your punishment and learn from it."

"That's easy for you to say. You're her favorite." I sulked, hardly above a whisper.

"As if you know anything about what I have done to earn favor with her! Do you think she is one to give reward to an untested slave? You know nothing of what I have endured. And how would you? You're always so busy talking about yourself!" She stood and picked up the wine bottle hastily.

I shrugged and stretched my neck uncomfortably, wrapped in the shawl she'd given me. Guilt overwhelmed me and I blurted out,

"I'm sorry!"

She stopped and turned back to me slowly.

I sighed, "I'm just tired. Thank you for all you've done for me."

"I do as I am commanded. That being said, I am happy to be able to ease your suffering, Zsash. And I am furious that Corvas has taken this ridiculous rivalry to the lengths it has gotten to."

"Why is he so upset about me? You said you can't be with other slaves, right? Why has he taken claim on you to such a degree?"

Her lips became a straight line and she looked down at the box in her hands. "He was always somewhat flirty with me. I never imagined for a moment that he was actually in love with me. At least, as close to love as he can get. He likes to win. To conquer things. He wants me because he knows he can't have me. And when you acquired...something he never had, I think it was a big hit to his pride."

"You mean when I kissed you?"

"Yes," she said. She stood and moved toward the door.

I realized something and asked quickly, "Wait! So...am I the only slave you've ever kissed?"

She stopped and turned to me with a blushing smile.

"You know, you really do have an annoying habit of making everything about you."

"That's not a no." I smirked.

She thought for a moment. Her tongue perched on her front teeth, until she turned to hide her smile.

"Goodnight, Zsash. Try to get some rest."

She shut the door and locked it, leaving me with her blue shawl to wrap around me. I couldn't tell what made me feel better, the warmth of a layer over my skin or the fact that it smelled like Khessi.

I slept.

I'm sure it was for at least eight or ten hours. There was no way to tell in the dungeon since there were no windows. I woke up well rested. More than that, I was energetic. I was still somewhat cold, so I decided to get my blood moving. With my wrists still chained, my options were limited. I was content to do pushups to get my temperature up. Time stretched on and I began a cycle of resting and doing exercises to keep warm. The Mistress would come back eventually to continue my education in appreciation. I had to trust that she had my best interests at heart. I would take the pain and the punishment with the most acceptance I could muster.

When she did finally come back she carried a full glass of wine. It felt like a whole day had passed. I honestly didn't have any idea how long I'd been in that room. I was doing pushups when she entered. She was dressed in a white corset and short skirt with white riding boots, an outfit I'd come to recognize as her riding wear. I stopped and knelt in front of the golden chair as the Mistress sat down.

"Get on your hands and knees and face that wall," she commanded, pointing to the right of me. I did and was immediately met with her setting her boot heels on the center of my back. It hurt some, being used as a footrest. Mostly just because of the beating from the day before. I straightened my back to the best of my ability, pushing through the pain.

"Oh, what a shame," the Mistress said looking at the floor where I'd fallen asleep. "Khessi forgot her shawl when she gave you dinner last night. See that you return it to her when you leave here, Zsash." Her tone was sly and full of knowing.

"Yes, Mistress."

"Are you ready for your second lesson, my sweet?"

"Yes, Mistress."

"Good. Then continue your pushups while I finish my wine."

I was momentarily confused. Then I moved one foot back, followed by the other, doing my best not to disrupt the Mistress's feet. I did a pushup with them squarely in the center of my back. Then another. And another.

"The second lesson in appreciation is service. I wish to see how well you can be of service to me."

I began to regret doing pushups earlier in the day and using valuable energy that I wish I had now. In no time, my muscles began to burn. But I kept going. I wanted to ask how many pushups she wanted or how long I would have to keep this up. No sound came from the Mistress. I started to sweat with effort, my muscles quivered. The pushups became slow. Each one was a strained battle for me to fight gravity and the added pressure of her legs. I took a deep breath and willed my body to continue. I focused on my breathing. Each pushup took everything I had, each time I completed it. And then I did it again.

Sounds of strain and effort wheezed out of me. It felt like an eternity until I heard the most wonderful sound.

The empty glass being set on the floor.

"That's enough, Zsash."

I exhaled an audible sigh of relief. Then pulled my knees back up so that I knelt with her boots on my back. It was still in a somewhat uncomfortable position after all those pushups but I started to get my breathing back under control.

"So, I was thinking about what you said last night. About the second thief." I waited for her to finish this thought for a few moments. "That's a strange turn of events and I don't think I believe you." My heart sank into the pit of my stomach. "However, there is one nagging detail I can't seem to get over. Though you are still very guilty and your punishment is far from ended, something else disturbs me. I am not missing five pairs, though we found five in your room. Nor am I missing six. Twenty-seven pairs of my underwear are missing. You don't happen to know where those other missing ones are, do you Zsash?"

My eyes widened in surprise. I was going to say 'No' but I remembered that she didn't like that word. Instead I said,

"I do not, Mistress, but if I were to guess, I would say perhaps the woman in grey has been visiting your chambers for some time."

"Hmm. It would seem that thieves abound on my property. Rest assured, I will sort the situation out." She took her boots off my back. My muscles rejoiced at the immediate relief from their pressure, no matter how slight it was. "Starting with you. Stand up, slave."

I stood. The Mistress rose from her golden bench, looking me up and down. My eyes widened in surprise when she grabbed my cock and began rubbing it softly.

"Hmm. This doesn't seem that impressive to me. Is this what makes you a such good fuck? Is this what gets all my interior slave girls wet? I don't think it looks that special, to be honest."

I didn't know how to respond. I stammered, looking between her face and what her hand was doing to me. *I* didn't know how to respond, but my body did. Blood rushed into my groin as the Mistress worked me with her hand.

"You know, I didn't give you permission to cum yesterday," she said in a teasing tone. Bewilderment swam through the pleasure in my mind. Her hand was so soft, trailing up and down me. After the flogging the day before, the skin of my cock felt extra sensitive and swollen.

"I'm so sorry, Mistress. That has never happened to me before. I couldn't control myself."

"It seems you have multiple issues. Your mouth and your cock both seem beyond your control," she said with amusement.

I didn't respond, since both statements were true.

"Do you think you're good enough to pleasure me?" she asked.

"I would no longer presume so, Mistress."

"There are Kings and Queens and an Emperor lined up who wish to experience having sex with me. And you think that I could be satisfied by you? A thieving, lying slave with a big dick?"

I searched for what to say but a moan of pleasure is all that came out. She looked down at my cock, now fully hard in her hand.

"Hmm, that's better. It looks nice enough. Good length. Thicker than most. Definitely above average."

I let out a small nervous laugh as she confirmed what I've always known about myself. I moaned again under the grip she had around me as she continued to speak.

"It's getting nice and hard for me. Even after being smacked around a little yesterday. Hmm, I guess it is very pretty. But, looks aren't everything," she purred, pondering. "I don't know. Maybe you do have something worthwhile here. Maybe I just don't know what I'm missing. Sit down," she ordered and gestured to the golden bench.

I did so immediately. The Mistress straddled my waist and knelt on the bench with her knees on either side of my legs. Her thighs brushed against me. Was she really going to...?

I shuddered in pleasure as she ran the lips of her pussy over the swollen head of my cock in slow controlled deliberation.

This wasn't happening.

How was this happening all of a sudden?

Oh, Goddess...

Slick heat encompassed the tip of my erection as she hovered her hips above me. I froze in arousal and fear, sucking in air through my clenched jaw.

"Is this what you dream about, Zsash?" She whispered as she slid me against her clit in agonizing slow circles. I saw desire behind her sapphire gaze. I held as still as I could. Willing myself not to thrust. I didn't dare do anything to anger her or ruin this moment.

She held me there, at the edge of her warmth, teasing me.

"Oh, Goddess..." I muttered. The Mistress brought her hand to my cheek, leaning in to kiss me gently.

That's when I felt her slide down over me. I groaned, letting my head fall back out of the kiss.

"Oh, fuck...oh, fuck" I panted. Agonized pleasure gripped me as I was enveloped in the slick tightness of her body.

"Ahhhh..." she sighed into my ear. "Maybe I do have a use for you, slave."

"Thank you, Mistress." I said, hushed and lusty. She began moving rhythmically on top of me. My hands went instinctually to her hips and she smacked them away.

"Get your fucking hands off me! I did not give you permission to touch me. No, you just sit there and let me enjoy you." Her taloned hands caressed over my shoulders. "I just want to see if this cock of yours can even get me off. But don't you dare finish." She said, sliding her hands down my chest. "If you cum inside my beautiful cunt, your punishment will be...severe. Do you understand how severe I can get slave?"

"I don't think I want to Mistress."

She laughed, leaning back a little and bringing new pleasure around my cock with the motion. She rode me hard. Fucking me. Taking me. Bringing moans from me that sounded primitive and guttural. Her pussy clenched down around me, milking my flesh with strong practiced muscles that owned every bit of my attention. Hot pleasure sizzled through me like electricity to by brain. Her hands ran over my skin, possessing my body. Touching my chest, my shoulders, my neck and up into my hair. I felt myself panting hard through my moans. She felt amazing. It was pleasure wrapped in silk that dripped milk and honey. And at her core, a heat that burned into me more than just need. It was wild pure carnal desire for flesh.

Training had not prepared me for Mistress Isavyne.

As much as I enjoyed being inside her, she only seemed to be mildly enjoying what I was doing. I dare say, she almost looked bored.

"Maybe I was wrong," she said while she rode me. "Maybe this cock isn't worth my time," she shrugged.

That snapped me out of my pleasure drunk state and I refocused. My own pleasure dimmed into the background. I tensed the muscles in my abdomen so that my cock would stand up and pressed deeper into her. Holding there for all I was worth. She sighed in pleasure at my renewed efforts. The Mistress grabbed a handful of my hair and led my mouth to her breast. I licked and ran my teeth over the nipple there while she rode me harder. At least she didn't sound bored anymore. I bucked upward against her as she began moaning. Sweat beaded over my body as I worked my cock in and out of her. Moans and panting breaths echoed loudly around the dungeon. Her sounds were not as loud as I was used to. The interior girls screamed with abandon when I took them. The Mistress seemed to be enjoying my efforts, but not wild with pleasure. It was a bit of a blow to my ego, but I didn't need to be the best she'd ever had. I just needed to get her off.

I could feel the tension in her body as she became more aroused. She was getting closer. I couldn't touch her with my hands, but I could change the angle if I leaned back more. So I did, bracing the both of us with my arms on the back of the bench. At that angle, I felt myself rub against the spot I'd been searching for inside her. Her blue eyes fluttered and she licked her blood red lips with hunger.

"Yes, yes like that. Right there," she ordered me through a cry of pleasure that I was determined to hear again. I flexed my hips higher, meeting her movements and rocking her back and forth above me.

"Grab my ass," she ordered, apparently deciding she wanted my hands on her now. I immediately searched beneath the white skirt for those perfect ass cheeks. I squeezed them, using her backside to pull her over me faster. I started to lose control of my focus as we sped up. I fucked her harder than I've ever fucked a woman in my life.

"Yes, that's it. That's it! Don't you dare fucking stop!" The Mistress cried out. Her wet pussy clenched me in a fluttering frenzy while I kept on pumping into her. She drenched my cock with a fresh wave of juices as she came. Her moans were throaty and wild as she throbbed deliciously around my cock. I clenched my jaw and I held my breath. I prayed to the Goddess that I wouldn't finish. I was so close, it would take only a moment more to set me over the edge.

Her hips rolled slowly to grind against me as she savored her pleasure for a minute more. The slowing of friction lowered the intensity and I exhaled in relief that I hadn't orgasmed against her wishes. My relief was followed by disappointment as she abruptly lifted off of me. She smoothed her skirt down over her thighs and sighed loudly. Smiling, she stretched like a cat in a windowsill waking from a nap.

"That was very nice, Zsash," she said, tousling a golden strand out of her face.

"Thank you, Mistress," I panted, thoroughly spent.

"Kneel at my feet, slave," she ordered. I knelt down on my knees in front of her white boots. She lifted her perfect leg to rest a spiked heel on my shoulder. "Place your hand on my ankle and worship my boot, slave." I turned my head and began kissing the leather. I could see her gold-crowned cunt glistening and pink beneath her skirt, while I licked the pristine white leather.

"With your other hand, jerk your cock for me so I can watch," she commanded. I shuddered in relief as I gripped myself tightly, still wet with her cum. It only took a few strokes before I was close again. I jerked myself hard and fast, kissing her boot and moaning. But, I wasn't going to make the same mistake I did yesterday.

"May I please cum for you, Mistress?" I begged between licking her boot and breathing hard. My brow dripped with sweat. She bit her lower lip and watched me with an intense look of satisfaction while she intentionally delayed her answer. I stopped my worship of her boot to look up at her, still pulling my hard cock mercilessly.

"Beg me," she said, pressing her heel into my shoulder harder. The pain made me impossibly more aroused.

"Please, Mistress, may I please cum?"

"More." She answered quietly.

"Please...Oh, Mistress, please. Please, please may I cum for you?" I was at the edge of finishing. Each movement of my hand making the tension more unbearable while I begged and worshipped her boot. I pleaded for release from the pressure, even with my mouth occupied against leather.

"Please....Mistress....please, please Mistress, may I cum?" I repeated for what seemed like an eternity.

"You may." She said finally.

"Oh fuck...Oh fuck...." I hissed through my teeth as I came. Her command had cracked open the barrier of my restraint

172

and pleasure now grabbed me by the throat. I cried out while my cock pulsed, spurting thick shots of cum till it dripped over my hand onto the floor. My other hand still gripped her boot to my shoulder as I arched my hips and thrust into my fist violently.

Oh Goddess, that was so fucking good.

Eventually, my grunts faded into sighs as I knelt before her.

The Mistress watched me with a satisfactory smile on her lips. My cries had ignited embers in her still gaze as she enjoyed watching me climax. My mind had not cleared yet, when she removed her boot from my shoulder. I looked up at her, my eyes still hazy and out of focus. She leaned over and kissed my shuddering lips, softly this time, with more compassion than our entire sexual encounter. Almost apologetically, she ran her talons through my damp hair.

Then she said, "I am pleased with your progress, slave. The third step to appreciation will take longer than the first two."

"Yes, Mistress. Whatever you command," I swallowed. My heartbeat slowly returned to a sane pace. Her face hardened as she spoke.

"You and Corvas will both serve as my offerings to the Cheritoth games for the Blossoming Celebration. The two of you will fight to the death and solve this rivalry."

Blood rushed to my ears. My heart caught in my chest. With eyes wide in new and sudden fear, I fought back a waver in my voice.

"But…I am not a fighter, Mistress."

"If you want to live, you will become one."

I nodded. "As my Mistress commands," I said, bowing my head.

"In the meantime, I have new chores in relation to your continued punishment. Since you could not keep yourself out of trouble when left unsupervised, you will spend your daytime helping Garsteel in the blacksmith shop from now on before giving me my bath. That should keep you plenty busy."

"Yes, Mistress," I said, instead of bringing up that I was no more a blacksmith than I was a fighter. None of that mattered to the Mistress.

"You're doing very well, my pet. Do not be discouraged just because what I ask of you is difficult," she said, running her fingers along my cheek before giving it a slap. The slap probably stung, but I didn't feel it.

"More than any other emotion, fear affects the actions of animals. Fear of pain. Fear of loss. Fear of death. You cannot escape the fear because you are an animal. However, fear is not a weakness unless you let it decide your fate. In the hands of a practiced slave, fear can be sharpened and wielded like a fine-edged weapon."

Landryl, *The Scrolls of the Goddess*

CHAPTER 11: SLIP

Have you ever had that moment the morning after a night of hard sex, where you forget what you did the night before and you sit up in bed too fast? That's what I woke to the next day. My stomach muscles were so sore. I laughed for a second, remembering why they hurt. Which hurt some more to laugh.

And then I remembered the rest.

Oh, yeah. I was going to die in three months.

It kind of took the fun out of the glory sex with the Mistress the day before.

I wasn't entirely sure what to wear to the blacksmith shop since I assumed that I'd be cleaning stables and such. I would most likely be sweaty and covered in shit. I opted for heavy boots, a pair of brown pants and a red shirt that already had a hole in the armpit.

The stables were attached to the blacksmith shop in one large building with two access points and walls to separate them. On the left, I could see into the blacksmith shop. A fire pit of embers burned and everywhere there hung metal. Swords, axes, various armor for the guards, a great many blades and tools used in the cane fields. In one corner was a great deal of gold plated weapons and armor. I assumed those must have been for the Mistress. The stables held enough stalls for perhaps fifty horses, though it was only about half full.

As I stood there waiting for Garsteel, I was startled by a soft pressure against my boot. I looked down to see a fox rubbing against my leg. It looked up at me with speckled amber eyes and cocked its head to the side, blinking expectantly.

"Well, hello," I said, leaning down to pet behind its ears. I'd never seen a fox this close up. I expected it to run off after a few moments, but it didn't. It just sat at my feet and let me pet it. He had dark orange fur and a white tipped tail, with fluffy cheeks and a smile tucked under his pointed black nose. I rubbed his ears together and his eyes shut happily.

"Careful," a voice called my attention and I stopped petting the fox. I looked up to see Garsteel walking out from one of the horse stalls. "That little shit'll start following you everywhere if you give him attention. I fed him once and he keeps coming back around. Damn thing thinks he's a dog, I imagine." As soon as he heard Garsteel's voice, the fox ran to him and jumped up into his arms. Garsteel scratched the fox's ears affectionately. "This is Tark. He guards the shop. Keeps it free of vermin."

I hadn't ever met Garsteel but I had seen him before. He was the slave who had been staring at me in the dining hall while smoking his pipe months ago. Garsteel was taller than me and wider with a barrel of a chest. He had a little bit of a fat, jolly belly on him despite how much muscle he had, which was significant. He was clearly the sort that had worked hard physical labor his entire life. He dressed in black leather pants and a white cotton shirt that was smeared with ash. A black head scarf covered his hair except for his long grey ponytail trailing down his shoulder. I noticed deep scaring at his wrists from being in manacles and wondered if his back bore the scars of a disobedient slave, like mine did.

In his ear, he wore a silver hoop that I almost missed since it blended with his hair so well. He also bore a fancy silver collar, clearly a personal gift from the Mistress. It didn't exactly match the rest of his appearance. His dirty, worn and weathered skin made the silver collar stand out. He met me with a broad smile that gleamed behind his ruddy skin as he arched an eyebrow at me.

"So, the one gold slave, is it?" he set the little fox down and then folded his arms over his chest.

I laughed and shook my head. "How did everyone find out about that?"

"Oh, well, you know how prevalent gossip is. Anything different that makes you stand out becomes gossip-worthy. You've had more than a couple instances that have gotten you attention." He stepped out from the horse pen and shut it behind him.

"You seem a little too seasoned to be spreading gossip," I said.

"Well, I don't spread gossip much, but I sure do enjoy listening to it. Keeps me entertained. Seems a few of the slaves around here like to talk about you."

"I don't know why. I'm pretty boring," I shrugged.

"Really? A slave who mouthed off at the auction and got himself bought with one gold coin? Boring?"

"Yeah, well…" I shuffled my feet, both uncomfortable and proud that I was being talked about.

He continued. "Who shared a coveted kiss with a household slave."

"Nothing happened."

"Who pleasured half the interior slave girls into a panting nasty mess."

I shrugged. "Okay, that happened," I laughed with no small amount of pride.

"A bath slave who got into a tussle with the guard captain and lived? Who now has an ultimate fight to the death in the Cheritoth?"

"Yeah…" I looked down at my shoes again. I weighed these factors in my head. I guess I had managed to be gossip-worthy in the last few months. I was also secretly thankful that either my theft of the Mistress's underwear had gone unknown by the rumor circle or at least Garsteel was nice enough not to bring it up.

"You're the most entertaining story we've had on this estate in a long time. Most of the rest of us just do our work. Eat, sleep, drink, fuck a little here and there. Nothing legendary."

"That's a shame. What will you all talk about after I'm gone?" I joked, but a little sullen bitterness crept in.

"You planning on going somewhere?"

I sighed. "Well unless a miracle happens for me, I'm assuming I'll be dead after too long."

"Yes, that would be a shame." He pursed his lips and nodded. "Well, your ass is mine until that time anyway. I'll put you to work here in the stables and in the smithing shop. Are you good at anything?"

"I used to think so." I said softly, my tone melancholy as my thoughts had stolen my good mood from me.

His brow furrowed for a moment and his eyes narrowed some in, I'm assuming, irritation.

And then he slapped me in the face.

It was more jarring than painful. But it surprised the shit out of me and flipped my sadness to sudden anger.

"Knock that self pity shit off! You don't have time for it. Come on, I'm asking you a serious question. What are you good at?"

"I don't know!" I shrugged, stammering. "Uh, music and art I suppose. Singing, percussion, sculpting..." I thought about it for another moment. "I'm pretty good at sex but I doubt that's going to come into play."

"Less likely," he shrugged. "So, sculpting and percussion. I can work with that." He waved for me to follow him. We walked out of the stables next door to the smithing shop. Tark followed us with light feet, pattering past us to sit on a perch above the coal pit. He curled up in a ball with his tail wrapped around him and watched us lazily from above.

I hadn't noticed while standing outside how dark it was in the shop. Canvas shades were pulled down low over each of the windows, only allowing in dim light from outside.

"It's so dark in here. How do you see what you're doing?"

"Your eyes will adjust enough. It needs to be dark to see the colors in the metal."

I followed him over to the large fire pit where a few pieces of metal sat in the embers, heating up. "You've never done any blacksmithing have you?"

"None."

"Well, here is your first lesson."

He tossed me a pair of heavy leather gloves and put on a pair of his own. Then he picked up a set of iron tongs and began pointing at some of the blades.

"Shaping metal is an easy enough idea to grasp. Mastering it, well, that's going to take us much longer than three months. But we'll start here. When iron gets hot it will start to glow. First red, then orange, then yellow, then white. The hotter it is, the easier it is to manipulate, but it can also ruin the strength of the metal. The best color for drawing out the metal, which is what I'm going to have you do, is this." He took the tongs and reached for a sword that was mostly orange with a slight tint of yellow. "This point right between orange and yellow is the best temperature for lengthening metal. You'll need to do more at the tip to give it a point. For now, you'll just do this." He set the glowing half of the blade on an anvil next to the fire pit. Picking up a hammer, he began a series of strikes to the metal in three hard bursts. Clang, clang, clang. Rest. Clang clang clang. Rest. "You're wanting to push the metal toward the tip. Hit it a few times then move about a half inch lower and repeat it. You get the idea."

"Yeah," I nodded. He set the blade back in the fire and handed me the tongs and hammer.

"Off you go then."

Picking them up, I wondered if I might get more tan just standing near the fire. My skin felt like it was baking. I picked up the sword blade with the tongs and began to imitate what he had done.

"A little harder, Zsash," he said.

"I hear that all the time," I said with a wink over my shoulder at him. He scoffed and smiled against his will.

"I know you think you're joking, but rhythm is rhythm. In the bedroom or music. Being a blacksmith has a fair amount to with pacing yourself at tempo so your strikes are even."

"Yeah, girls love a blacksmith," I laughed with a smirk.

"Brother, you don't even know. Keep at it," he laughed.

And I did.

Strike, strike, strike, rest. Strike, strike, strike, rest. After a bit of that, I moved my hammer a half inch lower. Strike, strike, strike, rest. Strike, strike, strike, rest. Repeat forever.

"Now, you want to make sure your work is always heating while you shape the others. If you only worked on one blade at a time, it would take you forever to finish one. Have a few blades heating while you work on one. Once that one has started to cool back to red, put it back in the fire and start working on another one."

He pulled out one of the blades himself and started to work on another anvil nearby. It took me about ten minutes of blacksmithing to realize four things I hadn't known before.

One, this blade was going to take forever.

Two, my arm was already killing me.

Three, I was certainly still being punished.

Four, I liked Garsteel.

I hammered on those damned swords all day. They were actually getting longer. Less like square pieces of iron and more like blades. It was slow going, which made it nice to have someone to talk to while working. We discussed how he had belonged to Queen Crystavieve before the Mistress inherited him. How he'd known Mistress Isavyne since she was a baby. It seemed odd and made me uncomfortable, the idea of telling him about my various sexual encounters with her. The way he talked about her was much more paternal. He was still humble and submissive but in a proud, protective way. He spoke with great enthusiasm about Mistress Crystavieve.

"The Mistress and her mother used to fight a lot. But I think she still has a lot of regrets about her mother's death."

"How did her mother die?" I asked over the clang of metal.

"She was killed by another Master over business. A real smooth-talking piece of shit king named Trumble. The cane industry is huge, much more than I can wrap my head around. I think Master Trumble thought he could kill Queen Crystavieve and force the—then—Princess Isavyne's hand with intimidation. It did not work out so well for him. That fucker certainly tasted the fire of Mistress Isavyne's anger." He laughed as he pounded out a few more strikes on his iron.

"Has she killed many other monarchs?" I asked.

"Not many. The Mistress isn't some cold death dealer, but she also doesn't tolerate games. She may not kill many, but I'll wager there's more than a few Masters with scars from our beloved Queen."

I found myself pounding metal instead of flesh for the first time in my life. Blacksmithing is an art of patience. Like painting or sculpture, except you're painting with a tiny brush or sculpting with only one finger. Garsteel showed me how to use the smaller hammers to get detail out of a piece of metal. And how to narrow down the tip of the sword to make it pointed and sharp.

"You're really going to use this technique once we're making daggers or the small points of some of the gardening tools," Garsteel said to me. "But, the guards need blades to fight off the beasties in the far edges of our property."

"Like wyrlings?" I asked.

"Hmph, wyrlings," he said through a frown and his nostrils flared with disgust. "They follow the water. Whole packs of them traveling along the sea and streams. I don't know how there got to be so many of them. At first it was just runaway slaves with some creature in them. The ones out there now are bred in the wild.

Raised as beasts with no sense of civilization or the Goddess's law. They rape and eat the flesh of any creature they can get their hands on."

My mind suddenly flashed to the sea wyrlings and how they had started to bite and tear at me. How they almost tore me to pieces, even while seducing me. I hadn't realized until just then how disturbing the idea of being eaten was to me. I felt a little shudder run down my back.

After working on the swords for most of the day, both my arms were burning for me to stop using them. I had to keep trading arms to keep striking. It had taken me the better part of the day, but one of the swords was finally getting to be somewhat sword-shaped, when Garsteel looked with concern out the window.

"You should probably grab some food and get clean in order to give the Mistress her bath."

I looked out the window and seeing the darkening orange color of the sky I knew I didn't have any time for food. I placed my hammer down and mumbled something about seeing him tomorrow. Then I ran out of the smithing shop.

Racing through the rose garden toward the castle, I passed by interior and grounds slaves on their way to the dining hall. My empty stomach cried out bitterly in envy.

As I passed the fountain, I saw movement from the rose bushes that grabbed my attention enough to get me to stop. It was just the faintest rustle that could have been the wind or a rabbit. I wouldn't have even heard it if I hadn't been standing right there with so much silence. I glanced over to see a streak of grey running away from the rose bushes and around the castle wall. The same grey figure I'd seen in the Mistresses room the night Corvas had nearly had me beaten to death. It was the thief!

If I'd actually thought about it, I probably wouldn't have followed. I was exhausted. Both my arms were basically useless. I needed to get the Mistress her bath on time. But I ran after the figure, chasing it around the castle. They made their way between the thorny branches of the rose bushes that crawled up the stone walls, hiding.

"Stop! Thief!" I shouted, as if I had some kind of authority. The movement stopped suddenly. I frantically searched the bushes.

"Reveal yourself! You're caught!"

"Am I?" said a soft high voice from the thorns in front of me. The thief leapt toward me from the bushes, amazingly, she hardly rustled a branch. Her hands punched me in the chest hard enough that I fell backward. I landed roughly on my back and looked up to find a woman dressed in grey, crouched across my body. Her feet were tucked together making a little L shape at the top of my thighs while her hands pressed down on my chest. And though she weighed next to nothing, I found myself held there. Something about the way she balanced herself against my joints kept me from raising myself from the ground.

The grey hood had fallen back, revealing pale white skin. Not fair, but sickly pale white. Her head and face were covered with the same grey material as the rest of her clothes, except for her eyes. Bright shimmering eyes the color of pink topaz burned down at me with amusement. They appeared to glow against her light skin. A single lock of pale, white hair had escaped the grey head scarf under the hood, dangling down toward my body.

"I cannot tell if you are very skilled or very stupid to keep catching up to me like this" the thief mused.

"I seem able to occupy both standards simultaneously." I smiled up at her, then tried to raise myself again with no result. She let out a series of small jittery squeaking giggles that sounded like a child's laughter mixed with the chittering of a squirrel.

"You are just adorable, aren't you?" she said. Her mouth moved below the fabric in what I assumed was a smile. "What a shame."

She shook her head, then small warm hands wrapped around my throat. I struggled but couldn't seem to get out from under my tiny attacker. Two thoughts occurred to me as I felt my throat being crushed. First, why did everyone try to kill me? And second, maybe I shouldn't fight it. It was either here or public humiliation in the ring. At least this would be private. It also had the benefit of going out with a woman laying across my body. It was not exactly what I had in mind for my death, but it could certainly be worse.

I am embarrassed to say that during those five to ten seconds while she choked me I came to the conclusion that I would be all right with this as my end.

But the Goddess seemed to have other plans.

Garsteel appeared and grabbed the woman from behind, pulling her off of me. I sat up and coughed to regain my breath. Garsteel had the woman's throat in the crook of his arm and he attempted to bring his hand over his bicep. She tucked down and slipped out of his grasp. Tumbling forward she then sprang up, holding a slip knife. It flew from her hand in a swift graceful motion toward Garsteel.

"No!" I shouted. To my surprise, he rolled his shoulder out of the way and dodged to the side. Moving his hand toward his belt he suddenly held several slip knives of his own. They were dark black solid metal blades. More crude than the secret blade I'd found on the beach. But they flew true. He threw two at the pink-eyed woman and then armed himself with a third. She dodged one and caught the other. Her gaze then snapped over to me where she threw the knife.

I'm not exactly sure how I did this, but I caught it! I guess it could have been due to all the nights I spent playing with the knife in my room. It surprised of all three of us, I imagine.

I readied the knife in my hand to use it if she attacked me again.

The pink eyed woman shifted her head slightly to the left, as sounds of feet approached from the front of the castle. She pulled two more knives from her belt and ran toward Garsteel. I ran toward him as well in an attempt to help him fight her off. As she got close enough to engage him, she jumped over him instead with an incredible leap that cleared both of us by two body lengths. She then ran and we followed.

"Thief! Thief on the grounds! Guards!" Garsteel shouted as we chased after her. She was so fast. Unnaturally fast. In moments we lost sight of her. The guards were there just as swiftly and pursued the intruder.

"Let me see that knife," Garsteel said as the guards ran off. I handed it to him and he inspected it. "That's a fine piece of work. Too fine."

"Its balance is perfect. Have you ever seen metalwork that good?"

"Not often, and not in a slave's hands, that you can be sure of," he balanced the knife on the tip of his thumb for a moment. He let it stand straight and vertical before flipping it around his hand and back into his palm.

Then he said heavily, "No way that's some wyrling bitch running around on her own. That slave channels something fast and was gifted with blades of incredible quality. It means she's trained as an assassin for one of the royals. Is that the woman who you bumped into the night Corvas and his boys gave you that sound beating?"

"Yes. Just like I said."

"I will let the Mistress know what happened tonight when she returns, and that it seems you were telling the truth."

"Thank you!" I said, feeling elated. Someone else had seen the woman in grey! Garsteel could verify that I hadn't lied to the Mistress. This made me happier than I had been in a while. "I don't understand, though. She was taking the Mistress's underwear. That doesn't sound like an assassin to me."

"There are plenty of creatures in this world that need a scent to track prey. You give hounds an article of clothing to track if you want to find someone. If someone was going to train something to attack a Queen, you might give it a piece of intimate apparel."

"Goddess...What can we do to protect the Mistress?" I asked.

"You'll do nothing. I'll make sure it's taken care of. Now, you get on up to the tower and get her bath ready. I'll come get you in the morning."

I nodded. I wanted to help, but I realized that it wasn't my place. And again, what exactly was I going to do to protect the Mistress? She was plenty strong all on her own and she had a contingent of guard slaves. I'll admit, I had a small, terrible prayer that maybe Corvas would die fighting wyrlings before the blossoming celebration so that I wouldn't have to fight him. I doubted I would get that lucky, though.

After the ordeal, I went up to the tower and expected to find the Mistress there, displeased with me. However, when I got upstairs, the Mistress wasn't there.

I ran the bath and waited for an hour. The Mistress did not show up. That was unusual. Most of the time if the bath was cancelled she would leave a note or send Khessi. I wanted to tell the Mistress about the thief and how it was the woman I had seen before. Hopefully, Garsteel would back me up on what had happened. After a few hours, I went down to Khessi's office to find out if the Mistress was still coming to have her bath.

Khessi's office was empty as well. Where were Khessi and the Mistress? I supposed it was not as though they needed to give me warning if they were both going to be gone, but I was filled with a sudden and strange concern for their whereabouts. What if they were in trouble somewhere? I tried to brush this off as my blood still being up from the thief attacking me.

"Shit…" I huffed as I passed a school of yellow and blue fish that followed my footsteps.

"The Mistress took Khessi with her on a business engagement," a voice said from behind me. Sira appeared holding a feather duster and ran it up the front of my shirt.

"Do you know when they are getting back?"

She scoffed, "Not for a day or so, I think." She ran the feather duster lower and between my legs.

"Stop," I said, knocking it away.

"Why don't you tear my clothes off and take me on this desk, right here?"

"What?"

"I'd like it if that bitchy household slave could smell our sex every time she counts the Mistress's gold," she laughed and tried to kiss me. Anger rose in her eyes as I pushed her away.

"I'm not really in the mood," I said coldly.

"Mood? Are you kidding me? You've been in the mood for months."

"Well, I'm not right now."

"You don't have moods, bath slave! You're a fuck machine. That's all you're good for and it's what you like to do anyway, so what's your problem?" She reached between my legs but I grabbed her wrist, pulling it away from me.

"I said stop, Sira."

"Goddess's tits! Are you actually sweet on the household slave, Zsash? She's not interested in you, you know. She's not interested in anything except pleasing the Mistress."

"Look, some other time, okay? I've got a lot on my mind right now," I said, trying to keep my tone light.

"No. You're going to fuck me now!" she sneered.

I'd never seen her features look uglier.

"I think you're overestimating my interest in fucking you. You're a nice enough girl, Sira, but you're not the Mistress. Don't presume that you can order me to do anything. Just leave me alone! I've got to get back to work," I said, knowing I had no work left to do. I walked past her a few steps before she shouted at me.

"Hey, Zsash! From now on if you want get off you can go fuck yourself! Because you're not getting any from me anymore! And you sure as shit aren't getting any from the other girls!"

I turned back to see her long-lashed eyes wide and nostrils flaring. I almost laughed at how worked up she had gotten over not getting her own way. I didn't realize my dick was something to throw a fit over. I opened my mouth to say something shitty. I then realized none of it mattered. I turned back around and left Khessi's office, ignoring the rest of her tirade.

The next morning I was awakened by a grizzled face way too close to mine for comfort.

"Time to train, pretty boy!" Garsteel said loudly.

I bolted upright and moaned at the sudden pain moving had caused in my stiff arms. Garsteel reached into my wardrobe and began grabbing random clothes and throwing them at me. A white shirt and pair of pants, my boots from off the floor. One of the boots hit me in the face.

"Yeah, yeah. I'm up!" I said, standing and stepping into the pants. "For fucks sake, you don't have to get me out of bed like it's on fire."

"Hey, that's a good idea."

I regretted saying that.

He's joking, right? Oh please Goddess, don't let him set my bed on fire.

The sun had barely crept over the horizon. The morning air was chilly, though not freezing. It was the type of morning that begged for a hot cider with breakfast. That thought made my stomach grumble as we headed for the blacksmith shop.

"What are we doing up this early?" I groaned, following him.

"You're going to learn how to use slip knives."

"Um, all right."

"You showed a lot of promise with them last night. Since you don't have a lot of time to learn, you'll need to practice."

"I'm not sure how much promise I have with fighting. I've always been really proficient at getting my ass kicked."

"I think you're going to learn pretty damn quick since your life is on the line."

"If you say so," I shrugged.

"I did say so. And," he turned around to face me. I stopped in my tracks so I didn't bump into him. "You can knock off that sad puppy routine you've had going on."

"She's sending me to die. I'm little upset about it."

"Yup. It's upsetting to realize you're expendable. But she's giving you a chance to save yourself. Don't be a pussy about it."

His stern look cracked into a smile on the side of his mouth. And I laughed.

"All right, all right. Teach me how to use the knives."

I followed Garsteel into the blacksmith shop where there was a pile of slip knives on the wooden bench. They resembled a heap of small black metal bits that looked as though they were castoffs from various projects. I picked one up and noticed immediately that its balance wasn't anything near as perfect as Secret or the pink topaz girl's knife. In the corner was a large leather doll, human in form, with red and purple lines running down in a pattern like roots. Garsteel picked up a slip knife and threw it. The black metal whistled through the air and landed in the small painted dot that fashioned the eye of the leather man. He threw a second slip knife that hit it in the other eye. Two knives stood straight out where the eyes of the man would have been.

"Nice," I nodded my head. "The old poke 'em in the eye defense. It's a classic."

"Slip fighting isn't for guards and warriors," Garsteel said, continuing to throw knives with accuracy into the leather body. "It's for our kind of fighter."

"And what kind of fighter are we?" I asked with cynicism.

"The sneak. The assassin. The opportunity killer. Slip fighters use speed and accuracy, over power. Slip knives are small, delicate blades. Easy to flip and curl around your fingers. That can add speed and velocity to a strike. They are not built to slice through muscle or bone, but to slash veins and sever tendons. The idea is to inflict mortal wounds with minimal damage. Understand?"

I nodded. "I do. Go on."

"The man is a puppet on strings, but the strings are on the inside. Cut the right strings and the puppet won't move." He threw another knife into the leather man's shoulders. "Cut the right arteries and the puppet bleeds out." Another knife landed in the leather man's throat. "You know the human body right? You know muscles and the pathways blood takes?"

"Yes. Quite thoroughly, actually, because of massage training." My interest piqued as I started to grasp what he said. I was pretty sure I could do this kind of fighting.

"Ha! Massage," Garsteel laughed. "Death by massage," he chortled with a blade in his hand, before sending it flying into the groin of the leather man. I swallowed, uncomfortably.

And so, I trained. I trained like a fucking maniac. I hammered steel, threw blades and of course, bathed the Mistress every night.

By the end of the month, a day of smithing no longer hurt my arms. With my new strength, the slip knives rocketed from my fingers the more I worked with my hands.

I was obsessed with learning the knives, not just because my life depended on it. I was learning that I might be good at something I never conceived of previously. I was learning that I might not be terrible at fighting. My hand-to-hand fighting was still terrible, but I could throw the shit out of those knives!

The Mistress still seemed like she had more important things on her mind. To be honest, I didn't have much left in me by the end of each day. Silently soaking in hot water each evening with the occasional massage and refilling wine was really all right by me. Though I bathed her every night, she didn't speak to me much those days. She also didn't engage any of my sexual skills. I was upset about that for a moment until I thought about how much energy it would take if she actually did request it.

I became increasingly worried about the Mistress. She didn't seem her usual, teasing self. She would sit staring into the distance with an intense furrow in her brow.

Khessi, too, was a rare sight during that time, not that she wasn't around. She continued to flitter around the estate doing her daily checklists. However, I was occupied all day as well. The most I could do was nod or wave as I passed her. We didn't really get a chance to talk during this time, either.

Each night, I would lay in bed exhausted, but fiddling with the knives. Twirling them around my fingers, learning their balance. Learning how to manipulate the blade to hide in my palm or throw it when I wanted to.

Day after day, I was consumed by metal and heat.

I started to develop a kinship with the iron in my hands. I thought to myself that I was like the metal. A man can be like a piece of iron. Raw, without purpose. Set a fire to him, get him hot. Enough strikes and pressure and he'll either break or be tempered. Grind him to the core and he starts to get an edge to him, until one day, he has become something else.

Something sharp.
Something dangerous.

"Do not think that because the Goddess shines her face upon you that it will always be so. Be grateful for every kindness you receive and every hurt as well. For they are all experiences that you have been graced with as an alternative to death."

Riquora, *The Scrolls of the Goddess*

CHAPTER 12: GIFTS

The day before we were to head to the palace, Garsteel told me we wouldn't train that day. Honestly, I had no idea what to do with myself given the choice. I'd been busting my ass for the last three months so hard that to rest felt lazy and like a waste of time.

It was one of the first warm mornings after winter, so I pulled on my silver pants that were still in my closet. They were lightweight and comfortable. No shirt or shoes. I wanted to feel the breeze on my skin and the grass in my toes. I wanted to enjoy the day. As I was headed down to get breakfast, I walked past a large mirror and for the first time in three months, really stopped to look at myself.

My first thought was that I'd seen the reflection of one of the guards out of the corner of my eye. Turns out, it was me.

I looked good! I had definition and muscle I'd never seen before. I was still not as bulky as the guards, but my arms and back muscles were, well, impressive. Not the muscle of warriors exactly, but the muscles of a man who worked with his hands and body all day long. All that hammering had paid off. Muscles stood out when I turned my forearm over. I flexed my arms to see how they changed when I raised them over my head. I stood there marveling at my new definition in the mirror in what was probably the vainest maneuver ever.

Which, of course, was the moment Khessi came around the corner and caught me flexing at myself in the mirror. I tried unsuccessfully to look casual as I lowered my arms.

"What are you doing?" she said, raising her hand to cover the laughter on her lips.

"Nothing," I answered, feeling my face flush. "I was just... heading down to breakfast."

"You seem to have been keeping very busy these last few months," she said with calculated tones.

"You, too."

" What I mean is, you look...well." Khessi exhaled as she looked me up and down. I stood up a little straighter.

"You look beautiful," I said. "But that's no surprise. You always look beautiful."

She brushed a lock of hair behind her ear toward a blue flower that decorated it. The blue in the flower made her eyes stand out. She wore a dress of forest green accented with purple gems and a shawl that wrapped around her shoulders. The diamonds of her restraints glittered in the morning sun. Her lips were the color of lilacs.

"Shall I walk with you for a moment?" she asked. "I was hoping we could talk."

"Of course," I offered my arm to her, casually flexing. She took it and we began walking down the long corridor toward the main door.

"Have you ever been to an imperial gathering? Or any gathering with many members of royalty?" she asked me.

"No imperial gatherings. Master Azur would occasionally entertain a few monarchs at the training house, but no more than ten, I suppose."

"Conducting oneself in the presence of the courts is far different than here on the estate. I wanted to give you a few guidelines to follow."

"Sure. This is your arena so I'll take any tips you can give me."

"First piece of advice. Always stay close to the Mistress."

"Okay." I nodded.

"Second, maintain the utmost humility and formality."

I scoffed. "But of course."

"Third, don't speak unless directly addressed."

"It's like I was born for palace life." I chuckled but stopped as she gripped my arm harder with concern.

"I mean it, Zsash! No talking unless spoken to. Obviously not to the monarchy, but not even to other slaves."

This made me pause.

"Why shouldn't I talk to other slaves? Maybe it would be nice to make some friends at the palace."

"No one at the palace is your friend. Trust me. Even if they wish to be. They are all potential enemies to be used by their monarch. Do you understand? You don't need to develop any new friends *or* enemies in the other estates."

"I got it. Should the Emperor himself address me, I will look to the Mistress before I answer."

Her eyes widened and she exhaled, "Goddess, let's hope that doesn't happen!"

"I'm sure the Emperor has better things to do."

"Emperor Dukkar has a special interest in the Mistress. Goddess forbid he actually proposes marriage to her," she looked around, idly clenching her jaw.

"Why would that be so bad? Wouldn't marrying the Emperor be the best thing a Queen could hope for?" I shrugged.

"Things are not so simple. The Mistress does seem to like him. But, she favors Master Braxian as well. We'll have to see if either wins her heart."

"Well, she's pretty sharp. I'm sure she can figure out which man has her best interests at heart."

"Let's hope." Khessi sighed. "I just wanted to tell you, that I hope you..." She struggled with the words. "I wanted to wish you luck tomorrow."

She stopped walking and turned toward me. Her eyes stared down and her head slightly bowed. The rim of her lovely eyelashes kissed the tops of her cheeks. She licked her lips.

"Khessi, if I survive this, could you and I..." I weighed my words, "...talk more? I know you have concerns about what others will think."

"Slaves don't mingle with the household slave. It's just not common."

"Well, fuck being common!" I barked, and she looked up at me with a smile. "They're all cowards. They're afraid you'll tell the Mistress something unfavorable about them. I don't have anything else to fear. The Mistress already knows the worst of me."

"And the best," she added.

"I have nothing to hide anymore. Why would I shy away from being your friend?"

She smiled again, still not daring to look into my eyes. "That would be nice," she said softly.

I lifted her chin to get her to look at me. "Khessi, you have been so kind to me, many times when you've had no cause to. You've been good to me when I've treated you like shit. And I would like to learn more about you. I promise I can stop talking about myself from time to time."

"Sadly, there is nothing to know about me really. I just serve the Mistress."

"No! Goddess, no!" I said more forcefully than I'd planned on. "I know you have dreams and thoughts beyond your service in there. You are more than your orders. Of course, you do as the Mistress commands. But you are compassionate when you don't need to be. And loyal before it's reciprocated. You're kind when you've no cause to trust. Especially to someone like me."

I released her chin and she leaned her smile in toward me as if to tell me a secret.

"You know, Zsash, perhaps it is because I'm not supposed to carry favorites with any slaves of the estate, but you have endeared yourself to me somehow…"

I was surprised to find her eyes glossy with emotion. Slowly, intentionally she lifted up onto her tiptoes and kissed me on the cheek. Her breath warmed my skin and I felt flush. It was completely unlike our previous encounter which had been desperate with passion. This moment drew me in as so precious and fragile that it made my heart hurt. Her hand rested on my clean-shaven face for what I felt would be the last time. The unfairness of that resonated in my chest and made me feel bitter.

A moment later she lowered herself back to the ground with a nearly tangible disappointment at the absence of her mouth on my skin. She reached up and plucked the blue flower from her hair and placed it in my hand. A favor. A symbol of her affection. I was overwhelmed with sadness but I was also grateful.

"Thank you." I whispered.

"Take care of yourself," she said. Then she turned with a swish of green and purple and walked back the way we came. From that moment on, one of my biggest regrets was not grabbing her around the waist and pulling her lips against mine. I should have kissed her. I should have fucking kissed her! Just one last time before I died. I would go to my death regretting not taking that opportunity.

The fact of my impending death suddenly became more real to me than ever before. I was probably going to die tomorrow. It's silly really, to be surprised by it. Everything in this world dies. Everyone knows this, but it never really seemed like a real possibility.

My thoughts of mortality led me to wander the grounds of the estate. Lost in thought, I wandered through the cane fields, watching grounds slaves harvest the plants. Vibrant pink flowers grew on the long reedy shafts that were trimmed into one basket, while the shafts of the plant were cut and loaded into bundles. I traveled away from the ocean, uninterested in running into more wyrlings along the beach.

I found myself in a lightly wooded area beyond the fields. I realized I moved that way because of the colors. The red and pink of the cane fields slowly faded into green grass and blue flowers. I looked at the blue flower in my hand from Khessi and realized that this must be where she got it from. As I walked further into the blue flowers at my calves I saw a grove planted with a row of blood red trees. Their long vines and thin branches hung down almost to the ground and swayed softly in the cool evening breeze. Tucked in the center of these trees were a series of white stone columns that held intricately carved rooftops. Red beaded curtains that resembled the trees color, veiled the eight entryways to what I realized was a temple. This was a temple to the Goddess where slaves could come to pray.

I wished suddenly that I had spent more time talking with my creator. It seemed an empty gesture to beg for forgiveness now. But, I wanted to leave this world as best I could. My heavy feet carried me to the first of the eight entryways. I ran my hands over the cool beads that swayed calmly in the midday breeze and pushed them aside. I stepped past the beads and onto the stone floor of the temple and there she was.

The stone idol of the Goddess stood tall in the large white room. The slave priestesses of the temple carved beautiful statues of our beloved Goddess out of blue lapis with the most intricate detail. Bright sparkling rubies were set into the eyes and matched the red of her painted lips. Her fingers, too, were painted red to the knuckles on her hands and along her toes. This depiction of the Goddess was draped in a top and skirt made of long sweeping red velvet that hung down over her breasts and hips. She wore red pearls that hung from her neck and shoulders.

The idol stood on a stand of pure gold while the stairs below it were plain stone. Those steps were littered with offerings. Various flowers, many of them blue, crystals, pretty shells or rocks and even food were scattered down them. A row of eight lit candles lined the front stair. They cast a soft glow that played in the large rubies of her eyes, giving them a flash of life as they glittered in the flickering light. Resting directly in front of the Goddess's red tipped feet was a bowl filled with sacred water.

This is where I found Master Braxian knelt in prayer. He looked up at me with recognition in his eyes, even though we'd never spoken.

"Zsash?" he asked, pointing. He got to his feet and walked toward me. Good Goddess, he was fucking huge. He wore a navy tunic in a snakeskin pattern with diamonds lining the high collar. His undershirt split low in the chest to show off his superior muscles. Not on accident, I'm sure.

"Yes, Master," I said, bowing my head and placing my hands behind my back in submission.

"That's one serious scar you have," he said, gesturing at my chest.

"Yes, Master. I almost forgot it was there," I said with unintended sarcasm.

"How'd you get it?"

"During my placement trials. I was pitted against another slave of was obviously a better fighter than I was."

"Hmm," he said thoughtfully. "How are you feeling today, bath slave?"

"Very well, Master," I answered.

"That's a pity." He exhaled and stepped closer to me. He smelled like leather and...something else. It took me a second to figure out what it was. Chocolate? He smelled like leather and chocolate.

He smiled handsomely at me with sparkling teeth. The grin causing those charming little laugh lines at the corners of his eyes. He rested his hands on his hips and looked me up and down, evaluating me.

"You look like you'll put up a decent fight. Should be entertaining."

"Pardon me, Master?"

"Oh, I made a little wager with Queen Isavyne in regards to the fight you're in tomorrow. She bet that you'd win."

My heart swelled some, knowing that the Mistress wanted me to beat Corvas.

Then he said, "Do me a favor and lose, will you? I bet against you just to spite her."

"Uh, Master...You wish me to die then, in order for you to win a bet?"

"Well, only if it's not too much trouble." The Master of Diamonds smirked.

I would have thought he was kidding by his tone, only I don't think he was. His charm aside, he had actually just told me he wanted me dead. Did he know about how I'd served the Mistress? Was he, goddess help me, jealous? How could this Master feel anything other than self-confidence, bordering on narcissism about his appearance? There was no way he saw me as any kind of threat to his pursuit of Mistress Isavyne.

He continued, saying, "I'm really not sure you have much chance against that guard slave anyway. It was the smart bet to wager against you. No offense. I just really don't like losing."

I'm pretty sure my mouth hung open a little. He patted me on the arm with a nod, as if we were conspiring together. Like we were on the same team about my death so he could win. Then he walked out through the beaded curtain. He said over his shoulder, "Don't let me down, slave."

I realized as he left, I was trembling a little in rage. I would *not* just lay down and die because he didn't like to lose! In fact, it made me want to beat Corvas all the more. As if I didn't have enough incentive already. I wanted to win now so that the Mistress didn't lose her bet with him.

I knelt down in front of the lapis statue of the Goddess and pulled a small vial from my pocket full of pink cane crystals. It had been months since I'd used cane. This seemed like an appropriate time. If this was to be my last day, I wanted to enjoy myself.

I exhaled hard, trying to shake off my anger. I removed the stopper on the vial and tipped the cane crystals onto my tongue.

At the base of the steps was a white satin blanket and matching pillow for worship. I knelt down before the idol with my hands resting on my thighs, looking up into the face of the blue lady. The flower Khessi had given me rested in my palm.

"Goddess, please hear me. Please...." My head began to sing with the pleasure of the cane making my heart pound in my chest. "...I don't want to die. I know I am not worthy of your mercy. But I want..." I cringed as the selfish word escaped my lips. I restated. "I *beg* your help in victory. If you will that I die tomorrow, I ask only for the strength to die well. I do not wish to embarrass the Mistress further in death than I have in life." My words were heavy with the drug and I babbled out variations of this over and over. Tears began to slide down my face. It was strange to be crying in pleasure and fear simultaneously. The tears left trails down my skin that felt like streams of vibrating color.. The saltiness of a droplet made it onto my tongue. This caused a crackling sensation over my lips and down my throat. I started breathing heavier, caught in the pull of the cane. I followed the high through the pulsing in my veins. Suddenly every movement in my body caused tremors of pleasure. A breeze rolled through the empty hall and I sighed at how it caressed my skin. I hadn't gotten high in so many months that it seemed like my first time again. As I knelt there, melting into the white satin beneath me, I thought of Khessi.

My mind projected visions of her in a room of white light wearing nothing but diamonds. Silver fish cuffs swam at her wrists attached to her diamond collar by a shining silver chain. Her coppery red hair framed her clear, aqua eyes. Her perky breasts glittered with their diamond piercings. She stared at me through long black lashes as she ran her hands over her perfect skin. The scent of peach and rose haunted my senses across the hallucination in my mind. A flutter of images flashed through me of her mouth making numerous pleasurable shapes and sighs. Tasting her diamond-studded nipples between my lips. Feeling her run her mouth over my chest and down my stomach. Her hands gripping my back while I thrust into her. I would never feel that perfect peach scented skin against me again. Would never kiss those pink petal lips again. The cane let my imagination feel almost real. Almost. But she wasn't there.

I was alone.

When I opened my eyes again, I was in the same kneeling position I had been. My head was still a little fuzzy with the drug. When I moved to roll onto my hip, my legs creaked painfully as though I'd been in that position for hours, which I was pretty sure I had been. My feet were numb and nearly immobile from lack of blood. I looked around and noticed that the sun had gone down drastically.

Great. Precious hours had fallen out of the hourglass just like that, over a little hit of cane. I spent my last day alive laying around high. I felt like such an asshole. Maybe I didn't deserve to live. I stretched and massaged my legs for a moment until the tingling of my numb limbs ceased.

When I returned to my room, I saw that there was something resting on my bed. It was a large, beautifully carved box with a note written in the Mistress's handwriting. It read,

No bath tonight. Get some sleep.
Inside this box, you will find your proper clothing for tomorrow.

Letting the note fall onto the bed, I turned my attention to the extravagant gift. I ran my fingers over the carvings. Images of a forest were depicted on its lid, with wolves standing among the trees and bushes. I marveled at the detail as I took in the full piece. If I had been handed this box alone as a gift I would never have been worthy of it. However, what I found inside was more fantastic still. Upon opening the box I first found a white long-sleeved cotton shirt, a new one to replace the one that I'd pretty well destroyed with blacksmithing.

Also in the box was a pair of black pants and a pair of soft leather boots made of deer skin. What I pulled out next was heavy black leather. It was a doublet, covered in a green knotwork pattern that traveled up the front of the chest and onto the shoulders. Not only was it a beautiful garment, but an extra layer of protection in a fight. I was so enthralled by the doublet, that it took me a moment to notice that there was another gift at the bottom of the box.

It was a belt made of thick leather with a silver buckle at its center. All across it rested slip knives and they were all like Secret. The full belted set of knives was just like the one I'd found on the beach. I realized that this was the set the knife had fallen from. Neat rows of silver and black slip knives lined the belt at an angle all the way around.

I put the belt on right then over my silk pants. The solid weight about my hips made me feel strong. Complete, somehow. I ran my fingers over the hilts and couldn't help myself. Pulling two from the belt, I flicked them through my fingers, running them over my hands and across my palms. Their edges sent tingles through my skin as they brushed across it. So sharp. I was filled with that awareness that comes to your senses when something is dangerously edged.

They were beautifully, perfectly balanced. Superior craftsmanship like the one the thief in grey had left behind. I threw one across the room into a wooden plank in the wall. The blade sunk into the beam with ease. It made throwing so much easier than the blades I'd been using to practice. They were weighted so perfectly they made my throwing better and more accurate.

I imagined Corvas, his gloating face over me as I choke on my own blood. I threw the second slip knife and it landed an inch from the first.

Placing my new gifts back in their box, I set it on the floor next to my bed and stared out the window. I listened to the distant waves of the sea as the stars twinkled in the infinite dark blue sky and the moon cast rays of white light into my tiny room. I began to feel something I should not have been feeling. Something that I had no business feeling, really. But, against my will it had crept in.

I'd started to hope.

"For those unworthy of their Master's love, the Cheritoth was created. A slave who is of no use to their estate is stripped of their skill title and unmade. The Unmade know only the shame of their worthlessness, coupled with the sure fact that their death will be painful, public and before the eyes of the entire Kingdom."
Dornic, *The Scrolls of the Goddess*

CHAPTER: 13: CHERITOTH

I didn't sleep the night before the Cheritoth fight. I laid in bed staring out the window at the night sky. I watched the stars and moonlight and let my fears feast upon my brain. I knew I was tired the next morning but the knowledge that this was my last day to live kept the exhaustion at bay.

I knew I was hungry and should eat something, but it felt like having food in my belly would make me slower in the fight. I decided not to go down to the dining hall.

I showered and shaved, splashed my neck and chest with some oils. I got dressed. The clothes fit me my body so perfectly that it made moving in them effortless. Not too tight to constrict movement, just tight enough to look really smashing. The belt at my hips was heavy enough that I felt its weight present. It seemed to add a center-point to my gravity, a middle balance in my body that made me feel better weighted the same way the knives felt balanced in my hands. I didn't have as much sparkle as Khessi but in my own way, I was just as well dressed, enough to make an impression at the Imperial palace. For a moment, my ego faltered as I realized the Mistress was probably more concerned about making sure I represented her well than making me feel special. Either way, I did feel special. In the face of such overwhelming fear I took that positivity and ran with it.

I'd only just completed getting ready when Khessi approached me. She looked absolutely stunning, of course.

She was draped in blue fabrics that shined iridescent in the morning light. Her eyes were made up with intricate hues and lined in black. In her perfect hands, she held a set of ugly iron shackles that didn't match her. I knew they must be for me.

"Aw, more presents? You shouldn't have!" I said, trying to lighten the mood.

"The Mistress wants to make sure that you and Corvas will not be able to fight before it is time," she said flatly.

"I was kidding. I just...I understand." I nodded and held my hands out.

She bound my wrists with reluctance. "The carriage is outside and you will be leaving shortly," she said.

The carriage was a new level of spectacular I hadn't yet seen. Apparently, the Mistress only brought it out for special occasions. Pale ash wood, trimmed with gold and a red velvet interior, with long, rectangular cut glass windows glittered against the morning. Gold lanterns hung at the sides of the carriage, although they were not lit. Hitched to the front were four flawlessly white horses in black and gold bridals.

At the back of the carriage were two benches. Corvas was already chained to one of them, with a bag over his head and hands bound like mine. I looked to Khessi who did her best not to look at me.

"Thank you for everything," I told her. She turned to me. Her mouth opened as if she wanted to say something, but Garsteel approached us and she turned away from me and got into the carriage.

"Up you go." He nodded to the bench next to Corvas. I stepped up into the carriage and took a seat. I couldn't see his face but I could feel Corvas's reaction to my presence. I hadn't realized it, but it was probably wise that we were bound and bagged. I felt his hatred for me fueled by three months of obsession oozing off his aura.

Garsteel secured my chains to a ring in the floor beneath the bench. He looked at me before placing the bag over my head and gave me a nod in solidarity with a reassuring smile. I replied with the same before my head was covered by black fabric.

A few minutes later, I heard the Mistress greet Khessi and exchange some instructions for while she was away. The carriage rocked lightly when she entered the cabin. Moments later, the carriage began to move and we were on our way to the imperial palace.

Or so I assumed since it was not like I could see where we were going.

The journey was long and boring and by the end of it, I had to pee something fierce. I was starting to debate if I could get away with dangling my dick over the edge of the carriage and relieve myself. Then I began to register sounds around me.

Voices, music, horses and carriages. The smoky scent of burning wood and cooking meat along with rich smells of wine caught on the breeze. My empty stomach started to mumble complaints to me.

As soon as the carriage stopped, I felt hands on me. Quick metallic squeaks and tugs at my chains told me that my bonds were being undone from their secure base. I was pulled roughly by two pairs of hands.

"You two! Stand!" A rough voice barked too close to my ear. I did so and was pushed forward as soon as my legs were under me. "Walk!" The voice said again.

I tried to feel my way down to the ground while being half pushed off the side of the carriage. They kept the cloth over my head. Corvas was pushed and pulled down right behind me. We both managed to get off the carriage and onto the ground. Below my feet felt like a cobblestone path of some kind.

The bag was roughly pulled from my face, flooding my eyes with bright white light. When my eyes finally began to adjust I realized I was standing next to Corvas. He eyed me hatefully for a moment. It was only a second, but he seemed a little taken aback with the change in my physic. My attention was pulled to the Mistress who stood in front of us.

Master Braxian stood with her. They whispered between themselves, and Braxian placed an affectionate hand on the side of the Mistress's cheek. I wondered when he had joined our party. Had he been in the carriage with the Mistress? Maybe he only just arrived and joined her. I didn't realize I was almost glaring at him.

Master Braxian smiled at me broadly and clicked his tongue in my direction and gave me a wink. I don't know what my face did but I don't think I hid my feelings very well. I was somewhere between confusion and disgust.

My vision was still a little blurry, but I noticed a figure approach Mistress Isavyne with his arms open wide in a greeting. As he came closer, my eyes began to clear as well and I got a clear look at the Master before me.

The King of the Cheritoth was not what I expected. Master Lovol was a legendary swordsman and renowned through the land for his abilities as a warrior and battle strategist. He wore a beautiful ornate silver sword on his hip. That was a fantastic accessory to his full length, corseted gown.

King Lovol wore a billowing layers of emerald green, cinched together with an emerald corset. A high collar of iridescent green feathers framed his charming features and a brilliant emerald necklace dangled at his throat. In the arch of his upper left ear was a piercing boasting a smoky grey diamond. His eyes were lined in a black charcoal and shaded with green and glittering makeup up to his plucked, well-shaped eyebrows. His lips too, sparkled black which made his white teeth shine all the more. He had short, spiky hair that I would have mistaken for black if he weren't standing in the sunlight. Backlit by daylight though I could see that his hair was a deep shade of purple. Though, the trait that disturbed me most were his eyes. They were silver. Not grey, but metallic silver irises with no pupils, cold orbs of wintery brilliance that pulled a shiver from me in the heat of the day. I could see clearly the side of him that made an intimidating fighter. I imagined his silver gaze calculating and breaking down a fighter's tricks to nothing.

As a Master, Lovol could present himself however he chose, though it was not well accepted in all parts of the monarchy for a man to wear a dress. I would suppose if you're a man who enjoys wearing women's clothes, it doesn't hurt to be the biggest badass with a sword in the land, either. I'd heard tales of Lovol expressing his displeasure with the judgments of others at sword's edge.

However, he did not strike me as a cold-blooded killer. His features were a mysterious blend of handsome and feminine, while his smile was fierce and full of joy.

He extended a black leather-gloved arm to Mistress Isavyne, and when he spoke his voice was rich and deep and full of charm.

"Isa! My love!"

"Lovol," the Mistress smiled broadly.

Lovol placed a hand upon the Mistress's face and kissed her.

He really kissed her.

The only other Master I'd seen the Mistress allow to have any intimate gestures toward her was Master Braxian, but Lovol kissed her fully and passionately as two old lovers remembering a long forgotten romance. I am sure Master Braxian noticed this as well.

Miraculously neither managed to stain the other with their respective lip colors as they parted their kiss. Lovol smiled broadly at the Mistress and then turned to kiss Braxian. The Master of Diamonds turned his cheek slightly at the last moment to avoid being kissed on the mouth. He received a small, black kiss on the corner of his mouth. Braxian managed to do this in a charming way, without being rude. However, it clearly stated his preference in gender while kissing. Lovol didn't seem to be fazed or upset by this. He kissed Braxian's cheek with a gentle peck of friendship.

"Please friends, join me in the high viewing box with his most Imperial Majesty. It would be my pleasure to entertain you today!"

"Of course," Mistress Isavyne nodded.

A single respectful nod was all that came from Braxian as he wiped the black smudge with his shirt sleeve.

The Mistress declared, "I have brought two for the games today." She motioned toward Corvas and myself.

"Oh excellent, excellent!" Lovol cheered and looked us over. I honestly could not tell you if he eyed Corvas and I with lust or just professional evaluation. "Both look strong. Able-bodied and bright-eyed. It seems a shame for one to die." His dark lips pressed into a line for the smallest moment before he turned his shining smile back to his guests. "But you know how the Emperor is. It's not real entertainment until there's blood spilt." He laughed shortly then nodded at the guard slaves standing next to us and the bag was placed back over my head again.

"Oh, come on!" actually made it out of my mouth under the bag before I was pulled forward by my chains by unseen hands and lead away. After a while, the cobblestone of the main entry road changed to dirt under my feet. The sounds of excitement and arrival faded. New sounds of metal against metal and dirty smells permeated this new area. We crossed through a doorway and into a stone building of some kind. There were voices in here. Rowdy shouts and taunts began all around us. I heard pounding on metal bars and clapping of hands. I was suddenly thankful for the bag over my head as I was hit by small rocks and some dirt. The slaves were throwing things at us. I also heard something that took me off guard. Growls, hissing, and various animalistic noises mixed with the voices of the unmade slaves. I couldn't see them, but I wondered how many were wyrlings or close enough. Channeling was not forbidden in the Cheritoth and even encouraged so that the audience would see a better fight. Feral shouts from male and female voices melded together. It gave me a chill of fear as I imagined the damage they could do to me. Corvas suddenly didn't seem so scary. Fragments of taunts caught in my ears.

"Look at these two sad sacks of..."

"Gonna fuck that little piece..."

"Come on over here honey!"

"Is it a boy or a girl?"

"...dead meat mother fu...."

"....if I get my hands on that pretty ass..."

"...don't look better than us now do..."

"You're gonna bleed, bitch!"

"Tear'em apart!"

"Shut the fuck up!" The guard pulling my chains shouted. He was met with laughter and a sea of various versions of "fuck you".

The cages of unmade slaves finally ended and I was brought to a stop. I heard a door open and I was pushed forward. The bag was taken from my head and the shackles unlocked.

"Wait here until the gate opens and you hear the trumpets signal you to the ring. Don't make us come get you or you'll be entering the competition minus a hand," said a guard slave. He backhanded me across the face to make his point clear, then turned and left. The door closed solidly behind him and I heard it lock.

Slowly, I took a look around. It was dark, which was nice since I'd just been in the dark and my eyes were already adjusted. The only light in the room was a small lantern near the door. I was standing in what seemed to be a large empty holding cell. It was about ten feet wide and the same tall. Stone walls surrounded me except for a dirt floor beneath. The farthest wall was made of two large wooden doors that I figured would open onto the arena. Above me were the thunderous sounds of the crowd, monarchs and slaves pouring in for the day's entertainment. Once they all settled there was some kind of announcement that I couldn't quite make out any words to. I thought it would probably be a minute before I was called. I didn't want to go into the ring with a full bladder. I opened my pants right there and relieved myself in the corner on the dirt floor.

Then distant trumpets and cheering began. The Cheritoth had officially started. I flipped out two knives from my belt. My knife Secret, and one other. All of the slip knives in the belt looked the same, but I had gotten used to the feel of Secret in my hand. Her handle was a little rougher from her stay in sea water. I nervously began twiddling it through my fingers.

"First fight?" a low voice said from the dark of a corner. I was so shocked that I threw the other knife in my hand before I had time to think about it and readied Secret to throw next.

Chains shook to life on the far side of the room where the voice had come from and a figure stepped forward.

A slave stood, chained to the wall. He was cuffed at each limb, the neck, and the waist. Each shackle was attached to a thick chain set into the stone wall behind him. He wore simple grey pants held up by a thick black multi-buckle belt. He was shorter than me with hair the color of raven's wings. He stared at me through his long hair that hung in his face. Once in the faint light from the lantern, I saw that his eyes were bright speckled amber and slitted like a cat's. It made him look like a black-furred lion.

His shirtless chest boasted well tanned, thick muscle. He was riddled all over his skin with bruises. The highlight of these was on his right shoulder. Dark purples and blues streaked in a halo down his arm and shoulder. The edge of his lip was bloodied and dried down the edge of his chin as well. I approached him with caution.

"You want your knife back?" he asked. It could have sounded threatening in the right setting. Though his appearance was somewhat fearsome, he seemed calm and matter-of-fact.

"Yeah. Thanks." I stepped forward and took it back from him.

"It's pretty. Great balance, too." He handed it back to me. The long black nails on his hand were one-third the size of my blade. There was some blood on the knife when he handed it back to me.

"You surprised me." I said in apology.

"I get that a lot," he nodded.

"Did I hit you?"

"Don't worry about it," the lion slave said with a shrug. Just then, I heard trumpets sound. My pulse rushed and adrenaline pumped.

Oh, Goddess. This is really happening...

"That's not for you. The doors will open first. Then they'll trumpet you out. That's the trumpets for a different fight."

"Right, okay..." I mumbled.

Feeling awkward in the silence of the moment I asked, "So what are you being punished for?"

"Oh, this isn't punishment." He smiled with a wince as he stretched his arms a little. "This is just where they're holding me until my next fight."

" Are you dangerous?" I asked.

"Occasionally," he chuckled. His laugh was a dry, somewhat desperate sounding baritone. And I had to still myself not to take a step back. He had two long teeth in front and two shorter, but still elongated, teeth on bottom. I'd heard that Cheritoth slaves were encouraged to channel. Since they weren't expected to live long, channeling energy from a creature made the fights for entertaining and they lasted longer in battle. But I was fascinated with this transition. The in between of a slave who is becoming a wyrling but hasn't fully transitioned into the animalistic madness that comes with it.

"Have you won many battles?" I asked, with all my inexperience showing.

"Yeah. I'm working my way up to being a crowd favorite."

"I've never won a fight before. I'm not really a fighter," I shrugged.

"For what it's worth, you throw like you mean to kill."

"How bad did I get you?" I asked again.

"I said don't worry about it," he answered, more firmly this time. The last part of his statement trailed off as he licked his lips, looking away.

"Is there…" I started, then rephrased with, "Are you all right?"

He laughed, loudly. His laugh sputtered out a cough near the end and he tried to regain his composure. I felt like a jackass.

"Forget it. Sorry, I said anything."

"I'm not laughing at you," he finally got out. "There's not a whole lot of compassion around this place. I can't recall the last time a stranger gave a shit how I was. Thank you for asking, though."

"Sure," I smiled, tightly.

"How about you, my sensitive brother? How's life working out for you these days?" he asked with a touch of sarcasm.

"Well, I guess we'll just see in a little while, won't we?"

"Yeah. I suppose we both will."

There was a heavy pause as we both took in that thought.

"Any regrets?" he asked me.

"Just one really." The thought of Khessi brought a bittersweet smile to my lips. "But at least I got to steal a kiss from her once or twice."

"Ah," he nodded. "Seems like it's always about a woman."

"Do you have a lady?" I asked him.

"Well, 'lady' seems like a stretch for them but yeah, I've got two, actually."

"Two women? At the same time?" I raised an eyebrow. He nodded, smiling. "That sounds like a lot of work."

He laughed really hard that time.

"Don't hurt yourself," I scoffed. "Which one of your girls do you like best?"

He shook his head, "Impossible to say! They're both so different. One is passionate but sassy. The other is fierce and fearless. I could no sooner choose a favorite eye…" He paused, looking away, sadness clinging to his tone. "Or a favorite hand."

"That's some loyalty you have there."

"Well, they've earned it."

"You seem tough. I'm sure you'll defeat the slave they have you fighting."

"Well, it's not even odds. I'm fighting three others."

I blinked. "That hardly seems fair."

"No, it isn't. But that's the Cheritoth for you."

I suddenly felt upset at the notion that this slave I'd just met might die. It got my mind off of my concern at the moment that I might die.

"Do you think you can beat them?"

"I'm not sure. It would be tough enough beating the champion of the arena, let alone two others. It's all hand-to-hand combat, but he's just a killing machine. It doesn't much matter that he doesn't have a weapon. He knows as much about fighting as I do. And he's never lost a fight. He's a real son of a bitch. Zulyin's been the Emperor's champion for three years running."

At the mention of the hated name, a sense of cold washed over my heart. I was suddenly aware of the scar on my chest. Zulyin, the bastard who had nearly cut me in half as a boy. I ground my teeth a little as I slid Secret back into my belt. I reached down into my boot and pulled three of the black iron knives I'd hidden there for backup. I looked down at them in my hand.

"Take these," I said through my clenched jaws.

"I'm fine with my claws."

It was then that the heavy wooden doors began to open. A tunnel led out from the doors that emptied into bright, white-hot sunlight. He was much more injured than I had seen in the dark. Dark red cuts were all around his feet and calves. One cut of bright red in his forearm still bled and I figured that must have been where I caught him with my blade. I brushed the guilt behind my urgent need for him to accept my help. I squinted, knowing that time was short before they would trumpet for me to come out.

"Would these help you?" I pushed the blades toward him.

"Well, probably but..."

"Then take them! Please, I want you to..." I thought about what I wanted. All manner of terrible bloody deaths for Zulyin flickered through my mind. All too complicated to explain.

"....I want you to win!" And then I added, "For your ladies!"

He tilted his head, hesitating a moment more. He took the blades from me and tucked them into the thick belt at his waist.

"I don't like unpaid debts, friend. There is no way I can repay this," he said.

I looked out into the sunlight tunnel, then back at him. I decided on a price.

"There is something you can do for me." I leaned in toward him and whispered in his ear until the trumpets sounded. They rung through the cell sharply, letting me know I was out of time. When I backed away he gave me a confused look.

"I don't understand, but I'll do my best," the lion slave smiled.

"Thank you," I sighed. "Strange, that it actually makes me feel better."

"Well, you're welcome," he said.

"It was a pleasure meeting you," I said, putting a hand on his shoulder.

He nodded, his yellow lion's eyes now illuminated in the light.

"You as well, Zsash. The Goddess guide you."

"You, too," I nervously smiled. Then I turned and faced the light to walk down onto the Cheritoth arena. It wasn't until later that I realized and regretted that I had never asked him for his name.

"Desperation is a fantastic motivator. Some of the most impressive acts are achieved under great duress. It is better that you should be frantic, than comfortable. No slave has ever achieved anything of great worth by being comfortable."

Loash, *The Scrolls of the Goddess*

CHAPTER 14: BLOOD

When I emerged from the entrance, the air around me erupted in thunderous applause. I waved and smiled blindly. The ground beneath me crunched under my new boots. I thought vainly that I was going to get my nice outfit all dirty.

The arena smelled faintly like rot and garbage. Looking down, I realized that the crunching beneath my boots was actually glass. Suddenly, I was thankful for the heavy soles of the boots. Lifting one boot, I saw glass slivers stuck all over the bottom. The glass seemed to only go about ten feet from the door. I was grateful that I wouldn't have to be dancing on glass during this whole fight.

At first, I couldn't really see anything past a few feet. I'd had my head in a bag for most of the day and then put into a dark room, after all. My eyes dilated furiously and I squinted in an attempt to ease them into it a bit. I kept walking forward, waiting for things to come into focus.

When they did, the first thing I saw was that the arena was huge. Set in a circle, probably two hundred feet across. The second thing I saw took some of the fire out of my step. It was a grounds slave loading a severed leg into a wheelbarrow along with a mess of other limbs. The grounds slave then grabbed a bag of dirt and sprinkled it on the ground to soak up the pool of blood there.

Feeling he had sufficiently covered the mess he threw the bag back into the wheelbarrow with the body parts and carted it away.

Twenty-foot-high stone walls surrounded the main pit of the arena. And above them, rows and rows of on-lookers. They all were shouting, clapping, eating and drinking. Across the arena, in front of me, I saw Corvas walking toward me. He was wearing his leather armor and holding a sword. Fuck.

As quickly as the cheering had started it all stopped. I looked around as the crowd stared behind me. Just above where I had come out was a large purple canopy that covered a series of chairs. They were fancier than the rest of the stone seats. Under the purple canopy I saw a man with long, dark blue hair. He was dressed in the same purple as the canopy. He held a hand up in a gesture for silence that was immediately obeyed. I realized the man in purple must have been the Emperor.

From the distance I was at, all I could tell about the Emperor was that he was tall, certainly taller than me. He wore a black and silver vest under the purple coat. Both the coat and vest were decorated with bright silver buttons and a ring sparkled on his index finger.

I fell to my knees and bowed, pressing my forehead to the dirt as Corvas approached to stand next to me. Laughter erupted from the masses but the monarchy seemed to enjoy my act of humility.

"Slip knives?" Corvas scoffed, eyeing my belt. "What does a pleasure slave know about how to knife fight?"

"I know it's all about where you stick it."

"I'm going to take my time killing you, you know that? You're going to die screaming, cocksucker!" Corvas spat at me.

I stood slowly, keeping my head bowed respectfully.

"I don't know what was nicer. The last three months without having to hear your voice or not seeing your fuck-ugly face!" I said under my breath.

Ready and pumped for the fight, he pushed me hard in the shoulder with both hands.

Three months ago, that same jab would have pushed me over and made me stumble. Now I didn't even budge from the hit. I had time to savor the surprise on his face for a flicker of a second, right before my knuckles flew into his mouth, splitting his lower lip open.

"Stop!" The Emperor called from above us. We both faced forward, looking up at the Emperor. Behind the Emperor, Mistress Isavyne sat under the canopy along with Master Lovol, Master Braxian, and a few other monarchs. Coppery red hair caught my eye near the corner of the canopy and I saw Khessi was there too, watching. She was far away, but I recognized the look in her eyes. It was similar to when we buried her fish. She looked distraught and holding back tears.

The Emperor's voice projected through the acoustics of the stone circle. We could hear him clearly. I knew enough about acoustics to know, however, that from where we stood I would have to speak up for him to hear me. The Emperor propped a boot up on the edge of the wall and leaned on it casually.

"I am told that this is a long awaited fight between you two. Your Mistress claims it is quite the rivalry. Tell me what grievance you have that has led to this."

"Yes! I seek to protect the honor of the Mistress's household," Corvas began . As he spoke, I realized two things. First, my own anger toward him. In fact, I don't know if I'd realized until that moment just how much I hated Corvas. For everything he'd done to me since I'd arrived at the estate. I realized that more than anything, I wanted to kill him. I wanted to live.

And second, I saw the Emperor lean forward with a strained look on his face. The Emperor's eyebrows knitted with confusion and his head leaned an ear toward the field. It occurred to me that nobody had heard a word that Corvas had said. Places like an arena, you have to speak up to be heard.

My voice boomed through that arena like a clap of thunder. I used the same voice I'd used on the auction block when desperation had taken hold. I used it now to grab the attention of the masses.

"Oh, great Master Emperor! Highest lord and ruler of Atlaind. Before the Goddess, I submit my will and body to the beautiful Mistress Isavyne. The Phoenix Queen blesses us all with pleasures that set us to burn. I am not fit to gaze upon such golden radiance as the Mistress of cane and fire."

The crowd loved it. Cheers rattled from all above and around us. I watched Corvas glare at me from the corner of my eye. His lower lip bled a drizzle down his chin from where I'd punched him. The Emperor raised his hand and the crowd became silent again.

"Yes, yes. Very pretty talk. But your love for your Mistress does not tell me of your hate for this slave. What dispute can a slave possess?"

Before Corvas could even think of a response, I said, "I can possess nothing, oh great Emperor. But the Mistress has charged me to protect her property. Myself and her lovely household slave, are included in that." I paused for a moment looking at Khessi. She stared at me and I wondered if it was the last time I would look into those eyes.

I tore myself away from staring and continued.

"But this proud and disloyal slave has picked fights with me since my arrival. He has abused his station as Guard Captain to see me beaten on numerous occasions. Why, the last time it took him and an entire group of guards to beat me. *Me!* A bath slave with no fight training to speak of, pitted against the guard captain. But I survived! " The crowd went wild. Everyone loves a good story about the little downtrodden slave standing up for himself. "Through the mercy of the Goddess and the grace of Mistress Isavyne, I was spared!"

Corvas tried another lame attempt at out talking me. His voice cracked with the amount of effort he put into it.

He shouted, "No, no, I was defending Khessi! He was trying to..."

I effortlessly talked over him. My voice was like a great boot stomping out the tiny anthill of his pathetic shouts. Like so frequently happens to me when I get worked up, my mouth was irrevocably out of control.

I hadn't realized I was pacing behind my enemy. I circled Corvas with the bloodthirsty stalk of a lion.

"I am not a warrior! But I have come to fight. To finish this feud he started. As the bath slave, I am charged by my Mistress to wash. To make things clean. Well then, today let me wash my hands of this rivalry! Let me be clean of his slander! And let me bathe in his *blood!*"

The outpouring of sound the crowd made could not be contained by even the vast arena. Cheers and stomping rattled the entirety of the arena. I bowed low and dramatically before the Emperor who nodded in approval. I positioned my best sly smirk on my lips. I possibly flexed my muscles. I bolstered my masked confidence, ignoring my thundering terrified heartbeat behind applause. Behind the Emperor, Khessi had a hand over her mouth in a gesture that I knew was her hiding a smile.

"Oh, but my apologies, Corvas. Please, tell his most glorious Emperor of your pittance with me."

I glared at Corvas with a wry smile, extremely pleased with myself. If he could have killed me with a look, his eyes would have torn me to pieces. Corvas proceeded to try and reiterate his version of my terribleness. Nobody could hear him. I leaned toward him and put a hand to my ear, pretending to strain to hear him from right next to him. I then shrugged and shook my head comically. That elicited a roar of new laughter. If they couldn't hear him before, they certainly couldn't now. His voice shredded with effort until the Emperor waved for Corvas and the crowd to quiet down. I thought Corvas might cry with frustration.

"I think we all get the idea." The Emperor said and lifted a glass to us and added a dismissive hand gesture that caused the crowd to quiet. "May the Goddess smile on…"

I lost what the Emperor was saying as Corvas turned toward me with a snarl.

"Your little show doesn't change anything, you know! I'm going to kill you, you vain, worthless prick. I'm going to cut you apart, piece by piece until you scream and beg for death in front of everyone here!" His hand gripped his sword eagerly. Beads of sweat already formed on his brow.

"....when this glass breaks."

That was the last part of what I heard the Emperor say while I was distracted by Corvas. I really wished I'd been listening and turned and actually said aloud, "What?"

I was just in time to watch the Emperor drop his glass. It fell to the arena ground and shattered. I guessed too late that it was the signal to begin the fight.

Corvas didn't waste any words. He drew his sword and slashed at me in one swift move that I narrowly dodged. His attack came again and again. I stumbled backward. I rolled back onto my shoulder and heard the blade strike the sand behind me. I stood up and did the only thing you can do when someone with a large sword chases you.

I ran.

I felt pretty stupid for showing off as I was spectacularly running away. I chanced a glance behind me and saw that he was right on my heels. Goddess, this was going to be very stupid if I died five seconds after that speechifying. I looked for an opening as my hands flew to my belt and I readied two knives, their blades against my forearm while I kept my fists up. My first thought was that I needed to take away his sword. Without that he couldn't cut me into little pieces.

I found my footing while I ran. I waited until my left foot touched down solidly before spinning to throw the knives at him. My aim was apparently not as good while I ran for my life. The knives sailed past him as he dodged easily out of the way. Seeing my pause in running, he swiped low, slashing at my leg. The edge of the sword caught shallowly at the back of my calf on the outside. It thankfully cut more pants and superficial skin than muscle. Pain shot across my leg, but it didn't matter. I continued to run. Grabbing two more knives from my belt, I rounded another spin when I got the opportunity. My marks flew straight. Straight into his armor, that is. The knives made a pathetic pinging noise as they bounced off the garment and disappeared into the sand. It was a good thing I would never live through this, because I didn't know how would I find these damn knives again . Ten knives seemed like a lot initially when I imagined them all flying into his throat. With only six left I suddenly found myself wondering why I had given away my backups to that random slave I'd never met. Curse my giving nature. It was going to be the death of me.

I drew two more knives and feigned a turn to my right. I saw Corvas anticipate my move and raise his sword high above his head, preparing to chop down at me. At the last moment I spun left. I released both knives toward his exposed armpit. The blades sunk true and deep into his arm. Corvas cried out, the sword instantly falling from his hand as the tendons in his right arm had been cut. The two glittering handles peeked out from the red soaking up his shirt. I wasted no time.

I turned and kicked his legs out from under him as hard as I could. His large frame brought him down fast. It knocked the wind out of his lungs. Corvas made a tight gasping sound, struggling to get up though he couldn't breathe.

Remembering every bruise and broken bone I'd endured at this man's hands I knelt over him and began punching him in the face. Adrenaline surged through me while I hit him again and again. This seemed like it went on forever but I probably only got five or six punches in. Blood oozed from his mouth, and in a desperate moment he spit a mouthful of blood at me. I turned my face from it. That gave Corvas the moment he needed to push me off of him with his one good arm. He was on his feet so fast I didn't really see him stand up.

I struggled to scramble away from him so I could get to my feet as well. His boot smashed into the side of my face. I think he loosened some of those good chewing teeth in the back. I continued to squirm away from him. My brain was rattled and I fought to shake off the watering in my eyes. Corvas cradled his useless arm while he looked down at me with hatred. He reached to pull my knives from their home under his flesh, then thought better of it and left them there. Damn it. I was really hoping he would pull the blades out and bleed to death.

Instead, he brought his boot down as hard as he could on my ankle. In a white-hot moment like lightning, I felt my bones break under his foot. I screamed. The pain of it consumed all the energy I had left. He twisted his foot a little for good measure and leaned down to savor the terror in my eyes.

"Try running away now you little shit!" He spat in my face. The thunderous sounds of the audience suddenly crashed through my ears. I looked around the Cheritoth, squinting in the sunlight of the day. Monarchs and slaves all watching, drinking wine, eating snacks. Taking bets. Well, at least Master Braxian would be pleased.

I felt a streak of bitterness behind my horror that I was about to die. Lame and driven by naked fear, I pushed away from Corvas with my good leg and one hand. He laughed and leaned down to grab at me.

Two knives found their way into my grasp and I stabbed them down as hard as I could between his collar bones. I wasn't sure if they had severed arteries, but I hoped so. I'd certainly impaled one of his lungs. He gasped and stumbled back a few feet. He pulled one knife from his chest but left the other. The one blade he'd pulled dangled lazily in his hand for a moment before he tossed it away. Thin, bright red blood gurgled out of Corvas in bubbles. He fell to one knee trying to take in a full breath. Realizing the damage I'd just caused, he began scrambling after me. He clawed at my face desperately and missed me by a foot. I shimmied back from him, trying to get some distance between us.

If he was bleeding out, all I had to do was outlast him. Maybe five minutes? Two if I'd gotten him really good. Maybe he would drown on his own blood. I kicked and struggled from his grasp. I turned onto my belly to crawl away while he tried to grapple me.

It wasn't pretty, this fight for life. There was nothing graceful or noble in this type of battle. I crawled on my hands and knees like an infant trying to get away from Corvas, who choked and wheezed behind me. Two men clawing in dirt and blood to try and kill each other. It was so ugly it made my stomach retch. I wanted this to be done. I just wanted to not feel the shame of dying there, to not feel my foot shattered and flapping uselessly behind me. The worst part was that every time I looked over my shoulder, Corvas was there, gasping and crawling right after me. He was like some vile sea creature slithering in my wake. And he was getting closer every second.

I realized that this was my last moment to get to kill him. His eyes burned at me while he grabbed at my feet. I inhaled deeply, trying to shut out the pain while I slipped the last two knives into my hands. I aimed carefully, though there was little need since he was right in front of me. I remembered when Garsteel had thrown knives into the leather man when we were training.

I moved to throw my last two knives where they would bury themselves into his eyes and kill him.

The knives launched from my fingers. My form was perfect. My speed, lethal.

But at the last moment, Corvas grabbed my broken ankle and twisted it. The pain soared through my nerves, sending every thought in my brain into chaos. My fingers flickered with tension at the last moment, sending the knives off course. They flew toward his face. In a moment of self-preservation, he released my ankle to put his arm up to deflect my knives with his armor.

I was all out of knives.

All out of moves.

Again, I crawled. Like a child learning to walk, escaping death for a few more moments.

The end happened so fast I hardly had time to register it until it was all over. Sand grated roughly into the meat of my hands and knees as I desperately crawled away from the inevitable. This was pathetic. I drug my broken foot along. The pain was so intense with each unnatural movement it would be a relief to die. Suddenly, pain stabbed through my pants and into my knee. I hissed and looked down to see what I'd knelt in.

Broken glass. The glass the Emperor had dropped.

I'd managed to land in the broken shards of the goblet, which just seemed like an insult at this point. I looked back up to see Corvas over me. His unforgiving, sword hand gripped my throat as he began to crush the life out of me. But, it didn't hurt anymore.

Euphoria struck me. Thick pleasure ran over me in waves. For a moment I thought that it must be part of dying. That this was what death felt like. Then I realized that I'd felt this before. It wasn't some mystical spiritual moment pulling me to the breast of the Goddess.

It was cane. The Emperor had been drinking something with cane in it.

I wasn't dying.

I was suddenly…
wonderfully…
…beautifully…

…so fucking high.

My hand seemed to float down to my leg where new waves of color and sensation streamed from my injury. I grabbed the base of the shattered glass goblet. The long glass stem was still gleaming and unbroken. It glistened in the sunlight. It refracted with such beauty. The moment passed on in a glorious eternity as I realized my intent.

I thrust up toward his face. The length of thick glass pierced his eye with everything I had left. It struck with such force, I felt it hit the back of his skull and break inside his brain.

Everything went silent.

Corvas let out a convulsive shudder as a line of red trickled down to the tip of his nose. His body fell to the side with a sickening thud.

There was a long stillness while I stared in disbelief.

Applause and cheers of victory cut through my pulsing senses like an explosion. Somewhere in the back of my mind, I knew this was something I should be happy about, but I couldn't really keep my thoughts together as I spun away on a cloud of exhaustion and pleasure. Slumped and kneeling on the floor of the Cheritoth, I had two final thoughts before passing out.

One, the Emperor has good shit. Mistress Isavyne must have given him an extra special stash. And two, I really wish I'd kissed Khessi one last time.

"The most joyous is a day where you know you have done your duty to your owner. When there is no doubt that you have completed your commands without ego. To make your Queen happy with your service is to know your life's true purpose."
Landryl, *The Scrolls of the Goddess*

CHAPTER 15: GOLD

The afterlife was so fucking beautiful.

I walked through a peach orchard toward an open window where roses grew beneath the sill. Inside the window were beautiful household slaves baking peach pastries. They played and laughed as though they didn't have a care in the world.

Oh! I forgot to mention.
They were all naked.

One by one, the ladies started slowly and seductively feeding each other the pastries. A breeze rolled through the window, tossing gorgeous locks of hair and creating taught nipples from cooling skin. It played out slower than reality, every second that passed was twice its length so I could enjoy every second. Scents from the garden and the kitchen were caught and brought to me on the breeze. My mouth watered. One lovely brunette fed a dirty blond-haired girl. A golden drop of the pastry filling escaped her mouth and landed just above the blush nipple on her breast. Being a good friend, her dark haired companion leaned down and extended her tongue. She cleaned the area thoroughly. Very thoroughly. Several pairs...or trios...or...groups of girls were all apparently messy and continued to clean or create more messes on their friends. One girl who was holding a handful of sugar, licked her lips and kissed the sugar, creating a sugar-coated treat for a girl next to her. I thought that I must have died and this was my reward from the Goddess.

Sadly, I woke up.

My mouth was slicked with some liquid being drizzled between my lips that reminded me of honey. I licked my lips and opened my eyes. Almost all pain was gone from my body. Khessi was feeding me the tiny cup of healing potion like she had a few months ago, in the healer's wing. Khessi smiled softly when she saw my eyes open.

"Hey," I tried to say. My voice sounded dry and raspy. I looked around the room. We were in was some kind of guest room in an estate somewhere. Master Lovol's most likely.

Lanterns glowed with pink stained glass, giving the room a warm tone. A silver and bronze table was topped with glass bottles of wine and goblets, a basket of fruit sat on the table with the wine. A jasper bowl holding some kind of pink candy sat nearest the door. Across from the bed, about ten feet away was a long rectangular bath set into the floor. Steaming and full, the bath water had a milky opacity to it and rose petals floating atop. Rose candles burned all around it, offering more sweet smells to add to the room.

I had been stripped down and lay naked in the most comfortable bed I've ever been in. It was even more comfortable than the Mistress's bed, and that's saying something.

A glorious amount of pillows were piled up behind me to elevate my upper body. The blanket was heavy and warm . I then realized I was pitching quite a tent with my hard-on beneath the blanket. I cleared my throat as I saw Khessi notice.

"Sweet dreams?" she teased.

"Very sweet," I admitted, giving her a smirk. I made no attempt to hide my arousal. The texture of the blankets felt nice against me, giving light friction that made me wish she would put her hands on me.

"You're filthy," she said, smiling and looked away to place the small cup back in its box.

"Oh, come on. It's not the first time you've seen me without my clothes on."

"No, not that," she giggled, and leaned closer to my mouth, speaking in an articulated whisper. "You're dirty, Zsash..." And she let her words just hang in the air while my breath caught in my chest. Then she leaned away from me with a laugh.

"Dirty, as in, you're disgusting and covered with dirt and sweat and blood and Goddess knows what else. You need a bath before you are presented to the Emperor."

I sat up with excitement. "I'm going before the Emperor?" I smiled.

"Just let the Mistress present you. Bow your head and be humble and please do your best not to talk. For the sake of my sanity. Please?"

"Hey, you know me."

"Yes, that's what I'm worried about."

Khessi smiled and ran her soft hand over mine, the teasing smile melting away from her. She raised her eyes slowly to mine.

"You worried me. Several times during the fight."

"I was not...unworried myself," I said with humor in my tone.

My brow furrowed as I tried to think of something to say. Then I captured her face in my palm and kissed her. I kissed her with the urgency of a man gasping for air after being trapped below the water's surface for too long. She kissed me back intensely and I thought of my first training bath. Cane was nice and the pleasure it brought was amazing, but there was something incredible about how real everything felt this time. Nothing floaty or heightened, but real, tangible pleasure. It felt good, knowing that she wanted to kiss me too without any influence from something else. When she broke the kiss, she moved back from me.

"The mistress is expecting us soon so..." She said, blushing. "We should not keep her waiting."

I nodded.

When I pulled the covers back I found my ankle was nearly healed from its previous broken state. I tested it some. It still clicked funny when I moved it. The joint was swollen and painful when I put weight on it. I half hopped out of the bed, standing on my good leg.

"Do you need help?" she stood and moved around the bed to help me.

"I'm all right," I said as I winced and limped.

She rushed to help me and I sighed at having her arms wrap around me. I leaned in to kiss her again and she moved away with a smile.

"All right, all right! Bath first," she said sternly. "I'm not kissing you again in your current disgusting condition."

"Fair enough." I agreed, then headed toward the bath without thinking about my injury. In the short steps across the room, my stride went from slight limp to strong walk. I stopped and looked down at my foot. I made a circle motion with my ankle. It was still really painful, but it was basically healed in comparison to a few moments ago! Khessi cocked her jaw to the side, watching me.

"You're healing much faster than I thought you would," she said.

"Won't you join me in the bath? I might need, you know, help or something." I said, extending my hand out to her. She walked over to stand next to the edge of the bath.

"I guess it wouldn't be any harm if I took a bath with you," she said with a seductive tone I'd never heard her use. "After all, I've been thinking about what it would be like to run my hands over all those big, strong muscles you have now." She slid her hands up her skirt, raising it to her thigh. My breath caught in anticipation.

She kicked the tip of her toe into the water and it splashed across my face.

"But I don't think so. That water is going to be absolutely nasty by the time you're done washing. I will be taking a shower on my own, thank you. I will be back to collect you in one hour's time. Don't even think about making me wait." She turned and walked away with a bounce in her step.

I shaved my face and splashed on some oils. My original undergarments were gone, I assumed destroyed beyond repair. A new ensemble waited on the chair for me. Black pants, boots, and a red satin shirt.

I guess the Mistress really wanted me to look good, not only for presentation in front of the Emperor. Today was the first day of the Blossoming festival, the largest celebration of the year. The day when the first trees and crops start to sprout and bear new fruit and flowers. For the monarchy, it is a day of firsts. All Mistresses and Masters are supposed to do something they have never done before to create new experiences. They are encouraged to do as many new things as possible, the idea being to live life and experience the Goddess's creation in all its glory.

For the royalty that turn eighteen, it is the day they usually bed their first slave. Parties and indulgences are presented for the young monarchs so they can choose a slave they like.

There was a knock at the door and I answered it with haste. I felt my eyes get wider seeing the beauty that waited outside it.

Khessi looked incredible. She wore an under-bust corset of red and black striped satin, a garment that would have usually been worn to leave the wearer's breasts exposed. Instead, full bloom red roses covered her breasts. The skirt of her gown was a fall of rich red satin that extended to the floor and split up each side to expose her legs. Peeking out from the red fabric of her dress were gold strapped high heeled boots that traveled up to her knees. Her face was decorated in shades of black and gold makeup. The silver fish manacles had been exchanged for another set just as detailed. A different style of fish made of sparkling red stones on gold cuffs was attached with gold chains to a golden collar around her slender throat. Her scarlet painted lips smiled as I took in the sight of her.

"Goddess save me," I said while shaking my head.

"What's wrong? Is everything all right?"

"All right? Khessi, you look absolutely, stunningly beautiful. Do you have any idea how gorgeous you are?"

"The Mistress tells me so," she said, blushing.

"I'm sure she does. But…do you know it?"

"That's not necessary. But, um…" She seemed flustered. It was so cute to watch her search for the correct diplomatic response. "You also look quite…eh…well, that is to say, that you look very…quite…" She bounced from looking at me, to staring at her hands, to looking away from me. She then seemed to decide on a word. "…Nice."

I put my hand to my chest dramatically. "Wow! Well, thank you. It may take me a minute to recover from the staggering implications of that compliment."

"I'm not good at compliments. I'm better at critiques."

"Then I will take *that* as a big compliment."

She opened her mouth as though she intended to say something else, but closed it and turned to walk down the hall.

We entered a room at the end of the hall to find Mistress Isavyne waiting for us. She stood near a fireplace in a great sitting room. The light from the flames surrounded her with a vermillion glow. For the second time that night, I was brought up short by beauty.

She held so still I could have mistaken her for a porcelain statue. Her hair hung long in loose curls down around her. Her face was, of course, a flawless mask of classic beauty. Her crimson-painted bow lips smiled. Her blue sapphire eyes danced with the firelight. She wore a long strapless gown that wrapped around her luscious curves. I'll let you guess what color, or rather lack of color, it was. She dripped with diamonds along her neck, wrists, and hands, glittering and shining like the sun. In her hands she held a black lacquer box.

Mistress Isavyne raised a white-gloved hand and gestured for me to approach her.

"My sweet, handsome, Zsash!" she called to me in a tone of velvet honey. I wasn't going to complain, but I was pretty sure she'd had a couple drinks. Not drunk, but she was festive. She always got more cheerful with a glass of wine, for the most part. I'd been pouring her cup long enough to have figured that out.

She asked, "How did you describe me to the Emperor? The golden radiance of the Mistress of cane and fire? I had no idea you had such the heart of a poet, my pet."

"One needs not be a poet to see the poetry in your grace, Mistress."

"Come here, my lovely," she commanded me.

I stood before Mistress Isavyne and lowered my head. I felt so truly humble and unworthy and grateful. Goddess, I was just so grateful.

"Look into my eyes, Zsash," she said.

I did so, slowly. I steeled myself to meet her eyes. I looked into the burning oceans of her eyes and felt mine welling with tears almost immediately.

"You have become better than you were when I purchased you, Zsash. You have received your punishments well and done your best to learn from them, despite a few issues with theft and running that lovely mouth of yours."

I winced and looked away from her.

She took my face in her hand and brought my gaze back to her. "You have defeated an adversary that was becoming a problem for me and my estate. You defended the honor of my beloved Khessi. Not to mention, you entertained myself and the Imperial court greatly. You have earned a reward."

"More? Oh Mistress, you've given me so much already. I don't deserve…"

"Silence," she purred and I shut my mouth. "You've pleased me so greatly in the last few days, Zsash. Do not ruin it by speaking."

I cleared my throat and said, "My most sincere apologies, Mistress. I await your commands and desires."

Mistress Isavyne handed the black lacquer box to me.

"This is the last lesson of appreciation. Remember where you started, so you can appreciate what you've become. Open it," she ordered.

I nodded. What I found inside made my heart catch in my chest.

Settled in the red satin interior of the box was a beautifully crafted black leather collar. And fashioned to it was a gold coin.

No. Not just any gold coin.

The gold coin.

The same one that had purchased me. I knew this because it still bore the small red flecks of blood that had splattered on it during that first flogging when I was purchased. It had been dipped in some kind of clear resin to seal it, as well, so that I could always remember the circumstances of my purchase. So I could always remember how I was saved that day.

For the first time in my entire life, I was unable to come up with something to say.

"I am giving it to you. It is yours." And the way she said *yours* sent chills down my spine. I was the owner of one piece of gold. This was more than any slave in the Kingdom. I'd never even heard of a slave being given a gold coin. Khessi was entrusted with all the gold in the estate, but it wasn't hers. This was mine to do with as I please. I could sell it if I should so desire. However, I knew the honor of being given such a gift meant that buying something with it was out of the question.

"Khessi," the Mistress nodded, and Khessi took the collar from the box and buckled it around my neck. I felt complete somehow, that I matched Khessi in some way. Two slaves of red and gold on either side of a radiant white Queen.

"Thank you, Mistress." I finally said and bowed my head low. I put the collar on, feeling its solid weight around my throat like a medal of honor.

"Now, let's get to the celebration," The Mistress smiled, giving my face a soft but affectionate slap, as she'd grown fond of doing. "I need a glass of wine to go with this victory!"

"I have never been taken more times and in as many ways than during the Blossoming celebrations. It is an experience that can be unpleasant if you are not truly willing to serve all monarchy. Some slaves cannot reconcile the touch of one other than their owner. They find being used by another, foreign, strange, and upsetting even. If they are too rigid in their ideas of gender attraction as well. Because pleasure slaves are not exclusively used during the Blossoming celebration, another skill level slave might be commanded to pleasure a monarch. A guard slave or grounds slave may find being used sexually by a King or Queen, uncomfortable. But, for those who truly commit to fulfilling the pleasures of the monarchy, it can lead to unforeseen enjoyment. Do not fear to submit during this time. It is an ecstasy wrought with ragged desires and carnal delights beyond measure."
Misteryn, *The Scrolls of the Goddess*

CHAPTER 16: BLOSSOMING

Being a pleasure slave has exposed me to more than a few gala events even before being purchased. The training house would loan us out to large events when a monarch wanted more skin showing around their manor for the use of his guests. Those events were usually paired with drinking and a feast that spanned an entire dining room for monarchs to graze during the party. This way they could have any sensation at their fingertips. It was not considered a good party unless there was every category of physical indulgence. Food, drink, drugs, music, games, sex.

The imperial feast thoroughly dwarfed any and all events I'd ever witnessed in my life. It is difficult to explain the experience and do it justice, but I will try to recount as many of the sights and sensations there.

The heart of the celebration took place in the main imperial audience hall. It was a huge room of white marble. On three of the four walls were large windows, paned in silver and draped in vibrant purple. Outside each window, I could faintly see balconies and beyond that, the ocean.

From the ceiling hung ornate silver chandeliers, gracefully depicting rampant dragons. My stomach ached at the sight of rows and rows of delicious food. Everywhere were slaves holding trays of alcohol in small silver or crystal glasses. I saw a Master licking cane off of a slave girl's thigh while she whimpered and bit her lip. There were also slave posts. These were metal posts set into the marble that had one or more slaves chained to them. They all danced or touched themselves until a monarch decided to use them for their pleasure, which came in every variation of numbers and genders you can come up with.

To sum it up: food, drinking, drugs. Laughter, music, conversation. Gasps, moans, screams. A kaleidoscope of hedonism.

Though the room was fairly crowded with monarchy and slaves, I noticed that we never had to alter our course. The room parted for Mistress Isavyne. All eyes were upon her when she moved by them. I read so many expressions on those faces. Fear, lust, jealousy, admiration. There were only a few smiles that I figured might actually be in genuine friendship. Khessi and I walked about five feet behind the Mistress, flanking her either side. I did my best to mimic Khessi's manner as well as stride. We passed tables of so much lovely food I thought my stomach might have been audible over the sounds of the hall. I must have been staring intently at the food because the Mistress noticed.

"I have no use for you for a while, Zsash. Go eat and enjoy yourself. But do not be gone long."

"Yes, Mistress," I nodded and gave a slight nod toward Khessi as well.

I made my way to the nearest banquet table which was covered mostly in fruit. I snatched up a plate from the end of the table and quickly covered it with strawberries, pineapple, grapes and apples. There wasn't enough room on my plate for the slice of soft spongy white cake I found at the end. I just palmed that in my hand and walked to a nearby wall. I tried to stay of the way of the celebrating Queens and Kings.

I stuffed my face full of the cake and then began on the fruits. While I ate, I looked around the room. I didn't see the Mistress or Khessi anywhere and wondered for a moment how I would find them with everyone in here. I figured I had been instructed to eat and I would do so. I helped myself to a glass of wine as a good-looking young man walked by with a tray of them. I continued to comb through the crowded room for dresses of white or rose red while I filled the echoing chamber of my belly.

My attention was drawn instead to a woman who stared at me. She stood with such poise but stillness, silently, with no breath or tousle of hair. I actually felt my heart jump when I saw her move at the realization that she was alive. She finished drinking from one of the crystal glasses and threw it into a corner. It shattered against the marble floor a few feet away. It was immediately found by another slave who began sweeping up the glass. It seemed like this happened a lot.

The woman walked toward me with a slow swagger in her hips. She was attractive in a way that was more cute than beautiful, but still quite striking. Her facial features were delicate and lovely. She smiled at me with black-painted lips. White hair hung over pale shoulders accented with pink at its ends. She was petite while still showing lean muscle. A dark pink corset top pressed her small breasts into a cleavage arc that I can describe in no other way but fun. On her lower half, she wore a gray skirt and pink boots that looked like they would hurt to be kicked by. I only mention that because I was pretty sure she'd kicked me before. It was the pink topaz eyes that gave it away.

She was holding a large white rabbit, also with pink eyes. They looked well coupled together.

"Hail to your victory, Zsash. You were magnificent today." She lowered her hand from petting the rabbit and ran a finger slowly, and suggestively, over the gold coin at my chest. "Such pretty gifts your Mistress gives you." She then returned to snuggling the large bunny. I was a little surprised that she would approach me so boldly. Perhaps she wanted to see if I recognized her.

"Your gifts are very impressive as well. Your Master or Mistress must truly favor you."

"You flatter me," she bowed her head in acknowledgment, though her crystalline pink eyes held cool indifference. "Do you like my Kitten?" Her voice rose a register as she scratched behind the rabbit's ear.

"It's...lovely. Though, I'm pretty sure it's a rabbit," I said with sympathetic tones as if she may not know what it is. She raised her white eyebrow in amusement and laughed in that chittering giggle.

"Of course she's a rabbit! Her *name* is Kitten."

"Ah, that's...an interesting choice."

"I like rabbits. We have so much in common. Don't we?" She giggled and put the rabbit's little pink nose to her own. She was talking more to the rabbit than to me, I figured.

"What traits could a rabbit have that would be desirable? Aren't they just slightly cuddlier vermin? Like an extra fluffy rat?"

Yeah, that pissed her off.

"They are *nothing* like rats. They're beautiful! Fast, agile and *so* adorable. Not to mention…" She stepped toward me as if to show me the rabbit. She pressed against the front of my pants with her thigh. "Insatiable sexual appetite. They can't get enough of it."

"I see," I said as she ran brazenly ran her free hand down my chest to rest at the top of my pants.

"I like you, Zsash."

"That seems sudden. We've never met before." I added, hopefully making the point that I knew who she was.

"Oh, that doesn't matter! We're thick as thieves, you and I," she laughed.

She knew I'd been stealing as well. Great.

"Maybe we can practice your knife fighting sometime. I'm sure I know some moves you've never seen before," she purred.

I ran an idle hand over her hair and was shocked at the softness. So much like the thin, soft feel of rabbit's fur.

"That sounds lovely. What is your name and I'll see if the Mistress will allow me to train with you?" I asked, hoping to get a name to give to the Mistress on who had stolen the rest of her garments. She tilted her head forward as her snowy eyebrows raised in joyful surprise.

"You do not know who I am?"

"I was a little sheltered in the training house," I shrugged. "Are you a slave of some importance that I should know?"

Her smile broadened, "I am Tikora, household slave to his most imperial majesty Emperor Dukkar."

The bottom fell out of my stomach a little. The Emperor's household slave was stealing the Mistress's underwear. My tone backed up to respectful.

"Then I am deeply honored."

"Zsash!" Khessi's voice cut through the conversation.

I backed away from Tikora as casually as I could and took a step toward Khessi as she approached.

"Khessi!" Tikora smiled and it was returned with the cool white pearls of Khessi's most diplomatic expression.

"Tikora, dear. You look beautiful." The two hugged with practiced grace that just oozed with how much they hated each other. "I see the Emperor would rather have you in plain clothing for this occasion. In truth, I do envy that some. These gala dresses can get rather tedious with their extravagance."

"Indeed. The Emperor seems to emphasize function over frivolous appearance for some strange reason. It's almost as though he would rather I do my job than be trussed up in some ridiculously ornate guise."

"He is certainly wise. You know some Masters might just use a household slave for crude and demeaning sexual exploits. The Emperor clearly knows your true value," Khessi let out a bell-like laugh.

"So true!" Tikora agreed with clenched teeth. "I hate to think of how empty I would feel, how alone I might be, if I'd never been taken by the Emperor. It makes me sad to think that some slaves, even household slaves, might never know what it's like to serve so completely. Though, the day may soon come that you two will know that pleasure. I have heard that our houses may soon merge."

Khessi did not respond for a moment. Her feathery, black eyelashes batted a few times before she responded.

"I too, have heard such happy news. Of course, we can only wait and see what Mistress Isavyne says on the matter."

"Of course, of course. But how could she say no? The Emperor is the dream of all he graces with his presence. You know, though, Khessi, that when that happens…"

"*If,* don't you mean, sister?" Khessi corrected her with stretched smile.

"Yes! If, of course. *If* that happens, I would make sure you received all comforts upon your move to the imperial palace. I am very sensitive to the needs of the slaves in my charge. And I would find a suitable..." Tikora paused to look Khessi up and down before continuing, "position for you. Zsash too, of course! I can think of quite a few positions he'd be good at filling."

I stood there awkwardly during this exchange, slowly becoming aware that I didn't really want to be there for this conversation. It seemed that household slaves are somewhat catty with each other.

I interrupted before anything got uglier. "Uh, Khessi? Did the Mistress summon me to return?"

"Yes! She did." Khessi took my arm. She said to Tikora, "It was so nice to see you again. We'll have to do this again soon."

"Absolutely," Tikora smiled.

As we walked away, Khessi grabbed a glass of wine from a slave walking by holding a tray of them. She drank it in pretty much one gulp.

"I hate that bitch," she said under her breath more to herself than me.

"I noticed. I'm pretty sure she noticed, too."

"Please tell me you didn't say anything stupid in front of her."

"I don't think so. But, Khessi, she's the thief."

"What?"

"The woman I caught stealing. You know, when I was stealing. It was her. I think the Emperor had her stealing Mistress Isavyne's belongings."

"That's disturbing," Khessi sighed.

"Yeah. So, should I tell the Mistress?"

"Not right now. I'll approach her with it when we get back to the estate." She looked around the room at various slaves moaning and screaming in pleasure and pain while the monarchy taking delight in using them everywhere I looked.

"I hate the palace, Zsash. Being diplomatic is one thing. But it's exhausting always having to be on my guard like this."

"Don't worry. We'll just keep to ourselves until the Mistress wants to leave. Stay close to the Mistress, that's what you told me."

"Yes," she nodded, trying to pull her eyes from the onslaught of carnal desires around us. "Let's go."

Khessi led me across the room until we stood beside a set of stairs. Tikora had followed not long behind us and smiling at me, made her way up the stairs. At the top was a large marble throne. It was wide enough to seat two people side by side. This was the first time I saw the Emperor up close.

Emperor Dukkar, commonly called the "Boy Emperor" by less respectful monarchs, sat upon the throne. The title had been given to him because of how young he was when he received his crown. There was also the possibility because of his youthful boyish facial features. However, there was no doubt that Dukkar had long ago become a man. He had developed the stature and poise of his forefathers. He was tall, with strong shoulders. His pale skin was framed by long locks of dark blue hair. I noticed that even when his eyebrows arched in amusement or the curls of his lips rose in laughter, there was a sharp feel to his features. Rigid and calculated movement displayed frosty expressions. His blood red eyes were the only part of him that seemed to burn at all times. When he spoke, it was slow and with purpose, each syllable was drawn out over his tongue like he savored the flavor of his own words. He sat sideways on his throne, leaning on one arm and his legs crossed over the other.

Two nearly naked slave girls were chained to the base of the throne. They were running their hands all over the Emperor. One was a brunette, the other a redhead. Their long hair was pulled back into loose braids. Each girl wore a garment of metal that snaked from one breast around the back of their hips then crept down the front of their pelvis. A bright blue resonance stone was fixed over the nipple on the metal that cupped their breasts.

Another larger stone was set above the metal that trailed from their hips down to press against their clits. They moaned and rocked against the vibrations. They were begging him to fuck them. One had tears streaming down her face she wanted him so badly.

Occasionally he would fondle them lightly, play with their breasts or slide a finger into them. It would only last a minute until he seemed to lose interest, not enough to grant them release. Tikora watched with a satisfaction in their torment. Each time the Emperor finished fingering them, he would extend his hand to Tikora to lick his fingers clean, which she did dutifully.

The Emperor barely noticed the women with him. He watched something with intense interest on the dance floor. I looked out and realized it was Mistress Isavyne he was staring at.

On the dance floor that stretched out before the throne I saw the Mistress dancing with Master Braxian. I laughed when I thought about their conversation and I really hoped I'd cost Master Braxian a lot of gold, not to mention, some humility in front of the Mistress.

They seemed happy in their dancing. The Mistress had that little scarlet smile she wore when she was really enjoying herself. It was a smile that extended to her blue eyes, making her impossibly more beautiful.

At some point since I'd left her side, tiny silver flowers had been placed in her hair. I recognized them as blossoms that grew in the imperial garden. It was a tradition during the Blossoming Celebration that any monarch who wished to court another would give them one of these silver blossoms to wear in their hair. If the monarch wished to join with them, the monarch would dry and return the silver blossom during the harvest celebration. Around ten silver flowers had been placed in the golden locks of Mistress Isavyne's hair, symbols of the other monarchs who would like to pursue her romantically.

Master Braxian swept Mistress Isavyne in a spinning arc as they danced gracefully together. The ivory satin of her dress twirled around her curves to the music. Master Braxian whispered in the Mistress's ear. As they danced, he slowly reached up into her hair and pulled the flowers of other suitors from her golden locks and dropped them onto the dance floor. Several of the other monarchs did not look pleased with this display. That brought my attention back to the Emperor. He didn't exactly look angry, but there was something covetous in his expression toward the Mistress and I wondered if one of those silver flowers had been his. I knew Master Braxian was bold, but I didn't think he was that bold. To thwart the advances of an Emperor did not sound like a smart idea to me.

One of the crying slave girls at the Emperor's feet, the redhead, crawled onto his lap and lay back against him. She writhed her body on top of his in hopes that he would become interested.

"Tikora," he said simply with a wave of his hand.

Tikora grabbed the girl by her hair and pulled her viciously up from the Emperor. She began spanking the girl, hard. Pink hand-marks swelled up on the girl's ass almost instantly.

"Stand up!" Tikora shouted. "Put your hands on the throne!"

The redhead did so with practiced speed. Placing her hands on the armrest, she bent over sticking her ass up in the air. Tikora spanked her a few more times before sliding her fingers into the girl's pussy. Her hand was so slender, all four of her fingers slipped in easily. My pulse rose at the sight of the redhead practically getting fisted against the throne. The girl cried out and a smile drifted across her tear-streaked lips as she was finally getting what she wanted.

"You can't have him again! Not now. Maybe not ever!" Tikora declared, "But this is all you want, right? You're just a fucking whore who wants something in her holes, don't you?"

The girl couldn't form words. The vibrating stones at her pleasure points made the penetration irresistible. She muttered "yes" and "please", intermixed with her moans as she fucked Tikora's hand wildly.

Tikora was much different from what I'd come to expect out of a household slave. Khessi was all grace and class. Even when I'd seen her naked, she'd never come off slutty. Tikora was the exact reverse, though she, too, maintained an unmistakable balance and focus. There was a completely dirty freak factor to her. I'm not saying it wasn't a turn on, because it kind of was. It was just so opposite from Khessi that it was bizarre that she was a household slave as well.

Tikora looked down at me from the throne and smiled. She flicked white hair out of her eyes and licked her lips before winking at me. I looked away, suddenly feeling like I'd been caught doing something I shouldn't have.

As I looked away, I was met with Khessi's gaze. She raised a finely sculpted eyebrow at me.

"What?" I said indignantly. Khessi just shook her head a little at me.

"Zsash!" I heard a voice say. I turned to see blonde, gangly beauty wearing a long dress of sparkling violet. "Oh, Goddess! You look so different," she giggled.

"Basz!" I exclaimed, then turned to Khessi. "Do you think it would be all right if I left to have a conversation ?"

Khessi nodded, watching the Mistress still dancing with Master Braxian. "Looks like the Mistress will be entertained with dancing for a while. I'll come find you when you are needed again."

"Thanks." I smiled at her then walked toward Basz. She had filled out a little in the last year. She looked healthier and less boney. Her shining honey-colored hair had grown long and hung to her middle back.

"Your hair is so long!" I said, running my hand over it.

"The Emperor likes long hair," she smiled, flipping it over her shoulder.

"You live here in the palace, then?" I asked. "How is it?"

"It's good! The food is amazing. Sometimes I feel like all I do is eat when I'm not serving the Emperor. Though, I see your

Mistress likes to keep you in shape. You were never this muscled at the training house." Basz touched my arm and felt the muscle beneath my shirt. I think I blushed a little.

"Well, she's had me working as a blacksmith for the last few months."

"Wow! I bet you love that. I know how much you like to work with your hands." And she winked at me.

"And how is service to the Emperor?"

"He is a vigorous lover. Fortunately, he has enough girls that I am not used that often. We all kind of take turns and then rest up before our next use." She paused and pursed her lips as if trying to silence herself. Her eyes drifted up to the throne. The Emperor watched Tikora making the redhead cum. He touched the redhead lightly across the face, moving sweaty strands of her hair out of her face as she still begged him to take her. The brunette had spread her legs wide at the foot of the throne. I could see the resonance stone vibrating against her, driving her wild. She propped herself up with one arm to watch the other girls. Her other hand slid down her breast and down her body before she sank her fingers deep inside herself.

"He torments those two all the time," Basz said over my shoulder, and I turned back to her.

"And I thought I was insatiable. Is he really that good?"

She shrugged, "He is the Emperor." It struck me as possibly a flattering sentiment, but also an entirely non-committal statement.

"Did your Mistress decided to use you for your sexual talents or just stick you on blacksmithing?" Basz asked, trying to get both our attention off the spectacle on the throne.

I said pointing my thumbs back at myself. "No, actually she's mostly had me as the bath slave. I've only been doing blacksmithing for the last three months."

"Oh, no! A bath slave! Really?" she winced. "What a waste of a perfectly good tongue."

"Well, she's had use for that. Being a bath slave is not as bad as it's made out to be. Officially, I'm a bath slave. But, the Mistress has had use for some of my talents. And I've kept myself busy otherwise."

"Oh! Goddess," Basz said with wide eyes, noticing the gold piece in the collar around my neck for the first time. "Is that real gold?"

"It is," I said proudly. "The Mistress just gave it to me tonight."

"That is impressive, Zsash."

"I'm still kind of in shock about everything," I shook my head.

"I knew you were always meant for great things. What did I say? The Goddess was saving you for something special." She smiled warmly at me. Her eyes drifted to the throne. The Emperor was leaving the throne and exiting the hall. Basz's smile faded a little. She moved in and gave me a fiercely tight hug.

"I've got to go right now. But come find me later in the party, all right? If your mistress doesn't make you leave immediately, I'd love to talk more with you."

"Sure," I smiled. She kissed me on the lips quickly and walked away in her little awkward flat-footed duck walk.

The next hours were filled with Khessi and I waiting to see when the Mistress would be ready to leave. In the meantime, though, we wandered around and ate and drank and enjoyed ourselves. Khessi had the prettiest voice. I could listen to her talk about any topic for hours, which was fortunate that she seemed to know so much more about the imperial palace than I did. She told me histories of the architecture and the art on the walls, stories of previous emperors and their lineage with white dragons.

After filling a plate full of strawberries and taking two glasses of champcane, we went out on the balcony to get away from all the noise in the main hall. It was a perfect night out, cool but not cold. The night sky was clear and bright. The silvery orb of the moon reflected in the vast open water of the sea just off the palace. The quiet was only altered by the sound of waves.

"Ahhh, this is much better," Khessi sighed looking up at the twinkling stars above.

"I agree. Much better for talking," I added.

She laughed a little. "And what is it you would like to talk about?"

"Anything. Everything. I just want to know more about you."

"Like what?" She crossed her arms and eyed me with mock suspicion.

"Tell me about your life as far back as you can remember and then end it with us sitting down out here."

"That sounds frightfully boring."

"All right, tell me about the day the Mistress bought you. Why do you think she chose you?"

"Oh, I know why she chose me. I engineered it that way."

"And?" I goaded her on. Khessi smiled and looked away. "Come on! You engineered how a Mistress would buy you? You have to tell me this story, now. "

"All right," she sighed and looked me in the eyes. "I punched another household trainee in the face."

"You what?" I laughed in disbelief. "That's fantastic! You have to explain, though. I can't imagine you punching anyone."

"Well, I have to get really upset. Or desperate, I suppose."

"Okay, lay it on me. Tell me the tale of Khessi the stone-fisted household slave."

She bubbled with giggles. Real giggles. In fact, she snorted a little when she laughed.

"You have to remember that the Mistress was not as you know her now. She was young. Her mother had recently died. She said she wanted a household slave who could take care of the business so she wouldn't have to. Nothing is further from that now. But at the time, she had other concerns. The Mistress came in and was looking at all us new household slaves. She was looking more at the male trainees. I knew I had to do something to make myself stand out. So I turned to the girl on my left, and I shouted, 'Don't you dare speak that way about a Mistress!' and I punched the girl in the face."

I laughed, imagining it, as I nearly choked on a strawberry. "Goddess!"

"I'm not very good at punching, so I only bloodied her nose a little. I think I startled her more than hurt her. The Mistress told me later that she knew the girl hadn't said anything, but she was so impressed with my ingenuity that she knew she had to have me. She also added that she liked my tits and would like them better if they were pierced. That's basically how I came to service under Mistress Isavyne."

"Well, you do have a very nice...bouquet." I gestured to the roses over her breasts. I reached down and took her hands in mine, running my fingers over her soft skin. "These little hands look far too delicate to have punched someone. And cold! How are your fingers always freezing?" I asked, trying to warm them some. She shrugged.

"They don't feel cold to me," she smiled thoughtfully, looking down at my hands wrapped around hers. "You're very sweet, Zsash.

"I am, aren't I?"

"Are you sure you're all right with this friendship and talking idea you're on about?"

I looked at her, confused.

She continued, "You're an awfully physical slave and I'm just not sure you've thought about the long term implications of being my friend."

"Oh! You're wondering if I can be around a beautiful woman without needing to stick my dick in her?"

"Pfft! Classy as always," she said with raised eyebrows and finished her drink.

"Sorry. I mean, yes, of course I find you attractive. I'd have to be blind and stupid to not want to have sex with you. I'm currently only one out of two of those." I said. She laughed and set her glass down. "Of course I've thought about you like that. I'm a pleasure slave. Sex is kind of on our minds a lot. Are you gonna pretend you haven't thought about it?"

She looked away with a smile and cleared her throat.

"Well you know, you're decent enough looking, I suppose."

"Oh please. You'd be defenseless against my charms. I'm a Cheritoth winner, after all. Women find that irresistible." I leaned my shoulder into hers jokingly.

"Sure. Let's say for the sake of argument that I was interested. It doesn't matter. I'm not fooling myself into thinking I can just have a normal sexual relationship. I will not know a man's touch until I'm instructed to do so. I will be bred. Have a child that I will never meet. And after that? Maybe the Mistress will not decide to breed me again and I can have a normal, regular sex, if I'm lucky. You don't want to have to wait around for that."

"So, wait. What is it, exactly, that household slaves are forbidden to do?" I asked.

"We are not allowed to get pregnant."

I waited, expecting her to continue.

"That's it?"

"It's a pretty clear command. As if there needs to be more?"

"Actually, there couldn't be anything less! Do you know how many physical pleasures you can have that don't involve that?"

"No, not even if a man says he'll be careful. There's too much risk involved and I'm not willing to take the chance with anything that even could get me pregnant."

"So don't let men fuck the pregnancy hole!"

"Again, real classy," she sighed, laughing and shaking her head.

"Sorry, sorry, I just…"

"And I've already thought of that. But I don't want to do anal sex. It hurts for the woman."

"Not the way I do it," I said, raising a single eyebrow. Her mouth gaped open in shock for a moment. I softened my tone and regrouped. "Khessi, I don't want you to feel pressured to do anything with me or anyone. I just want you to know that you can have sexuality without having sex. That's all I wanted to point out, is that you have options."

"Like what?" she asked innocently. My head shook with all the suggestions I had on this topic.

"This is *so* weird for me that you haven't discovered this on your own that I can't tell if you're messing with me or not."

"I don't think I want to talk about this anymore. This may be your area of expertise but I am not like Tikora. I am not some slut!"

"I'm not saying anything like that and I'm not trying to make you uncomfortable."

"Well, you are," she said, standing. "I know I'm probably not your type of lover anyway. So, I'm going to go inside and check on the Mistress."

"Wait, wait! Just…" I stood up with her, placing my hands on her waist. "Please don't run away from me."

She stopped and looked up into my eyes. Her breasts were rising and falling rapidly behind their rose confinement and I found that she was staring at my lips.

"How would I even go about experiencing these types of 'options'? Every slave on the estate is afraid to even talk to me." She huffed.

"I'm not." I answered without thinking. "Will you permit me to show you just one thing? Just one idea of pleasure that you can have without breaking your commands? Just something quick and easy?"

She looked over my shoulder at the crowded hall inside and pursed her lips. "What did you have in mind?"

"Can I show you?" I asked softly as I moved in closer to her, running my hand over her jaw to bring her mouth to mine. I kissed her gently, massaging her lips with my own until I felt her finally relax. Goddess, she smelled incredible. I extended my tongue slightly to brush against her mouth. Cautiously, she opened her lips to me. Her hands gripped my shoulders, nervously at first. But as the kiss deepened, her mouth became hungry for mine. I held her waist close to me with one arm, while with the other I ran my fingers over the pale skin of her exposed leg. The high slit in the fabric let me find her satin panties beneath.

"Zsash!" she gasped and looked again toward the crowded party hall. "What if someone sees?"

"Shh, nobody is paying any attention to us. It just looks like we're kissing." I whispered against her mouth while I pet the front of her satin underwear. I felt the metal stud of her clit piercing beneath the fabric. Khessi moaned a little, then pulled me in to kiss her again. The roses over her breasts pressed against me, their thorns sticking my chest through my satin shirt the closer we got. My motions were slow and soft, rubbing between her legs till the satin began to get warm and damp. Her hips lifted toward my touch as I teased her gently.

I moved the satin panties to the side to feel her sleek smooth flesh beneath. My fingers brushed across her softly, slowly parting her until I could just barely dip a finger inside. I hovered at her entrance, dipping back and forth to build the tension in her body.

"Zsash...." She whispered breathily. She was getting so wet with just the kissing and shallow teasing I was doing. I trailed my fingers in lazy circles around the tight entrance of her pussy.

"You could ride my fingers if you wanted." I offered. "All without risk of getting pregnant. All without pressure to return any pleasure to me. I just want to be with you, Khessi."

It took all the control I could muster, but I removed my hand from under her skirt. Kissed her softly once more and took a half step back from her.

"If that's something you want." I said, a tremor of lust had crept into my voice. "You can have pleasure without breaking your rules as a household slave."

She stared up at me with lusty aqua eyes, her breath still elevated. Then she smoothed her skirt out and took another step away from me, clearing her throat. I noticed we'd knocked a few petals off of the roses with our kissing that were now on the ground.

"Well, that was very educational. I, um, I need to get back to the Mistress, though."

"Wait, you don't have to leave,"

"You can wait here or enjoy the party. I'll find you when it's time to leave," Khessi said with her best diplomatic voice.

I grabbed her hand . "Don't run away. We can talk about something else. I just wanted to..."

"I'm not running away," she lied. "I'm not upset. I just, don't know what I think about all this. And I really must see to the Mistress. We can talk more later."

"Okay," I nodded and let her hand go.

She turned and walked back inside. The noise from the party boomed for a split second before she closed the door.

Shit. I didn't mean to press the matter. It just took me off guard. I had always been told that household slaves literally were not allowed to ever have sex or personal relationships. Now to hear Khessi tell it, it was just a matter of not getting them pregnant, something I had successfully managed to not do for years. It started to make the whole Tikora fooling around with those girls make more sense. I was pretty sure that Tikora was fucking male slaves as well, but who knew what her little system that she had worked out was.

There was something else that I had wanted to get across to Khessi, but didn't seem able to as I got sucked into the other conversation. The truth was, I think I would have been fine with never having sex with her. I enjoyed being around her. She made me laugh, made me feel cared for and safe. There was a kindness and strength in her that made me...

Oh, Goddess...

That made me love her.

"All monarchs have their particular appetites. Some are physical. Food, sex, drugs. These are the easier appetites to fulfill. Discover how to prepare the food. What wine to pair with what dish. Foods they dislike, and so on. Learn what sexual preferences they enjoy. Again, what pairings they prefer, what they'd like to do or have done. Simple. You will find, however, that many appetites of the monarchy are mental and come in a labyrinthine assortment of desires. But it is no matter. If the hunger in your Master is complex, rare or costly to the slave, it should be your honor to service it to your last breath."

Thralldrix, *The Scrolls of the Goddess*

CHAPTER 17: FEAST

It was then that I realized, I was lost.

Not with discovering that I had feelings for Khessi. I mean literally. I had gotten myself lost wandering around.

I had started to walk out into the gardens behind the palace. A winding labyrinth of sculptures cut into the tall bushes out back. I had entered it seeking some solace. This I achieved, but I underestimated the complexity of the tree maze and was now all turned around.

I don't know how regularly others fall in love. I never had. Perhaps it was a hazard of being a pleasure slave. Many slaves confused sex with love in their youth, I was told. It had always been a clear line in my mind. Though I have love for my brothers and sisters at the training house and love for the Mistress, romantically falling in love had just never happened for me.

I thought it would be more sudden. That it would hit me upon seeing her the first time. It's true that she did make a big impression on me. Khessi always made an impression. She was beautiful and had a presence whenever she was in the room. It took a lot longer to sink in than the storybooks implied. For the sake of storybook romance, I will always recount that I knew she was the love of my life from the start.

A cool, crisp breeze rustled through the trees and brought with it sounds that tore my thoughts from their romantic wistfulness. Heavy breathing, grunts, and whimpers. Furious whispers and the wet smacking of skin. My curiosity led me around corners and bends of the maze until I turned in one that led to an inner courtyard in the center.

There was a large stone mausoleum. It was an open structure that could be walked through to view the above-ground marble caskets of the emperors entombed there. It was made of cut black granite that sparkled with quartz in the moonlight. The imperial heraldry, a white dragon made of pure marble, stood guard at the front and back of the building facing out to ward off enemies. On top of one of the white caskets, I saw a couple having sex.

The first person I recognized was the Emperor. His pants and boots were gone. They were laid neatly on the ground along with his folded purple frock coat. He wore only a white shirt with frilly cuffs that I assumed had been beneath his coat and vest. His hands were on the woman's hips and he was taking her slowly from behind. His long dark blue locks swayed as he thrust against her. The woman stood with her face away from me. One of her legs was propped up on top of the casket he pushed her against, opening her wider for his penetration. I noticed her long blonde hair and white boots first. She wore a white corset that pushed her breasts up so the Emperor could take his time fondling them. But it was the pair of panties that made it all come together for me. I'd spent months fantasizing over a similar pair. White satin panties, pulled to the side so he could slide into her around her garments. And when I figured out what the Emperor was whispering, my mind felt like it had shattered.

"Isa…Isa…." he panted over and over. For a moment my world spun out of control. I didn't think the Mistress had sex with other Masters. I suppose that since he was an Emperor, and maybe that didn't count. I also started thinking thoughts I had no business thinking, like how she had danced with Braxian and led him on, only to be fucking the Emperor on the same night. It was her right, I supposed. Then another thought struck me. What if the Emperor was raping her? Maybe this was against her will and no matter his crown, I should stop him and defend my Mistress. I listened for a moment. She was enjoying it. Sounds of pleasure echoed in the great stone structure as she begged for more.

"Yes, oh yes! That's it," she moaned. "Oh! Please fuck me, Master!"

The Emperor stopped and grabbed her face, turning it to look at him. He slapped her hard across her cheek.

It was Basz. The truth of what I saw struck me almost as if I'd been slapped as well. I recognized all the clothes she wore. The boots. The corset. The panties. They all had belonged to Mistress Isavyne. Stolen by Tikora, so that the Emperor could play out fantasies of being with the only Queen he couldn't get into bed.

"Don't call me Master right now! Say my name while I fuck you!" he barked. "Do it!"

"I'm sorry, M—" she almost said it again. He slapped her across the face. It smeared the red lipstick she wore in an attempt to try and match Isavyne's lip color. She shook off the slap and looked him in the eyes. "Please, Dukkar. Please fuck me."

"That's better," he nodded and released her long enough to turn her around to face him. He reached down between her legs, sliding his fingers into her pussy. Basz shuddered visibly. "You're so beautiful. I can't tell you how long I've wanted you. Wanted to taste you. To know how it feels to be inside you."

"I've wanted you, too," Basz said around her moans. She was a poor imitation of Mistress Isavyne but, I guess as far as surrogates go, it wasn't bad. I now understood why he'd made Basz grow her hair long. It wasn't gold. But the blonde would have to do.

The Emperor removed his fingers from her and grabbed her by the waist. He then lifted her up onto the stone casket, which put her at his hip level. He leaned down and lifted one white boot to his shoulder. He kissed delicately down the boot until he reached her calf. He then extended his long tongue to lick from the inside of her knee to the top of her thigh. He moved back and spread her legs apart, holding the crook of her knees in each arm. He leaned in close to her face, which pushed her knees up till they rested by her shoulders. With his forehead pressed against her cheek. He whispered in a dark tone colored with lust, "I love you,

Isa. I've always loved you. Ever since you found me. I knew you'd be the one."

"I love you too, Dukkar," Basz said, unsure if that was her line. It seemed good enough for him.

"Tell me you want me." He said while he pressed the head of his cock over her wet entrance.

She bit her lip and moaned, "I want you. I want you more than anything."

"Tell me you need me inside you."

"I need you inside me. Please, Dukkar, please take me. Please fuck me!"

"Ah, yes. That's it!" he hissed. "Say my name. Beg me to fuck you!"

An animalistic purr came from the Emperor as he slid inside her. He took her breasts in his hands and pinched at her nipples roughly while he fucked her on the graves of his ancestors, kissing his name on her lips while she repeated it. His tongue slithered into her mouth in kisses drowned in obsession. His clawed hands gripped her hips hard, pulling her against him all while whispering Isavyne's name. He pounded into her, aroused beyond going slow, grunting and occasionally snarling. Small, high-pitched moans escaped Basz with each of his movements, her makeup melting under her eyes with sweat as she tried to keep up with his excitement. He was lost in his own frenzied fantasy, murmuring mad desires to her.

"You take my cock so fucking good," he panted, his voice clenched between his teeth.

"Oh yes, please, Dukkar! You feel so good. Oh, please let me cum!"

"Yes. Yes, Isa. Give yourself to me. Cum for your Emperor my love!" He lowered his thumb to her clit, rubbing it with his thrusts until her legs shook and her moans turned to screams.

"Oh! Oh, I'm cumming! Yes, yes!" Her cries heightened to a crescendo as the Emperor thrust into her wildly. The Emperor also seemed to be close to reaching his finish as he impaled her again and again. Her face had just relaxed from her orgasm as he was at the height of his passion.

With unearthly speed, the Emperor grabbed Basz by the throat and pulled her to his mouth. His teeth sharp and glistening. She only had time for a short startled scream as he sank his teeth into her neck. He tore the flesh that covered her artery so that he could drink her blood while he came. He thrust into her several more times, coming hard as he drank the river of ruby gore that spilled from her throat. It soaked into his shirt and splattered the white garments she wore. A cry of shock and terror must have escaped my lips without permission because my open hands flew up to cover my mouth. A gurgle of blood surged out of her dying lips and her eyes fell on mine for the split fleeting moment before she stopped moving. Stillness claiming her lovely features forever.

Having drunk all he could from her, the Emperor pulled back to look at her frozen, horrified face. He sighed.

Looking down at her with something like pity in his eyes, he cooed, "Poor little bird. So beautiful. So fragile."

He then planted a kiss on her lips that smeared them dark. He released her body, letting it fall to the ground in a heap.

He took two steps away from the body. He stopped in an abrupt halt and turned his head to look at me. A slow, unnatural movement like the turn of a praying mantis. I cringed, trying unsuccessfully to conceal my horror. My limbs were locked down in terror. This was probably not the first time a slave had looked at him this way. He did not seem fazed by my presence or notice the state of my shock. My heart hammered in my chest as he stared for long moments looking at me with those disturbing red eyes. He raised a clawed finger into the air and squinted a little. Finally, something clicked with an expression of realization, and the monster spoke to me like he was an Emperor again.

"Oh! Zsash, is it? I wanted to tell you how pleasing your performance was today," he said with my childhood lover's blood still dripping from his chin. He looked at me for a response as he began licking clean his fingers. He didn't remind me of a mantis anymore, but a large cat cleaning its bloodstained mouth after a kill. So casual. Without a care in the world. I couldn't run. I couldn't come up with words. Instead, I found myself nodding. My entire body shook with fear and hate, making my hands tremble uselessly at my sides. He pulled a handkerchief from his pocket and began wiping his mouth while he looked me up and down.

"Thank you, your majesty," I managed to say with a shaking voice.

"What is it again that you do for your lovely Mistress?"

"I…uh…baths…" I stammered incoherently.

He smiled politely and all I could focus on were the points of his teeth. His hand rose slowly and lifted my chin between two fingers. It was so strange. He didn't seem to move fast at all but his hand was just suddenly on me. I just watched him move closer and closer.

"Speak up, boy. I know you know how to use that mouth," he hissed. I could feel how much stronger he was than me in the soft exchange. He wasn't even holding onto my chin tightly but even his light grip hurt. "Tell me. Do you pleasure your Mistress with that silken tongue of yours?" His voice sounded curious, but also angry at the concept.

"I'm her bath slave, sire. Just…just a bath slave." I suddenly realized that my answers were going to directly affect whether he chose to kill me or not. His grip on my chin seemed to loosen some.

"Yes, you have some skill for public speaking. A real entertainer, aren't you?"

I nodded wordlessly.

"And how would you entertain an Emperor?" he continued.

"Uh…I can sing. A song perhaps?"

"Indeed. Your throat does hold some fascination for me."

"Oh! There you are, darling!" A flamboyant call interrupted the terrible moment.

I turned to see Master Lovol with a goblet in his hand, swishing his beautiful gown through the trees. He gave a brilliant black lipsticked smile to us and fell into a small intoxicated bow toward the Emperor. "Your most glorious majestical majesty! I have been looking for *this* one forever. Isavyne would kill me if I'd lost one of her pets. Especially this one."

"Indeed? What did she say about him?"

"Oh, just that he's hung like a beast and that I should make service of him while I can," he said, running his hand down the front of my pants for a moment before bursting into laughter. He didn't seem to notice or care about all the blood down the Emperor's shirt but instead, carried on in high spirits.

Master Lovol leaned in toward the Emperor, speaking in mock whisper and said, "It has been some time since I bedded a boy and I thought I'd give this one a shot. Or maybe two, if he's good!" He laughed obnoxiously and took another drink. The Emperor rolled his eyes contemptuously as Master Lovol continued, "Unless you intended to use him for your pleasure first, my lord? I would not dream of depriving you."

"No! No, I have other guests to attend to. But," The Emperor raised his hand to my face and patted my cheek. His dark red eyes fixed on mine. "Give my best to your Mistress when you see her, slave."

"Yes, Master Emperor."

I nodded numbly. Master Lovol placed his arm around my shoulder and played with my ear seductively. The Emperor turned and walked away while Lovol took me another direction out of the maze. It only took a few turns until we stood outside the maze and I could see the balconies where Khessi and I had been. I turned my attention to Master Lovol, who I realized I was now in the position to service. Wrestling with my composure I straightened up and attempted a smile.

"What is your pleasure, Master?" I said, bowing my head and running my hands over his muscular chest in a numb attempt to keep up appearances.

"Oh, please," Lovol scoffed and batted my hands away. All traces of drunken tone vanished from his voice and manner. "If I was going to start fucking men, you would not be my first choice. You're not that pretty. Let's get you back to your mistress before you get yourself killed."

I was still in shock and babbling a little. I finally got out words. "Did you see what he did to her?" I asked, feeling my face drain of color.

"Yes, darling. I'm sorry you had to see that. His majesty is a creature of specific tastes."

"But he made her wear—" I stopped myself. I knew Lovol was friends with Mistress Isavyne. Maybe he thought I'd just caught the Emperor having sex with a slave. Maybe he didn't see him kill her. Or perhaps he had seen the Emperor kill a slave and it just wasn't a big deal in his eyes. Surely he did not know about Mistress Isavyne's garments being stolen and about the Emperor saying her name while he fantasized fucking and killing her. Surely her friend would help warn her against such a Master. Then again, I thought she was friends with the Emperor too, prior to tonight.

It became apparent to me that the Mistress did not fully know what the Emperor had been up to in regard to his obsession with her. I stared into the bizarre silver eyes of another magically enhanced Master who I didn't know if I could trust. Especially one who had also expressed a romantic interest in the Mistress. I decided not to speak of it. He had saved me, but I could not come up with a reason why. It was best to be cautious. I bowed my head in respect to him and walked back to the palace to find Khessi and the Mistress.

I didn't speak the rest of the night. The carriage ride back to the estate was a quiet one. The Mistress slept for most of it. The two seats in the carriage flattened out to make a single padded sleeping mat. Khessi and I sat cross-legged at her feet for the journey. Khessi was wrapped in a red cloak. I shook my head no when she offered me one. I leaned against the wall of the carriage and pretended to sleep, even as I could feel Khessi's concerned gaze on me. I just wasn't prepared to talk about anything. I'm sure she wanted to talk about our kiss and her sudden exit earlier, which was minimized by all that had happened in the hour after she left. So much new information floated around in my brain and despite my realization of feelings toward Khessi, all I could see was Basz. I could only see her face in that final moment seeing me and how her eyes faded black.

I didn't know who to talk to. I didn't know who would believe me or if that even mattered. Maybe the Mistress knew all of this and didn't care. After all, Basz was just a pleasure slave. An expendable pleasure slave.

Just like me.

"It is a mistake to try and interpret the actions of your Master. It is a natural mistake because the Goddess gave you a mind to reason and think. Your efforts are in a desire to obey. But it is still a mistake nonetheless because it also contains the audacity to believe that you can wrap your mind around how your betters think. No slave understands the complexity of their world or their desires. The good news is that it is not a slave's job to figure this out. Let your mind be calmed by the reassurance that there is only one goal you should bend your mind to. Do as you are bid and nothing more or less. All else is not your concern."

Riquora, *The Scrolls of the Goddess*

CHAPTER 18: MESSAGES

In the following week after the Blossoming Celebration and our return to the estate, a new glass had been made for the Mistress and set onto the wine glass rack in the bath chamber. It was an interesting piece. Artistic. The bottom was clear cut crystal like the chalices found in the imperial palace. Identical to those, in fact. At the top of the stem, near the cup, there was a splintered, angular break. Above that fragmented line, the remaining stem and cup of chalice were blood red crystal.

I probably should have been mortified, or at least sickened, to realize it was the remaining fragments of the glass the Emperor had dropped into the ring. The same stem of the glass I'd shoved through Corvas's eye. I just couldn't get myself to feel bad every time I filled that glass for her during her bath. I felt the opposite, actually. It made me revel in my victory.

Similarly, I wore my gold coin collar everywhere. I hadn't taken it off since I'd received it. Other slaves looked at me differently, now. They smiled and wanted to get to know me. I guess Corvas wasn't very popular with many of the other slaves, either. A few of the guards still hated me, but they kept their distance. I would like to think it was because of my much-improved muscles and reputation for killing guard captains. More than likely, it was simply that there was nothing they could really do about it.

When I slept, I had nightmares. I would dream that I was bound up in front of the entire court being whipped by Tikora. While I stood bound and helpless I would watch as the Emperor had his way with Khessi, making her suck his cock to get him hard, then fucking her while he sat in that huge throne. In the

271

audience, the Mistress just stood and watched while I begged for her to stop him. Every dream ended the same, with the Emperor taking Khessi until he made her climax and then tearing her throat open to drink her blood.

When I woke, I would always be covered in cold sweat and gasping to get air I couldn't take in. It seemed to take forever for me to take full breaths.

During the days I would think about Khessi. How would I tell her that I was in love with her? Should I tell her? Did she feel that way about me? Did I scare her off at the Blossoming Celebration? I had so many questions and I didn't know how to act on them. I wished we could just be like we had been at the party. Close. Talking. Kissing. Together.

It wasn't until I made it back to the blacksmith shop that I got called out on it while daydreaming and working metal.

"You are too damn quiet since you got back," Garsteel finally said while we were heating iron. "What is wrong with you?"

"Hmm? Nothing. Just working, is all. I'm focusing." I had been staring into the embers for a while and gotten lost in my thoughts. I looked at Garsteel and gave a close-lipped fake smile. "I'm good. How...how are you doing?"

He set the metal he was working on down into the fire and moved closer to me, cleaning soot off his hands.

"Please don't slap me again. I swear I'm not being a self-pity slave. I've just got a lot on my mind."

"You are the most chatty jerk-off I've ever met in my life. Everything that has ever passed through your mind in my presence has made it out of your mouth. There are things I didn't want to know, that no man should really ever know about another man. Things you can't seem shut up about."

"So?"

"So, something must be very wrong if you deem it too much to talk about. It means it's probably something you should get out of your skull."

"It's a lot. And no offense, but I'm not ready to talk about some of it."

"All right," he frowned slightly.

"But can I talk to you about one aspect of it vaguely? I don't want to give specifics."

"Yeah, that'd be fine," he shrugged the corners of his mouth and nodded.

"I have feelings for a woman."

"Khessi, right? I'm pretty sure everyone knows that, " he said.

"Shit, never mind!" I threw my hands up in frustration as I took a step away. I then let them rest on my hips as I shook my head.

"Oh, come on! Was that supposed to be a secret? You've been staring at her for months now like a starving dog looking at a piece of meat. Exactly how mysterious were you trying to be?"

"Well, I'm not even sure if she wants me to pursue her. And even if she does, how would I ask the Mistress for permission to be with her household slave?"

"Those are excellent questions that no other man on this estate has figured out how to answer."

"Great."

"But, then again, I don't see too many others wearing a gold coin around their neck. You want my advice? Tell Khessi how you feel about her and the rest will get figured out."

"That sounds overly simplified."

"Well, Khessi is the closest with the Mistress. If she wants to be with you, she'll tell her. All you have to do is let her know that you care about her and see where it goes."

"I don't even know how to say what I feel."

"Well, write it down. Aren't you some kind of poet of public speaking in the arena and shit?" he laughed, slapping my arm.

I smiled, laughing for the first time in weeks.

Garsteel chuckled and crossed his arms over his barrel chest. "Why don't you go find the lady right now? It's not like we need to train you as hard as we were. I'm sure the Mistress won't mind."

It took a few more times of his coaxing but I eventually took his advice and decided to go find Khessi. I went to her office and found it much more occupied than I'd expected.

I poked my head in for a moment but then stayed outside in the hall as I heard multiple voices. Like any good gossipy slave, I hovered in the doorway and listened. The Mistress was talking.

"It is such a pleasure to receive you. I had a wonderful time at the blossoming celebration. The Emperor is a most gracious host."

"He will be happy to hear you think so," said Tikora.

I held my breath. Slowly, I peeked back in again. Mistress Isavyne sat at the glass table, having tea. She sat on the back of a well-muscled male slave on his hands and knees. He was naked except for a black blindfold tied over his eyes.

There actually was a trick to being used as various types of furniture. It was something all slaves were taught when we are young. The body doesn't naturally maintain a flat surface. You have to lower your arms so that your shoulders are level with your hips. In this way, you can function as a chair, or table if needed. This slave didn't tremble or shift at all. It led me to believe he must have been some kind of official chair slave.

Tikora stood before the Mistress on the other side of the table, holding a silver canister. Khessi approached them, holding a gold teapot that matched the tea set at the table that Mistress Isavyne and Tikora drank from. Khessi wore a shiny black gown and her silver collar and cuffs again. She poured the tea flawlessly and without hitting the chains of her restraints against the glass teapot or cups. Her smile was frozen diplomatically on her painted lips in rigid politeness while she filled Tikora's cup.

"More tea, sister?" Khessi asked with razor-smoothed pitch.

"No, thank you. But I would take another sugar in mine. This tea is awfully bitter," Tikora mocked. The household slave to the Emperor blew delicately on her steaming tea and watched Khessi sharply while she dropped two cubes of sugar into the Mistress's cup first. Khessi then dropped one cube from slightly too high above the teacup, causing a tiny splash of subtle rebellion.

"So what is this message you bring to me?" The Mistress asked between sipping.

Tikora set her cup down with practiced precision and handed the silver canister over with both hands and her head bowed. The Mistress opened it and tilted it to one end. A scroll fell out. She broke the wax seal of the letter and spent long minutes reading it. Every slave in the room held still while she read it to herself.

When she was done, she rolled the scroll back up and set it aside, handing Tikora back the canister.

"Shall I wait for your response, Mistress?" Tikora asked, bowing her head.

"No. I will contact the Emperor with a more private message once I have had time to properly consider my response."

"As you command." Tikora bowed her head again deeply. She then reached for her cup and finished her tea in one gulp.

Setting the cup down, she turned again to Mistress Isavyne. "Do I have your permission to return to the palace, Mistress Isavyne?"

"Please do. Tell the Emperor that I am deeply moved by his words and will not keep him waiting long for an answer."

Tikora bowed low to Mistress Isavyne, then turned on pink-heeled boots to leave. There was no casual way to not be seen. I stood up against the wall next to the doorway and looked straight forward. Tikora smiled at me as she turned the corner, surprised to see me. She didn't speak but placed a finger to her lips to show silence as though we were in on a secret together. It made me feel dirty. I wanted nothing to do with her or her Emperor.

A moment or two after Tikora walked away, I heard my name called.

"Zsash, come in here," The Mistress said.

I guess I hadn't been as sneaky as I thought.

I walked into the room and went to the Mistress's side. She patted the slave beneath her on the head and stood up. He rose and walked out of the room and down the hall, all while still wearing the blindfold. I thought it seemed like a really neat trick. He must have done that a few times.

"Is it your intention to always get yourself into trouble by being where you shouldn't be?" The Mistress said before drinking more tea.

"No, Mistress. I came to speak to Khessi and did not want to interrupt your meeting."

"Oh, really? What did you need to speak with her about?" Her thin golden eyebrows raised in curiosity.

My mouth hung open while my brain raced to think up some reason I would have been in there to talk to her. "I just…uh, wanted to…thank her for all her support since my arrival and through my training," I replied.

"Hmm. Well? Do so and be done with it. She and I have much to discuss."

"Oh...um," I smiled at Khessi, who had sat down on the black couch. Her back was straight and legs crossed at the ankle in a poised position, she glanced at me out of the corner of her eye. "Thank you."

Khessi nodded her head. The Mistress clapped her hands together.

"Well, now you have done that. I suppose it's just as well you are here. I was going to summon you anyway. You heard most of that conversation, yes?" she stated.

"Yes."

"I will be writing a response to the Emperor immediately and I wish for you to accompany Khessi and Garsteel to the palace. The three of you will deliver my answer to his majesty personally and I expect you to be on your best behavior."

"Of course, Mistress."

"And when in doubt my pet, don't speak."

"Certainly, Mistress," I nodded.

That night in the bath, the Mistress was extremely quiet. But she drank. Glass after glass I poured for her, she drank without reserve. She finished two bottles of wine by the end of the bath. Eventually, while filling up her glass, I overstepped my boundaries out of concern.

"Are you all right, Mistress?" I asked.

Her answer was slow and without humor. "Shut your mouth and pour my wine, slave."

I did so.

When she was done, I helped her out of the bath. As I wrapped a towel around her, she tilted to the side and I caught her about the waist. Mistress Isavyne sighed heavily, placing a palm to her forehead. She cleared her throat.

"Carry me to my bed, slave," she commanded. I picked her up gently and carried her to the bed. Slipping her between the sheets and the comforter, I tucked her in. I waited for a few minutes since she didn't officially dismiss me. She was soon fast asleep, so I assumed I was good to adjourn for the evening.

The next morning we set off to the Imperial palace to deliver the Mistress's answer to the Emperor. The gold carriage had been brought out front for our journey. Two white horses were harnessed to it. Because this was an official visit, we were to dress in the colors of the Mistress. I was dressed in black pants and a white shirt. I also tucked two of my slip knives into my belt. I didn't want to appear overtly threatening, but there was no way I would be without protection of some kind around the Emperor and his rabbit girl.

Khessi looked gorgeous as usual. She wore a white top that criss-crossed fabric across her long, lean torso. Silver shells and diamonds decorated the top and sparkled merrily with her silver collar and cuffs. The skirt she wore was a light sheer fabric that fell like white petals around her hips.

The one I was not prepared for was Garsteel. Clean shaven and looking like a gentlemen, also in a white shirt and black pants. His sword rested on his hip casually and I wondered if I could have gotten away with wearing my entire slip knife belt.

"What?" I said and whistled at the blacksmith, gesturing at his attire. He smiled, shaking his head.

"Yeah, yeah. I clean up good," he smiled begrudgingly.

"You look quite handsome," Khessi said and gave him a quick kiss on the cheek.

"Thank you, sweet girl," he blushed a little.

"All right, you two, into the back," Garsteel said, clapping his hands twice.

Khessi and I climbed into the carriage and I was on my way back to the palace for the second time. I was not excited to be around the Emperor again so soon. Khessi sat holding a gold case that housed the scroll we were to deliver.

The carriage rolled with only a few bumps here and there down near the sea. Outside the window, the sun hung high and bright over the sparkling waves. I waited until we were clear of the estate to speak. Once we were, I figured it was safe to address the issue at hand.

"So?' I started.

"What?" She blinked.

"The Emperor asked her to marry him, didn't he?" I said more as a fact than a question.

"Zsash..."

"It's just like Tikora was talking about at the party. How he wanted to join their houses. That's what's happening, isn't it?"

"I don't know. She didn't let me read his letter to her, nor her response," she shook her head.

"Oh, come on! You know that has to be it! Do you know how obsessed the Emperor is with the Mistress?"

"He has favored her over all others for some time now, yes."

"So what was her response? Is she going to marry him? How fucked are we?"

"Well, we'll find out eventually!" She said, raising her voice a little at me. "No matter the content, our orders are plain. We take her answer to the Emperor and deal with whatever she's chosen to do."

I leaned in toward her, gesturing to the scroll case.

"Let's just take a look and find out. We have it right here."

"Are you trying to get yourself killed? It is one thing to act a fool and get yourself into trouble on our estate. It is something else entirely to meddle in matters between the Emperor and the Mistress. The Emperor owns all of us. He doesn't even need her permission to take our heads."

"Well, then I guess I hope she gave him a happy answer. Wouldn't it be kind of nice to know what sort of situation we're walking into?"

"It's not our place to…" She started to say, but I cut her off. I was irritated.

"Oh, horse shit! I am so sick of all of your tight-lipped diplomatic answers like you're above thinking the way I do. You're just as curious as I am. Don't pretend like you're not!"

"Of course I am!" She snapped then huffed with her arms folded across her waist. She then looked up, thinking of Garsteel above us driving the carriage. She quieted her tone some but her eyes blazed. "Of course I am just as curious as you! But you cannot just bound through life doing whatever you want!"

"What about leaving your shawl with me in the dungeon?" I whispered.

She blinked and her face calmed down somewhat.

"I've seen you break the rules when you think it's justified. Your loyalty is to the Mistress. You're still serving her best interests by knowing what is in that scroll and what we are about to walk into."

She looked at me, thinking. She moved to my side of the carriage, pushing me so she could be by the window.

"Move over," she sat next to me. "This is a terrible idea." She opened the scroll case and pulled out the scroll inside. It was sealed with a stamp of gold wax, bearing the Mistress's phoenix heraldry.

"Damn it," I let out a disheartened breath. "Never mind. It's sealed."

"All letters from monarchs have wax seals, Zsash," she said as if I was slow. "It's not difficult to get around. I'll need to borrow this, though." She caught me off guard as she reached toward me. It was nice to feel her touch again. I was suddenly aware of how close her face was to mine, and I ignored the scent of her skin as she reached under my belt and pulled out a slip knife. She wagged it at me with a smile.

"Tease," I huffed out at her.

She shrugged then held the seal up to her mouth and breathed long hot breaths onto the wax. After warming it with her mouth for a minute, she slid the edge of the knife under the wax until half of it came off the paper and it unrolled.

"Not our business, my ass. You did that way too well for it to be the first time."

"Oh, hush," she brushed off my statement with a shrug and began to read the scroll. I couldn't read her face while she did so, but it wasn't good. When she'd done, she rolled the scroll back up.

"Well?" I asked.

She handed me back the slip knife.

"It says she's accepting his proposal," she said with tight lips.

My heart sank. "How can she do that? He's a monster."

"Hush, Zsash. You can't talk like that. Ever," she said putting her hand to her temples like she was getting a headache.

"But he is!"

"Keep your voice down, please," she said trying to whisper.

"What about Master Braxian? Didn't it seem like she loves him? I mean, he's not my favorite choice but at least he's not..."

"It doesn't matter! She's marrying the Emperor. We have no say in it."

"I don't understand! Why would she save herself for so long? Why would she waste her time stringing along Master Braxian and putting on her ivory Queen virgin Mistress strut just to marry that terrible blood-thirsty....!?!"

"Zsash! Stop!"

Our argument stopped abruptly at a sound outside like stones hitting the side of the carriage. A moment later, something flew through the carriage window and into the side wall, bringing a scream of surprise from Khessi.

It was an arrow, crude and barbaric looking with an ugly, barbed tip and nasty, spiny fletching. The carriage swerved erratically, pitching side to side. I heard Garsteel let out a bellow of pain above us, followed by screeching of the horses. The carriage rocked suddenly, violently and tipped over onto its side. Khessi clung to my waist as the carriage toppled. We didn't fall far. Water and sand splashed into the carriage windows as it dragged to a stop. We must have veered into the shallows of the beach because water covered our feet, but the flooding did not continue. I pulled the two slip knives from my waist, holding them between the fingers of my right hand and caught Khessi with my left. Khessi's fear-filled eyes looked into mine.

"Are you all right?" I whispered.

She nodded, panting. She screamed again as the door of the carriage, now above us, was pulled open. A dark shape with wild fur snarled and reached down for us. I didn't wait to see more. I threw both knives toward the form above us. This close to it, my aim was perfect. My knives buried deep into each of the man's eye sockets.

"Pain is the lesson."
The Code of Slaves, *The Scrolls of the Goddess*

CHAPTER 19: BURNED

The creature with the daggers in his eyes fell backward. I heard him land hard on the earth outside with a splash.

"Stay here," I told Khessi. I stood and peeked my head out of the side door that was now open above us. I pulled myself up on top of the wreckage. The horses were dead, shot with multiple arrows. The wyrling I'd killed lay right outside. His body was decorated with mud and thick paints of orange. Dark fur bristled down his arms to the long black claws on his hands. He was beastly and feral.

And he wasn't alone.

A pack of thirty similar wyrlings were approaching us at a run, showing little to no notice of their dead comrade. I jumped out and grabbed my knives from the skull of the dead one. The horde was on me in seconds. I began slashing into the wall of meat attacking me. I killed at least three, but there were so many all at once.

They grabbed my arms and dragged me away from the carriage. I tried to punch at them, attempting to break free. But they were strong, much stronger than me. I struck one wyrling with green paint and a pair of tusks growing between his lips. He snorted and punched me so hard I thought I might black out. Falling to my knees, blood pouring from my nose, I fought to remember how to breathe.

Garsteel was brought up next to me. Arrows had pierced his shoulder, a leg, and his gut. Blood seeped from his wounds into the sand and he glanced at me with one bruising eye.

I was lifted brutally to my feet again. My arms were held in front of me while one of the wyrlings bound my hands tightly with a leather strap. They did the same to Garsteel. They had gotten hold of my knives and two of the wyrlings marveled at the shine of my blades. A third wyrling pushed them both in an attempt to take the blades. There was snarling, pushing, punching between them for a moment until they decided the first one would keep them. He was big and nasty, and it seemed there was a pecking order.

There was suddenly a tug at my throat. For a moment I thought they might strangle me to death until I realized one of them had pulled my gold coin collar from my neck. I made another lame attempt to fight them to get it back, an attempt that ended with a punch to my guts that sent me doubled over in the sand while they laughed. My forehead rested on the ground while I gasped and wheezed like a fish on land.

A new fear sunk into me as I heard a chant of taunts and appreciative noises erupt from the wyrlings. They had discovered Khessi hiding in the upturned carriage. She tried to fight back for a moment, but her hands were soon bound like ours. Dirty clawed hands pawed roughly over her beautiful face, smearing her intricate makeup, leaving streaks. Two of the wyrlings held her while the tusked one put his hands on her. I felt my face grow red with fury as he ran his hands over Khessi's pale flesh. More hands tore at her skirt and top, pulling at the fabric until her skirt was shredded and only her top remained, though askew. The tusked wyrling marveled at her pierced breasts that were now exposed and ran his black, spotted tongue over his lips.

I shouted something. Garsteel was next to me, telling her it was going to be all right. I don't know why it is our instinct to tell comforting lies when we're in trouble. It's not like we could actually guarantee any of our safety from our position.

Animalistic hands ran through her lovely hair. The tusked one brought his tongue, long and snake-like, out to lick one of her breasts. The trail of slime he left behind made me want to gag. She struggled against him, pushing away from them as best she could. One of them held her wrists, pulled aside his crude leathers at his waist and brought her bound hands between his legs. He thrust into her hands messily while she fought against them. The other tried to follow suit. He settled for pressing against her hip to gain pressure with her body, roughly grabbing her other breast to hold her more securely. The tusked one in front of her began stroking his cock and grabbed her by the neck in an attempt to get her to open her mouth.

There was nothing I could do. I struggled against the ones holding me, wishing they would kill me for entirely selfish reasons. At least if they killed me, I wouldn't have to live with the shame and pain of knowing that I couldn't protect the person I loved. That she had come to harm and pain and that I had been powerless to stop it.

The one wyrling using Khessi's hands must have been distracted because she suddenly got them free from his grasp. She was still bound, but in an instant, she used her delicately sculpted nails against the tusked one in front of her. She clawed at the flesh between his legs, making him scream and bleed with the short time she had to defend herself. The other wyrlings laughed at him. The enraged tusked wyrling brought his other hand up and punched her hard in the face. Grabbing her by her red hair, he pulled her away from his fellows down the beach.

I kept shouting her name.

No, no. Please Goddess, this can't be happening.

A new desire flashed in the tusked wyrling's eyes while blood trickled down his leg. I'd seen the look on Corvas, the look with intent to kill shown in his eyes. Khessi screamed and kicked into the sand as he dragged her down the beach and into the water. Her hands flailing uselessly against his muscled arms as he held her face down under the water.

I was screaming, fighting. It did no good. It all felt like a dream where sound was so intensely loud it was somehow muffled. All I could do was watch for what seemed like an eternity. It was also a startlingly short amount of time.

The tusked wyrling held Khessi's head below the water. Her arms flailed in panic, she clawed at his forearms, splashing convulsively while they all laughed. His face was full of malice and joy over this act of taking her life. After a minute, the violent splashing stopped. Her body jerked a few times. Then that terrible stillness set in. And all I could think of was the last look on Basz's face claiming Khessi's beautiful features.

That was the longest moment of my life.

Those filthy hands pressed at the back of her head, keeping her down, wreathed in long tendrils of her bright copper hair that spread out on the surface of the water. Waves bobbed her motionless body up and down. It may not have been the Emperor, but this was my nightmare.

That image was all I thought about while they dragged us through the wild along the coastline. They had to drag me. I didn't fight them anymore. Garsteel was silent beside me except for his labored breathing. It seemed a kindness that he might bleed to death before we found whatever end these savages planned for us.

Death was certain. All that remained was to discover what door the Goddess had planned for me to walk through as I left this world. Tears stung bitterly into my face in the setting sun. I both cursed and thanked the Goddess that Khessi's end had been somewhat quick. I cursed her for taking the life of such a beautiful woman but thanked her that she hadn't been raped before her death. And that at least she'd been laid to rest in the sea.

Like her beloved Glo.

It was dark when we arrived at the wyrling encampment. They had taken to hitting us with their spear ends and sticks to keep us walking. Fortunately, I didn't feel a thing. The encampment was between the forest's edge and the sea. Twenty or so tents were set up in a circle around a fire pit. Fish hung from a spit near the fire and several of the wyrlings were eating ravenously. Howls and screeches came from the hunting party as they returned home with their prey.

Female wyrlings ran out of the tents, calling out with hoots and catcalls. A few of the females grabbed and mounted a male immediately. They rolled to the ground behind us, fucking wildly in the mud. One female looked me up and down and then slapped me across the face, causing laughter from the bunch. I spit out a mouthful of blood at her. She seemed to enjoy it.

Our bonds were tied to long thongs of leather at the base of a wooden post at the edge of the camp near the tide. They already had our weapons, but then they took our boots and belts, as well. The sand was moist below my feet. It stung in the cuts I hadn't realized I had all over my legs. Shells and fragments in the sand poked into my feet. It all hurt but I hardly noticed.

They left us there and went back to celebrating the return of their warriors. When they were far enough away, I turned to Garsteel. His shirt was stained with blood. He looked up at me, his breathing heavy.

"Can you walk?" he said softly.

"It doesn't matter. You can't walk and I'm not leaving you," I replied, beating him to his next thought.

"I'm dead already. If you can get out of those bonds, you can get out of here. Get back to the Mistress."

"And tell her what?" I looked into his blue eyes.

He searched for something to say but couldn't. I couldn't go back. If I survived but Khessi and Garsteel had not? It was better to die with them.

As the sun set, the wyrlings came back and forth from the forests edge to stack piles of wood in the center of their camp.

"Zsash," Garsteel whispered.

I looked over to see he was using a piece of broken shell to try to cut through the leather. There were shells buried all across the sand. I dug around in it for a moment. I could only find long, six-inch spiral shells. Pointed, but not edged. I saved them, though. I thought that I might be able to stab one of our attackers with one if they came close enough. They were long and pointed, not much different than a slip knife in shape as far as throwing was concerned.

Garsteel broke a flat shell in half, then tossed the other half to me. Picking it up, I felt the sharp edge of the shell. We both began working on cutting our bonds immediately. It was not a fast process. Blood had begun to pool in the sand under Garsteel. My elation at the idea that we had a hope of getting out of here was dampened by how long it seemed to take to cut through our bonds. You'd be surprised how long it takes to cut through leather when you can only move your fingers about an inch. Garsteel gave me a strained smile while we both sawed at our bonds. His smile faded and I turned to look over my shoulder.

Four wyrlings grabbed him. One of them cut Garsteel free of the posts that held us. He didn't put up much fight as they took him away, his face ashen in the firelight. They didn't notice the shells or that we had been attempting to get free. Perhaps it was because it didn't matter. They dragged him to the center of their camp to the fire pit. A nauseous feeling twisted in my gut as I realized what they had captured us for.

We were food.

Garsteel realized it too. A final streak of frenzied energy let him kick at his attackers. He pulled at his bonds with renewed strength. The wyrlings placed him against a wooden post in the center with practiced ease, tying him with new restraints . He finally stood helpless, slumped against the restraints at the wooden beam. He stared at me from across the camp and raised his head high. He nodded to me with a little tremor of effort. He lifted his throat. He hoped they would cut it any minute now before setting the fire. I sawed harder at the leather that held my wrists. A few times, I missed the bonds and sliced my skin in a mad pace to get free.

My panic turned to frenzy as I saw them approach the fire pit with torches, setting flames into the woodpiles. They were going to burn him alive! His head remained high as the flames started to consume the kindling around his feet. The wyrlings shouted and danced around the fire in primitive celebration. Feeling the half shell, sharp and in my hand, I tossed it aside to pick up one of the spiral shells I'd saved. I tested the weight of it and realized there may be one thing I could do for Garsteel.

I took aim, feeling the balance for a moment. I threw the shell like I would a slip knife toward him, aiming for the artery in his neck.

I missed.

The shell was so much lighter than a blade, my aim had fallen short. The shell disappeared into the fire at his feet. Wildly, I searched around for another. Finding one almost immediately, I aimed again. My bound hands didn't allow me the same balance I was used to. I tried to adjust for it. I ignored the cries that heaved from his coughing chest. The smoke rose around him while the heat worked on him. I threw the second shell at his exposed throat with all the strength I could pull together. It hit hard and stuck in the post about a foot above his head. Tears streamed from his bloodied face and got lost in his stifled screams while flames licked the bottoms of his legs. I fell to my knees, hands digging into the sand in search of more shells. The screams and sounds of cheering reached a deafening level in my ears. It seemed like an eternity before I found another. This one was a longer and heavier. The weight and shape of it was as though it had been built to be thrown.

Please Goddess, please don't let me miss again.

I tucked my left hand around my right wrist and looked back. Blinking tears from my eyes I fought to wash my mind in cold focus. I tried not to see the flames engulfing my friend. His clothes were ablaze and his skin blackened. I ignored the roar of the fire. Ignored the cheers. Ignored the screams.

I threw the spiral shell with perfect spin and all the strength I had left in me. It sailed across the camp and into Garsteel's throat. I had hit the artery. Thick spurts of blood pulsed from his neck. With his other injuries, it didn't take but a few moments. I don't know if it was wishful thinking, but I thought I saw a flicker of relief cross Garsteel's face as he slumped into the bonds that held him in the fire.

The wyrlings didn't even notice.

Falling to my knees, drained and weak, all of what had happened was far too ugly and painful to deal with anymore. The fire continued to creep over his still form and consume him. I turned away from the fire pit and stared out into the sea. My sobs were lost in the lapping of the waves at shore.

I was a coward. I shuddered under the night sky with miserable cold. Never had I dreamt that I would miss the cold floor of the dungeon. But the icy night air coming off the sea made me wish I was back in my cell. Perspective is everything.

I tried to block out the smell of charring meat that made my stomach turn. But I couldn't shut out the sounds. The hissing of sizzling and then eventually sounds of ripping, tearing, cutting and carving. The wyrlings laughed and snarled into their meal. My empty stomach retched between my tears. I began to dig in the dirt for another shell. An edged shell. Not to continue cutting my bonds, just one more shell to take my life before I had to burn alive.

I should have done this at the training house. That morning while I shaved, I should have slashed my wrists and died in the bathtub. Maybe if I hadn't been stealing, the Mistress would have noticed her missing garments sooner and found Tikora out. Maybe she wouldn't have consented to marry the Emperor if she knew he'd been responsible for stealing her things. Goddess, why hadn't I told her what kind of monster he was? Why hadn't I told anyone? Maybe these were just the fearful denials of a slave that was never worth anything and should have died long ago but was just too stupid to realize it. Until now. Not even worth one fucking gold.

The large wyrling with the tusks approached me and set something next to me, on top of the wooden post I was tied to.

"Hungry?" he said in a gargled monstrosity of a voice. He set the swollen, charred head of Garsteel there. I tried not to look at it. Instead I noticed that the wyrling was wearing my coin collar. The gold piece glittered and stood out compared to the other furs and filth he wore. I glared at him with a sneering laugh bubbling insanely out of me. He looked confused at my sudden onset of humor.

"I really hope you're wearing that when the Mistress finds you," I told him. He kicked me in the side and let out a superior snort. Then he turned and walked back to the feast. I shook with anger and pain and disgust, thinking about all the terrible ways I wanted to kill him. I wanted to kill all of them.

I kept my face turned as far away as possible, anything to pull my mind from the sickening sights now haunting my mind. I would be next. This was how I was going to die. This was how the story of the one gold slave would end.

It was what I deserved. I was a terrible slave. The Mistress had spent so much time teaching me, making me better. But now Khessi and Garsteel where dead. And I would be, too. My pitiful life should have ended when I was almost cut in two as a boy.

As if providing proof that it was my time, I found a beautiful pearlized shell in the sand. I broke it in half, feeling the sharp edge against my fingertips. I tested it against the skin of my arm, ready to slice open my wrists.

Long moments went by as I worked to gather my courage. I was done. That was fine. What really pissed me off was that these disgusting creatures had killed two people I cared about and might not be punished.

Garsteel was one of the most good-hearted slaves I'd ever met. Without his teaching and friendship, I would have been dead back at the Cheritoth.

And Khessi...
Goddess, I'd never even told her I loved her.

Should I really just give up?

No.

No I shouldn't!

For a few reasons that included not actually wanting to die, but mostly and more importantly, *fuck them!* I was not going to quit! Maybe they would burn me alive and eat me, but not without a fight. If I could at least get my hands free enough to kill a few of them, that would be all right by me. Especially that tusked bastard who had laid his hands on Khessi.

I could see Khessi now in my mind. Pale skin against that incredible vibrant hair, still colorful while dripping wet. As always wearing the collar and cuffs the Mistress had bestowed upon her, wearing nothing on her bottom half but only the white top that exposed her belly. I could almost see her walking up the beach, holding a knife and cutting my bonds.

And then the most amazing thing happened.

I was rescued.

A cold wet hand covered my mouth and I jolted with surprise. Kneeling in front of me with dripping red curls and soaked in the sea water, was Khessi! I hadn't been imagining it. She was really here. My eyes squinted with confusion. I fought to find the words. A sob of relief escaped me as she placed a hand over my mouth. I caught in her small palm and pressed it against my face, kissing it.

"Oh, Goddess, I thought you were dead!"

"Shh…" she said softly and removed her hand from mine gently. "Where's Garsteel?" She asked, looking around the camp.

"Don't look," I said, trying to stop her before she saw it.

Her eyes rested on the severed head they had set above me. She gasped and looked down at me, shutting her eyes. When she opened them, she didn't look up at the decapitated head again.

"Come on, Zsash. We have to go," she said, holding back tears.

A primitive screech rang through the camp like the shrill squeal of a pig. One of our captors raced toward us. Of course, it was the ugly tusked one, wearing my gold coin collar. He held a stone knife and raised it as he approached us. I stood, shuffling to my feet in an attempt to get in front of Khessi. As he got to me and raised the knife, I heard the sound of breaking bone, which I expected to be mine.

It wasn't.

Mistress Isavyne stood before us. Long, golden hair hung loosely around her shoulders above a simple long white gown. Her lovely hand was around the wyrlings neck, holding him effortlessly by the throat.

"This one?" she asked Khessi, her tone mild for the situation.

"Yes, Mistress." Khessi's voice was unforgiving and we both glared at our attacker.

The Mistress crushed his throat in a single movement. His head tilted off to the side of his spine, only held there by residual muscle and skin.

Mistress Isavyne raised her other hand to my coin collar around his neck. She tore it from him before dropping his body. When she turned to me, I saw that her eyes glowed, lit by blue fire wreathed in orange flames. The air around her filled with the vacuum of her growing power. The Mistress took my hand in hers and placed the collar in my palm.

"Do not lose this again, Zsash," she said with ruby lips sparkling in the flame from her eyes.

"Yes, Mistress." I nodded, putting the collar back on immediately.

"Where is Garsteel?" she asked of her household slave.

Khessi gestured sadly toward what remained of our fellow slave. The Mistress stepped toward Garsteel's skull, looking at the severed head. For a long silent moment, she stared into the empty, charred eye sockets.

I felt the rush of heat coming off of her like a warm front moving in before a storm.

There was no sadness or disgust in her eyes. Her face did not contort with emotion but rather stilled into a beautiful mask void of sympathy. The only emotion I could read from her came from her eyes.

Mistress Isavyne's eyes began to glow.

Anger was too mild a word. She possessed a pure, unflinching rage that brought a glowing light to the blue embers in her eyes. Tears of fire and electric gold slid down over her cheeks. Her skin turned ashy and black in the fires that spread over her body. Her hair became bright molten gold, wreathed in flames that engulfed her entire body. Ashes drifted behind her while the fiery aura around her blazed. The fire burned away the dress she wore until all that remained was her now pitch-black skin, seamed with gold and a halo of flames.

The wyrlings had noticed us at the edge of their camp. They were gathering their fighters from the tent, looking at the Mistress with superstition and fear.

A few wyrlings ran in to attack the Mistress and I honestly cannot tell you exactly how they died. She moved too fast. I saw splashes of blood and limbs ripped from their hosts. Then, burning. All of them burned.

More wyrlings emerged from their tents and grabbed weapons to attack.

"Khessi, get him beneath the water. It's not safe here." the Mistress said with absolute calm. A dark tremor of heat waves resonated in her voice.

She then turned and walked into the heart of the camp. The flames around her grew larger, leaving her perfect body in the center of an unyielding inferno.

"Zsash! Hurry!" Khessi shouted, pulling me by the hand. We ran down the beach to the water. I turned again to see the shapes of many of my captors emerging from their tents. Shouts beginning to carry on the air mixed with a growing roar of flames and the piercing call of a bird of prey. The flames grew in a cylinder of power around the Mistress. I stopped for a moment at the edge of the water, my feet sinking into the sand while I stared with wide eyes . The fire grew quickly. It spread, catching tents and wyrlings all ablaze. They screamed and ran but none of the wyrlings could escape the speed of the expanding flames.

"Zsash! Come with me, right now!" Khessi shouted. "Hold your breath!" She grabbed my hand and pulled me further out into the sea. I had only a moment to suck in a large gasp of air before we plunged beneath the surface of the water.

"Second chances are rare in this world. If you are offered one, take it. You will not get a third."
Dornic, *The Scrolls of the Goddess*

CHAPTER 20: BREATHE

Khessi's grip on my hand was fierce as she pulled me deeper and deeper under the surface of the water. We swam twenty or thirty feet below the surface of the water and far out from the shore. She was stronger than I thought possible. Maybe that was just because I was so weak and had no grace without gravity to aid me. She seemed remarkably agile, though. We were far past the shallows now. I kicked my legs as hard as I could but she swam so much faster, I probably made her drag me along harder. I could have just gone limp and she would have hauled me down to the depths .

Struggling to open my eyes, everything was dark blue and shadowy shapes. A part of my brain realized that we were going far beneath the surface of the water and that we would need to breathe soon. However, I didn't want to be around for whatever would happen when the Mistress really let loose with her power.

A loud, sizzling bang shuddered through the ocean that would have been deafening had we been above water. A brilliant orange flash of light appeared above us, illuminating the surface with a vermillion glow. My mind was momentarily distracted from the fact that I was swiftly running out of air.

Radiant fire was everywhere above us. It felt like a dream. The whole world shimmered, suspended and washed in brilliant colors. I wished bitterly that I could see the destruction the Mistress would bring on the wyrlings. My chest tightened momentarily at the thought of Garsteel's end, followed by the vindication of knowing none of them would escape the Mistress's wrath.

Long seconds strung on and the fire did not die away. We could not yet resurface without being burned alive. I tried to pull Khessi closer to the top so we could breathe as soon as the fire abated. Between burning and drowning, neither sounded good to me. I watched little bubbles escape from me to freedom on the surface above.

Khessi kept pulling me back down, shaking her head. My chest started to hurt. The tension became unbearable. I stared at the hot surface above us, waiting for the second we could emerge for air. But it never came. Didn't the Mistress know we were drowning down here?

Khessi's eyes stared at the glassy surface as well, the light reflecting in her beautiful eyes, her face serene and lovely, submissive to her fate even now. I wished for such clarity but I couldn't think past the pain rising in my lungs, the burning pressure that made every muscle in my chest feel as though it was collapsing in on me.

Khessi looked at me suddenly and seeing my expression she moved toward me in a quick swish. She covered her mouth with mine in what I thought was probably a goodbye kiss. I could think of worse ways to die. If this was to be my end, my lips were cradled in those of the most gorgeous slave I have ever met. I'd take it. Submission finally came to me. I relaxed in that moment against her mouth.

I took in a breath.

Air filled my lungs somehow. Opening my eyes in shock and surprise, I realized Khessi was blowing into my mouth. It was a strange sensation. Some part of my panicked brain realized I should inhale through my mouth but not my nose. So I did. And I was fine. I pulled back to stare at her face with confusion. She smiled at me, her hair floating around her lovely face.

Starting to calm down some, I was able to look around my surroundings. The sensation of being underwater was something like flying, I imagine. The light from above illuminated the water everywhere and I could actually stare into the vastness of the sea for a hundred feet around me. Around us were some sea life here and there, varieties of silver and spotted fish of which I couldn't tell you any types. Looking at Khessi in the light, I noticed her hair looked different than it's usual bright red. It had more dimension in it. For a moment I thought it was just the shadows above us or a trick of the light through the water. But it wasn't. Her hair had purple in it at the crown of her head. I touched a floating strand of her hair before releasing it as she smiled at me.

Then out of the corner of my eye, I saw a flicker of what I thought was a large, colorful fish behind Khessi.

I was wrong.

The realization of what I saw made me let out a shout, wasting yet more of my precious oxygen. The shout bubbles scurried to the surface and I clamped a hand over my mouth as I stared at Khessi. It was as if I truly saw her for the first time. I realized how Khessi had gotten away after being drowned.

She'd faked it.

Khessi's entire lower half had become a fish tail. Her legs were gone and from her hips down was a long, beautifully scaled tail with the most brilliant colors of orange, blue and pink, highly similar to those of the fish she kept in her office. I stared at the glossy sheen and vibrant colors in her tail. It was beautiful. *She* was beautiful. She floated effortlessly, swishing her lower half back and forth slowly in the current.

In this short span of time, I realized that this was the rare and wondrous version of wyrlings. Those beasts who had attacked us, that was what happened to most slaves who couldn't handle the power of the creature they channeled. Khessi was what happened when a slave channeled a creature beautifully. Tikora channeled her rabbit successfully without turning into something terrible. I discovered the unspoken trait of household slaves and the reason their bloodlines were so important. Why they were trained separately from the rest of us and why breeding was so crucial for them. They could channel animals without becoming wyrlings.

I was lost in amazement until she moved toward me and covered my mouth with hers, filling my lungs with air again. No longer worried about drowning, I was flooded with emotions about the fact that she was still alive. Her lips already against mine, I raised my hands to capture the back of her neck as I kissed her. She seemed surprised for a moment, but then kissed me back. It was such a different sensation, kissing underwater. It was weightless and perfect.

The light from above stopped and we both looked up. Khessi released me from the kiss so we could swim to the surface with a few swishes of her tail. Her *tail!* Goddess, that was going to take some getting used to.

She peeked her head above the water and then motioned for me to join her. I raised my head out of the water and inhaled. Cool and crisp, the night air felt beautiful. My heart pounded with renewed strength at the fresh air. The shoreline was a distance off and no lights remained there. That seemed odd. seeing as that everything was just on fire a moment ago. The shoreline was black and utterly silent.

"Should we head back in?" I whispered to Khessi.

"Not here," she shook her head. "Let's get a little distance from here. She'll find us."

We swam underwater for a while, swimming further and further away. I tried keeping up at first until I realized it was actually easier to just go limp and let Khessi pull me through the water. Her tail propelled her so much faster than anything I did, and I realized I caused more drag by flailing my limbs around.

When I needed to breathe I would squeeze her hand and she would give me more air. We passed a lot of sea life on the way, amazing creatures I'd never laid eyes on. A sea turtle played in the bubbles of our path while schools of quick fish darted out of our way. It was magical.

Khessi seemed more at ease and at home here than I'd ever seen her. All the symbols of the ocean that the Mistress had allowed her to surround herself with made much more sense now.

Khessi brought us up on a beach a little distance away from the massacre. I made my way up onto the sand and filled my lungs. I exhaled all the fear and terrible things from the night. I was alive. I couldn't believe I was still alive.

Khessi stayed in the shallows of the water, not following me all the way onto the sand. I looked back and saw her laying in the surf, letting her tail swish and flip up out of the water. The colors of the morning sun reflected off her scales, making the colors shine vibrantly. Her lovely ass cheeks were raised slightly out of the water. I could see where her skin transitioned into the tail.

"Are you coming?" I asked nodding my head toward land.

"I don't want to get out just yet. I don't get to be myself like this very often," she said apologetically.

I nodded and joined her in the water. "I thought you were dead." I told her.

"I'm sorry. There wasn't time to explain. I saw an opportunity and I had to take it."

"How much time would you need really? You could have just said, *I'm half fish*, and dove into the sea." We both laughed.

"I'm sorry for other things." She said, looking up into my eyes. "I've been pushing you away for a long time. At first, I thought it was because of my duties. Then, because of Corvas and the Cheritoth, then at the Blossoming Celebration." She looked away then, biting her lip. "I think it might have started when you kissed me that first time during the bath lesson. But I have all these feelings about you and desires, that I don't know what to do about. I think, I want to be more than friends with you, but I don't know how. I've spent so long alone that I'm not sure I know how to do anything else."

She looked back up at me, looking at me for a reaction. I pulled her into an embrace and kissed her pink, sun-brushed lips. My hands wrapped around her hips as I touched her tongue with mine, tasting her delicately. My fingers first brushed skin and then down against the cool, smooth scales at her side.

"That's going to take some getting used to." I said, still running my hands down and over the tail. The scales ran from the top of her legs in a V just below her pelvis and under the fold of her ass cheeks, leaving her torso the same but transforming her legs into the single tail. "Definitely a first for me. And I thought I'd been with every kind of girl."

"Is it too strange? Strange in a bad way?" she asked, biting her lip.

I thought about it for a second. "Nah. I'm kind of a freak like that."

Her eyes widened, happily. She splashed me playfully with a flick of her tail. I was hit with a small wave that drenched my shirt again. I laughed sea water out of my mouth a moment before she wrapped her hands around my shoulders to pull me into a kiss.

The moment was cut short before I could tell her my feelings on the topic. Rustling grass caused us both to look toward the land for fear of enemies. We looked up to see a naked figure walking toward us from out of the trees. It was Mistress Isavyne. She moved gingerly, as if injured. I could see no blood or bruising on her body, but her movements seemed exhausted and weak.

In a shimmer of magic, Khessi had legs again. We both ran up to meet the Mistress and without her permission, I scooped her up into my arms.

"Good..." The Mistress mumbled, slapping my cheek affectionately. "Good boy, Zsash," she repeated, then she fell unconscious.

"Mistress?" I said in a panic. "We've got to get back to the estate."

"She must have burned too hot. Jaideen will know how to help her," Khessi said, running her hand over Mistress Isavyne's arm and then her forehead. "Start carrying her toward the estate," Khessi ordered. She took off the remaining shreds of clothing she wore.

"What are you going to do?" I asked.

"I'll make better time swimming back. I'll get Jaideen and a carriage and come find you! Take care of her, Zsash."

"Right."

She nodded and without more discussion, turned and leapt into the sea. I wanted to run, but I knew that was stupid. I started walking toward the estate at a brisk pace.

"Hold on, Mistress," I said. "We'll get you home."

I walked for hours, I think. Everything in my body hurt with exhaustion, injury, and hunger. My body screamed for me to lie down and die. Each step was the last one I could take, but then the next one was. Despite what my body said, I was not about to die. Not now.

First of all, I would not die before getting the Mistress back home safely. Second, I did not survive the auction, the Cheritoth, the Emperor and wyrlings to die now. Also, the woman I was in love with had feelings for me! I was not about to die now that there was actually some kind of hope for us. Lastly, I had just discovered that she had a freaky magical power that was somehow the most exotic and sexy thing I've ever seen. I was pretty sure if I played it right, I was going to get to have sex with an enchanted fish girl.

There was no way I was dying now.

The Mistress breathed in short, quick bursts. Her face scrunched in pain and she stirred restlessly in my arms. She looked ill. Her skin was a dull, light blue-grey shade, lacking its usual luminous quality. Even her golden hair looked tarnished somehow. Her rose red lips had faded and cracked to withering white petals. Her bones seemed to poke sharply into my grip as if she'd lost muscle. The Mistress was not a bony woman. Her curves had always been one of her most attractive qualities. To see her so colorless and emaciated made my heart hurt.

It seemed like forever, but I finally saw a carriage coming toward us down the beach. It was a white carriage with black horses. A slave I'd never met before drove, snapping the reigns with urgency. As the carriage pulled up in front of me, Khessi and Jaideen jumped out.

"Give her to me, quickly!" Jaideen shouted.

I did so and he carried the Mistress into the carriage. Khessi got in as well and closed the small door. I crawled on top to sit with the driver. He turned the carriage around and we rode back to the estate at full speed.

The Mistress was taken directly to her chambers while Jaideen continued doing some strange healing practices on her that I didn't fully understand. He covered her with crystals. Amethyst and quartz were laid all over her body. A large geode of amethyst was placed under her bed. Spices were burned and oils applied to her forehead. I was allowed to sit in the corner of the room and watch over her but I couldn't help much. One by one, all the slaves of the estate came in and laid blue flowers from the shrine of the Goddess around the bed, praying to the Goddess for the Mistress to be all right.

It took a few days, but finally, the Mistress opened her eyes. Her voice was weak and dry sounding as she called for Khessi. I couldn't make out what the Mistress said to her.

"Open the windows," Khessi said, looking up the other slaves in the room. Jaideen was busy with oils and crystals. I rushed around the room and opened all the windows as far as I could. When I looked back, I saw that the Mistress had started crying.

"Khessi..." she said weakly through soft sobs. "Khessi! Don't let them go to waste," she cried out.

Khessi grabbed the bottle of healing potion in the red box. She pulled out the glass bottle of pearlized honey that I had been graciously given a few times.

"Easy now, Mistress," Khessi said softly while she collected the Mistress's tears into the bottle. Each tear left a golden opal trail down the Mistress's cheeks. Jaideen stood next to me while I stared in amazement. The healing potion I'd been given were actually the healing tears of the Mistress.

She didn't cry for long but Khessi caught every tear and put the stopper back in the bottle just as Emperor Dukkar entered the room. Anger and fear rose up in me at the sight of his sharp, pale features. I began slowly making my way around the room to stand near Khessi. The Emperor didn't pay any attention to me or the other slaves. His blood red gaze was bent with concern and fixed on Mistress Isavyne.

"Isa!" he said, removing his frock coat as he went to her bedside. He ran a hand over her face. "Thank the Goddess you're all right."

I was startled as he kissed her. Every slave in the room looked awkwardly around at each other. The kiss didn't last long but it was far more intimate a gesture than I'd seen them exchange before.

"I'm fine," the Mistress said. "I simply used up a lot of power all at once. I'll be all right."

"Please, let me nurse you back to health at the palace. I will ensure your every comfort," his voice was soft as he sat on the edge of the bed next to her.

"That is too kind of you, my lord, but I would prefer to rest in my own bed."

"Of course," he nodded.

The Mistress struggled some to sit up. Khessi moved to help her, but the Mistress waved her off.

"My apologies to your majesty that my slaves were unsuccessful getting my response to you in regards to your marriage proposal."

Khessi and I exchanged worried glances.

"It is nothing," Dukkar said, waving his hand. "We can discuss it further when you are well."

"No. That's just it," Mistress Isavyne sighed. "There really isn't anything to discuss," she said, her tone apologetic.

Emperor Dukkar looked at her unblinking for a long moment. Then he swallowed and looked away.

"I am very fond of you," she started.

"I understand," he interrupted, his tone icier than before.

"And of course, I do value your friendship greatly."
Mistress Isavyne put a hand on his arm. "You are a handsome man with wealth and power. Any Queen would be lucky to have you. But I find that I am still restless in my heart. In good conscience, I could not accept your proposal without knowing if I truly love you. I do not know if I could love you the way you deserve."

"Perhaps you could grow to love me. Give us time to know each other better, so you can get to know the man instead of the emperor."

"I will continue to consider. But I do not wish to hold you back from finding an Empress."

He stood. He put his frock coat back on and straightened the sleeves.

"Tell me, though, has Braxian influenced your decision in this at all?" the Emperor asked.

The Mistress tilted her head slightly. "I keep my own council in these regards, my lord. Master Braxian has made his intentions known to me, much like yourself. But he does not influence my actions, Dukkar. No man does."

Even weakly sitting up, the sapphire eyes of the Mistress burned bright with defiance at the implication that her will could be influenced.

"I just worry about you," he crooned. "Braxian is quite charming in his manipulations. But his motives in business and at court are erratic. I know he has pursued you since his miraculous return from illness and I can see how you might be tempted by his endowments. But powerful Masters seek financial gain above all else. That much even more, if the woman they seek to tame is rich and powerful. I hope that he does not seek your gold and virtue over your heart."

The Mistress smirked and the temperature in the room rose became actively warmer.

"Unlike yours, dearest Dukkar? Whose desires for me are pure as they are virtuous, I am sure. Do not fear for my powers of observation, my lord. I see much."

"My apologies. I have offended you." He bowed his head slightly. "And while you are not feeling well. I will not press the matter further." He smiled at her, taking her hand in his. "My offer will always stand if you should change your mind. I still have high hopes that you will one day accept my proposal. You would make a magnificent Empress, " he said, his lips tight over clenched, pointed teeth.

"I will keep it in mind," she nodded.

Emperor Dukkar kissed the back of her hand, closing his eyes and inhaling the scent of her skin deeply. Then he turned and left the room without another word or backward glance. I inhaled deeply and my heart thundered with quiet fear. It hadn't even realized I'd been holding my breath.

"The First Code: My life for my Master.
The Second Code: Submission is peace.
The Third Code: Love is my duty.
The Fourth Code: Pain is the lesson.
The Fifth Code: Channeling forbidden.
The Sixth Code: Unworthy but never unwilling.
The Seventh Code: Forgiveness is earned.
The Eighth Code: Behold my gifts in every form."

The Code of Slaves, *The Scrolls of the Goddess*

CHAPTER 21: REWARDS

I don't know what happened that convinced the Mistress to turn down the Emperor's proposal. I had never told anyone about the horrors I witnessed at the palace with Basz. Perhaps Master Lovol told her about the encounter. Perhaps Master Braxian changed her mind like the Emperor said. Perhaps she just came to the conclusion that she didn't want to marry. No matter the reason, I was relieved that our estate was not about to join with the Emperor's.

I was ordered to rest and heal from the ordeal until the Mistress had use for me again. So I slept. I probably spent the better part of three days lying in bed, resting and healing. I had some bruising and cuts and all of my muscles felt sore and stiff. Strangely enough, this felt almost normal . I was rather used to being in various stages of healing at this point, so I'd learned to shuffle around in pain fairly well.

Between the carriage flipping over and being brutalized by the savagery of the wyrlings, Jaideen said he was surprised I wasn't in worse shape.

Khessi seemed uninjured. I assumed that her wyrling powers had somehow made her heal quicker than me.

On the third day after the ordeal, I woke to find a letter slipped under my door. I immediately recognized the handwriting as the Mistress's. It said,

Zsash,
Clean yourself, eat, and meet me in the garden
by the fountain.

I was excited at the thought that the Mistress was feeling better and wanted to see me. I took a shower and shaved. I put on a pair of black pants and the red satin shirt with the gold coin collar, then headed down to the gardens.

When I found the Mistress, she still looked more pale than usual, but her lips had regained their sanguine color and she looked healthier. She was wrapped in a sheer white sheet, her hair shining gold in the sunlight.

"Mistress," I said while bowing before her. "You look like you're feeling better."

"Much better!" she said in a warm tone, though I still sensed her exhaustion below it. "Sit next to me, pet." She gestured to the stone bench she sat on. The fountain splashed pleasantly near us while I waited for her to speak.

"I have new orders for you, slave."

"As the Mistress commands," I nodded, smiling. She smiled back.

"You are no longer to be my bath slave," she began. For a moment, worry crept over me as to what exactly that meant. She continued, "I need a blacksmith far more than I need a bath slave. You will take up Garsteel's position for the foreseeable future. This also includes removing yourself from the bath slave quarters and taking over the blacksmith quarters."

"Yes, Mistress. I did not know he had private quarters."

"They are not well known. He resided in a small shack not far from the shoreline. A private place that is somewhat hidden on the estate. You are welcome to anything Garsteel had there and may stay in his room. Also, I hope that you will be able to adjust to companionship as you will not be the only slave staying there."

"Of course, Mistress. I have lived with multiple slaves for most of my life. This will not be a problem," I answered. Secretly, the idea of having living companions again was exciting and sounded much less lonely.

"Good," she sighed and whistled to the rose bushes across from us.

A scruffy, point-nosed little face emerged from the roses. Tark jumped merrily up into my lap and waited impatiently for me to pet him. I felt my chest catch as I thought about Garsteel and how the little fox would never see his friend again.

"I thought you two would get along." The Mistress smiled broadly while I scratched under the fox's chin.

"Really? Why is that?"

"Well, I know how you have a thing for redheads." A little knowing smile curled her lips. I laughed and felt my cheeks get hot. Mistress Isavyne set Tark on the ground. He gave a little yip, sniffed his tail in a circle twice and sat down, staring up at me. "I don't need any blacksmithing done for a while. Take your time and get settled. Continue to rest and heal and I will summon you when I require your services."

"Yes, Mistress," I stood up, bowed formally. "Thank you."

I turned and followed the white-tipped tail of the red fox. I had to jog to keep up with Tark as he scampered through the cane fields toward the sea. He was fast and clearly didn't seem to notice how much slower I was.

After jogging down to the beach, I stopped to try and get my breath. He continued trotting away.

"Stop, will you?" I shouted.

His ears perked up, hearing me and he stopped, turning back to look at me. He let out a huffy little gruff sound in impatience but came back for me.

Once I could jog again, he led us down near where Khessi and I had fallen asleep on the beach after burying Glo. However, he turned away from the sea and moved toward the rocky cliff face, and disappeared behind a large bush with fanning leaves. When I moved the leaves to the side I saw that it led into a break in the rock wall.

Looking into it, I saw that it was a crack that ran up the entire cliff face about two feet wide. It was enough for a fox and just enough for me to walk through sideways. It didn't look like any place a person would naturally want to go. That was probably how it had stayed hidden.

I walked cautiously through the maze in the wall. It was not a straight path, instead it twisted this way and that into the rock. About twenty feet in, it finally opened up into a large underground grotto that contained a hidden beach. The roof of the grotto was hundreds of feet high and with a large hole in the center that opened to the sky. Basically, it was a massive cave with a hole in its ceiling. Most of the cave was filled with beautiful turquoise sea that lapped at the white sands on the beach. Green plant life clung to the rock walls here and there. The shack sat in a shady spot in the grotto, under a rocky and mossy overhang.

Calling it the shack was intentionally misleading, as this was nothing I would have referred to as a shack.

It was a sea cottage, made of wood beams and white stone. The roof was made of ceramic tile the same turquoise blue color as the water that surrounded the beach. Bright blue fabric was draped over the windows and around columns that lined the front and side porch. The porch was made of long slabs of white rock extending down into and under the water like a dock. On the porch were two chairs and a small circular table near the outside wall where the roof overhung. There was also a large stack of firewood protected by the porch roof, and an above-ground fire pit sat a few feet away. The fire pit was a four-foot-wide ceramic bowl lined on the outside with more blue glass tile and full of lumps of ashy wood.

Not far away in the water, I saw bubbles begin to rise and the water stirred. Tark's ears pricked up and he let out a little ruff with a foxy smile. A moment later, a streak of color arched out of the water.

Khessi, with her tail trailing after her brilliantly, leapt into the air for a moment then dove back under.

I smiled when I saw her and made my way toward the beach and down the dock. She swam up to meet me, staying in the water where the stone dock extended under the surface. Her smile was radiant in the sunlight, swishing her tail back and forth slowly in the twinkling waves.

"What are you doing here?" I asked.

"I was commanded here. The Mistress said these are to be my new quarters."

I couldn't believe it. Unable to get the ridiculous grin off my face, I put my hands on my hips, pretending to think.

"How strange. The Mistress commanded that I too should live here as well." I gestured to the cottage. "Strange that she didn't mention you living here."

"Indeed. She did say that I might have to get used to an annoying live-in companion."

"Well, I assumed you'd just live in this bit of ocean here and I'd take the cottage."

"I'm willing to share. You should come in. The water is warm," she said, swishing back from the dock some.

"Eh, I don't know. I don't want to get my nice pants all wet."

"Then take them off," she grinned with a cute flip of her wet hair. I shrugged, then slid my pants off in two quick motions. She laughed at me as I walked down to meet her in the water.

The temperature of the water was perfect. Not hot, but just cool enough to be refreshing. I didn't really want to swim, but the water felt too good not to get in. I stepped in until it came up to my ankles, then sat down on the stone slab. Laying flat on the dock, I could do a slight back float in the shallow water while still feeling the stone beneath me. Putting my arms back behind my head, I stared up at the circular opening at the top of the cave and saw blue skies skirted with thin clouds. Sunlight warmed my face and the water around me. It all felt so amazing.

Slender fingers ran over my toes and across my foot under the water, causing me to raise my head. Khessi moved slowly as if savoring the touch of my skin while she positioned herself between my legs. She touched me so softly with her palms and fingers grazing my knees, then my thighs, causing goose bumps and other things to rise.

"Khessi…" I half laughed, starting to become aroused but also nervous for some reason. "What are you doing?" I asked as her hands moved up the sides of my bare hips and over my torso.

"Would you like me to stop?" she asked, all coy and sweet.

"Not at all. I was just wondering what happened to that conversation we had about you being uncomfortable."

"Well…" She tilted her head to the side and began lowering her hands with cruel and slow precision. "I thought about what you said."

"And what conclusions did you come to?" I said, trying to keep my voice casual.

"I could just show you my conclusions," she suggested, letting her soft, delicate fingers glide from my hip bones down to the muscles of my groin. I held my breath as I went from casually interested, to at full attention in a matter of seconds.

"Sure…" was all I could really get out. She ran her hands slowly over my stiff cock. I let my head fall back and exhaled while she explored me.

Khessi was different than any lover I'd been with. She was tentative, slow and purposeful in her movements as she stroked me. Hers were not the hands of an experienced lover who knew how to get men off. But there was something even more precious in that. Curiosity and affection were in her hands as she touched me all over, making my body hum with pleasure. My sighs bounced off the cave walls and mixed with the lapping of the waves.

I felt her stop for a moment, so I looked down at her to see if everything was all right. Her wet hair hung around her shoulders like melting copper. Her brilliant colorful tail flipped casually in the shallow water. She placed a hand on either side of my hips and looked up at me for a moment, licking her lips. I watched with anticipation as she lowered her mouth to the head of my cock. Her breath was so warm beyond the cool water. She took her eyes off me to look down, then licked across the head experimentally. My breathing quickened. I tried not to move as she licked long, scalding wet lines from the base of my cock to the tip.

"Ah, fuck!" I said clenching my teeth with my arms still captured behind my head. She smiled up at me wickedly. "That's so not fair," I told her around my shuddering breaths.

"We can work on what's fair later." She smiled, then lowered her wet pink lips over the tip. My jaw dropped open with a moan and I ran my hand over the back of her neck. She went lower, taking me further into her mouth a little at a time. She started sucking me softly, letting her tongue swirl lazily around my flesh. She gripped my hips lightly, as she slid her lovely mouth over my shaft at a slow, steady rhythm. Moans and hissing gasps escaped me while the pressure in my cock swelled. Each sensual movement pushed me further toward the edge of my desire. The cool water splashing against my body contrasted so beautifully with the heat of her mouth. She took me to the edge of her throat, again and again across her moist lips. She wouldn't give me the speed I wanted, so it was a slow build. Soft moans vibrated from her mouth, turning me on even more. Finally, I felt the tension in my body start rolling me toward release.

"Khessi, I'm gonna cum," I said, just above a whisper, giving her the opportunity to stop. I didn't want to finish in her mouth if she wasn't expecting it. She held my hips more firmly and sped up her movements. It still wasn't fast, but the new sensations sent me over the edge. My cock pulsed between her lips while her tongue stroked me. My toes curled to a point and I gripped her neck tighter, while every muscle in me tensed. Long lustful moans escaped from my chest with every breath. Pleasure coursed through me as I came inside the warmth of her mouth. I felt her swallow as she continued to suck me until I finished.

I laid there panting, staring up at the blue sky while my head spun and I tried to catch my breath. I felt her release me from her mouth, followed by the sound of a splash. I looked down to see that she'd gone back in the water.

"Hey!" I shouted, slowly getting to my feet. I waded down into the water and dunked my head under for a moment, getting my hair wet. Letting the water cool me as it evaporated on my skin. I looked around for Khessi.

"Okay, that's still not fair! You don't get to do that and then just swim away!"

She appeared in front of me a moment later, looking somewhat shy but also pretty proud of herself.

"Was that all right?" she asked. "Did I do it correctly?"

"That was fantastic," I said. I wrapped my arms around her waist. "You didn't need to do that but you are certainly welcome to whenever you like."

I pulled her close and slid my arms behind her back, under her tail and scooped her up out of the water and into a kiss. Khessi wrapped her arms around my neck, kissing me back. She pulled me to her and twisted in my arms to get closer contact with me. I felt the piercings at her nipples pressing against my chest and my desire began to stir again. The kiss slowed to gentle embers and our mouths moved apart an inch as we both took a moment to breathe.

"I've been wanting to do that for a while now," I said.

"So have I," she smiled and ran a hand over my face.

It struck me suddenly that there was something missing from her. I was startled that I hadn't actually noticed before. Then again, I was distracted by an amazing new home and having my dick sucked, so give me a little credit for not being the most astute.

"Where are your collar and cuffs?"

Khessi laughed. "The Mistress said I do not have to wear them here. That I am only required to wear my bonds while at the estate or on business for her."

"Does it feel strange without them?" I asked.

"Yes, but it's a good strange. The kind of strange that I could get used to. Like being with you."

"So, what led to this sexual liberation you're embracing now?"

"Well, I talked to the Mistress about how I feel about you."

"And how is that?" I asked, wide-eyed.

She paused and looked away from me, a blush creeping into her cheeks.

"I don't know exactly when it happened." She said, reclaiming her household slave tone from the giggling girl I'd seen a moment ago. "But I seem to have strong feelings toward you...and desires."

"And what did the Mistress say about that?"

"She said that I am free to interact with other slaves as long as it doesn't interfere with my duties and how I run the estate."

"Interesting. Any ideas on how you'd like to interact with me in the near future?"

She kissed me. Again and again. I kissed her back just as much. I just wanted to hold her and feel her against me forever. I'd not been able to express to her how I felt or touch her the way I wanted to before. Now that I could, I didn't want to stop.

The next day was filled with the task of going through the shack and emptying it of anything we didn't want and then moving in our things.

There was something strangely comforting about going through Garsteel's living space. In some way, it was the best method to say goodbye to him. I'd tried not to think about the gruesome passing he had and my part in it. I wasn't ready to think about the situation yet and I hadn't told anyone how I'd put him out of his misery on the fire. I don't think I ever will. It all hurt too much to discuss. However, going through the items of his life made me feel better about his death.

The interior of the shack was small but cozy. There was a little kitchen with a wood-burning stove for both cooking and heat. There was a small sitting room with two comfortable couches. The sitting room was also lined with bookshelves, though it was a humble collection. There were some books on the shelves that the

Mistress had apparently given him, which surprised me, as I didn't know Garsteel had known how to read. There was also a hammock that stretched across the window. It looked like this is where Garsteel had slept.

We didn't actually end up throwing out that much. Many of the kitchen items he had, we intended to keep. I thought the Mistress had been generous to me initially. Garsteel had pots and pans for cooking. Ceramic jars, jugs, cups, pitchers, plates. Also, his own silverware!

The largest room in the house was the bed chamber. It looked as though Garsteel never slept in that room. It seemed he preferred the hammock. The bed chamber was still fairly small but would fit two people quite comfortably.

The bed was a thick mattress on the floor covered in lots of blankets and pillows. There was a large hook in the ceiling that held a canopy that draped sheer white fabric down around the bed to protect the sleeper at night from any bugs that might get into the house. The fabric of the canopy was held open by satin ropes attached to two more hooks set into the walls on either side of the ceiling hook. There was also a small closet in the room full of wooden boxes containing all kinds of junk. Much of it looked collected from the beach over the years Most items were water damaged like they'd washed up on shore.

It took very little time to load up the things from my room. Khessi, on the other hand, had so many things I wasn't sure we would be able to fit them in the cottage. The Mistress had gifted her above all things, clothes. Her collection was not going to fit in the small closet of the bed chamber. That turned into where we put my things. We ended up pulling out some of the bookshelves in the sitting room and adding bars for her to hang her clothes. The sitting room became a sitting closet, somewhat. I moved the hammock out onto the back porch.

As I was going through the closet in the bed chamber, though, I found a wooden box among other boxes.

"Damn, Garsteel," I said to myself. "I guess you did entertain the ladies in your time."

There were numerous lengths of soft rope. I dug down into the box to find more rope than I would probably ever need. I also found a black box with two blue, glowing resonance stones. As I picked one up, the heat from my skin made it begin to vibrate softly. It had a hole drilled through the center, making it a bead around the size of a walnut that could be strung on the rope to be held over various sensitive points. I decided if I got the chance, I would use these on Khessi.

That chance turned out to be much sooner than I had thought.

While we sat in front of the fire pit that night under the stars, drinking wine I may or may not have acquired from the Mistress's bath chamber, Khessi asked me a question.

"Does being a pleasure slave make you better at sex than other lovers?" She asked. I looked up at her in the firelight. Such a beauty. She was wearing a white cotton shirt and skirt with a red satin under-bust corset that matched a set of sexy satin red heels.

"Well, it makes me more experienced." I tried to answer without bragging. "But *better* is a subjective word. I have more varied interests than most slaves, I suppose."

"Like what?" she asked, the innocence of her question playing all across her face.

"Well, for example, I enjoy the use of rope bondage during sex."

"As in, you like to be tied up or you would like to tie me up?"

"Either is fun. But currently? I'd like to tie you up."

"Hmm. I've seen it done on palace slaves but I've never tried it. The Mistress is fond of chains and leather when she has tied me up. Of course, hers are more for punishment than pleasure, usually."

"Would you like to be tied up with satin ropes sometime?" I asked, pretending like it was just a casual musing. Khessi finished her glass of wine and set her face with determination.

"I have decided that I am no longer going to run away from my sexuality. So, yes. I think I would."

She stood and slid her skirt down over her hips, revealing red satin underwear. She pulled the white top shirt off over her head, leaving her wearing just the red under-bust corset and underwear. Well, and that pair of red high heels that tied in a bow behind her ankles.

"Will this do or do you need me completely naked?" she asked.

"Oh, uh..." I stammered. I hadn't realized she intended us to get right to this. "No, no that will be just fine." I said, setting my glass down.

We didn't say much as we went back inside the shack to the bed of blankets and pillows. I fetched the box of ropes and resonance stones I had found earlier.

Tying her up took time. That was part of the enjoyment of ropes, taking the time to appreciate the knots and twists. Not only how they held the subject but how they looked in them. It's extremely beautiful. I chose red satin ropes from the box to match with her undergarments. I tied her torso in a net pattern that went from her neck and around her breasts. Not squeezing them, but just enough to tantalize them with the friction. I was careful not to touch her skin as I laced two ropes between her legs over her panties. I pulled them tight between the folds of her sex to ensure they would squeeze her just right when she moved.

"They go there?" She asked surprised.

"Trust me." I winked at her, flashing a smile. I brought the same ropes snuggly up between her ass cheeks, causing a little 'Oh!' sound from her. Once her torso was secured, I had her lie back on the pillows. They kept her propped up fairly well so that she was at an incline but still leaning back. I then brought a new length of rope through the netted harness I'd already built around her torso and began to wrap rope around each wrist. From there, I had her bend her knees to attach her wrist to the ankle on the same side. I was careful not to entangle her high heeled shoes as I wanted to leave those on. Once finished, the ropes kept her effectively in a spread open position. Her ankles were bound to her wrists and those were secured to the netting around her body. The vibrant red ropes against her pale skin were gorgeous. I brushed her long coppery hair back over her shoulder to expose her lovely, perky sparkling accented breasts in their rope cage. I knelt back on my heels and picked up my glass of wine while admiring my work.

"By the Goddess, that's fucking sexy," I sighed and took a drink. "Are you comfortable?"

She shifted in the ropes a little, then nodded. "It seems like I should be uncomfortable, but I'm not."

"Good."

"What would you like to do to me now?" she asked.

I raised an eyebrow.

"Hmm.Well, it would only be fair if I returned the favor from yesterday..." I took another sip of my wine and leaned slowly in to kiss her. When I did, I let some of the wine drizzle out of my mouth as we kissed. Her tongue brushed across my lips, tasting the wine. Her murmuring sounds of desire turned to full moans as my hands cupped her breasts. I felt the ropes shift as she rocked her hips, the ropes between her legs rubbing her clit in reward.

"Oh my!" she said breathily between kisses. "I see why the ropes go there." I hid my smile, lowering my mouth to a sparkling nipple. I licked wine off her body as I went, running my tongue roughly over the pink point of her breast as it became firm in my mouth. I let my tongue and teeth play with the diamond stud that decorated it. My fingers pinched softly at its partner. Khessi arched her back, pressing her breasts into my hands. Her attempts to move caused her little success, thanks to her bonds. Hungry moans sighed out of her, urging me on. She wanted me to give her more. To bring her to climax.

But this was to be fair.

And yesterday, she was slow with me. She'd taken her sweet time, quite on purpose, I might add. So I would be returning the favor. I'm probably a bad man for how much I enjoyed teasing her.

"Does it feel good?" I asked softly, while trailing kisses down her corset. My fingers ran light patterns over the back of her thighs, gliding my fingertips toward her ass cheeks.

"Yes," she moaned, biting her lip. My kisses ran lower and lower until my lips rested just above her panties. Then I moved away from her.

"Zsash!" She protested, bringing her head up from where she'd been staring at me. I reached into the rope box, searching around.

"Yes?" I said innocently. I took out a resonance stone and brought it back with me to the bed, hiding it in my closed hand. It began to vibrate softly. Her shock turned to curiosity as she stared at my closed fist and what I was hiding.

"What is that?" she turned her head slightly. I brought the bright blue jewel up to her nipple, running it around the pointed tip. The vibration of the stone was slow and steady as I placed it against her skin.

"It's a resonance stone," I said over her gasp.

"Where did you get that?" she exclaimed before another moan took her voice. Her nipple piercing clacked pleasantly against the blue gem. The tempo of the vibrations slowly climbed the more they were in contact with the heat of her body.

"They were in the box with the rope. And they are all ours to play with whenever we want."

"Do you know how expensive those…" she started to say, but I lowered the stone to the front of her panties. Her hips jumped as she let out a cry of pleasure.

"Shh, shh, shh. I don't really care how expensive they are." I said with a shrug, hushing her concerns away. Her eyebrows knitted in frustrated desire while I ran the stone slowly over her satin-covered clit. The heat between my hand and her body made the stone begin to vibrate stronger. Khessi rocked against the ropes as the building pleasure in her clit consumed her. I leaned closer to her again, kissing her gently.

"I want you so badly, Khessi. I've wanted you since we first met," I whispered, then claimed her lips fully against mine in a kiss that made me groan with anticipation. I pressed the stone more roughly against her panties while she bucked her hips against it as best she could. But she couldn't get the pressure she wanted with her thighs bound. I traced the stone around and up and down, avoiding giving her what she needed to climax. Not until her panties had soaked through did I finally bring the now strongly vibrating stone over her clit and held it there.

"Mmhmm...oh...yes...Yes, right there." she whimpered while her pleasure intensified. I stared into the beautiful, almost pained, facial expressions she made. Only every once in a while did I look down at my work between her legs. I could feel her tension building to release. Her hands opened and closed, gripping her ankles, pointing her toes in those beautiful fucking red heels. She was so close. I knew she would cum if I kept the stone right there.

So I didn't.

I pulled the stone away from her clit a few seconds beyond what she would need to finish.

"By the Goddess, Zsash!" she shouted at me, irritated. I laughed a little.

"Trust me. It's all going to be worth it."

"You just want to tease me!" she said pouting, "Which is entirely unfair! I didn't tease you this much!"

I set the resonance stone down next to me and lay down on my stomach between her thighs. She stopped talking, now watching every move I made. I looked up at her giving her a half smile while I gently pulled her damp panties to the side. The two pieces of satin rope still effectively held the outer petals of her pussy open for me, effectively presenting her exposed swollen clit.

I sighed. "You're right, I suppose. I wouldn't want anyone to accuse me of not being *fair*. So let's make things just exactly fair, shall we?"

I slid my other hand onto the opposite thigh and lowered my mouth to her dripping center. I licked her softly at first, though she didn't really need warming up. She moaned each time I tasted her, moving my tongue in short lapping strokes across the pink nub of her clit. She rocked against my mouth, her head tossing from side to side on the pillows behind her. I pulled at the ropes in my hand, causing more gentle friction around her flesh as the rope net cradled her. While I licked her clit, I took my hand from her thigh and began rubbing my fingers against her entrance. I decided to use just one finger, since I could already tell she was very tight. I let my middle finger slip into her, pushing inside more with each stroke of my tongue. She twisted in pleasure against the ropes, moaning louder.

"Please stop teasing me. Please let me cum!"

I removed my mouth from her and looked up into her eyes.

"I'm no Master! You don't have to ask my permission." I said, moving up toward her face again but still keeping my finger inside her. I braced myself with an arm behind her head and leaned down to kiss her. She kissed me back greedily. My thumb rested on her clit and I began rubbing it while I pushed in and out of her.

"Oh Goddess!" she cried out. "That feels so good!"

I was getting so turned on by watching her. My cock was hard and pressing uncomfortably in my pants.

I whispered against her lips, "You're so fucking gorgeous tied up like this. I want to make you cum on my hand, sweetheart."

Her response was a string of *yes* and *more* and *don't stop* all wrapped in the most sensual moans. She was so wet and trying to get more inside her, so I added a second finger. As I slipped it into her and stretched her more fully, her cries turned from breathy to throaty with hunger. She gasped at the new sensation and looked into my eyes. Surprise and wonder played across her face.

Her skin was flushed and her slightly parted lips were a sleek rosy pink. Her nipples stuck out hard and begged to be touched, as they were teased by the barricade of red corsetry and rope. I felt my own lust clawing up inside of me and I began touching her more roughly. Rocking her body against mine and kissing her. I crooked my fingers upward to give her what I knew she had been looking for, finding the spot inside her that would make her cum. I pressed into her faster now, tapping my palm between her legs while I ran my lips over her whimpering cries. Her thighs trembled with effort as she relaxed in her bonds and her body submitted to the ecstasy. I kissed her through her first cries as she came. Her pussy rippled around my fingers in spasms of pleasure and she dropped her head back, crying out my name.

Her ignited cries of passion slowly dwindled back to embers. The throbbing continued to bring short gasps from her for several minutes. I ran light kisses over her shoulder while her breathing slowed back down.

"That was fucking beautiful." I whispered to her while my fingers continued to caress her gently.

A few moments later, I withdrew my hand and let her catch her breath. Her body was covered with a sheen of sweat. She was so gorgeous like this, her hair messy and in her face. Her eyeliner smudged. Her skin pink and aroused. All her inhibitions about sexuality were gone. The poised, graceful diplomat had been taken over by desire.

"May I have a drink of wine please?" she asked through a still racing heartbeat. I reached for the wine and brought a sip to her mouth. She drank a few gulps then resumed panting as I took the cup away.

"Do you want more?" I asked.

"Yes, please."

I lifted the cup back to her mouth but she turned away.

"No. I meant…not wine." Her eyes were glossy with lust and after all that, I had no willpower to say no. I stood and set the wine down. I unbuttoned my pants, took them off and threw them into the corner. I was painfully rock hard and my cock ached to be touched. I stroked it a few times while I knelt down in front of her. Hunger still reflected in her gaze.

"What would you like?" I asked.

"I don't know, I just, want you inside me," she answered.

"We'll have to be careful if we're going to follow the Mistress's one rule."

"I trust you," she said, sitting up more. "Do you want to untie me or…"

"Mm, yes. I will in just a minute." I said, pulling her panties to the side again. I leaned over and kissed her, rubbing the tip of my cock against her pussy. Goddess, she was so wet. "I want to try it this way for a moment since I have you all tied up anyway." I'd loosened her up but she was still extremely tight. We kissed softly and I felt her relax.

"Oh, yes…" she whispered, absently gripping her ankles. "Please let me have you."

"Tell me if anything hurts or if you want to stop. All right?"

"All right." She nodded.

"I'm going to try and go slow. But…I don't know how long I'll be able to do that."

I began to move my hips in a slow circular motion. I worked into her shallowly, dipping deeper a half an inch at a time. Her eyelids hooded with each thrust and she moaned at having me inside her. I tried to focus on being gentle. It took every ounce of my effort not to bury myself into her on the first stroke. I just kept breathing slowly to keep my pace while I watched her. I was caught in a cycle of watching my cock slide between the tight petals of her sex, then following her moans up to those lovely lips and finally getting lost her eyes. My breathing became ragged as her body closed in around me each time I went deeper. It wasn't until I sank fully into the tight, wet folds of her pussy that I cried out. We held still there for a long moment. My forehead fell onto her shoulder as I panted heavily, overwhelmed with sensation and emotion. I was still staggered at the fact this was *actually* happening. I rose up and looked into her lovely passion-fogged eyes to find her mouth tilted in a sly smile.

"What?" I asked, confused.

"You want me so bad, pleasure slave. Who would have guessed I could get *you* so turned on." she grinned and bit her lower lip.

All manner of retorts skipped through my mind as I narrowed my eyes. Instead, I flexed my cock inside her, giving her a little thrust.

"Oh, Goddess..." she exhaled and I set my jaw smugly.

I leaned against her with my hand in the small of her back, pushing her down against the pillows. I began moving into her with rhythm. The new friction brought sighs and moans from both of us.

"Oh fuck, Khessi," I cursed between my teeth at how good she felt. My thrusts were slow, staying deep while she adjusted to having me inside her.

"I can feel you stretching me. That feels so good." She moaned.

"We're just getting started." I panted and kissed her again.

Pleasure rippled through her each time I entered her. Khessi's mouth hung open in a series of *Oh* noises. I loved how she looked tied with the ropes, her corset pushing her breasts up for me to touch and taste. I ran my hands over her, every sight and texture building my arousal. I took a moment to lean away from her and reached for the resonance stone I'd laid on the bed. I held the stone against her clit while I fucked her. I didn't want to climax with her still in the ropes. But I wanted her to. I wanted to make her cum as many times as I could.

In a few moments of the added vibration, her moans turned to wild cries. The heat of our bodies made the stone vibration so strong it began numbing my fingers to hold it. The sounds she made were incredible. I could tell how close she was. I pounded into her faster, while her eyes shut tight. Her cries got louder as every muscle in her body tensed.

"Oh, Goddess! Yes! Oh, oh, Zsash!" she cried, as her pussy clenched around me, slicking my cock with a new wave of cum from deep inside her. I exhaled with a smile on my lips, as her body trembled in ecstasy.

"Oh yeah, that's my girl. That's what I wanted." I whispered while she throbbed around me. I fucked her gently as her moans turned to soft sighs, coming down from the aftershocks of her orgasm. I was shaking with the effort it took to not finish inside her. But I was elated that I'd gotten her to cum again and proud of myself for not breaking the one rule.

I pulled out of her slowly, then began kissing her neck, her shoulders and finally, her lips.

"Are you all right?" I asked. She nodded her head, stars still floating in her eyes. "Wait here just one moment and I'll get you out of the ropes," I said. She nodded again with a little smile on her face.

It only took me a moment to return with a silver knife from the kitchen. I carefully lifted each rope I intended to cut away from her skin before doing so, until she was free of all bonds and only wore her corset and panties. I was still hard and wanting more but I was so satisfied with getting her off twice that I would have been happy to just jerk myself off and fall asleep. This was all more than I ever expected to experience with her to begin with.

As soon as she was free of her bonds, Khessi wrapped her arms around my neck, pulling me into another kiss. I kissed her in return, feeling the warmth of her skin against my chest.

She then gave me a little push backward toward the bed, breaking the kiss.

"Lay down," Khessi demanded softly, her voice just above a whisper. I could tell she wasn't done with me yet. I lay down on the bed, taking her original position against the pillows. She stepped out of her drenched panties, kicking them to the side, then straddled my hips. Positioning herself over me, she let the head of my cock rest between her legs.

"We don't have to do any more. There are plenty of other ways for me to finish," I said.

My dick yelled at my sensitive heart to shut the fuck up.

I ignored him.

"I know we don't have to." She said, still breathing hard. My hands traced over the curve of her thighs as she hovered just above me."But I want to. Do you think we can?"

"It's risky but, I think so." I nodded.

"Good," she said, and sat down on my cock, taking every inch of me inside her in one slick stroke. I gasped and let out a long groan of surprise and pleasure. I grabbed her hips with both hands and waited to see if I was going to cum right then.

I didn't.

I sighed in relief, looking up at her. Khessi's oceanic eyes were steamy amidst the disheveled vibrant strands of her hair. She began to move her hips, slowly at first. She splayed her fingers across my chest, pressing her hands into my skin while she shifted her hips back and fourth to ride my cock.

"I love how you feel inside me," she sighed. "I can't believe I went without this for so long."

"Well for what it's worth, you can have me whenever you want."

"I want to cum for you again." She said, biting her lip.

"You're in control. Use me. Take me how you like."

She smiled softly, beginning to ride me harder. Taking her pleasure from me. Her hands gripped my shoulders while our moans filled the small bed chamber.

"Oh, fuck yes! Ride my dick. Make yourself cum all over my cock!" I said, loving how her hips rolled each time she moved on top of me.

She arched her back and ran her fingers through her long hair. Her lovely breasts bounced with her movements and my fingers crept up the red satin corset to reach them. Massaging her tits was getting her all worked up again. I was sure I could get her to finish, but I wasn't sure I could do it before her gorgeous body sent me over the edge. I needed to cum so badly!

I reached up and wrapped my arms around her waist, pulling her down against my chest. I kissed her neck while still playing with one breast and holding her waist against mine. She started to buck her hips while she rode me and raised her knees higher. I held her hips in place as I rolled us over, so that I was on top. This way I could have more control over when I pulled out of her.

I pushed her knees back toward her shoulders, spreading her wide so that I could take her deep when I felt her climaxing. But I wanted to tease it out of her. Also, going slower would let me prolong my orgasm.

So, I pulled my hips back some, giving her only a few inches in short quick thrusts, letting the head of my cock just barely kiss her entrance so I could tease her clit with each stroke. She started panting in long gasps while I did this. I kissed her again while she moaned around my tongue. I kept her wanting more for long minutes that tortured my flesh. But also kept me from reaching satisfaction. The depth of my penetration increased slowly with the passion of my kisses. I felt her pleasure coiling inside her until her moans were pitched with such desperate desire I knew she would climax.

Unable to keep myself to the shallow thrusts any longer, I fucked into her deep and hard without thought of stopping. Her body was so open to me, inviting my touch and hungry for me as much as I was for her.

"That's so good. That's so fucking good. Oh Goddess, Khessi!" I said with strained and ragged breathing. She gripped my shoulders tighter while her cries pushed me further. "You're so fucking tight! You're gonna make me cum!" I moaned.

"....yes, yes, yes, yes...." She repeated over and over.

Her pussy walls started to flutter around me. She whispered my name alongside her quickening breaths.

Khessi screamed in pleasure as she clawed at my back, clenching and squeezing around me. I grabbed her ass, holding myself above her with the other arm as I kept fucking her. My pulse thundered in my ears and behind my eyes. I panted into her neck with her hair brushing over my lips. Pleasure burst through all my senses. My orgasm took me over like a jolt of lightning crackling through my body. I only had a second to pull out before I erupted. Without saying a word, her hand was on me, jerking me hard and fast in the space between our bodies. I moaned helplessly in waves of pleasure as I came. Shooting my cum in fast bursts that coated her hand and dripped into the apex of her legs. I released all the tension I'd felt into a drifting haze of pleasure that consumed my senses until there was nothing but the sounds of our breaths drifting back to normal while we lay wrapped in each other's embrace.

Sleep claimed us both there. With no energy to do anything else, I whispered, "I love you, Khessi."

I don't remember if she responded.

The next morning I woke to an empty bed. I sat up in the mess of blankets, rubbing the sleep out of my eye with my palm. I yawned and then exhaled into a dramatic frown. I huffed a little, looking around for the beauty I'd fallen asleep with.

"Khessi?" I called out. Little clawed feet scampered over the tile and Tark stood in the doorway, staring at me. "Not the redhead I was looking for." I told him. He sighed and walked to the window, curled himself into an orange and white ball and closed his eyes.

I found Khessi out in the water, swimming. I joined her to wash off since I still had sweat and Goddess knows what else on me from the night before. I'm sure I didn't smell the best. She swam up to me and handed me a bar of soap.

"That's the last time we fall asleep like that before cleaning up. I'm surprised you didn't wake up when I left since we were basically stuck together."

"Eh, yeah. Sorry about that." I began to soap up, washing my body clean of the most wonderful night of sex I'd ever had. "How are you doing this morning?" I asked.

"I'm a little sore, but rather pleasantly so." she smiled.

"Good." I said, stuck in my own thoughts as I lowered into the water to rinse off the lather. "That's good."

"That's good?" She blinked, crossing the water to me. She moved in close to my face and wrapped her arms around my neck.

"Yes. Good. I am happy that you are the opposite of bad."

"Hmm. And how was last night for you? I mean, I'm not a pleasure slave or anything but..." she shrugged.

I kissed her before she could finish that thought. When I broke the kiss she wouldn't look me in the eyes.

"Last night was unequivocally the best night of sex I've ever had in my life."

She looked up at me with doubt. "But...that can't be true. You've had sex with the Mistress, right?"

"I don't think I'm the best lover for the Mistress."

"Really? But men fall all over themselves to be with her."

"You know, it sounds good in theory. She's of course very beautiful. But the reality of it is way more effort than I could pull off on a daily basis. She is extremely difficult to get to orgasm." I smiled at her. "I prefer to enjoy sex with a partner that is easy to make cum."

"Oh, so I'm easy?"

"Yeah..." I shrugged, smiling.

"Oh! Really?"

"Yeah. You're *so* easy. Like, first day of pleasure training skills easy."

"Hmm. Well, I suppose there are worse things."

"Actually, that's possibly one of the best things ever. Having a man who knows how to get you off that must be worth..."

"At least one gold," she said playing with the coin at my collar.

I nodded. "Yes, that's worth at least one gold, I'd say."

*   *.   *

For more details on the upcoming novels, audiobooks, and photography Subscribe & Follow!

www.facebook.com/Atlaind

www.Instagram.com/MistressCK

www.twitter.com/mistress_ck

www.etsy.com/shop/AtlaindEroticFantasy

www.youtube.com/c/MistressCK

Make Your Mark by joining us on Patreon!
www.patreon.com/MistressCK

Printed in Great Britain
by Amazon

46121455R00185